Richard Kadrey has published seven novels, including *Sandman Slim*, *Kill the Dead*, *Aloha From Hell*, *Devil Said Bang*, and more than fifty stories. He has been immortalized as an action figure, and his short story 'Goodbye Houston Street, Goodbye,' was nominated for a British Science Fiction Association Award. A freelance writer and photographer, he lives in San Francisco.

RichardKadrey.com

By Richard Kadrey

Sandman Slim
Kill the Dead
Aloha from Hell
Devil Said Bang

SANDMAN SLIM

RICHARD KADREY

HARPER
Voyager

Harper*Voyager*
77–85 Fulham Palace Road,
Hammersmith, London W6 8JB

www.harpervoyagerbooks.com

This paperback edition 2013

Published by Harper*Voyager*
An imprint of HarperCollins*Publishers* 2013

A catalogue record for this book
is available from the British Library

ISBN: 978-0-00-744598-1

This novel is entirely a work of fiction.
The names, characters and incidents portrayed in it are
the work of the author's imagination. Any resemblance to
actual persons, living or dead, events or localities is
entirely coincidental.

Printed and bound in Great Britain by
Clays Ltd, St Ives plc

MIX
Paper from
responsible sources
FSC www.fsc.org **FSC** C007454

For Nicola

ACKNOWLEDGMENTS

Thanks to Ginger Clark, Diana Gill, Emily Krump, and Holly Frederick, and Jack Womack who dodge CHUDs everyday. Thanks to Nicola Ginzler and Pat Murphy, who continue to ignore the missing cemeteries. Thanks to Dino De Laurentiis, Lorenzo De Maio, Ed Wacek, and Igor De Laurentiis, who are the ham in a dinosaur-and-porn-star sandwich. Thanks also to the guys at Night Shade, the Liminals, Gus, and Kathy.

Thanks especially to Tom Waits for letting me carjack some of his beautiful lyrics. If I die first, you can have my bones for a xylophone.

Thanks to Sergio Leone, the Shaw Brothers, Werner Herzog, David Lynch, Takashi Miike, and Richard Stanley for killing pretty.

Just judge of vengeance,

grant the gift of forgiveness,

before the day of reckoning.

– DIES IRAE, REQUIEM MASS

The dumber people think you are, the more

surprised they're going to be when you kill them.

– WILLIAM CLAYTON

I WAKE UP on a pile of smoldering garbage and leaves in the old Hollywood Forever cemetery behind the Paramount Studio lot on Melrose, though these last details don't come to me until later. Right now all I know is that I'm back in the world and I'm on fire. My mind hasn't quite kicked in yet, but my body knows enough to roll off the burning trash and to keep rolling until I can't feel the heat anymore.

When I'm sure I'm out, I struggle to my feet and shrug off my leather jacket. I run my hands over my lower back and legs. There's no real pain and all I feel are a couple of blisters behind my right knee and calf. My jeans are a little crispy, but the heavy leather of my jacket protected my back. I'm not really burned, just singed and in shock. I probably hadn't been on the fire too long. But I'm lucky that way. Always have been. Otherwise, I might have crawled back into this world and ended up a charcoal briquette in my first five minutes home. And wouldn't those black-hearted bastards down under have laughed when I ended up right back in Hell after slipping so sweetly out the back door? Fuck 'em for now. I'm home and I'm alive, if a little torn up by the trip. No one said birth was easy, and rebirth would have to be twice as hard as that first journey into the light.

The light.

My body isn't burning anymore, but my eyes are cooking in their sockets. How long has it been since I've seen sunlight? Down in the asshole of creation, it was a dim, perpetual crimson-and-magenta twilight. I can't even tell you the colors of the cemetery where I'm standing because my vision goes into an agonizing whiteout every time I open my eyes.

Squinting like a mole, I run to the shade of a columbarium and crouch there with my forehead on the cool marble walls and my hands over my face. I give it a good five or ten minutes then lower my hands to let my eyes get used to the bloody-red light that seeps through my lids. Little by little, over the next twenty or so minutes, I open my eyes, letting in minute amounts of glaring L.A. sun. I mentally cross my fingers and hope that no one sees me hunkered down against the wall. They'd probably think I was crazy and call a cop, and there wouldn't be a damned thing I could do about it.

The muscles in my knees and legs ache before I can open my eyes all the way and keep them open. I sit down against the cool building to take some of the strain off. Though I can sort of see now, there's no way I'm marching off into full daylight for a while. Instead, I stay in the shade and take stock of things.

My clothes are burned, but wearable, if you ignore the burning garbage smell. I have on an ancient Germs T-shirt that my girlfriend lifted from a West Hollywood vintage shop for me, worn black jeans with holes in the knees, a pair of ancient engineer boots, and a battered leather motorcycle jacket, strategic points of which are held together with black gaffer's tape. The heel of my right boot is loose from when I'd kicked the living Jesus out of some carjacking piece of shit after he dragged some screaming soccer mom to the pavement at a stoplight. I hate cops and I fucking hate goody-goody hero types, but there is some shit I will not put up with if it happens in front of me. Of course, that was back then, before my trip down under. I wasn't sure what I'd do if I saw the same scene today. I'd probably still put a boot into the car thief, but I don't know if I'd let him walk away.

Right now there's something more important on my mind—the fact that these are the exact clothes I was wearing when I got demon-snatched. When I'd hit the pavement down under I'd been naked. That got me my first big laughs, stumbling around trying to find my footing before I puked myself in front of an audience of fallen angels. After that, the laughs were mostly about my physical abuse and humiliation at the hands of one devil dog or another. Trust me on this—Hell is a tough room.

It's been a long time since I've seen these clothes. I go

through my pockets to see if there's money or anything useful. There's not much. There's nothing in my pockets but twenty-three cents and an empty pink matchbook with the name and address of a Hollywood bail bondsman printed on it. I don't even have the keys to my apartment or the old Impala my father left me.

I feel just above my right ankle and a genuine wave of happiness hits me. The black blade is still there, strapped to my leg with strips of basilisk leather. I put my hand over my heart and can feel the chain under my T-shirt and the fat gold Veritas coin that hangs there. The fact I'm on Earth at all means that I still have the key to the Room of Thirteen Doors, even though I can't touch it or see it. So, I managed to smuggle three things back with me from Hell. That's no small feat. Of course, none of it alters the fact that I have no money, no ID, no wheels, my clothes are half burned off, I don't have a place to stay and no real idea where I am, except for the fact that this tombstone trailer park looks and feels like L.A. I'm off to a damn good start. I'll be the first hitman in history who has to panhandle for bullets.

I make my way slowly, still half blind, to the front gates of the cemetery. Near them, I cup my hands in the water flowing from the top of a contemplation fountain. I take a drink and splash water onto my face. It feels as cool and perfect as a first kiss. Right then it hits me. This isn't some devil's illusion, a glamour or some game designed to crush my spirit. *I'm really home.*

So, where the hell is everybody? Outside, I catch sight of the one thing I've been hoping to see. North from where I'm standing, in the distance, are the big white letters of the Hollywood sign. Perched high on the dirty brown scrub hills, it's never looked so beautiful. In the other direction, toward Melrose, a car hisses by every now and then, but there are way too few. And there are no people on the street at all. There are some small houses off at an angle from the cemetery gate. The green lawns are decorated with lights, plastic reindeer, and an inflatable snowman. Wreaths on a few doors across the street. *Holy shit, it's Christmas.* For some reason, this strikes me as the funniest thing in the universe and I stand there laughing like an idiot.

Someone slams into me hard from behind. The hilarity ends abruptly. I spin around and I'm face-to-face with a young executive type. Brad Pitt's stunt double handsome, with a haircut and black double-breasted jacket that together cost more than my car. Where the hell did he come from? I've got to shape up. Downtown, no one would have been able to creep up on me like that.

Brad Pitt takes a couple of stiff steps back. "What the fuck?" he yells, like it's my fault he walked into me. It's not that hot out, but he's sweating like a racehorse and his movements are quick and jerky, like a broken windup toy. He looks at me like I just killed his dog.

"Calm down, Donald Trump," I say. "You ran into me." He wipes his upper lip with the back of his hand. There's something tucked in his palm, and he's so twitchy he drops it. Brad starts to lunge for it, but takes a step back instead. Lying on the sidewalk between us is a plastic bag with about a hundred little ice-white cocaine rocks inside. I smile. Welcome to Christmas in L.A. Say hi to Saint Nick loading up for a party I'll definitely be skipping.

I look back at the guy, and before I can say anything, he reaches into his jacket. I latch onto his arm just as the stun gun comes out. I snap his wrist back and twist outward, taking him off balance and slamming him hard onto the pavement. I didn't even think about it. My body just went on autopilot. Guess some part of my brain must still be working right.

Brad Pitt isn't moving. He went down on the stun gun and it's still jammed into his ribs. I kick the thing away and touch the side of his neck. Even out cold, his pulse is fast. Who says crack isn't good for you? He's wearing a small Christmas tree pin on his lapel. This makes me think about Christmas more, about being somewhere without friends and how I could use a Secret Santa of my own right now. I figure that my new friend is about as close to a Good Samaritan as I'm likely to find outside a cemetery off Melrose. I quick check to see that the street is still clear, pocket the stun gun, and then drag him into the cemetery, behind some hedges.

Turns out, the guy is Santa, the Tooth Fairy, and the Easter Bunny all rolled into one. His eel skin wallet is fat with hundreds, at least a few grand worth. Even though the twitchy son of a bitch was so ripped on coke and paranoia that he tried to electrocute me for nothing more than standing on the street, I feel a small twinge of guilt as I rifle through his pockets. I've done a lot of questionable things in my time, but I never actually mugged anybody. Not that this was technically a mugging. Brad Pitt here attacked me. In another time, helping myself to this guy's gear would just fall under the heading of "Spoils of War." Besides, I need this stuff. I'm back with nothing. No friends that I know of and no real plan.

I help myself to his cash, his Porsche sunglasses, an unopened pack of Black Black gum, and his jacket, which is a little tight across the shoulders but not too bad a fit at all. I leave him my half-burned leather jacket, his credit cards, car keys, and the big bag of Christmas crack. I'll just add this incident to the list of sins I'll have to atone for later. Ten minutes back on Earth and I'm already adding to the bill.

I crack open the pack of caffeinated gum and chew a piece as I walk. I can't seem to get the taste of burning garbage out of my mouth.

It feels like I'm walking on someone else's legs, wobbly and disconnected. I trip over a couple of curbs and almost jump out of my skin when I step on a squeak toy some kid left in the street. Chuck Norris, I'm not. But the blood starts flowing and my legs start feeling like part of my body again. Other than that, I'm not walking with any purpose or direction. I want to go home, but what if Azazel has sent up some of his pet spiders—the bloodsuckers as big as rottweilers? I'm not ready to face that just yet. I pull the chain out from under my shirt and unclip the Veritas coin.

The Veritas is about two inches wide, silver and heavy. Around the edge in Hellion script it says HOME SWEET HOME. Good. It's awake and snotty as ever.

One side of the coin is stamped with the image of the morning star—Lucifer—and on the other side is a round, many-petaled flower sort of like a chrysanthemum. It's an asphodel, a Hellion word that translates as "evensong." The flowers sing hymns that the fallen angels used to sing in Heaven. After belting out off-key hosannas all day, getting all the words wrong, they strangle themselves with their roots every evening and die. The next day, they resurrect and start all over again. This has been going on down there for probably a million years and most Hellions still think it's a knee-slapper. Hellion humor doesn't travel well. Plus, except for Lucifer and his generals, most of Hell's troops make the Beverly Hillbillies look like the Algonquin Roundtable.

Holding the big coin on my thumb and forefinger, I flip it thinking, *Hollywood or home?* The Veritas comes down asphodel side up. That's it, then. The Veritas never lies and gives better advice than most people I know. I put it back on its chain and turn north for Hollywood.

It's over a mile to the Boulevard. I'm exhausted by the time I get there, and the payoff isn't exactly what I was hoping for. Sometime while I was gone, Hollywood

Boulevard had a nervous breakdown. Vacant storefronts. Trash dissolving in the street. Nothing but ghosts here— shadows of runaways and dealers huddled in padlocked doorways. I remember the Boulevard full of wild kids, drag queens, manic Dylan wannabes, and tourists looking for more than their next fix. Now the place looks like a whipped dog.

I'm beat from walking on these stranger's legs and I'm sweating in Brad Pitt's jacket. I should have taken the idiot's car. I could have left it on the Boulevard, safe and sound. Though, more likely, I'd have tossed to keys to one of the street kids slouched against the buildings, just to see if there was any life left inside some of those dead eyes.

Walking deeper into Hollywood, I pass Ivar Avenue and see a funny sign flanked by burning tiki torches. BAMBOO HOUSE OF DOLLS, it says. I remember the name. It's an old-school kung fu movie with a women-in-prison twist. I saw it when I was Downtown. The devil steals cable. Who knew?

The Bamboo House of Dolls is cool and dim inside, and I can take off Brad Pitt's sunglasses without wanting to faint. There are old Iggy and Circle Jerks posters on the black-painted walls, but behind the bar it's all palm fronds, plastic hula girls, and coconut bowls for the peanuts. There's no one in the place except for the bartender and me. I grab the stool at the end of the bar, farthest from the door.

The bartender is slicing up limes. He pauses for a second

to give me a nod, the knife loose and comfortable in his right hand. That other part of my brain kicks in, sizing him up. He has close-cropped black hair and a graying goatee. He looks big under his Hawaiian shirt. An ex–football player. Maybe a boxer. He realizes I'm looking at him.

"Nice jacket," he says.

"Thanks."

"Too bad the rest of you looks like you just dropped out of the devil's asshole."

Suddenly I'm wondering if this is some Hellion setup, and if I can reach Brad Pitt's stun gun or my knife in time. He must see it on my face because he gives me this big deer-in-the-headlights grin and I know that he was kidding.

"Relax, man," he says. "Bad joke. Looks like you had a shitty day. What are you drinking?"

I'm not sure how to answer that. Yesterday, I'd been hunting for water that sometimes dripped through the ceilings of limestone caves under Pandemonium. Mostly I drank a Hellion homebrew called Aqua Regia, a kind of high-octane red wine mixed with a dash of angel's blood and herbs that made cocaine seem like Pop Rocks. Aqua Regia tasted like cayenne pepper and gasoline, but it was there and I could hold it down.

"Jack Daniel's."

"On the house," says the bartender, and pours a double.

There's strange music playing. Something odd and tropical, with fake bird chirps every now and then. There's a CD case on the bar. A Hawaiian sunset on the cover and the name "MARTIN DENNY." I put the chewed Black Black in a cocktail napkin and sip the JD. It tastes strange, like something a human might actually drink. It washes the last of the garbage taste away.

"What the hell is this place?"

"Bamboo House of Dolls. L.A.'s greatest and only punk-tiki club."

"Yeah, I always thought L.A. needed one of those." I'm in a bar, but something's missing. "I forgot my cigarettes. Think I can borrow one?"

"Sorry, man. You can't smoke in bars in California."

"When did that happen? That's ridiculous."

"I agree completely."

"At least I'm home for Christmas."

"Close. But you missed it by a day. Didn't Santa bring you anything?"

"This trip, maybe." I sip my drink. So, not Christmas, after all. Just Christmas enough to keep the streets deserted so no one saw me crawl home. Lucky me.

I ask, "You have today's paper?"

He reaches under the bar and drops a folded copy of the *L.A. Times* in front of me. I pick it up, trying not to look too eager. Can't even read the headlines. Can't focus on anything but the date at the top of the page.

Eleven years. I've been gone eleven years. I was nineteen

when I went Downtown. I'm practically an old man now.

"You have any coffee back there?"

He nods. "That's how you missed Christmas. A lost weekend. I've had a few of those."

The coffee is beautiful. Hot. A little bitter, like it's been brewing for a while. I pour the last of the Jack Daniel's into it and drink. My first perfect moment in eleven years.

"You from around here?"

"I was born here, but I've been away."

"Business or pleasure?"

"Incarceration."

He smiles again. A normal one this time. "In my reckless youth, I did six months for boosting cars. What were you inside for?"

"I'm not really sure, to tell you the truth. Mostly wrong place, wrong time."

"That'll put a smile on your face." He refills my coffee cup and pours me another shot of JD. This bartender might be the finest human being I've ever met.

"So, why'd you come back?"

"I'm going to kill some people," I tell him. I pour the Jack into the coffee. "Probably a lot of people."

The bartender picks up a rag and starts wiping glasses. "Guess someone's got to."

"Thanks for understanding."

"I figure that at any given time, there's probably three to five percent of the population that are such unrepentant rat-fuck *pendejos* that they deserve whatever they get."

He's still wiping the same glass. It looks pretty clean to me. "Besides, I get the feeling you might have your reasons."

"That I do, Carlos."

He stops wiping. "How did you know my name was Carlos?"

"You must've said it."

"No, I didn't."

I look over his shoulder, at the wall behind the bar. "That trophy on top of the cash register. 'Carlos, World's Greatest Boss.'"

"You can read that from here?"

"Apparently." The thing with his name popping into my head? That was weird. Time to go. "What do I owe you?"

"On the house."

"You this nice to every aspiring assassin who wanders in here?"

"Only the ones who look like they just crawled out of a burning building and didn't even get their jacket dirty. And I like repeat business. Maybe now you'll come back sometime."

"You want someone who, like you said, just fell out of the devil's asshole as a regular?"

"I'd love it." He looks away, like he's trying to think of the next thing to say. "There are these guys. White boys. All tattooed, like Aryan Nation or some shit. They're coming around, wanting money for protection. A lot more money than I can afford with a little bar like this."

"And you think I can do something about them."

"You look like someone who might know what to do in a situation like this. Who wouldn't be . . ." That look again, groping for words. "You know . . . afraid."

I could tell it was really hard for him to say that. Is this why the Veritas sent me here? I'm back a couple of hours and already I'm into karmic payback? And with the carnage I have planned, but haven't even started? No, that didn't make any sense.

"I'm sorry. I don't think I can help you."

"How about this? Free drinks. Free food at night, too. Good burgers, ribs, tamales. You eat and drink free until the end of time."

"That's a really nice offer, but I don't think I can help you."

He looks away and starts wiping glasses again. "If you change your mind, they come on Thursdays, in the afternoon, when we're getting deliveries."

I get up and head for the door. When I'm halfway there he says, "Hey," and slides something down the bar at me. It's a pack of American Spirit browns, the nonfiltered kind. There's a pack of matches tucked under the cellophane wrap.

"Take them," he says. "I can't smoke in here, either."

Slipping on Brad Pitt's shades, I ask, "You have anymore of these back there?"

"No."

"You're a hell of a first date, Carlos." *Damn. When someone gives you his last cigarette, you owe him.*

Martin Denny bird chirps follow me to the door.

Turns out, I don't need the shades for long. It must have been later in the day than I thought when I went into the Bamboo House of Dolls. As I leave, the sun is almost down and lights are coming on all along the Boulevard. I've always liked Hollywood better at night. The streetlights, headlights, and flashing signs outside the tourist traps blur away the straight lines and hard right angles that ruin the place. The Boulevard is only ever real at night when it's both bright and black and there are promises hidden in every shadow. It's like it was designed and built specifically for vampires. For all I know, it was.

Yes, there are vampires. Try to keep up.

I count to eleven as I walk deeper into Hollywood. Eleven parking meters. Eleven hookers looking for their first post-Christmas trick. Eleven actors I never heard of on eleven stars in the sidewalk.

Eleven years. Eleven goddamn years and I'm home with a key and a pocketknife and a coin that won't buy me a cup of coffee.

Three, five, seven, eleven, all good children go to Heaven.

Gone eleven years and I make it back the day after Christmas. Is someone trying to tell me something?

I pull out one of Carlos's American Spirits and light up. The smoke feels good in my lungs. This body is starting to feel like mine again. Like me. I'm just not sure about the rest of the world.

Who the hell are all these people on the Boulevard the day after Christmas? How am I supposed to blend in with them? There's a nice guy at a bar a few blocks from here. He was just doing his job, but he had a knife in his hand and all I could do was count all the ways I knew to kill him.

It hits me then how unprepared I am for being back, how everything that made sense Downtown is strange here, wrong and ridiculous. All the skills I developed—how to draw an enemy in and how to kill, all the magic I'd learned or stolen—suddenly feels feeble and foolish in this bright and alien place. I'm steel-toed boots in a ballet-slipper world.

I finish off the first cigarette and light another. The world is a much louder and stranger place than I remember. I need to start doing and stop running around screaming inside my own head. Brooding is for chickens, as my first-grade teacher used to say. Or maybe it was Lucifer. Homily reciters all kind of run together for me.

I need to concentrate on what's important, like my sure and certain plans to find and kill, in as painful a way as possible, the six traitorous snakes who stole my life. And something worse. It makes me weak inside to think about it. It's a woman's face.

Her name is Alice. She's the only bright thing I ever loved, the only person I ever met worth giving a damn about. If Heaven ever meant anything, she should be married, probably now to some skinny leather-pants guitarist she has to support with temp jobs in those fluorescent-tube high-rise dungeons along Wilshire. Or she'd have gone straight, married a dentist, squeezed out a minivan full of crib lizards, and gotten fat. That would be okay, too. But none of those things are going to happen for her. Nothing nice happens to murdered women, except that maybe someone cares about how they got that way.

If Alice was still around, would she even recognize me under all these scars? There was a mirror inside the entrance to the Bamboo House of Dolls, but I'd been careful not to look at it. Walking along the Boulevard, I take quick glances at my reflection in the dim glass of dead storefronts. I'm bigger than I was when I went down, heavier with muscle and scar tissue, but still thin by human standards. I can still recognize the rough outline of my face, but it looks more like stone than flesh. My cheeks and chin are chiseled out of concrete; my eyes are dark, shining marbles above lips the color of dirty snow. I'm a George Romero zombie, except I've never been dead. Just vacationing in the land of the dead. Suddenly I want to get my hands around the throat of fat Alice's imaginary husband and squeeze him till he pops like a balloon.

That stops me cold.

It's the first time I've fantasized about killing anyone outside the Circle. What a stupid and dangerous thought. Exactly the kind of thing that will steer me away from the real job and maybe get me killed. Then I'd be right back in Hell with nothing to show for it and wouldn't that be a lot of laughs?

That leads me back to the $64,000 question: Why did the Veritas send me this way? It's interesting being back on familiar turf, but I could have brooded back at the cemetery. That's why it's called a "cemetery." And I didn't need a bartender to offer me a job or give me free smokes. With a pocketful of Brad Pitt's hundreds, I'm Richie Rich with a knife in his boot. So, why am I here?

I'm walking and smoking on a block that's two open liquor stores, an empty secondhand bookstore, a dead record store, and a shuttered sex shop. As I'm speculating on how fucked up a town has to be when it can't even keep a dildo-and-porn shop open, the inside of my skull lights up like God's own pinball machine.

I have my answer. I know why I'm here.

He's turning off the Boulevard onto Las Palmas, waddling on his little legs a short way up the block to a place called Max Overdrive Video. At the front door, he has to juggle things for a minute—transfer a cup of coffee to one hand, grip the top of a bag of doughnuts in his teeth, and do a little ass dance so he can work the keys out of his pocket and let himself into the store.

I watch him from across the street, just to make sure that I'm not imagining things. As he enters the place, I get a nice backlit shot of his face.

It's Kasabian, one of my friends from the old magic circle. One of the six on my list.

Santa brought me something, after all.

Max Overdrive Video occupies both floors of an old Hollywood town house, the kind of weekend getaway kept by the gentry back in the forties and fifties, when this area was the most glamorous place in the known universe. Kasabian is moving around inside Max Overdrive like he owns the place. I think I should go and ask him if he does.

It's full-on night now and I'm surrounded by fat, ripe shadows. I cross the street and pick a plump, dark one around the side of Max Overload, next to a health food restaurant. I glance over my shoulder to make sure the street is clear, and when I'm sure I'm alone, I slip into the shadow. The key tickles inside my chest and I emerge into the Room of Thirteen Doors.

I cross to the Door of Ice and quietly step out of the shadow on the other side.

I'm in the far back of the store, in the porn section. The lights are off back here, so I get a good look at the rest of the place.

There's a door to an employee restroom on my right, tucked back behind the porn. Just beyond this section is a chained-off stairway leading upstairs. Neat racks of DVDs and bins of VHS tapes fill the rest of the store. I guess that's something that's changed in the last eleven years. Even the porn in the back is all discs. The only tapes I can find are piled carelessly in the sale bins. VHS is dead. This is something good to remember since I don't want to sound like the Beverly Hillbillies when I'm talking to regular people. I should sit down and make a list of everything I missed while I was gone. If you can't smoke in bars anymore, what other atrocities has the world committed?

Kasabian is up front, behind the counter, going over the day's receipts. He lost some hair while I was away, but he's made up for it by getting fat. He'd always been a little chubby, but now he'd taken on a truly odd shape. Not like one of those guys who grows a big belly and man boobs. He just seems to have expanded horizontally, like a balloon filled with too much air. It's admirable in its own weird way. His chin and gut are defiant in the face of gravity, making him look more like Frosty the Snowman than Orson Welles.

I walk slowly down the main aisle toward the counter, checking the corners of the room, making sure we're alone. Kasabian is deep in thought, crunching numbers. When I'm halfway to the counter, I take Brad Pitt's stun gun from my jacket pocket and hold it behind my back.

"Evening, Kas. Long time no see."

He starts and knocks a pile of receipts to the floor. I stop where I know he can see me, but also where the lighting is weak enough that I'm pretty sure he can't see my face.

"Who the fuck are you? Get out of my store. I don't want any trouble."

"It's right after Christmas, Kas. Don't you ever take a day off?"

"Everybody's on vacation. Who are you?"

"Did you have a merry Christmas this year? Did you sing 'Happy Birthday' to baby Jesus? Maybe pick up something at Baby Gap?"

"What do you want?"

"Know what I did for Christmas? I cut a monster's head off. Then I did the same thing to the guy who owned the monster."

"You want money? Take it. It was a lousy day and I've already deposited all the Christmas money, so you're shit out of luck there."

Kasabian has been a drama queen from the first day I met him, so I can't resist hitting him with a Vincent Price moment.

"I don't want your money, Kas. I want your soul," I say, stepping into better light to give him a clear full frontal.

It gets exactly the reaction I was hoping for. His mouth opens, but he doesn't make a sound. One of his hands comes up to cover his open yap, stifling a silent scream. He steps back from the counter, his eyes wide.

Forgive me, God and Lucifer and all you angels high and low, but this is fun. This is an e-ticket roller coaster.

"Shut your mouth, Kas. You look like one of those blow-up sheep in the back of porn zines." I stop about ten feet from the counter, just letting him feast on me. "What did you get me for Christmas? Right, you gave it to me eleven years ago. Damnation. The gift that keeps on giving."

His hands are down now and he's leaning on the counter like a drunk trying to decide whether to fall on his face or his back. I thumb on the stun gun.

"It's okay. I know you don't have anything for me. But I sure as hell have something for you, Kas. Climb up on Santa's lap and I'll show you."

I take a baby step closer to the counter and Kasabian takes one back. Then he does the funniest thing. He raises his hands and there's a gun there—a .45-caliber Colt Peacemaker. Wyatt Earp's favorite gun. He gives me five of the six slugs in the chest and belly, completely ruining my moment.

I drop to my knees, vision going black. The stun gun falls to the floor and I follow it down. I can feeling my lungs drawing in air. I can feel my heart beating. Both organs seem more than a little confused by what's happening. Death is settling over me, soft and warm, like a down comforter fresh from the dryer. My heart stops.

SOMETHING FUNNY HAPPENED to me when I was Downtown. I got hard to kill. When I first arrived there, I was the first and only living human to ever set foot in Hell. I was a sideshow freak. Pay a dollar and see Jimmy, the dog-faced boy. Later, when they got tired of slapping me around, examining me, and displaying me like a pedigreed poodle, they thought it might be fun to watch me die. They made me fight in the arena and they made a big deal out of it. Imagine the Super Bowl every week or two.

Naturally, the location being Hell and the setting being an arena, there was a lot of cheating going on. Hellions don't like losing bets any more than humans. Before almost every fight, a bribed trainer or attendant would show up with a sneaky little gift. They slipped me special weapons. They gave me diabolical drugs. They whispered fiendish spells into my ears. It all helped, though it didn't make me Superman. I was knifed and speared. I was burned. I was almost torn in half by a giant crab-thing that bled fire and screamed in the anguished voices of all the souls it had devoured. My ribs and skull were beaten to Silly Putty.

But I didn't die.

I don't know if it was the spells, the drugs, the Aqua Regia, or just clean living, but I was changing. Every time I should have died but didn't, I got stronger. That meant that the next attack had to be harder, faster, even more ferocious than the one before. After a while, I actually looked forward to the beat-downs. Each one changed me and that change meant that I was immune from a similar attack next time. By the end, I was a flesh-and-bone, armor-plated Dirty Harry.

By the time the ruling-class, old-school Hellions and nouveau celebutante fiends decided it was time to get rid of me, it was too late. I was too strong and by then I was doing more interesting things than killing in the arena. I was freelance-killing Hellions out of the arena, and that meant I was protected from on high by forces far darker than your run-of-the-mill tail-and-pitchfork type.

On the other hand, I'd never been shot before.

"Stark?" says Kasabian from a million miles away. "Is that really you?" He laughs quietly, nervously. "Mason is going to shit himself."

My left hand shoots to the side, grabbing the .45's still-warm barrel and driving it into the floor. Kasabian's fat finger is still looped in the trigger guard, so he comes down with the gun. Meanwhile, my right hand flickers to my boot and tears free the black bone knife. I twist my body toward Kasabian and bring down the knife in a smooth arc. Kasabian's head tumbles to the floor and rolls away like a pumpkin. His body flops to the floor.

From beneath the Disney new-releases rack, Kasabian's head begins to wail.

"Oh God! Oh Jesus, fuck! I'm dead!" It's quality wailing. Downtown, I became kind of a connoisseur of wailing and this is prime stuff.

"I'm dead! I'm dead!"

Crawling shakily to my feet, I pick up Kasabian's shrieking melon by the hair, tuck the .45 in the back of my jeans, and grab his leg by the ankle with my free hand. In a situation like this, when you want to clear away the evidence, you want to drag the body. You might think it's faster to toss it over your shoulder in a fireman's carry, but lifting a limp body is like wrestling with two hundred pounds of Jell-O. It wiggles, shifts, and refuses to stay still. Dragging is slower, but much less aggravating.

I carry Kasabian upstairs, his head still screaming blue

murder and his heavy torso bumping along behind us.

The second floor is one big room. It's large, with a nice big window on one wall, but sparsely furnished. There's a bed, a couple of desk chairs, and a table piled high with tape decks, DVD burners, and a big color printer—a mini video-bootlegging factory. I drop the body by the door and set his head on the worktable. The gun I toss on the bed. Kasabian is still shrieking like a banshee, which is pretty good for a guy with no lungs.

I grab a chair and drop down in front of him. Digging the cigarettes out of Brad Pitt's now-bloody jacket, I light one up and blow smoke in Kasabian's face.

"Smell that? That means you're not dead."

He stops screaming and looks at me. Then he spots his body on the floor and starts caterwauling again. I take a slow drag and blow an extra-long cancer cloud right in his face.

He gets quiet and finally seems to focus on me.

"Stark? You're dead."

"Tell me, Kas, how does it feel to wake up in the worst place you can imagine? Of course, you're luckier than me because you know why you're there."

"Fuck you! You think you're sneaky? You used magic. The whole Sub Rosa will know you're here. Mason will know you're here. He'll kill you."

I make a game-show-buzzer noise.

"Guess again, fat man. This knife doesn't disturb the aether and doesn't leave any magical traces. Pure stealth tech, which is sort of its point. That, and not killing its victims unless I tell it to."

"Oh God, look what you did."

"God's away on business, Kas. Talk to me."

He looks up at me with big moon eyes. "I thought you were dead. When you disappeared, we all thought you were dead. I mean, what Mason did, it worked?"

"I was alive and in Hell for eleven years, so, yeah, you could say it worked."

"How could you live through something like that? Mason was right about you."

"What did he say?"

"That you were the only other really great natural magician he'd ever met."

I have to smile at that.

"Sounds like Mason. I mean, it comes off like a compliment. But he calls me a great magician so he can call himself an even greater one."

I turn away like I'm checking out the room, but really my gut is killing me. I'm burned and bruised where the slugs went in and I'm pretty sure I have a couple of cracked ribs. They'll probably be all right by morning, but I'm not going to do much more walking around tonight. And I'm not about to give Kasabian the satisfaction of knowing I'm in pain.

"It must be true, though. You survived all those Hellions and you came back."

"Wringing your neck is what brought me back. Yours

and the others'." The old anger comes boiling up, but I don't want to lose control. It'll scare Kasabian too much and he'll be useless for information. I need to catch my breath. I can't plan anything running around barking like a mad dog.

"For your information, I didn't use any magic Downtown. Our magic is a joke down there. It doesn't work. You might as well be shouting brownie recipes." I take a calming drag off the cigarette. "I don't even remember much of the magic we did in the Circle, but I did learn a trick or two down under. Hellion magic, and every bit of it is designed to make you cry all the way home."

"Are you gonna kill me?"

"Did you happen to notice me cutting off your head? If I wanted you dead, you'd be dead."

"Why did you come after me? Is it about the girl?"

"I don't want to talk about her yet."

I can't talk about her yet.

"What do you want, man?"

"I want all of you. You were all in on it when Mason sent me down."

"I didn't do anything."

"Right. You just stood there. You knew what was coming and you just stood there."

"We didn't know what was going to happen."

"But you knew Mason was going to off me."

Kasabian starts to say something, but he looks away.

"What did Mason promise you?"

"The sun and the moon. All our dreams come true, if we stayed out of the way and zipped our lips. It was hard stuff to refuse."

"So, you said yes, then Mason screwed you and dumped you here. What a surprise. That's why you're about the last one in the Circle I need to kill."

"Why?"

He frowns, like me not killing him first hurts his feelings.

"Because you're a fuckup. You're a third-rate magician and a second-rate human being. That's why Mason and the others left you at the altar. You're excess baggage."

"You want to find the others from the Circle and you want me to help you."

"I want a lot of things, but let's start with that." I shift around on the chair, trying to find a position that doesn't hurt my ribs. I don't find one. "Where are the cool kids hanging out these days?"

"Are you crazy? Do you know what any of them would do to me if I told you?"

When I was Downtown, I learned a lot about making threats. Make them big. Make them outrageous. You're never going to kick someone's ass. You're going to pull out their tongue and pour liquid nitrogen down their throat, chip out their guts with an ice pick, slide in a pane of glass, and turn them into an aquarium. But you have to be careful with threats. Some Hellions and humans don't know when to back down, and you might have to actually follow through. It didn't happen often, but it was always a possibility.

"You know what I'm going to do to you?" I ask quietly and evenly. "You see that body over there? I'm going to drag it to the deepest, darkest part of Griffith Park and leave it for the coyotes."

"Please don't do that!"

"Then talk to me about the others. Where's Mason?"

Mason had been the leader of our magic circle, which made me Mr. Green Jeans to his Captain Kangaroo. He was a talented magician and never passed up a chance to remind you of it. He came from money. At least he acted like he did. The truth is, none of us really knew much about his life outside the Circle. Parker did, though. They were tight. Parker was a thug with a boxer's build and just enough magical ability to make him really dangerous. Mason saw the possibilities in someone like that and made the guy into his pet pit bull. Mason never got blood on his hands because Parker was only too happy to do it for him.

Mason also made a point of calling me Jimmy, James being my given first name. No one else ever called me Jimmy because I wouldn't let them. I've always gone by Stark because the rest of my name had always been an issue in the family. I don't know how Mason found out the rest of my name.

"Are you kidding? Does it look like I hang out with Mason anymore? I rent porn and Schwarzenegger to halfwits," Kasabian says. "I've hardly seen him since that night and, to tell you the truth, I'm glad. After you were gone, those demons, or whatever they were, charged him up with power. Superman stuff. No, more like the Hulk. He changed, right in front of us. His skin, his bones, his whole body turned weird. It kind of glowed and it looked like there were things crawling around under his skin."

"Sounds like they gave him an assload of nebiros."

"What's a nebiro?"

"A parasite. They live off the energy of whatever they infest. The only reason the host doesn't drop dead immediately is that the nebiros excrete supernatural energy. They shit magic. It supercharges the host, keeping him and the parasite alive. Hellions eat those things like popcorn. I didn't know they worked on humans."

"Whatever happened, he wasn't just Mason anymore. He was Mason and something else. Like God's older brother, who takes God's money, steals his car, and fucks his girlfriend. That's Mason now. A guy who isn't afraid to pants God. He took off and took Parker with him."

I know that he's telling the truth. In the same weird way that Carlos's name popped into my head back at the Bamboo House of Dolls, I know that Kasabian is telling me the truth. It's not reassuring to know something without understanding why you know it, but I'll figure that out later.

I flick ashes off the cigarette and place it between Kasabian's lips. He puffs on it a few times and that seems to calm him down. When he's done, I set the cigarette down in an ashtray on the table. I don't want to finish it after he's touched it.

"I'm going to have a lot more questions for you over the next few days. Maybe weeks. However long it takes to settle this. Be straight with me, keep telling me the truth, and I might just give you your body back."

"Sit here and wait for Mason to get me. What a sweet deal."

"Work with me and he won't be around to get you."

Kasabian's expression goes blank, like he's staring off into the distance at something I can't see.

"You're right, you know. I am a fuckup," he says. "All the rest of them, they got power, money, and cushy jobs. But they cut me out. I got nothing."

"Then you have every reason to want some payback, too."

"Don't you think I would have if I could? Look at me! I even had to steal this stupid store just to earn a living. Then a dead guy comes in and cuts off my head. Yeah, I'm the one who's going to put down Mason Faim."

"No, I am. You just point me at him."

"I told you, I don 't know where he is. He's gone. He's Kayzer Soze."

"What about the others?'

"You're asking a lot, man."

"No. I'm asking for exactly what I'm owed." I take a smoke again. I don't want to get into the next thing. "Tell me, Kas, like your life depended on it. Who killed Alice?"

Kasabian's eyes dart back and forth in his head like they're looking for the eject button. I recognize the look of panic. It almost feels like I can hear his heart speed up. But he doesn't have a body, though maybe he's still somehow connected to it.

"You know about that? All the way down there and you know about that?"

"Talk to me, Kas. The coyotes are calling."

I look at the floor, but I don't move. If I move, I'm going to break like glass. I can't stand talking about her. I raise my gaze to meet Kasabian's. If he had a body, he would have bolted.

"I don't know much. It's not like Mason or anyone stops by to talk over old times. I get the same rumors as everybody else. I heard Parker did it."

"Mason sent him?"

"Parker doesn't shit unless Mason tells him it's okay, so yeah, Mason must have told him to do it."

"Why? After all these years, why would he do that?"

"I don't known, man. Seriously."

I stare into Kasabian's eyes and know he isn't lying. He's absolutely panicked as I come over to him. When I take the burning cigarette out of the ashtray and let him finish it, he looks so relieved I think he's going to cry.

My Alice is dead and I'm alone.

"Tell me about the store," I say. "How many employees are there?"

"Four or five. College kids. They come and go. It changes with classes and holidays. Allegra is the only one with any brains."

"Who's she?"

"She manages the place. I don't like being down there with the customers."

"She runs the place so you can stay up here and bootleg movies."

"We do what we have to do to get by. I bet you did some dirty trick or two when you were in Hell."

"You have no idea," I tell him. "What time do you open in the morning? Does Allegra open the place?"

"Ten. Yeah, she does."

There's a closet behind the door to the stairs. I push the stairs door closed and open the closet. It's mostly empty, except for waist-high metal storage shelves. I drag the body into the back of the closet, then bring in Kasabian's head. I set him on top of the shelves. He says, "I'm a little claustrophobic."

I look around the room. He can't stay out in the open, in case someone comes up here. There's a small bathroom, but there's no way that I'm having Kasabian share my morning pee. Sitting on the bottom of one of the shelves is a small portable TV. I plug it in and turn it on while fiddling with its old-fashioned rabbit-ear antenna. A local news show comes on and I put the set on the shelf with Kasabian.

"Maybe this'll ease your pain."

Kasabian frowns. "You're a real prick, Jimmy."

"But I wasn't always, was I?" I close the closet door halfway and stop. "You ever call me Jimmy again, I'll nail this door shut. You can complain about claustrophobia for the next fifty years in the dark." I close and lock the closet door.

I sit down on the bed, exhausted and in pain. It's been an eventful day. I landed here with nothing and ended up with a nice new jacket and a pocket full of cash. I even have somewhere to crash and wash my face. The American dream.

I stretch out full on the bed and something else occurs to me. "I guess I'm in the video biz." *Damn, I even have a job.*

I want to go and wash off the blood that's drying on my belly and chest, but when I try to stand, my cracked ribs shoot to the top of my pain threshold and convince me that I can wait until morning. I shrug off Brad Pitt's jacket and lie back carefully. The moment my head hits the pillow, I'm out.

Alice had short, dark hair and almost black eyes. There were rose thorns tattooed around the base of her long neck. She was slim and it made her arms and legs look impossibly long. We'd been going out for three or four weeks. While we were lying around in her bed one night, out of nowhere, she said, "I can do magic. Want to see?"

"Of course."

She jumped out of bed, still naked. Candles and light

from the street slid over her body, shadowing the muscles working under her skin, making the tattoos over her arms, back, and chest move like dancers in some eerie ballroom.

She went to her dresser and drew a curly little mustache on her upper lip with eyeliner pencil. When she came back to bed, she had a top hat and a deck of cards. She sat down and put on the hat, straddling me on top of the covers.

"Pick a card," she said. I took one. It was the jack of diamonds. "Now put it back in anywhere you want. Don't let me see it." She made a point of closing her eyes and turning her head away.

"It's back in, Merlin," I said.

She waved a hand over the deck and mumbled some made-up magic mumbo jumbo and fanned out the deck across my stomach.

"Is this your card?" she said, holding up one of the cards.

It was the jack of diamonds. "Right as rain," I told her. "You're the real thing, all right."

"Know how I did it?"

"Magic?"

She flipped the deck so that I could see the cards. It was fifty-two identical jacks of diamonds.

"That's not real magic," I said.

"Fooled you."

"Cheat. You distracted me."

"I have the power to cloud men's minds."

"That you do."

She slid under the covers still wearing the top hat and mustache and we made love that way. The top hat fell off, but she wore the mustache until morning.

The night after her card trick, I told Alice about magic. I told her it was real and that I was a magician. She liked me well enough by then not to fifty-one-fifty me to the cops, but she looked at me like I'd just told her that I was the king of the mushroom people. So, I pinched the flame off one of the candles she'd lit and made it hop across my fingertips. I charmed old magazines, dirty shirts, and Chinese-restaurant flyers up from the floor, formed them into a vaguely female shape, and had them strut around the apartment like a fashion model. I made my neighbor's yowling cat speak Russian and Alice's tattoos move around like little movies under her skin.

She loved it. She was like a kid, shouting, "More! More!" What she didn't want was anything serious. Every civilian I'd ever shown magic to had the same response—how can we use it to get rich? Let's manipulate the stock market. Turn invisible and rob a bank. Throw on a glamour so that cops can't see us.

Alice didn't ask for any of that. I showed her magic and that was enough for her. She didn't instantly wonder what the magic could do for her. She loved the magic itself, which meant that she could love me because I wasn't likely to make anyone rich. We hadn't been going out that long and she wasn't sure about me yet. It didn't matter. I was already nine-tenths in love with her and could wait for as long as it took for her to come around.

It took two more days.

She showed up at my door with a box from a run-down magic shop in Chinatown.

"I can do magic, too," she said.

"Let's see."

The magic box was about the size of two matchboxes. She lifted the top off. Her middle finger lay inside the box, wrapped in bloody cotton around the bottom. The finger wiggled. Stiffened. She held up her hand so the severed finger flipped me the bird, the cheapest of cheap gags. Of course, she hadn't chopped her finger off. She'd slid it up through a hole in the bottom of the box that already had cotton and fake blood inside. It was about the stupidest thing I'd ever seen.

I kissed her and took her inside. We never talked about her moving in. She just came in and never left, because she knew this was where she should be.

Later, when Alice and I were in bed and still drunk from our one month anniversary party, I told her that I had a dream where we were on a road trip, eating lunch in some anonymous little diner. She told the waitress that we were driving to Vegas to get married by an Elvis impersonator and held up her engagement ring for everyone to see. It was the magic store box, still on her finger. When I finished telling her the story, she bit me lightly on the arm.

"See?" she said. "I told you I can do magic."

I SNAP AWAKE at the sound of the door slamming downstairs. I sit up, relieved that the pain in my ribs is gone. The good feeling is short-lived, however, when I realize that the room looks like a bad night in a slaughterhouse. The bloody jacket and shirt are still on the floor where I dropped them. I'm covered in dried blood, a lot of which I've managed to smear in a crimson Rorschach blot all over the bed while I was asleep.

I toss the jacket and shirt onto the dirty sheet, pull it off the bed and onto the floor. In the bathroom, I use up most of a roll of paper towels scrubbing the blood off me. The bullet wounds are just black welts surrounded by psychedelic-blue-and-purple bruises. If I twist the right way, I can feel the .45 slugs nestled inside me, like marshmallows in Jell-O salad. I'll probably have to do something about getting them out, at some point, but not now.

The wet paper towels I toss on the sheet with the bloody clothes. In a little storage cabinet under the sink, I find a roll of black plastic garbage bags. Tear one off and stuff the bloody remains of last night's square dance inside.

It hits me then that I still have a problem. I've just thrown away half of my clothes, leaving me with nothing to wear but taped-together boots and scorched jeans, which are starting to crack and come apart in places. For a second, I consider stealing the shirt off Kasabian's body, but that's too disgusting even for me. Plus, opening the closet door will just start his head screaming again.

I toss the room, tearing open boxes, looking for a lost and found or something one of the college kids might have left behind. I hit the jackpot—a whole box of store T-shirts is stuffed in the back, under the worktable. The shirts are black, with MAX OVERDRIVE VIDEO printed in big white letters on the back. Printed on the front is a fake store name tag that says *Hi. My name is Max.* Cute.

I stand by the door for a second, listening to Allegra move around downstairs. I can almost see her in my mind's eye. She's young. Bored and annoyed at having to open the store so soon after Christmas. I get a sense of brains and something else. Something she's trying not to think about as she straightens the shelves and counts the cash in the till. Quietly, I open the door and start down the stairs, then turn around and go right back up. The .45 and Brad Pitt's stun gun are lying on the floor. I stuff them under the mattress, then head back down.

Allegra is by the door, backlit by the light through the window. She looks to be not much older than I was when I was carried off to Oz. Maybe old enough to drink. Maybe not. She doesn't wear much makeup. Black around her eyes. Gloss on her lips. She's thin, with darkish café au lait skin. She'd look like Foxy Brown's little sister, except her head is shaved smooth. Her coat and skirt are thrift store hand-me-downs, but her boots look expensive. An art school girl with priorities.

She looks up as I unlock the chain at the bottom of the stairs.

"Morning. You must be Allegra."

Her head snaps up in my direction. "Who are you? Where's Mr. Kasabian?"

"Kasabian had to leave town. Some kind of family crisis. I'm an old friend. I'll be in charge of the place while he's gone."

That wasn't the right thing to say. Allegra is angry. She tries to hide it with surprise, but doesn't pull it off.

"Really?" she asks. "Have you run a video store before?"

"No."

"Ever run any kind of retail operation?"

I come up front and lean on the counter, checking the floor for blood as I go. Only a few drops that I can spot. I tend not to bleed for very long, and it looks like Brad Pitt's clothes soaked up most of what leaked out of me.

"Let me clarify. When I say I'll be in charge, that doesn't mean I'm going to actually be doing anything. I'll mostly be gone or working upstairs."

"Ah," she says, even colder than before. She knows exactly what Kasabian does up there and she doesn't approve. An L.A. girl with a conscience. They're about as rare as unicorns.

"Not doing anything is Mr. Kasabian's management style, too. You'll fit right in." Her heartbeat kicks up and her pupils dilate. Why the hell am I noticing these things?

She frowns, looks down, then up at me. "Please, don't tell him I said that."

"Your secret is safe with me."

Her breathing slows. She relaxes, just a hair. "Can I ask you a question?"

"Sure."

"What the hell is wrong with your clothes?"

"Yeah. I had a little accident coming into town," I say, giving her a sheepish grin. It's a look that girls used to like when I was young and not entirely unhandsome. Talking to a cute human girl that I might have flirted with in my former life, I forget for a second that I'm no longer young or handsome. I shift to what I hope was a more neutral expression.

"I might need to pick up some new things. What do you think?"

"Don't bother. I hear that arson is the new black." She crosses her arms, giving me her best defiant look.

"Stark."

"Stark. Just the one name then, like Madonna?"

"Or Cher."

"Okay, Mr. Stark . . ."

"Stark. No 'mister.' Just Stark."

"Okay, Just Stark. Here's the thing—I quit. I can run this place in my sleep, but Mr. Kasabian obviously doesn't trust me enough, so he brings in some, if you'll excuse me, thug buddy to keep an eye on me? No fucking thanks."

"The last thing I'm here to do is keep an eye on you. The

truth is, I don't have any place to stay and Kasabian told me I could crash upstairs. The running-the-shop thing is purely honorary. As far as I'm concerned, you're in charge. Run the place any way you like."

"You still look like somebody I probably shouldn't know."

"Yeah, you said that." I take a step toward her, waiting to see if she'll take a step back. She doesn't. Nervous, but brave. I like her already. "Listen, a thug is someone who's out for no one but himself. Me? I take care of my friends." Alice's face flashes in my brain, a reminder of how empty a promise like that can be. Good intentions and a dime won't get you a damned thing in this world. Reluctantly, I push Alice back into the dark. "Stay here and I guarantee that you'll work in the safest video store in L.A."

"Gee, that's not at all terrifying."

"Also, whatever Kasabian has been paying you, I'll give you a fifty percent raise."

Now I have her attention.

"You can do that?"

"There's no one here to tell me I can't. I figure, as long as I'm technically in charge, I can pay people whatever I like."

"When will Mr. Kasabian be back?"

"I have no idea. You know how these family things are. It could be a while."

She nods, looks down, then up at me. "Okay. I'll stay. For now."

Hallelujah. "Thank you, Allegra."

"You're welcome, Just Stark."

I WAIT FOR an hour upstairs, until the store fills with the lunch-hour crowd. When there's enough ambient noise downstairs, I figure that I can check on Kasabian and be covered if he starts screaming again.

He's right where I left him on the shelf. When he sees me, he doesn't scream. He just moans.

"For chrissake, put a bullet in my head or change the goddamn channel!"

On the set, some daytime talk show is playing. An older guy in a suit and a bottle blonde are talking about an actress I never heard of and a pasta maker that's going to change everyone's life.

"Please, turn this shit off."

"I don't know. That sounds like one damn fine pasta maker."

"Fuck you."

"Do you have a car?"

He stares at the TV, ignoring me. I reach over and turn down the sound.

"The keys are in my right hand pocket," he says.

I tilt his comatose body to the side so I can reach into his pocket. Got 'em.

"What kind of car is it?"

"Give me back my body."

"Where's Mason?"

"I don't know."

"I don't believe you."

"Trust me, if I knew how to send you to Mason, I'd do it in a heartbeat. Then I'd ask him to let me watch as he ripped your balls off."

I turn the talk show back up and lock the closet door. Muffled profanity comes from inside.

I grab the garbage with the bloody clothes and sheets and head down the stairs to the store. Allegra and another kid are behind the counter, busy with customers. There's a rear exit to the store in a small storage room behind the porn section. I get out the bone blade and try a trick that worked in Hell. Placing the tip of the blade into the lock, I push it inside and turn. The lock clicks open.

Behind the store is a short alley with a couple of Dumpsters. I toss the garbage bag and head for the street.

It's nice out. Sunny, but not yet hot. I feel a lot more human and settled today, just another normal guy with a .45 tucked in the back of his jeans, out to run some errands. I counted Brad Pitt's money last night and it came to twenty-two hundred bucks, so I'm sure I can get everything I need.

I keep pressing the little unlock button on the key chain and my good mood evaporates when Kasabian's car finally chirps. A white Chevy Aveo with a dented trunk. Only rental companies buy white American cars, which means that not only is Kasabian's car a piece of shit, it's a used piece of shit. But who's more pathetic, the guy who drives a used piece of shit or the guy who steals it?

IT'S WEIRD STARTING over from zero. It changes the scale of your ambitions. Instead of fantasizing about what kind of mansion you'll buy when you win the lottery, you ask yourself, *Do I own socks? Do I have a toothbrush? Do I have a shirt that's not covered in blood?*

Money is strange, too, if you haven't used it for a while. Hell is mostly a barter economy. Especially among the high and mighty, having to buy something is a massive social faux pas. It means that you don't have anything good enough to trade or you aren't clever enough to swindle your way to your heart's desire. Brad Pitt's wad seemed like a fortune when I counted it, but I blow through most of it in a couple of hours.

The big money goes for a few choice items. A new pair of Caterpillar steel-toed boots, because steel is always a good idea. I also pick up a long, light overcoat. There's a reason spies and private eyes wear trench coats in all those old movies. They're big enough to hide a multitude of sins, especially the kind with bullets. I pick up a long, charcoal-gray silk overcoat at a West Hollywood rent-boy boutique. Anything heavier than silk will look ridiculous in L.A., and wearing a black overcoat is nature's way of telling you to lay off the Bauhaus.

Down on Melrose, the movie biz show-offs and trust-fund bikers meet at smart cafés for lattes and burgers that cost as much as a face-lift. Out in front of the cafés stretch long, gleaming lines of $40,000 Harleys that have never seen a speck of dust or a splash of mud. As much as these clowns set off the self-righteous parts of my white-trash ego, I know there's one good thing about them. They demand the best bike gear available.

At a bike shop that's laid out more like a museum than a store, I pick up leather race pants and an armored moto-cross jacket. After getting shot and almost stun-gunned, I like the idea of having a layer of Kevlar between the world and me. I also get a Kevlar jacket liner, a kind of long sleeve mesh shirt with armored panels sewn in. I'll wear the liner under the overcoat and hope it's not so bulky that I look like a robot in a bathrobe.

I put on my new boots, pants, and the motocross jacket in one of the dressing rooms, and toss my burned stuff into the trash on the way out of the store. That's just about the last of it, I think. The last physical connections to my former life. The only thing left is the Germs T-shirt, now full of blood and bullet holes, stuffed under the mattress back at Max Overdrive. Maybe I should have tossed it with the rest, but Alice gave it to me, so it stays with me until I crash and burn for good.

When I parked the Aveo earlier, I left the .45 under the driver's seat. I do a switch when I get back, putting the .45 in the bag with my new coat and leaving the Aveo's keys on the seat. Maybe some desperate-for-wheels kid will find it, or a few homeless guys can turn it into a condo. I carry my bags down Melrose to do some car shopping.

There's only one way to steal a car and not feel guilty about it, and that's to steal the most expensive car you can find. That way, you know that it carries the maximum insurance possible, so whatever happens, the owner is covered. I pick out a black Mercedes S600, go around to the driver's side, and using my body to block the view, stab the bone knife into the lock. I hold my breath. The car chirps once and the lock pops. I slide in with my bags, jam the knife in the ignition, and the engine purrs to life. I do a check of the mirrors and windows. No one is even looking at me. Stepping on the gas, I guide the Mercedes into the afternoon traffic.

THE BUILDING IS like the Sphinx—eternal and unchanging—exactly as I remember it. Same wrought-iron bars bolted over the first floor windows. The chicken-wire-embedded glass in the upper floor windows reveals dusty curtains and tattered window shades. The building manager's window is easy to spot: there are shreds of the gold-leaf letters that once spelled out the safe company's name. Instead of a curtain, the manager's window is covered in foil. I've always wondered what goes on in there that he's so desperate to keep out the light. Someday I'll have to find out.

I watch the building for the time it takes me to smoke

three cigarettes. Nothing unusual or even interesting happens. Cars drive by. An old woman wanders by pulling a couple of tired-looking Jack Russells.

I'm not sure about the wisdom of walking into the place in broad daylight, but I'm not getting any demonic vibes off the place. I snap the Veritas off its chain and give it a quick flip inside the car. Should I go in or not? The coin comes down with the morning-star side up. The Hellion script around the edge reads, *Go back to the store and talk to the pretty girl.* Nice. My magic coin is trying to get me laid. While I appreciate the thought, the timing stinks. I get out of the car, tuck the .45 under my jacket, and jog across the street to the building.

As usual, the front door is locked, but the side door, by the loading dock, is wide open. There's a freight elevator to the right of the entrance. I pull down the upper gate, which closes the elevator's wooden jaws, and hit the third-floor button with the side of my fist. The elevator jerks and starts to climb.

I could have stayed across the street and walked in here through a shadow. I could have walked through a shadow straight into my apartment. Fuck that. This is my home. I'm going in through the door.

When the elevator hits three, I roll up the gate and sprint right down the central corridor, then cut left. My place is at the end of a hall just long enough to let me get a running start. The door is the original, solid steel and balanced perfectly on two heavy metal hinges. I wouldn't have thought about doing this before, but I'm a bit stronger now. I take a few long, running steps, swing my leg up, and slam my heel into the door. It pops open, the rusty lock mechanism spinning through the air like a metal Frisbee. I have the .45 up and in front of me, ready for anything.

"Well," says the two-hundred-year-old Frenchman from his easy chair. "It fucking took you long enough."

HE STANDS UP from a battered, green recliner. He's a little taller than I remember and a little heavier, but he still has the same salt-and-pepper beard and close-cropped hair, the same impressive Roman nose and dark eyes that, at different times, might belong to your favorite uncle on Christmas morning or to the pissed-off ex-thug who's about shove a power drill through your forehead.

I just look at him. Normally, I like hearing Vidocq shout "fuck" because he pronounces it "fock." On the other hand, of the top ten people I didn't expect to find here, he's the entire top five. I stay put, not moving to the right or left, orienting my body so that, if I have to, I can make it out the door without looking.

"Vidocq? What are you doing here?"

"That's how you greet a friend after all these years?" he asks, setting the battered book he'd been reading on the floor. "I've been waiting for you, keeping your home safe. You think I wanted to squat in this concrete shithole?"

I raise the .45 and aim it at his head. "How did we meet, old man?"

"Ah, you don't think it's me, no? You think this is some trap. I might, too, if I were you." He picks up a tumbler filled to the top with wine so red it looks black.

"You and I met at a saloon. It's closed now. Blood Meridian. This was before you met lovely Alice. We were both at the bar, each chatting up the same pretty girl, who stood between us. Neither of us had more than a few dollars then, so we'd employed a small memory charm on the bartender so that we could pay for drinks with the same money over and over again. When we realized what the other was doing, we forgot the pretty girl and talked about what and who we were, what and who we knew, paying the poor bartender with the same few dollars all night."

"No great loss, from what I remember. The girl was pretty, but kind of wasted."

"So were we, as I recall. Our sudden loss of interest offended her."

"Next lifetime, I'll buy her drinks and listen to her all night long."

"Next lifetime."

The gun suddenly feels heavy in my hand. I lower it. Vidocq, a head taller than me and half again as wide, comes over and crushes me in a long bear hug.

"It's good to see you, boy," he says.

Like the building, Vidocq hasn't changed a bit. He

looks about forty-five, but is old enough that he can tell you what guillotines sounded like offing the aristocracy during the French Revolution.

I look around the room. It doesn't look right. Where's all my stuff? Where's Alice's?

"How long have you been living here? Where is everything?" I ask.

"Alice moved out a few months after you disappeared. I saved your things and the things she left in the bedroom."

"Where did she go?"

"She moved in with a friend in Echo Park. That's where she was when the terrible things happened."

"Mason murdered her. You can say it." I feel stupid, but I have to ask him. "The friend she moved in with, was it a girl or a guy?"

"No, a girlfriend," he says. "Alice had lovers after you were gone, but none of them were very serious. You broke her heart. She wasn't the same girl."

I go over to the counter that separates the living room from the kitchen. The teakettle on the stove looks familiar, but not much else. And I'm not sure about the kettle.

"You checked up on her?"

"As much as I could. She didn't really want to see anybody from your old days together. Certainly, no one associated with magic."

That sounds like her. She didn't like Mason or anyone else in the Circle. After I was gone, she'd want to get as far away from magic as she could. But she didn't run far enough. I should have told her to leave town if something happened to me. I should have given her an escape plan. But what could happen to me? I was a golden boy. I was bulletproof.

I say, "Thanks for trying. And thanks for keeping the place. I don't know what I would have done if I'd come in and found some asshole stranger sitting here."

Vidocq picks ups the bottle of red wine from the coffee table, gets a glass for me from the kitchen, and fills it to the rim. He fills his glass, raises it, and we both drink. I sit down on the couch.

"So, how are you? What have you been doing since I've been gone?"

"I've been working. These days, the work is all I have," he says. "Thievery pays for the tools, and the work shows me the mind of God. Stealing is a lot like alchemy, you know. In each, we each try to find what is beautiful and hidden and make it ours."

"This is funny. The whole time we've known each other, I don't remember you staying more than a few weeks anywhere. It's hard to picture you here as a rent-and-electric-bill guy."

"Don't insult me. I wouldn't pay a penny for this hovel. I used an old gypsy potion, a *vin de mémoire manquée*. I painted the walls, the windows, floor and ceiling, *et voilà!* Your home no longer exists. It is not seen or remembered, except, of course, by our funny sort of people. The Sub Rosa."

The Sub Rosa. I haven't thought about the Sub Rosa in a long time.

Vidocq is Sub Rosa. So are Kasabian, Mason, and the rest of the Circle. I'm Sub Rosa, too, though back in the day I never thought of myself that way, even though there are maybe a few thousand of us walking around Southern California.

Sub Rosas are the secret people who look just like you, but are different. They bank where you bank. They stand behind you in line at the coffee shop. They panhandle you for the money that you suddenly and inexplicably *have* to drop into their grimy hands. Some of us also talk to the dead. Some see the future, trade souls like baseball cards, or bribe angels for a peek at God's to-do list. Mostly, Sub Rosas are the people regular people aren't supposed to know about. It's not that we don't like you; it's that you have a habit of burning us at the stake when you notice us.

Vidocq's alchemical supplies and burglary gear cover nearly every surface—racks of potions, books and scrolls in Latin and Greek, alembics, test tubes, and grinding stones. On a table in a corner are the baubles he's stolen on commission—netsukes, loose diamonds spilling from courier envelopes, passports, and computer discs. It was one of his less successful experiments that turned him immortal. He's spent the last hundred and fifty years stealing things to fund his research for a cure.

"Thanks for watching the place. I'm glad you have it," I tell him. "I couldn't live here without Alice."

He nods solemnly.

"Where will you live?"

"I'm crashing at a friend's place. There's a bathroom, a comfy bed, and all the movies you can eat. You should come by and see it."

"It sounds charming."

"I'm back here to kill some people, you know." I blurt it out, trying to get the words out fast. "I'm going to take out the whole magic circle."

"I knew that when you walked in. And I understand. I won't even try to talk you out of it, but there are things you should know before you start."

I can tell this is going to be a Real Talk. I light a cigarette as Vidocq pours more wine.

"I did something much like what you're doing, many years ago. Long before you or your grandparents were born. Revenge is never what you think it's going to be. There's no pleasure and glory, and when it's done your grief remains. Once a man does the things you're talking about, he will never be the same, and he can never go back to who he was before. Worst of all, no matter how many enemies you kill, you are never satisfied. There is always one more who deserves it. When it becomes too easy to kill, it never ends."

"You stopped."

"The desire is still there, even though all the men are dead, the ones I killed and the ones who passed away during the many years I restrained myself. Worse, when it was over I had to leave Paris, get on a ship, and come here to the land of cheeseburgers and cowboys. You are starting down a bad road, my friend."

"I appreciate the advice. Don't worry. I'm not here to ask for help."

"Don't be stupid. Of course I'll help you. We must always look after our friends, even when they are foolish. Especially when they are foolish."

"Thank you, old man."

"*Salut,*" he says, and holds out his glass. I clink mine into his.

When I finish the cigarette, I take out the knife I used on Kasabian and pry up some boards under the coffee table. The oilcloth wrap containing my father's guns is still there. I pull out the bundle and set the guns on the table, one by one. A good copy of an 1861 Navy Colt revolver, modified for modern .44 caliber shells. A heavy Civil War–era LeMat pistol. A Browning .45 semiauto my granddad used on D-day. And a Benelli M3 shotgun. They all need a good cleaning before I can use them.

Something flashes through Vidocq's mind. I only catch a fragment of it before he pushes it away. Seeing it feels like a migraine coming on, a knife behind my eyes.

"What's wrong?" asks Vidocq.

"There's something funny going on with my head. I keep feeling and hearing things I shouldn't. Like right now you're sweating and your heartbeat is going up. Like maybe you're a little afraid."

"You're back here from Hell, talking about murder, and you're pulling guns from under my floor. Shouldn't I be a little frightened for both of us?"

"There's other things, too. I've turned kind of death-proof. I can get shot, ripped apart, dropped in a Cuisinart, and I just get up and walk away. I don't understand what's happening to me."

"You fall into the Abyss a young magician and you emerge as Superman. How is that possible?"

"You're the one with the all the books. You tell me."

"Perhaps, like me, you were cursed with an inability to die."

"What happened to you wasn't a curse. You just decided it was. Besides, if anything, those Downtown demonfuckers would make me easier to kill so I'd get back there quicker."

"Perhaps it's simple biology. You're the first living man to have entered Hell. Your condition might be a natural biological response. A side effect of having been in that awful place. Perhaps you should be grateful that you have this new gift to accentuate your natural magical abilities."

"I don't trust it. It means something I can't figure out. Or it's a setup. Nothing that happened down there was for my benefit."

"We'll know in time, then. Your friends in Hell will be after you soon, I suppose?"

"Eventually, but not now. There's a war going on down there. It's fucking chaos."

"Lucky you."

"Lucky me."

I get a dish towel from the kitchen, bring it back to the living room, and use it to wipe the dust from each gun. Even though I had them in the oil wrap, I can see traces of rust. I'll have to clean them for real later.

"So, what was it like in Hell? Did you try to escape? You were always such a clever magician."

"Clever magic doesn't get you much down there. Even when I got stronger, I couldn't cast the simplest hex until I started learning Hellion magic."

"Is that how you got away?"

"No. I was the property of Azazel, one of Lucifer's generals. He made me his designated hitman. He said that Alice would be all right, as long as I played along."

"And then she wasn't all right."

"I don't know how I knew, but I did. It's like these new things I can hear and feel." I gulped some wine. "Before I left, I cut out Azazel's heart and left it on his altar."

"How did you get out?"

"A key. A key to anywhere in the universe I want to go."

"Do you have it with you?"

"It's right here," I say, putting my hand on my chest like I'm about to say the Pledge of Allegiance. "Over my heart. I took his knife, cut myself open, and put the key inside. Now I can walk through shadows to the Room of Thirteen Doors. Go anywhere I want, anytime I want. Back to

Hell. Maybe Heaven, too. I don't know. I haven't opened all thirteen doors."

"You put the key inside you? And it was made with Hellion magic? It will poison you."

"Everything that happened to me for eleven years poisoned me. You think one little key is going to make a difference now?"

"This isn't good, Jimmy."

"Please don't call me that. I don't have that name anymore."

"So, you are still afraid of them. Afraid they can find you through your name?"

"Not if no one uses it."

"Your name is who you are. It's your family. It connects you to this world. You can't give it away so easily." He took a long gulp of wine and said, "Wild Bill."

"Especially, don't call me that."

Vidocq is one of the few people who know that my full name is James Butler Hickok Stark. That's Wild Bill Hickok's name, except for the Stark. I learned to shoot and appreciate guns young because we're supposed to be direct descendants of Wild Bill, the greatest shootist of the American West. "Stark" was tacked on sometime after those prairie towns became cities to keep idiots from showing up at the door wanting to touch great-great-granddad's legend. Or worse. There were more than a few fights and even some gunplay. The funny thing is no one knows for sure if we really are connected to Wild Bill. Supposedly, he left a few little bastards behind in Kansas and Missouri, so it's possible. But it might just be a tall tale. My family never let facts get in the way of a good story.

"Wild Bill is dead. I'm just Stark."

"That is your family, your identity. You can't just walk away from your name."

"I can and I have. I'm looking for Mason. He gave me to the Hellions for power and now I'm here to pay him back. Do you know where he is?"

"No one sees Monsieur Faim anymore. Like God, he is a great mystery. What will you do if you find him?"

"Kill him."

"And then what?" Vidocq sets down his glass and steeples his fingers. "What you want may not be possible. Mason is a very powerful man these days. Very well protected."

"I've gotten through to plenty of well-protected Hellions. And I learned a few things along the way. Want to know what the first lesson was?"

"Tell me, please."

I pick up a little vial of mercury sitting on the coffee table and shake it, watching the light glint of its silver surface.

"Up here in the City of Angels USA, magicians worry about good and evil. White magic versus black."

"All magicians think about those differences."

"Not Downtown they don't. Hellions understand something we don't. That there is no white magic. There is no black magic. There's just magic. You can kill with a healing spell as easily as with a curse. If you were having a heart attack right now, I could do a spell to slow your heart and keep it from beating out of your chest. I could regulate your blood pressure, bring it up or down. But I can use those same spells if you aren't having a heart attack. I can turn down your blood pressure until you pass out. Slow and stop your heart. And you'd be just as dead as if I'd hexed you."

"This isn't Hell, boy. People will know. There are rules up here."

"Not for me. I don't even know if they can read my magic up here. If it will even disturb the aether."

Vidocq picks up, and then sets down his wineglass with a thud. Loudly, he says, "Then why don't you use it? Go on and do a location charm for Mason right now."

I set down the mercury and look around the unfamiliar familiar room. "I can't. I don't know what will happen. The magic might not show up at all, or it might go off like fireworks at the Super Bowl. I can't take a chance on anyone knowing I'm back."

Vidocq smiles and wags his finger at me. "So, for all your power you have no power at all. That's a little funny, don't you think?"

"I have guns."

"Yes, you'll conquer the whole Sub Rosa with guns. More Roy Rogers bullshit."

I think about that for a minute. "There are things I used in the arena. I'm going to have to get some weapons made. I need to find someone who can work with metal."

"You must let me help you," says Vidocq intently. "Let me help keep this plan of yours from going too far. I know that you've come back to Le Merdier, this world of shit, but where else is there for you to go? You must live here. You must have a name. You must be a man again."

What's that old Sunday school warning about how if you fight dragons too long, you can become one? That's been spinning around in my head for years, long enough that I know I'd rather be a dragon than a sheep to the slaughter. Maybe, in some kinder, gentler version of the world, I could walk away from the Circle, get Zen, and forgive them for what they did to me. But I can't forgive them for Alice. Never for that. Maybe I'm not worth killing for, but she is.

"I should go. I have to meet someone," I lie. I set the guns back in the oilcloth and wrap them up. I'm feeling a little ashamed of myself, like I'm letting down the old man. Without looking at him, I ask, "Want to meet up tomorrow?"

"Of course."

I make it out the door before he can give me another French bear hug.

I STEER THE Mercedes west toward the one other place in town that makes my skin crawl almost as much as the old apartment.

I turn off Sunset and onto Laurel Canyon Boulevard. The change from Hollywood to Beverly Hills is always sudden and startling, like flipping a switch. Bus fumes and strip-mall nail salons transform to trimmed green lawns and stately homes. This isn't movie-star Beverly Hills, but the older part. The homes are large, but not bloated parade floats. It looks like grown-ups might have lived here.

After crossing Mulholland, I turn right into a maze of streets all named Doña. Doña Isabel. Doña Marta. Doña Sarita. When I find the right Doña, I park and sit for a minute, thinking. I should have seen something like this coming. Things had been going too easy since I got back. Brad Pitt wasn't my fuck-you welcome back to the world. This is.

There's no need to get out of the car, but I do anyway, and cross the street to the empty lot where Mason's house—the place where our magic circle used to meet— once stood. The vacant land looks corrupt and out of place in this perfect landscape, like a starlet showing rotten teeth behind her million-dollar smile. Tall weeds grow through the sandy soil. There's a faded sign with the name of a real-estate developer and a "Coming Soon!" message on top, but it doesn't look like anyone has set foot anywhere near the lot in years.

The sun is going down fast. When a breeze picks up, I feel a chill. I know it's all in my head. Even at Christmas, L.A. isn't that cold, but it doesn't stop my teeth from chattering.

Night is coming on fast. I walk back to the Mercedes, get in, and light up one of the last few cigarettes from the pack Carlos gave me. I look at the empty lot and wonder what happened there. It doesn't look like the house burned. From what I remember, this neighborhood is on bedrock, so it probably didn't fall down in a quake. It just went away. I know I should go over and walk around to see if I can find something that could point me to Mason and the others. But not tonight. The shit and sulfur smell when I was dragged to Hell through the basement floor are coming back strong. I stay in the car, and when the last of the cigarette is gone, I flick the butt onto one of the manicured lawns and drive away.

I DITCH THE Mercedes a few blocks from Max Overdrive. At another time it would break my heart to have to leave such a brilliant machine behind, but L.A. is an all-you-can-eat car buffet, and now that I've seen what the knife does to locks and ignitions, I'm never going to starve.

I grab the oilcloth bundle with the guns and the bags with my new clothes. When I get to the store, it is closed, but I rap on the glass and Allegra lets me in.

"Damn," she says. "You clean up pretty good."

"Thanks." It feels nice being complimented by a human woman. The few kind words I'd heard in the last eleven years usually came from Hellions that looked like something a snake had just thrown up.

"Did you lose your key?"

"I forgot it. I haven't had to carry one for a while."

"Where did you live that you didn't need keys?" She looks at something in her hand that's beeping at her. It looks like a TV remote fucked a little typewriter and this is the bastard offspring. She types something on the tiny typewriter with her thumbs, and smiles.

"What's that you're playing with?"

"You've never seen one of these? It's a BlackBerry."

"Is it like a phone? But you're typing with it."

"I've got it now. You've been in a coma since the seventies. No. Abducted by aliens."

"You nailed me. *Klatuu barada nikto.*"

"*The Day the Earth Stood Still,* right? That was one of my favorites when I was a kid."

"Me, too. So, why are you typing on your BlackBerry thing?"

"Just BlackBerry. Like you, Just Stark." She turns the little device so I can see it better. "You can talk on it or you can send text messages. It's like e-mail, only it's instant. You've heard of e-mail, right."

"Sure. But why would you type something to someone? Why not just call them?"

"Sometimes texting is more fun. Or, like now, if you're sending someone an address, it's nice to have it in writing."

"What's that on the screen?"

"It's Google Maps. I looked up the address so I could give Michelle directions." She clicks and the little screen changes. "See, you just get on the net and enter the address."

"You have the Internet on that? If I got the Internet, I could look things up on it, right? Names, places, history?"

"First off, you don't get the Internet. It's the Web, and you don't get it. You use it. And, yeah, you can look up anything you want."

"Can I get one of these?"

She looks at me like I really have spent a decade with Martians.

"Of course. You just have to figure out what kind you want." She types a few more words into the BlackBerry and puts it in her coat pocket.

"Thanks," I say.

"No problem. I've got to go and meet some friends. Can you lock up after me?"

"Sure. Good night."

"Night."

I haven't used keys for a while. What a stupid damn thing to say. I could see it in her eyes. She's wondering if I'm flat-out crazy or a recent jailbird. Worse, she's wondering if I've done something to Kasabian. Plus, she's wondering about what's wrapped in the dirty oilcloth. I'll have to start locking the upstairs door. I'll have to do something about her suspicions, too, but I don't know what, and I'm not going to figure it out tonight. I take my bags and the bundle with the guns upstairs and drop them on the bed. Tomorrow I'll check into the BlackBerry thing. Having the Internet or Web or whatever with me will help me catch up on the world and keep me from sounding like a newly landed Martian.

I go over and open Kasabian's closet.

"Morning, sunshine. Sleep well?"

There's a cheesy infomercial playing on the TV. Some guy in a chef's uniform is waving kitchen utensils around.

"You ever see these knives, man? I just might have to get a set. They cut right through soda cans and bricks."

"If I ever start eating bricks, I'll come by and borrow them. You had any thoughts about our conversation last night? Like, where I can find some of the old crowd?"

Kasabian doesn't look at me, but keeps staring at the TV. "They never rust, you know. And you never have to sharpen them. They're amazing. They're almost magic."

"You're really not in a position to be fucking with anybody right now."

He finally aims his eyes up at me. "Think so? See, I think I'm in exactly the position where I can do any goddamn thing I want. You want to kill me? Go ahead. I wasn't exactly having an E ticket life before and now I don't even have that."

"You're not getting back your body. Someday maybe, but not right now."

He turns back to the TV. "Did you meet Allegra? That is one sweet little piece of art girl scooter pussy. It's not like I fucked her yet or anything, but New Year's is coming and I figure some champagne, a couple of roofies, and I'll finally know if the carpet matches the drapes."

"Whether you mean any of that or not, you really are just puke on two legs."

"I don't have any legs, asshole." He nods toward his body. "Aw, did I offend the serial killer? I'm so sorry.

Murder anyone today? Cut off any friends' heads?"

I recognize the pose, the B-movie defiance. I tried the same thing in Hell. It's hard to scare someone who thinks he has nothing to lose. The trick is to remind him that there's always something left to lose. For some, it's family or friends. For a creep like Kasabian, demonstrating the possibility of future loss is easy.

I get his gun from the bed, wrap it in a towel from the bathroom, and fire off three shots in the direction of his body.

"Are you fucking crazy?" he screams. "I need that!"

"All of it? You've got two knees, two kidneys. That's a spare for each."

"Fuck you, you fucking fuck."

"You want to answer some questions or do you want me to play William Tell?"

"You know, this, right here, is why it was so easy for Mason to sell you out and why the rest of us didn't really care."

"Why was that?"

"Because you're such a dick." He raises his eyebrows at me, hoping I'll react. I don't. "Back with the Circle, Christ, you were just a punk kid and you had all this power. More than any of the rest of us, including Mason. But did you care? Hell no. It all came too easy for you. The rest of us had to kill ourselves studying to get the simplest spell to work. Most of the time, you didn't even pretend to study the books. You'd just make up something on the spot and angels would fly out of your ass. Do you know how that made the rest of us feel?"

"So, you sent me to Hell because I hurt your feelings?"

"No, because you hurt Mason's. You never let up on the guy."

"If I gave Mason a hard time it's because he deserved it. Always going on about being a great dark magician. He didn't want to learn anything from magic. He didn't even want to have fun with it. He just wanted to be Lex Luthor. I might not have given him so much grief if I'd known what a little hothouse flower he was."

"See? You're still doing it. But for all your bullshit and your show-off magic, Mason beat you, didn't he? You could pull magic out of the air, but he ended up with real power and you ended up blowing demons for eleven years. Every night, before I go to sleep, I cherish the look on your face as they dragged your ass down to Hell."

Without looking where I'm aiming, I pop off a couple more rounds in the direction of his body.

"Stop it! Stop, goddammit! What do you want to know?"

"Same thing I wanted yesterday. Where's the rest of the Circle?" I toss the gun onto the bed. God, I want a cigarette. "Let's try a different approach. You're right here, so where's Jayne-Anne?"

If Donald Trump and the Wicked Witch of the West had a kid, it would be Jayne-Anne. She looks like a librarian with some money and good taste in clothes, but underneath the Versace, she's Godzilla with tits. She isn't as powerful a magician as Mason, but next to him she's the most focused and ruthless and, in her way, scarier than bad dog Parker.

"I don't know. I heard she's got some kind of movie-business gig."

"What about Cherry Moon?"

Crack open a pedophile's piñata and Cherry Moon is the candy that falls out. She's a Lollipop Doll, one of a gang of girls who take their manga and anime a little too seriously. They all want to grow up to be Sailor Moon and Cherry had the magical skill to do it. Last time I saw her, she was in High Gothic Lolita drag, radiating rough sex and looking all of twelve years old.

"Also don't know about her. Someone said she's running some kind of spa or plastic surgery thing for rich assholes."

"I'm glad to hear that everyone's using their new power for such worthy causes."

"We've all gotta eat. Not me right now, but generally."

"Where's TJ?"

He rolls his eyes when I say the name. "That fucking hippie. After the Lurkers grabbed you, he bawled like a little girl for days. Some people aren't cut out for real life."

"Lurker" is what the Sub Rosa call any secretive magical, mystical, or monstrous freak that isn't them. A naiad is a Lurker. So are zombies and werewolves. Undercover cops are secretive and sometimes monsters, but they aren't Lurkers. They're just pricks.

"Where is he?"

"Sucking dirt in Woodlawn. The little faggot hung himself a week after you went bye-bye. Guess he couldn't get the monsters out of his head."

Poor dumb kid. TJ was even younger than me. He would have been sixteen or seventeen back then. But Kasabian is right about one thing; some people aren't built to see the dark side of magic or deal with the vicious parts of life. TJ never belonged in our little wolf pack. In a way, I was glad he was gone. I hadn't been looking forward to hunting him down.

"I guess we covered Mason and Parker last night. Mason's gone and he took Parker with him. Do I have that right?"

"Yeah. And don't ask me about them because I don't know. People see Parker around town sometimes. Usually right before some other nosy magician gets his neck broken."

The thought of an attack dog like Parker and a Darth Vader wannabe like Mason running wild with heads full of Hellion hoodoo does not take me to a happy place. And the two of them could be holed up anywhere, from Glendale to Bhutan.

"You been out to the old house yet? Pretty, isn't it?"

"What happened to it?"

"Don't know. Maybe Mason took the house with him. Did you find anything good when you went inside?"

"Inside what? The house is gone. What's there to find?"

"You simple son of a bitch. The basement's still there. You've got to go underground." Kasabian gives me an appraising look. "What, did you just drive up and leave? Pretty tough, tough guy."

Beautiful. Now I have to burrow like a groundhog into Mason's basement to the same room where he summoned those things to take me Downtown. Nothing can possibly go wrong with this plan.

When I turn to leave, Kasabian yells at me.

"Hey, asshole. I gave you information. At least let me have a cigarette."

"I'm out, so tonight we both suffer. I'll pick up more tomorrow."

I step out of the closet, and just before I close the door, I say, "I almost forgot. Your car was parked in a two-hour zone and I was afraid you were going to get a ticket, so I gave your car away."

"You what?"

"Sweet dreams."

I SIT ON the edge of the bed wanting a cigarette, but unable to summon the will to go out and find a store that's still open. The bullets in my chest ache, almost like someone shot them in there. I think one of the slugs is scraping against a rib. I get up and scrounge around the room, moving furniture, opening cabinets, and digging through piles of empty DVD cases. Finally, at the bottom of a box filled with mangled porn tapes—I don't want to even think about how they got that way—I find a bottle of cheap, no name vodka in a plastic screw-top bottle. In high school, we called drinks like this Devil's Rain after an old horror movie. That strikes me as pretty funny, under the circumstances. I screw off the top and take a drink. The vodka burns my throat, and tastes like Windex and battery acid.

I can't believe that some small, ridiculous part of me feels kind of sorry for a pig like Kasabian. To spend your whole life brownnosing and riding on the coattails of smarter and more talented magicians, then having them dump you like the prom date who wouldn't put out right as they become infused with who knows what kind of power, has to sting. It has to be the final confirmation of all your worst fears, that you really are the chump you were always afraid you might be.

I, on the other hand, was exactly the prick Kasabian said I was. While he was struggling with kindergarten levitations and Mason was compulsively showing off some new spirit conjuration or fire blast, I bullshitted my way through magic the way I bullshitted my way through everything else, pretty well.

Magic really was always easy for me. At my fifth birthday party, I floated the family cat over to Tiffany Brown, a redhead I had a crush on, and dropped it on her. Tiffany didn't get the joke and that was the end of my first romance.

When I was twelve, the teacher had us make clay animals

in art class. I squeezed together some fat little birds. Then I made them fly around the room and out the window. I got suspended for a week for that one, though no one could explain to me exactly why.

I didn't even know I was doing magic back then. All I did know was that I could do funny tricks and make the other kids laugh.

My family never talked about it, but they knew what I could do. I was dangerous when I got sick. I'd break windows with a look. My fevers started fires. I only learned that what I was doing had a name when my father gave me an old, leather-bound book titled *A Concise History and Outline of the Magickal Arts*. I knew right away what I was. Not a warlock or a wizard. That was Disney stuff to me. I was a magician. A few years later, I found out there were other magicians and some invited me into their tight little Circle. Then they tried to kill me.

Sitting on Kasabian's bed, drinking his lousy vodka, I can picture Jayne-Anne, Cherry, Parker, and Mason sitting high above the city in one of those houses that hangs over the side of a hill on spindly spider legs, daring the earth to throw an earthquake their way. Each of them knows they'll survive. Even without magic, they'll survive, because that's their greatest talent. And soon they'll be up on another hill, looking down on us losers. They're strong and we're weak because we won't do the things they did to get up to the top of the hill.

They're right, of course. We won't crawl through the

shit, and over the bones and bodies of the dead. By their definition of the word, we really are weak, no matter how much we'd like to imagine ourselves being as cold and hard and determined as they are.

On the other hand, it might be fun to crawl up the hill one night and strap some dynamite to the spider legs holding up their houses. We'd jump on the roofs, like kids jumping on sleds in the snow, and ride down the hill until their bright, candy-colored mansions crash into the sea.

Between the bullets in my chest and the talk with Kasabian, sleeping isn't going to be easy tonight. Kasabian's vodka is pretty much poison, but it'll quiet the noise in my head and that's good enough.

When I finally drift off into alcohol dreamland, I'm back in Hell, lying in the dirt on the floor of the arena. My belly is slashed open and I'm holding my innards in with my hands. The beast I'd been fighting, a silver bull-like thing with a dozen razor-sharp horns, is lying dead a few yards away. They always had me fighting weird animals. I didn't know for a long time that it was another Hellion insult. They made me a *bestiari*. It was a Roman thing—a fun way to use their dumbest, gimpiest, most cross-eyed fighters. *Bestiari* weren't good enough to fight people, so they fought animals. Why waste a human gladiator on someone who had just as good a chance of cutting off his own leg as stabbing his opponent? Plus, it was fun watching bears eat retards. Still is, really.

A couple of Hellion arena slaves roll me onto a stretcher

and take me backstage. In the fighters' quarters, a wizened old Hellion gladiator trainer shuffles over and hands me a bottle of Aqua Regia. That's medical care in Hell. A hospital in a bottle. Later, the same old Hellion comes by with a needle and werewolf-hair thread and sews me up.

Later that night, Azazel, my slave master, sends for me. Fresh wounds or not, when he calls, you go. At least he's reasonable enough to send a couple of burly damned souls to carry me to his palace on a litter.

None of the palaces in Hell come close to Lucifer's in size or beauty. Lucifer lives at the top of a literal ivory tower, miles high. You can't even see the top from the ground. The joke is that he built it that high so he can lean out the window and pound on Heaven's floor with a broom handle when he wants them to turn down the choir.

Lucifer's four favorite generals have their own palaces.

Azazel is Lucifer's second favorite general, so his palace is second only to Beelzebub's in size and beauty. Beelzebub is Lucifer's favorite general. While Azazel's palace is made entirely of flowing water, Beelzebub's is mud-and-dung bricks covered in human bones. Not what you'd call pretty, but it makes a statement.

Inside Azazel's palace it's all Gothic arches and stained glass, laid out in classic cathedral style. A carpeted nave leads to an altar at the far end where a mammoth clockwork Christ buggers the Virgin Mary every hour on the hour.

"You're going to use those arena skills of yours to kill Beelzebub for me," says Azazel.

"Don't I rate a night off? I'm held together with Silly String and good wishes."

He smiles, showing his hundred pointed teeth. "Perfect. Then no one will suspect you. More importantly, they won't suspect me." He hands me something, a sharpened piece of spiral-cut metal, like a long ice pick. I've seen it before. It's General Belial's favorite weapon. "Leave that behind, but be sure to dip it into Beelzebub's blood first." He pauses. "And wear gloves. I don't want your human taint all over it. They have to think that Belial did it."

"Beelzebub's palace is a fucking fortress with about ten times more troops and guard animals than you have. And he knows I work for you. His guards will never let me get near him."

Azazel shows me his teeth again. He likes doing that. It used to make me want to pee my pants. Now it's just a ritual, like a dog biting another dog's throat to remind it who's the alpha.

Azazel reaches into his robes made of shimmering golden water and pulls out a heavy brass key. "Have you ever heard of the Room of Thirteen Doors?" he asks. "This key will take you there. The room leads to anywhere and everywhere in the universe simultaneously. Including Beelzebub's bedroom."

He hands me the key. It's heavier than it looks and weirdly soft. I realize that it's not made of brass after all. It's living skin over bones.

"In one hour, you'll enter the Room of Thirteen Doors

through a shadow behind this altar. From the room, you'll go out through the Door of Fire. That's a killing portal. It will take you right to your prey. Once you've killed Beelzebub, leave Belial's weapon and return here."

I turn the key over in my hands. I should be horrified by it, but I'm not. There's something animal-like about the key, like it's a pet that wants to please its master.

"You're thinking that I've given you your means to escape, aren't you?" Azazel asks.

"Me? I love it here, boss. Why would I ever want to escape?"

He touches the edge of the key with a fingertip.

"Lucifer can leave Hell and travel easily through the cosmos, while the rest of us are bound here, cursed by the heavenly enemy. I've found a way out. Not for me, but for someone like you. However, you should remember not to go too far. Though I can't leave Hell, I have some influence in your world, among those humans dedicated to Hell. Cross me, try to escape from me, and something awful will happen to the one you love. That pretty girl you left behind. Do you understand me?"

"I understand."

"You're not leaving here. Someday maybe, but not right now and not for a good long time." Azazel turns and starts away. "Keep the key next to your body. That way, it will know to open the room to you. Wait an hour before you go. I need to be somewhere public when it happens."

An obedient little slave, I do as my master tells me.

I wait an hour and slip into a shadow behind the altar. Passing into that utter blackness feels like falling through cool air.

I find myself in a semicircular room that, surprise, contains thirteen doors. Each door seems to be made from a different material. Wood, water, air, stone, metal. More abstract things, too. The Door of Dreams moves and writhes, reshaping itself from second to second. There's a sound from the far side of the room. I go to the only unmarked door and listen. There's something moving behind the door and it knows I'm here. Something growls and scratches to get at me. Then there's a shriek, a long, keening, furious animal sound that hits me like a knife dragged through my skull. Right then and there I know I'm going to do whatever Azazel wants and kill any damned Hellion he tells me to. I'll be his servant as long as he leaves Alice alone and never, ever asks me to go through the unmarked door.

I wake up with the taste of Hell in the back of my throat. I know it's just the bad vodka, but that doesn't help. My head is full of monsters and I'm one of them. I sit up smelling sulfur and I want to kill something. I want a Hellion to burst through the window so I can take this bone knife and cut its black heart out. There are so many questions left. It feels like I've been doing nothing but talking since I got back. I need to do something. I need to hurt something. I need to kill Azazel, but I've already killed him.

I'm afraid. I'm so fucking afraid. I don't know what's

worse, Hell or this stupid world where I'll never be at home. But I need to keep talking to people. I need to keep asking the right questions. And I've already missed maybe the most important question of all.

I roll out of bed and slam the closet open, nearly tearing the door off its hinges. Kasabian lets out a yelp and turns his eyes up at me. I pick up his head in both hands and hold him so that we're eye to eye.

"I have one question for you and I swear to God and the devil and everything holy and unholy that if you fuck me around for even one second, I will drop you in the ocean right now. Do you understand me?"

"Yeah." He barely whispers the word.

"Where's Alice's body?"

"I don't know."

"Don't lie to me!"

"I swear, I don't know. Jesus, even I'm not that fucked up. Parker would know. He killed her. Parker's the one that can tell you."

There's real terror in Kasabian's eyes. I'm still holding him up, squeezing him tighter than I thought. His cheeks are red and starting to bruise. I set him back on the shelf and lean against the wall.

Kasabian stares at me like he's never seen me before.

"What are you, hypoglycemic or something? Go eat a muffin, for shit's sake."

"I'll bring by some cigarettes later," I tell him, and close the closet door.

At least I got to ask the big question, but I'm not any less agitated. Kasabian was telling the truth a minute ago; I could see in his mind that he would have made something up if he could have thought of a convincing enough lie. That means I can't find Alice's body until I track down Parker. I'm still so wound up from having Hell in my head all night that I need to break something, and soon. I hate it when I get this way. Do they have anger-management classes for hitmen?

Allegra's voice comes from downstairs. I didn't hear her come in. She's talking into her BlackBerry. I look around for a clean shirt and realize that I forgot to buy some yesterday. I steal another Max Overdrive shirt from the box and go downstairs quietly. I'm not in the mood for this, but I need to do something now so that I don't have to do something worse later.

Allegra is still on the phone and has her back to me. She doesn't hear me come up behind her. When she turns around and sees me, she jumps a little.

"Jesus, you're quiet," she says. Then, into her Black-Berry, "No, not you. Let me call you back." She takes off her coat, stashes it behind the counter, and begins setting up the money and register for the day. "I thought you were upstairs. I heard noise."

"I had a movie on. *Dust Devil*. You ever see it?"

"Isn't that a horror flick?"

"Sort of a horror movie crossed with a spaghetti western. You ought to take a look. The girl character dumps her boyfriend and then spends the rest of the movie trying to get away from a ghost world killer who's sort of in love with her. She runs, but she's no coward. She fights back and stays brave. You'd like her."

"Thanks. I'll have a look." She gives me a distracted smile.

"Listen, I'm sorry if I said anything stupid last night. I haven't been in the city in a long time. I grew up here, but it might as well be the dark side of the moon."

"I feel that way sometimes, too."

"There's something else you're wondering about. You're wondering if I'm an ex-con. The answer is yes."

"Oh." She busies herself breaking open rolls of coins and putting the change in the register. "I only wondered because of, you know, the scars."

"Would it help if I told you that I didn't go away because of something I did, but because of something someone else wanted?"

"Are you, like, on parole?"

"It's more of a work-release thing. If things work out, I won't be going back at all."

"I had a boyfriend who did time."

"A dealer, right?"

She looked up at me, her expression shifting from interest to suspicion. "How did you know that?"

"A long time ago, I had a girlfriend named Alice. Your eyes are like hers were when I first met her. There's this funny thing that happens to girls' eyes when they've been in love with a dealer. It's a real particular look. More than not trusting people. It's like you're trying to figure out if they're the same species as you, like they might be a snake in a people mask."

She's still looking at me, sizing me up, and trying to classify me as animal, vegetable, or mineral. "Can we maybe change the subject?"

"Sure. I just wanted you to know the truth. I'm not a snake. I'm just a person like you."

She turns a key on the register, clearing yesterday's transactions and getting ready for today's. "But it's not the whole truth, though, is it? You're not like Michael was, but there's still a little bit of the snake thing going on behind your eyes."

"What do you expect? I'm from L.A."

She laughs. I can hear her breathing steady, her heart slow. Her fear doesn't disappear; she's too smart and wary for that. But she's not going to call the cops or stab me in my sleep, and what more can you ask of a pretty girl?

I start upstairs, but turn back to Allegra. "What day is it?"

"Thursday. It'll be New Year's in a few days."

"We should get some champagne for the store. And those popper things, too. They look like little bottles. Take some money out of the till and go buy whatever you think is fun."

"How much can I spend?"

"Buy whatever you want."

"Hey, those were nice leathers you had on yesterday. Do you have a motorcycle?"

"I might just pick one up today."

WHEN I WAS Downtown, Galina, one of Azazel's vampire drinking buddies, liked to regale me with stories about what it's like to hunt humans. She would go into exquisite detail, mostly to spoil my dinner. Sometimes to screw me up before a fight in the arena. She had a gambling problem.

Galina told me that most vampires work hard to keep a low profile. They dress, act, and often get jobs like regular people. Most vampires only feed once a month, at the new moon. A month is the longest vampires can go without fresh blood, unless they don't mind shriveling to something that looks like hundred-year-old beef jerky.

There are the other vampires, too. The kind they make movies about. Mad-dog, Dracula-Has-Risen-from-the-Grave psycho killers. They hunt every night just for the sheer meat-market thrill of it. The craziest ones don't even wait for night. They hunt during the day. Streaking from shadow to shadow, they snatch people right off the street and feed on them behind Dumpsters or in crack houses, next to the other addicts.

These vampires hunt for kicks, but not for fun. They hunt for rage. They hunt because something inside them is broken, and no matter how much new blood they fill their bellies with, it turns to fire in their veins. They hunt and kill because they need to, because if they didn't, they'd tear their own heads off. Just like any fix, the calm that comes from the kill doesn't last long, but for a few minutes or maybe an hour, the fire fades to a single glowing ember and they're at peace. Until they need to hunt again.

If I learned anything Downtown it's this: I'm not a vampire, but I am a junkie. And every junkie needs a fix.

A DELIVERY VAN is pulling away from the curb outside the Bamboo House of Dolls. I go in and see stacks of whiskey in boxes, steel beer kegs, and Carlos by the bar, flanked by three lanky skinheads. One is in a bomber jacket, one is in a T-shirt of some black metal band, and the third, a huge skinhead, is in a German military officer's coat.

Bomber Jacket jerks his head toward me. "We're closed!"

"Just a quick one, sweetheart," I say. "So I know you love me."

Bomber Jacket pulls out—can you fucking believe this guy?—a Luger pistol, like he thinks he's Rommel. Quicker than he can react, I scoop up one of the beer kegs and underhand it at him. It slams into his chest and knocks him across the room. The Luger flies out of his hand and lands on the floor somewhere near the bar.

The shaved ape in the officer's coat starts across the room at me while the black metal skinhead pulls an impressive shank from his boot. Just to make things fun, I go straight for the one with the knife. This confuses the ape, who turns just as I reach his pal, whose arm is straight out, trying to pig-stick me. It's been a long time since I've gone up against a human, so I don't know if I'm really fast or if these geniuses are really slow, but I slip past the skinhead's blade and pop him in the elbow, hyperextending the joint just enough to hurt, but not to snap. While little birdies are still flying around his head, I grab his arm and do-si-do around him, swinging him into the ape just as he comes up behind me.

But the ape is too huge to go down. He staggers back a step then lunges at me, faster than I expected. Fast enough to get hold of my jacket and throw a fist as hard as a tire iron into my jaw. I don't want to get into a real fight with this guy because I'm more interested in his partner with the knife. When he loads up for another John Wayne punch, I grab one of the squat, bottom-heavy glass candles off the bar and smash it into the side of his head. That sends him staggering back to the opposite wall, where he slides down like a pile of bloody laundry.

The guy with the knife is back on me. He has just enough brains to know not to try to stab me straight on, so he's going for a slashing attack. His arm blurs back and forth, then down, then up, trying to catch me off guard and bleed me. I parry his blows, letting one land on my forearm or shoulder occasionally. This is what I've wanted, a real chance to test the Kevlar armor in this jacket. He's working up a pretty nice sweat, coming at me with all he's got. Still, he's easy to dance around, easy to block. His face is contorted and frantic with anger. As long as I let him get a shot in every now and then, I bet he'll keep coming until he dies of old age or a stroke.

The guy I hit with the beer keg hasn't moved, but the ape is getting back to his feet. Time to wrap things up.

As the black metal skinhead slashes down at my head, I reach up with my right hand and grab the knife. There's a familiar ache, like electricity and heat, as the blade slices deep into my palm. I slam the heel of my left hand up under his jaw, staggering him, then twist my right hand, snapping the blade cleanly off his knife. As the ape rushes me, I go low and shove the broken blade deep into his thigh. He howls in pain and falls against the bar.

Damn, it feels great to hurt idiots.

None of the skinheads is getting up for a minute, so I look around for the Luger. Carlos is behind the bar, frozen in place, like he's not sure if he's more afraid of me or the Nazis on the floor. I spot the gun under a stool at the end of the bar and kneel to get it.

Good thing, too.

A blue-white ball of plasma misses me by a few millimeters and explodes against the far wall.

I wheel around and see him. It occurs to me that I might have been having a little too much fun before. I hadn't thought to check if there was another skinhead in the storeroom. I snatch the Luger from under the stool, but it doesn't help because the new skinhead does something a lot more interesting.

He holds up his right hand. There's something with a glowing end. Gnarled like a short tree branch. It extends from his hand and wraps around his forearm to his elbow. It's a piece of a Devil Daisy. I don't know the real name. Devil Daisy is just what I called them. I haven't seen one in a long time and that was in the arena. That's all I get to think before he blasts a tongue of blue-white dragon fire at me. I'm still afraid to use magic. All I can do is dive to my left, rolling over some tables and chairs and landing on the floor. The second shot goes wide, as does his third. Still, I feel the heat and skin-crawling static as each shot streaks by.

This is some powerful magic the skinhead is packing, but it's obvious from the way he's waving the branch around that he doesn't fully understand what it is or how to use it, beyond a dim aim-and-pray strategy.

My theory that he's not in control of the weapon is confirmed when the ape yells something and the guy with the Devil Daisy turns and almost blows his own foot off. It's the Three Stooges with death rays over there. The one I took the Luger from yells, "Asshole!" He gets to his feet and he and the ape, limping, with the knife still in his leg, get the skinhead I hit with the keg between them and drag him out the door. The one with the Daisy backs out of the place, holding the branch out like he's covering himself with a gun.

"What the fuck was that?" yells Carlos.

"The Nazi asshole must have had a flare gun," I lie.

I walk over, drop the Luger on the bar, and push it to Carlos. "Merry Christmas. Don't say I never gave you anything."

"What am I supposed to do with that?"

"I don't know. Put it up next to the tiki dolls."

"I don't like guns. Is it loaded?"

I pop the clip out, check it, and slide it back in. "Yeah. Keep it behind the bar. Those guys are going to come back. Not tonight, but sometime soon."

"You think so?"

"Definitely."

"I still don't want it," he says, and pushes the Luger toward me. I flick on the safety and shove it into my jacket pocket. Carlos nods toward me. "You're bleeding," he says, and hands me a clean bar towel. I wrap it around the hand I used to grab the skinhead's knife. The hand still hurts, but it'll stop bleeding by the time I walk outside.

Carlos leans on the bar. "So, what are you? Special Forces? Some kind of ninja?"

"Yeah, I'm the ghost of Bruce Lee. You have a cigarette?" Carlos shakes his head. The moment is still burning bright for him, but it's over for me. The rage has gone south and now I have a bigger problem. No question I was shot at by a magic weapon, but it was used by someone who had no idea what he was doing. I consider the possibility that Mason sent the skinheads, not to shake down

Carlos, but to ambush me, only that doesn't make any sense. If Mason decides to send a hit squad for me, he'll make sure they know exactly what weapons they're packing and how they work.

So, what devil Kris Kringle is handing out death rays to pinheads?

"Can I borrow your phone?" I ask. Carlos hands it to me and I dial the number of my old apartment. Vidocq picks up.

THIRTY MINUTES LATER Vidocq and I are sitting in a doughnut shop on Sunset drinking coffee and eating. He's paying. I'm close to tapped out. At least I spent Brad Pitt's money well. Before Vidocq got to Donut Universe, I'd examined the motocross jacket for damage. The Kevlar did a pretty good job. None of the knife slashes made it through the armor down to me. All the damage was to the leather, and I could fix that with gaffer tape.

"I've heard of power amulets like guns, but not like the one you describe," says Vidocq. "But I think I know someone who will. I'll introduce you soon."

The Frenchman puts a paper bag on the table. I take a bite of my Bavarian cream.

"What's that?"

"Look for yourself," he says, and pushes the bag at me. I open it and look inside. It's full of shirts.

"They are yours. You look like a fucking child in those

video store things. You should wear your own clothes. They will help you remember who you are."

I roll down the top of the bag and put it on the seat beside me. I suppose I do look stupid in these shirts. In my head I'm still nineteen. Time is stuck there and it's like a punch in the balls every time I look in the mirror. At least no one will bother me for ID when I buy beer now.

But I don't want to look at what's in the bag right away. Part of me wants to burn everything Alice and I left behind eleven years ago. Another part wants to leave it all right where it is, frozen in time, like bugs trapped in amber. It never occurred to me to wear any of my old clothes again.

"There was something weird and familiar about that amulet and I've been trying to remember what since I left the club."

Donut Universe is a twenty-four-hour place with an outer-space theme. There's a big plastic UFO suspended from the ceiling over the display case. The girl working the counter is a green-haired pixie who looks somewhere between twelve and thirty-five. She's wearing sequined antennae that bob up and down when she talks. The grown-up part of my brain imagines that she tears the stupid things off and tosses them in the backseat of her car the moment she's finished her shift. The nineteen-year-old in me wonders if she sometimes wears the antennae when she screws her boyfriend, and what it's like to look up and see her and those sequined balls bobbing up and down over you.

"There was this one time Downtown when a couple of big, horned Hellions dragged me out of bed in the middle of the night. Azazel was my boss, but these two worked for Mephistopheles. The general with the fire palace. Lucifer's third favorite general. His boys took me to the arena. It was after-hours, but there were a couple dozen Hellion posh types in the stands. They wanted a private show starring the living boy, which I knew meant that I was about to get my ass kicked.

"My favorite weapon, a *na'at*, was on the ground. A *na'at* is sort of like a spear, but it morphs and changes into a lot more than a spear if you know how to use it right. Like everything else down there, the name is a Hellion joke. They call a *na'at* a 'thorn' because its full name, *na'atzutz*, is the kind of bush they used to make Christ's crown of thorns.

"Across the arena from me was something all draped in black. When it came closer I saw that it wasn't dressed in black. It was black, nothing but black. It was like a hole punched in the world. And it kept shifting and changing shape, like a sheet on a clothesline on a windy day.

"It just stood there, so I went for it. I threw a few feints, trying to draw it into a fight, but it didn't move. It didn't even turn when I moved around it. The *na'atzutz* is spear-shaped. When I took a quick, hard shot at the thing's head, the *na'at* went right through it, like it wasn't there. But when the thing raised its arm to push me away, it was like getting hit by a dump truck.

"The *na'at* extends over ten feet when you open it all the way, so when the thing came at me, I let the *na'at* out to its full length and swung it like a flail. It went right through the thing again. I wasn't about to let it lay into me again, so I did a Muhammad Ali and danced around the arena, trying to figure out what to do next. I didn't know how to fight something I couldn't even touch.

"Then the black thing took something out of a pocket. What it held up was a lot like that amulet back at that bar. Only it knew how to use it. First, it shot at my feet, kicking up dirt and blinding me. Then it shot circles all around me, so I couldn't run. It could have burned me anytime it wanted, but it was taking its time, playing for the Hellions whooping it up in the good seats.

"After all those years and all that happened to me and all the things I'd killed, this laser-toting bathrobe was going to kill me. And I think it would have if Azazel hadn't stormed into the arena. He started screaming at Mephistopheles and I thought the real fight was going to happen in the grandstands. Neither one of them was backing down and some of Mephistopheles' buddies pulled out knives.

"A minute later, who strolls in but Lucifer? That shut everyone up damn quick.

"The thing you have to understand about Lucifer is that he hardly ever talks, and when he does, it's never much more than a whisper. When half the universe is hanging on to your every word, you don't have to shout.

' "This is over,' he said. 'Go home. Mephistopheles, come to my tower in the morning.' And that was it. Those Hellion hotshots couldn't get out of there fast enough. Then he went to the black thing and said something to it. The black thing didn't move. This is *Lucifer* giving the thing an order, and it just stood there. How is that for titanium balls? A couple of minutes later, the thing walks away across the arena and vanishes like smoke.

"I'd only seen Lucifer a couple of times and I'd only spoken to him once, but here he came right up to me and told me to go home to bed, and that none of this ever happened."

"What do you think it means?" Vidocq asks.

"That amulet got me thinking. Whatever had it must have been some colossal hard case because it tried to stare down Lucifer. Mephistopheles obviously knew the thing because it was his party. So . . . what if Mephistopheles knows he can't win the war Downtown and is recruiting some dark-magic types to help him move up here to Earth?"

"I thought that you had the only key that could allow them into this world."

"That's where it all falls apart. Except for Lucifer, no one can get out of Hell without the key, and I still have it."

Vidocq sips his coffee and makes a face. "The shit you people drink." He slips a flask out of his coat and pours a good portion of the contents into the cup. The next sip of coffee makes him smile. "It sounds as if you need to find those little Nazi boys and make them tell you where they get their toys."

"That's the second thing I need to do. The first is getting into Mason's place. Want to come along?"

"Breaking and entering? Now you are my friend again. I will show you how a good thief earns his daily bread."

"Sorry, man. There's no actual house to break into. It's just a basement, and that's buried under tons of dirt. But we can get in through the room."

Vidocq shakes his head. "You use guns when you should use magic and you use magic when you should let an old man pick a lock for you. You are a mixed-up boy, Monsieur Butler."

"Please don't say my name."

He holds up a hand by way of apology and reaches into his coat pocket. "Take this."

"What is it?"

"Someone you should meet. Dr. Kinski. He is an interesting man, and used to dealing with people of our kind. You shouldn't walk around with those bullets in your belly. The lead is bad for you."

"Thanks," I say, and put the number in my pocket. "I'll give him a call."

"So, when are you we paying a visit to your friend Mason?"

"Tonight. Late. I don't want anyone seeing us. We'll use the key to get in, but I want a car there, too, in case things get weird."

"Now you are thinking like a thief. Fewer guns and more exits. We'll cure your cowboy ways yet."

He doesn't notice that I ditch the bag of shirts under the table when we leave.

"HI. I'M CALLING for Dr. Kinski. I want to make an appointment."

"I'm sorry," says a soft female voice on the other end of the phone. "Dr. Kinski isn't accepting any new patients right now."

"I'm a friend of Vidocq's. He gave me this number."

"You're Eugène's friend? The traveler? How is it to be back in one place?"

"Unsettling."

"A rambling man. How romantic. Did you get what you wanted out of your trip?"

"If by 'get what you wanted' you mean a bunch of bullets, then, yeah, I hit the jackpot."

"Were they big bullets?"

"Big enough that I noticed."

"If it's an emergency, I might get the doc to look at you today."

"Tomorrow'll be fine."

"Love a man who'll bleed just to make a point."

"What's your name?"

"Candy. What's yours?"

"Stark."

"You sound like a Stark."

"Is that a good thing?"

"It's not a bad thing."

"I'll take that as a vote of confidence."

"Take it with cream and sugar, if you want. The doc doesn't have any openings tomorrow. He'll call you when he does."

"Thanks."

"Thank Eugène."

"I'll tell him you said so."

"You better." She hangs up.

AT EIGHT, I go over to the Bamboo House of Dolls. Carlos is all handshakes and smiles. "Anything on the menu," he says. "From now until the end of time." I order *carne asada* and Carlos brings me the meat with beans, rice, and guacamole. It's like God left his lunch in the microwave and you get to finish it. By ten, the skinheads haven't come back, so I thank Carlos and head back to the video store.

I OPEN KASABIAN's closet and let him puff away on the cigarette I hold down for him. His severed head doesn't bother me so much anymore. It's creepy, but familiar, like a three-legged dog.

"What's in the basement?" I ask.

"I don't know."

"Would you tell me if you did?"

"I'd tell you politely to kiss my ass. It's over there across the room, so I'll have a good view."

"You know I'm here to kill the Circle. You don't have to be part of that. Tell me something useful. Something I can use."

"Fuck you sideways, shitsack."

"I'm trying to find a reason not to put a bullet in you."

Kasabian smiles like a cat that just took a crap in your shoes and is waiting for you to find it. "I don't know what's down there, but I know this: Mason might be crazier than a sack full of dog's balls, but he kicked your ass to Never Never Land 'cause, unlike you, he thinks ahead. Is there something in the basement? I have no doubt. Do I know what it is? No. But I'm sure of one thing: it'll make you cry, and I'm looking forward to hearing all about it."

"I guess I'd be bitter, too, if I saw all my friends turn into gods while I was still the bum on the corner, hoping they'd throw me a nickel."

"See? It's that asshole thing that's going to get you killed soon."

"Did I hurt your feelings again? Sorry. When this is over, I'll send some flowers to your inner child."

I STEAL A Porsche 911 on Sunset and pick up Vidocq a little after two. I drive us to Beverly Hills and park where we can see the vacant lot where Mason's house once stood.

I sit there for a minute, scanning the street for teenyboppers or insomniac joggers.

"Are we going?" Vidocq asks.

"In a minute." I take out the Veritas, put it on my thumb, and give it a little flip. In my head is the question *Is this a good idea?*

When I turn the coin over, it reads in Hellion script, *When you jump off a cliff, is it better to land on jagged rocks or burning lava?* I know this one. The answer is obvious: It doesn't matter where you land. You just jumped off a cliff.

I lead Vidocq to the edge of the vacant lot, near a streetlight where the shadows are deep and wide enough for two. "I've never tried this with another human before. It might be a little weird. It'll feel like you're falling, but you're not. If this works, just step into the room like normal."

"What will happen if it does not work?"

"I have no idea."

Vidocq gets out his flask and takes a big drink. When he's put the flask away, I take his arm and pull him into the biggest, darkest shadow I can find.

There's a moment of coolness in the transition, and we're inside the room. Easy as a broken leg and we're both still in one piece.

Vidocq looks at me, eyes darting around the room. "It worked, then?"

"Two arms, two legs. It worked."

His lets out a breath and looks around, a little awestruck. "We're at the center of the universe. The cross-roads of creation."

"I suppose. I never thought about it that way. For me, it was just the emergency exit out the back of a burning building."

Vidocq turns in a slow circle. "My God. It really is a room full of doors."

"Thirteen. What did you expect?"

"I assumed the doors were a metaphor. Each door would be a way to describe a different state of being."

"No. It's just a lot of doors."

"Clearly. Where does this one lead you?"

"They change, depending on where I want to go. It's all about associations. The Door of Fire leads to cha-otic places, usually dangerous. Wind is mostly calm, but changeable. Dreams leads to, well, dreams."

He points to the thirteenth door. "Where does that one go?"

"I never opened it."

"Why not?"

"Because it scares me shitless, and, anyway, that's not how we're going. We're going through here."

"What is this?"

"The Door of the Dead."

MASON'S BASEMENT SMELLS like a straw doormat that's been left out in the rain too long. It's also pitch-black.

Vidocq takes a glass vial from his pocket and blows on it. The room fills with light. Who needs a flashlight when you have your own personal alchemist?

Paint is peeling off the basement walls and ceiling in jagged sheets. Thick roots grow down from the lot above and creep across the ceiling and walls, like black and brittle arteries. A knot of roots has rotted away the plaster from one wall, leaving exposed lath. The furniture sits exactly where I last saw it years earlier—tables, chairs, and a sofa woolly with mold.

In the center of the room is what remains of the magic circle. Some of the chalk is still visible where it's melted into the rotten floorboards. The burned stubs of candles are still lying around the circle, like the last people in here left quickly and never came back.

I can't get hold of any one feeling. It's like my brain and my guts and my heart are stuck in a speeded-up, old-school king fu fight. Different parts of me want to run off screaming in different directions. One part of me wants to puke quietly, but thoroughly, in a far corner of the room. Another part of me wants to rip the place apart, board by board, brick by brick. The weakest, smallest part of me, the one I seriously don't want to hear from, is nothing but apologies and regrets. *Sorry, Alice. You told me not to come here, but I did. Then everything else happened.*

One part of me that's left is the ten o'clock news. That's the part I hold on to. The cold camera eye. Just take in the scene and report the facts. These ruins aren't my private apocalypse. They're the haunted-house ride at Disneyland. Digital spooks and Dolby stereo moans. About as scary as a basket of kittens.

"What are we looking for?" asks Vidocq.

I shrug.

"No idea."

We move around the room, looking for a clue or a sign that points to something more than damp wreckage. I move furniture and trash away with the toe of my boot. I don't want to touch anything.

"I don't know if we're going to find anything interesting in here. Mason always hinted that he had a hidden room where he kept all his important stuff, but none of us ever found it."

Much as I don't want to, I lean against a mildewed wall. My head is suddenly spinning. Voices and faces shoot through me, like streaks of lightning. I can even feel echoes of the Circle, all of them, even my younger self, trapped in here. I've heard of dark magicians doing this. Sometime in the past, Mason hermetically sealed the room from the rest of the world with a kind of barrier hex. He didn't want what he was doing to leak out into the aether. It might let other magicians know that he was horse trading with Hellions. A lot of scary things passed through this room. A lot more than the few beasties that dragged me Downtown. Some I can see and feel, but others are just blurs that I can't get a fix on. The inside of their heads is all hunger and knives, like insects. I'm not sorry that I can't get any farther inside. I'd been getting used to sensing other people's thoughts and feelings, but the intensity of this place makes the experience new and weird again. Suddenly I don't want to be here anymore.

"Ha!"

Vidocq is in the corner of the room with one hand pressed up against a the ceiling and the other pressed into a small divot in the wall. The opposite corner of the room scrapes open, dragging on the junk that's accumulated in the door mechanism over the years. "I said that I would show you how a good thief earns his keep!" Vidocq says happily. With his bottled light, he leads the way into the hidden room.

The hidden room is in a lot better shape than the other. There's a lot of power in the hidden room. It's protected by much more powerful spells than any of the rest of the house. Every inch of the walls, floors, and ceiling is covered with multicolored runes, sigils, and angular angelic and Hellion scripts.

Vidocq is studying the place with grim intensity. He runs his fingers over the wall and they come away black. He sniffs the dust on his hand, touches a blackened finger to his tongue.

"What is it?" I ask.

"Ivory black," he says. "Made from burned bones and animal horns."

"Is that bad?"

"It's a traditional pigment. It goes back thousands of

years." He moves his light over the walls and holds it up to the ceiling. "This symbol? Painted with cinnabar—a mixture of mercury and sulfur heated together. Cobalt and aluminum chloride, also heated, make this blue. Here is antimony yellow. This particular red comes from boiling the iron oxide found in blood. All these hues, these colors, were made skillfully with chemicals and great heat." He holds up his light and turns three hundred and sixty degrees, taking in the whole room. "Everything in here was born in fire."

"Bring the light over here, will you?"

Vidocq carries the light to where I'm standing. There's strange writing on the wall, but it's not Hellion. It's something I've never seen before, like cuneiform that's been gashed into the wall with a meat cleaver. A symbol painted in bloody iron oxide covers the rest of the wall. It's a circle that wraps around and around its own interior, folding in on itself. It's a labyrinth, an ancient symbol of the deepest, darkest secrets and Final Jeopardy–hard knowledge. Something shimmers at the center of the labyrinth. I dig my fingernails into the soft plaster and pry out the treasure.

It's a Zippo lighter. On the front is a kind of cigar-chomping hot, rod devil's head done by an artist who signs his name "Coop." I turn the lighter over and click open the top, looking for a message, an inscription, or anything that might point us to what Mason was doing down here. There's nothing. I flick the Zippo closed. It's just a lighter.

Vidocq takes it from me and examines it closely under the light. In a minute, he shakes his head and hands it back to me.

"Maybe your friend Mason is a person who enjoys practical jokes?"

"He likes a good 'fuck you,' but I don't remember him being much for jokes."

"Then, we are missing something."

I toss the Zippo up and down in my hand a few times, enjoying the weight of it. "What's a lighter for?"

Vidocq scrapes his feet on the dusty floor. "To give us fire."

I hold the lighter up, click the top open, and strike the flint once. The room fills with light. Way too much light. It leaks from the walls and the floor. We have to wrap our arms over our eyes to keep from going blind.

Something brushes my arm. Dirt swirls from the floor as wind explodes around us, getting stronger by the second. For a minute I wonder if I'm hallucinating, feeling some stranger's memory. Then Vidocq stumbles into me, blown over by a sudden gust, and I know this is all real.

I move my arm down as my eyes adjust to the light. It's pure white and keeps moving, like ripples on the bottom of a swimming pool. The walls look like stretched skin and something is trying to come through them. We can see the silhouettes of faces and arms as they reach for us, straining at the thin wall flesh. The bodies writhe and twist, unable to hold a shape very long as they press in on us.

Arms like roiling packs of snakes. Bodies like the skeletons of fish and birds. Faces that seem to be all teeth, all nails, or screaming from the ends of arms, where the creatures' hands should be.

Vidocq shouts, "Can't you take us out of here?"

"We need a shadow, but the light's everywhere."

Vidocq flings open his coat. Vials containing his potions, rows and rows of them, are sewn into the lining. He pulls out one after the other and hurls them at the grasping hands. I get the skinhead's Luger from my pocket and fire off a few rounds at the silhouettes. They don't even seem to notice.

I grab Vidocq's sleeve and pull him toward the door, firing the Luger until it's empty. Vidocq keeps throwing his vials. Every now and then, an arm or a monstrous face contorts in pain from our feeble attack, but the wall goblins come roaring back at us a second later.

At the door, Vidocq shoves me away. "Let me go!" he shouts, and tears his arm free. He's back inside the possessed room, with the walls just inches away from him. He reaches into the very bottom of his coat lining and pulls out a bottle the size of his brandy flask. Screaming, *"Tas de merde!"* he smashes the bottle on the writhing mass of arms and fangs and throws himself back into the room with me, knocking us both to the filthy floor.

The secret room is on fire, but the creatures in the walls are still trying to get at us, only they seem to be trapped behind an invisible barrier. Unfortunately, the fire is not.

The rotten wood in our room ignites the moment flame gets near it. In a few seconds, the place is blazing like Nero's Roman holiday. The good news is that a burning room creates a lot of excellent shadows. I grab Vidocq and drag him down into a deep slash of darkness at the edge of the Circle. We emerge, stumbling into the Room of Thirteen Doors, eyes tearing, lungs burning with smoke. I don't stop moving, but guide Vidocq through the Door of Memory and out onto the cool and silent streets of Beverly Hills. The Porsche is at the other end of the block. We run for it.

By the time we get there, Mason's vacant lot is cracking open and flames are shooting two stories into the air. By the time I get the car started and do a screaming one-eighty, the whole lot has collapsed in on itself, shaking the street like an earthquake and blasting a fat orange fireball into the night sky. I floor the Porsche, taking the first turn out of Beverly Hills on two wheels.

THERE'S AN UNLIT parking lot behind an out-of-business movie multiplex between Hollywood Boulevard and Selma Avenue. I park in a far corner so no one can see us from the street. I'm still rasping. I know it's the smoke in my lungs, but it feels like I've been holding my breath since we got out of the ground. When I kill the Porsche's engine, we can hear the scream of fire trucks echoing off the buildings all the way across town.

"Sounds like a lot of them."

Vidocq snorts. "They always look after the rich. It's the same in all cities in all times, all over the world."

"What was in the last bottle you threw back there?"

"Spiritus Dei oil. A venerable old catholicon, and poisonous to almost any Hellion or Lurker beast. Very hard to find. That was my last bottle."

"Sorry, man."

"Don't worry. The man I said I'd introduce you to will have more."

I take the Zippo out of my pocket. "What am I going do with this thing?"

"Keep it. My exceptional knowledge of magic and the transmutation of elements tells me that it is not an ordinary lighter."

"It's a stupid vessel for such a powerful talisman."

"Perhaps it was created for someone Mason knew would be drawn to it."

"You think Mason left it for me?"

Vidocq shrugs wearily. "I don't know. But it does seem more *votre modèle* than the other members of your Circle."

"Yeah. I walked right off that cliff. But maybe the lighter will tell us something."

"Let us hope."

"So, you think Mason knows I'm back."

"You just blew up his home. He might suspect something."

I open and close my hands on the steering wheel, holding it tight. "I'm not ready yet. I barely have my feet on the ground."

"Opportunity always comes too early or too late. But with what you found tonight, you are one step closer to your heart's desire."

I flip open the top of the lighter and strike it once. Vidocq jerks away, banging his shoulder into the door. The little flame flickers, but nothing else happens. I want a cigarette, but my throat and lungs feel like hot gravel. I close the lighter and put it back in my pocket.

"When we meet this guy with the Spiritus Dei, I'll pay."

"Excellent. I was about to suggest that very thing. You should meet him as soon as possible."

"You think?"

"*Absolument*. He is a man who knows and possesses many useful things. And I think soon you will need more than your Sundance Kid guns to stay alive."

AFTER I DROP off Vidocq, I stop behind a nearby Safeway, wipe the Luger for prints, and stuff it in the bottom of a very full and very smelly Dumpster. I don't want the Luger near me. Who knows what crimes those Nazi freaks committed with it.

The Bamboo House of Dolls will be closed by now, but I need something to drink. I ditch the Porsche a block from

Donut Universe, get a large black coffee and a couple of old-fashioneds, and walk the few blocks to Max Overdrive.

I've finished the coffee and one of the doughnuts when I reach the store. The lights are on. The front door is open and the glass shattered. I throw away the food, pull Azazel's knife from my boot, and go inside quietly. The place is a wreck. Racks are turned over and discs and cases are scattered everywhere. The cash register, though, looks untouched, so it wasn't thieves or crackheads who got in.

I kick through the broken glass and discs wondering who would want to just trash the place when I see a shoe sticking out from under one of the upturned racks. I grab the rack and flip it over. Allegra is lying there. She's a mess. Her clothes are torn and her hands and face are bloody. I put my ear against her chest and am relieved to hear a slow and steady heartbeat. She weighs practically nothing, so I pick her up and carry her to my room. The door at the top of the stairs has been kicked in. I set Allegra on the bed and cover her with a blanket. When I go into the bathroom to get a wet cloth, I see something a lot scarier than the ghouls in Mason's basement. The door to Kasabian's closet is ripped off its hinges. He's gone.

I clean the blood off Allegra's face and drape the cool cloth across her forehead. When I push open her eyelids, her pupils are wide and they stay that way. A concussion. Not good. She moves her head and groans a little before pushing my hand away.

"What happened? I'm cold."

She's going into shock. I wrap the sheet around her. "You're hurt."

"Mr. Kasabian left. He looked dead, but he said good-bye."

"I'm taking you to the hospital."

She sits upright. Almost. She gets halfway up and drops back down.

"No hospital."

"You have to. You're hurt."

"No hospital. They might call the cops."

I didn't see that coming. "I'm taking you anyway."

That's exactly the wrong thing to say. Allegra grabs my arm, pulls herself up and tries to slap me. It's pretty impressive for someone who's gasping like a dying goldfish.

"No hospitals! No cops!"

Having finally gotten the point, I help her back down on the bed. Scraps of paper, half-eaten burritos, and ash-trays full of cigarettes are piled on Kasabian's worktable. I paw around the debris until I find the phone. I dial Kinski's number. Someone picks up on the sixth ring.

"Is this Candy? This is Stark."

"Stark? Lovely to hear from you. Tell me, Stark, do the clocks on your planet work like ours? Because the ones here on Earth tell me that it's late for chitchat."

"Shut up. I have a civilian here and I'm pretty sure she's been hurt with magic. I don't know how bad, but I think she's got a concussion. Kinski is the only doctor

I know about in L.A., so I'm bringing her to see him. If he isn't there when I get there, I'm going to be extremely unhappy."

"Okay. Do you have the address?"

Fucking brilliant. I'm threatening people I don't know, but need, at an address I don't have.

"Give it to me." She does.

"See you soon," she says.

I carry Allegra downstairs and leave her by the front door. Outside, I scan the street for transportation. I want something big so that Allegra can lie down, but mostly it's Japanese compacts and Detroit Tinker Toys. Down by the corner, I see what I want, a shiny red Escalade. The problem is that two guys are sitting inside. Still, it's worth checking out.

The guys are talking and laughing, passing a joint back and forth. Not a care in the world. I hate the idea of carjacking for one simple reason. It's a dog crime. A crime for morons and any little shitsack with the fifty bucks to buy a Saturday-night special. Still, I want the Escalade and I want it now. I look back at Max Overdrive, but Allegra's inside and I can't see her. As I turn back to the van, there's a glint from the rear driver's side window that I missed before. The glass is gone. The window is broken. The van is stolen. Hallelujah. I'm not carjacking. I'm regifting.

I go for the passenger first. He's so ripped that when I grab him, he's in full rag-doll mode, loose and relaxed. That's a good way to hit the ground if you're ever thrown—or pulled—from a vehicle. Only I toss him about ten or fifteen feet farther than I meant to. I've been boxing giant fire-breathing jellyfish and Hellions with skin like titanium. What do I know about fighting humans?

The driver is a pimply scarecrow with a Mohawk and a dirty Sex Pistols T-shirt ripped just so. He looks like a twelve-year-old dressed up like Sid Vicious for Halloween. When his buddy goes flying out of the van, his buzzed brain finally realizes that something is happening. He starts fumbling in his waistband for his gun, but his pothead reflexes aren't helping him. He might as well be wearing oven mitts. But I'd rather not get shot again if he manages to get all his digits working.

While he fumbles I grab the top of the door frame, kick off the edge of passenger door, and slide across the Escalade's roof, landing cat quiet on the driver's side. Speed Racer finally has the gun out, cocked and pointed at exactly where I'm not anymore. I lean in the open window, grab him by the neck, and haul him out, pinning his gun arm to his body. When he struggles, I bounce his head off the side of the van. Just once. Dazed and docile, it's easy to flip him over my shoulder, carry him around the van, and dump him near his friend. His gun I toss down a sewer grate.

Back at Max Overdrive, Allegra is on her feet, shaky as a newborn calf. I scoop her up in both arms, carry her to the Escalade, open the back, and lay her out flat.

"No hospitals," she says.

"I know."

"Where are we going?"

"For ice cream. What's your favorite flavor?"

"Fuck you."

"That's my favorite, too."

The two guys I tossed out of the van weren't complete idiots after all. They did a decent job of bypassing the Escalade's alarm and cutting into the van's keyless ignition. I twist a couple of exposed wires together and the Escalade purrs to life. Stepping on the accelerator, I cut the van across two lanes of traffic, twist the wheel, and aim the Escalade down Hollywood to where it crosses Sunset.

This isn't a situation where red lights, yellow lights, or anything that slows us down are acceptable. But what kind of a spell do you use to change the timing on traffic lights? If I wasn't such a freak-show attraction, I'd know something like that. Or I'd be able to fake it the way I faked my way through magic in the old days. All I can think of right now is a Hellion controlling spell, something I'd throw at an opponent in the arena to take control of their body and keep them from murdering me for a little while longer.

As the light turns yellow at the intersection ahead, I bark out the spell. Literally bark. High Hellion is mostly a bunch of low, guttural verbs and nouns strung together with growling adjective gristle. It sounds like a wolf with throat cancer.

I get the spell out as the light goes from yellow to red. As I finish the spell, it flips back to yellow. Then the light explodes, the housing suddenly white-hot shrapnel that hits the Escalade's roof like metal hailstones. The light's support pole is pretty much gone. So are the overhead lines that send juice to electric buses below.

Sorry, commuters. Tell your boss to fuck off tomorrow. Some terrorist asshole blew up all your vital crosswalk signals.

The second and third lights explode, too. The fourth just kind of sizzles, spits sparks, and goes out. I don't even look after that. It's flare guns and Roman candles all the way down to Sunset.

THE ADDRESS CANDY gave me is in a strip mall that hadn't been there before I went Downtown. I pull the Escalade into the parking lot and help Allegra out of the back. She insists on walking on her own, which I choose to see as a good sign. Doc Kinski's office is tucked between a fried-chicken franchise and a nail salon with signs in Vietnamese and dyslexic English. I double-check the address. It checks out.

The office is a blank storefront with blinds covering all the windows and the words EXISTENTIAL HEALING on the door in gold peel-and-stick letters. I try the door, but it's locked. I start pounding and the door swings open almost immediately. A tiny shaggy-haired brunette in tattered black jeans and Chuck Taylors stands there.

"Candy?"

"Stark?"

From the way she talked on the phone, I was expecting a big blond Judy Holliday type, not Joan Jett's little sister.

"Bring her inside. Doc is waiting."

The inside of the clinic is as bare as the outside. A couple of junkyard desks, with a not very new-looking laptop on top of one. A file cabinet covered in real estate stickers, Half a dozen metal folding chairs and a pile of *Sports Illustrated* and *Cosmopolitan*s, probably pulled from the Dumpster behind the nail salon.

This is the office of Vidocq's angel of mercy?

I'm seriously thinking about taking Allegra out of here and to a real hospital, no matter what I promised her. Then Kinski walks out of his exam room.

"What are you waiting for? Get the girl in here," he tells me. I do.

Kinski is as impressive as his office isn't. He's tall. A little taller than me. Like me, he'd been a lanky boy, but the years have added a few pounds to his middle and etched lines like a desert riverbed around his eyes. But he's still handsome. You can tell that when he was young he'd been the kind of good-looking that made girls forget about their boyfriends for the night and made guys want to punch him in the face on principle.

Allegra is too wobbly to walk anymore. I pick her up, follow Kinski into the next room, and set her down on a padded exam table.

He touches her head and cheeks. Takes her pulse at her

wrist and her neck and moves each lid back for a look at her eyes. Allegra squirms on the table and tries to push him away.

"You hurting?" he asks.

"Yeah. My head."

"Anywhere else?"

Allegra shakes her head.

"Okay. I want you to try and relax. Just breathe in and out real deeply. Can you do that?"

She nods, takes in long breaths, and lets them out slowly. Kinski puts one hand lightly on her forehead and keeps it there. He pats himself down and finds something like a piece of blackened jerky from his breast pocket.

"Chew on this," he says, putting the jerky between her lips.

"What is it?" she asks.

"You'll like it. It's dried fruit. Tastes good."

She chews and he keeps his hand on her, staring down like he's listening for something. I hear it, too. Her breathing and heartbeat slow abruptly. Her body relaxes. Kinski shoots me a quick glance like he knows that I can hear it, too.

"She's out," he says to Candy, and turns back to me. "What really happened to her?"

"I don't know exactly. I came back and the place was broken into. I think by a guy named Parker. He's another magician. Some magic things were missing."

"What kind of things?"

"A guy. Part of a guy, really."

"Part of a guy. Okay. Are you fooling around with stuff over there that's going to make this girl's condition more complicated? Any potions or herbs related to necromancy? Are you playing with any resurrection rituals?"

"Never."

"Okay. But you come in here with an injured girl and tell me that some magic part of a guy that you don't want to talk about gets stolen and I start thinking zombies. And that is some serious stuff."

"It's nothing like that. The guy wasn't dead. I was real careful about that."

"So careful this girl's skull is cracked."

"Can you fix her?"

"I've fixed worse." He looks over at Candy. "You want to get me the things, honey? I want to make sure this girl is all the way dozing before I take my hand off."

"How many do you want?"

"I think six should do it."

Candy gets six fist-size objects from an old medical cabinet. Each of the objects is wrapped in dark purple silk. She sets them on the exam table next to Allegra and un-wraps them. They're six shiny pieces of some milky-white stone.

Kinski lets go of Allegra, takes two of the stones, and places them on each side of her head. Candy places others over her heart and in her hands. Kinski puts the last piece, the smallest and nearly flat, between Allegra's teeth.

He gets old, unglazed clay jars from under the table,

pours several oils onto his hands, rubs them together to mix them, then smears the dark potion on Allegra's face. The oils smell like jasmine and wet pavement after a rain.

Candy gives Kinksi a carved wooden stylus and he draws symbols, strange letters, and runes into the oil. I lean in to get a better look at the markings. He's drawing a spell on her, but I don't know what kind. I've never seen one like it before. I recognize the characters surrounding the central circle and seven-pointed star, however. The symbols are an old angelic script. Enochian. Azazel taught me some spells from ancient books written in that script. Kinski can't be a Hellion because only Lucifer can walk out of Hell. But Hellions have plenty of human lapdogs. Lurker groupies and satanic assholes. Kinski can't be one, though. Vidocq would know and he'd never send me to the guy. Still. I slip my hand under my coat and touch Azazel's knife.

Kinski sets down the stylus. He's finished the spell and the stones around Allegra begin to glow. They shine right through her. I can see the outline of her veins and arteries, muscles and bones, and her beating heart. Kinski is chanting quietly. I try to listen to the words, but all I want to do is cover my eyes. I put one arm over my face and get hold of the knife with my other hand.

I can feel someone pressing against me from behind. It's Candy. She leans against me and lightly touches my arm, the one holding the knife.

"It's okay," she whispers. "Relax. Everything's going to be okay."

Her voice is like honey and heroin. Sweet and sleepy. My shoulders unknot. My legs get weak. My whole body relaxes. But I don't let go of the knife.

The stones' light fades suddenly. The room is back to normal. I turn, expecting to see Candy behind me, but she's over by the table, helping Kinski wrap the stones in silk and put them back in the cabinet. He pushes up each of Allegra's eyelids and takes her pulse like a regular doctor.

"She's going to need to rest awhile before she can be moved. Candy, can you stay with her? I want to speak to this young man."

"Sure, hon."

I follow Kinski out through the waiting room to the parking lot.

"You have any cigarettes? I'm out," he says.

I hold out the pack for him to take one. Light it for him. He looks older and more tired under the streetlights.

"So, you're Eugène's fair-haired boy."

"And you're his Florence Nightingale. Nice light show back there."

"It gets the job done."

"Nice office, too. Did you get that stuff at one garage sale or did you shop around?"

"Eugène said you had a mouth on you."

"Look, thanks for what you did back there, but what do you want? I'm expecting to see a hospital or a clinic and I walk into a peepshow booth full of stuff that fell off a garbage truck."

He chuckles. "Yeah, sometimes I think we might take the humble-healer thing too far."

"Is Allegra going to be all right?"

"She'll be fine. Her head's probably going to hurt for a day or two. It's not the injury, it's just something that happens to civilians when you blast their bones back together like that."

"It's my fault she's hurt."

"I assumed that. Eugène said there were some ugly people looking for you. Guess they found her instead."

"I'm going to find them. And no one's going to blast their bones back together."

"You take care of that girl in there first. You might be hell on two legs, but she needs taking care of. Throw a sheltering spell on her. Get Eugène to give her some protection charms."

"I should have done that when I first moved into the store."

"You fucked up. So fix it. Here."

He pulls a pencil-size piece of lead from his side pocket and puts it in my hand.

"Now you don't have any excuse. You can draw the circle and do any spell you want."

"I haven't done that kind of magic in a long time."

"What kind of magic have you been doing?"

"Killing things, mostly."

"That'll make you friends. Try a shielding spell later. Maybe having the lead in your hand will trigger some muscle memory and it'll come back to you. If you can't make it work, call me. I'll talk you through it."

"Okay."

"You should call me anyway. Let me take those bullets out of you. Five, isn't it? Maybe they won't kill you, but they can still cause an infection."

"If they do, you can just fix me with your rocks."

"Rocks? Oh. Those. No. Those are glass."

"I've never even heard of glass like that."

"That doesn't surprise me. Those are some of the rarest objects in existence. I don't suppose you'd let me take those slugs out tonight?"

"No thanks. Maybe when I'm done."

"That's what I figured."

Kinski flicks the remains of his cigarette out into the dark lot and looks at his watch. "Your young lady is probably back on her feet by now."

"What do I owe you?"

Kinski shakes his head. "We'll settle up when you let me take out those bullets. And listen: Candy gets kind of pissy when unexpected calls come late at night. Her people get twitchy after dark. But she gets over it. You have any problems, you need anything and Eugène can't help, you call me."

"You don't even know me. Why would you do that?"

"I was young and reckless and stupid once, too. Maybe between Eugène and me, we can keep you alive long enough to wise up."

"What did you do that was so reckless and stupid?"

"I'll tell you that when you let me get those bullets."

"I was in Hell," I say, and I have no idea why, except that there's something about Kinski that reminds me of my father. He's bringing out some weird, little-kid part of me that wants to confess my sins and ask for forgiveness. Only I don't want forgiveness, from anything or anyone. But right now I can't stop myself.

"I was in Hell for eleven years. Most Hellions had never seen a live human. I was the most exciting thing happened to them seen since they were booted out of Heaven. When they got done with me, when the torture and freak shows and rape got boring, I killed things for them. I was really good at it."

"I knew there was a reason you are the way you are. I guess a season in Hell is a better excuse than most."

"Vidocq told you?"

"Relax, boy. It's L.A. We've all got secrets around here. And we know how to keep them."

"Who are her people?"

"Excuse me?"

"You said Candy gets pissy about unexpected, late-night calls. What does that mean?"

"Oh," he says, and opens the clinic door. "She's a Jade. But we're working on it."

Candy walks Allegra out of the clinic while I open up the Escalade. We both help her get inside and stretched out in the back.

"Thanks," I tell Candy.

"You're welcome."

I start the engine, but she keeps standing there. She gestures for me to roll down the window. I push the button and the glass slides away. She steps up onto the running board and leans into the car, just a few inches from my face.

"Doc told you about me. I can tell. I want you to know you don't have to be afraid of me. Eugène likes you. Doc likes you. That means I like you. We're all family now. All the funny little people who live in the cracks in the world."

People say that Jades are like vampires, but really they're more like human tarantulas. When you get bit, you don't swoon in Bela Lugosi ecstasy; you're paralyzed while something in the Jade's saliva dissolves you from the inside. Then they drink you, leaving you as hollow as a chocolate Easter bunny. I haven't been this close to a Jade in a long time and it's freaking me out a little.

I say, "I used to kill your kind."

She grins.

"I used to kill yours. See? We already have something in common."

"Is the doc a Jade or something?"

"Doc? Wow. In the history of wrong guesses, that was about the wrongest wrong guess since ever."

"You're not like the other Jades I've met."

"What? I'm not all slinky and seductive?"

"No, you're cute enough. You're just not much of a monster."

"That's okay. I think you're monster enough for both of us."

Allegra sits up and looks around.

"Are we home yet?" she asks.

"I should go."

"Yeah, you should," says Candy. She gives me a peck on the cheek and jumps down off the van. Kinski comes outside; she runs over to him and slips under his big arm as he holds it up for her. She waves as we pull out of the parking lot.

I should have known that Candy was a Jade back in the exam room. That trick she did with her voice, almost sending me to sleep on my feet, that's Black Widow 101 stuff. She sure didn't come on like a Jade, except for one thing. That kiss on the cheek came from lips as cold as any dead thing I've ever touched. So, why did I enjoy it so much? After being a monk for most of eleven years, any attention from a cute girl, alive or dead, will get under your skin. There's the good news. The bad news? On top of everything else, I might be turning into a necrophiliac.

WHEN ALICE AND I got together, I wasn't the only one with secrets. One night, after a particularly long evening of bruising sex on the couch in our un-air-conditioned living room, she blurted out, "I'm rich."

"What?"

"I'm filthy, balls-out, stinking rich. My whole family is, though they've probably disinherited me by now."

"So, you might be rich, but you're not sure?"

"No, I'm rich. Even if they forget all about me, I have a trust fund worth more than some Central American countries."

I sat up and reached for the coffee that had gone cold on the table.

"You do not."

"I'm in the DAR. I have my grandmother's gold rings and diamonds in a safe deposit box. Hell, I own a tiara."

"And you've never worn it to bed? You're holding out on me."

She locked onto me with her serious face. I always had to shut up when she used the serious face.

"I never told a boyfriend about any of this before. You're the first."

"Why me?"

She hit me in the stomach, half joking and half annoyed. I almost spilled coffee all over the couch.

She said, "I love you, ass-brain. I want you to know all about me."

"You already know all about me. My family doesn't have any money. But I can make a good chicken-fried steak."

She sat up on one elbow.

"Why aren't you rich? Why aren't all magicians rich?"

I shrugged and lay down beside her.

"Partly it's keeping under the radar. Partly it's tradition. A sort of code or something. What's cool about being rich if you do it by reciting a few words? Most rich Sub Rosa are connected to some kind of legit business. The rest of us just skate by. We just use magic to cut some corners. And that's the point. I'm not rich, but I know I'll never starve because I can order a burrito and make the counter person think I've already paid."

"Aim high, dude."

I kissed her hard and she crawled on top of me.

"So, when do we get to blow your grandma's money on drugs and hookers?"

"That's the tricky part. Grandma was old money. Old money hates rich kids, even rich grandkids. I don't get a dime until I'm thirty."

"Thirty? That's geologic. That's Jurassic Park."

"Anyone can make it to thirty, if they're not a complete dipshit. That's the deal. We're rich and all we have to do is make it to thirty."

I looked away, playing it straight.

"That's a long way off. I don't like making big promises."

Alice sat up on me.

"No, you have to. Promise me."

"Hey, I'm kidding."

"Promise me."

"Okay. I promise not to die until I'm thirty. Happy now?"

"Almost. And you can't die first."

"Jesus. Where's this coming from?"

"My parents. Say it."

I grabbed her arms in my hands and held her tight.

"I won't die first. I'll live to be a hundred and leave card tricks and Japanese cartoon porn on your grave every year on your birthday. Happy now?"

"Completely," she said, and smiled.

"So, when can you bring that tiara home? I've never tied up a DAR girl before."

Parker killed Alice a month before she turned thirty. At least I got to keep part of my promise. I didn't die first.

ALLEGRA'S APARTMENT IS on Kenmore Avenue, just south of Little Armenia. Her building is a converted seventies-era motel called the Angels' Hideaway. Dying palm trees out front and a pool full of black water out back. The management knocked down half the interior walls, turning two dingy motel rooms into dingy, but decent-size apartments. They'd either hired the laziest contractors possible or real style visionaries because they'd left the orange shag carpet on the floor and the glitter stucco on all the walls.

Allegra's keys are in her pocket. She's walking now, but kind of clumsy. I pickpocket her keys, open the door, and find the light switch. There's a dark green sofa against one wall. She walks over on her own and flops down, leaning her head back against the wall.

"You want anything? Water? Coffee? A drink?"

She shakes her head. I want a cigarette, badly, but the room reeks of fresh air and nonsmoking vibes. I give up and sit down next to her on the sofa.

"You said I'd be safe if I stayed."

"I thought you would," I tell her. "You should have been. I fucked up."

I'd meant to get Vidocq to splash around some of his voodoo water and slap a protection charm around the place. But I got so caught up with hunting Mason that I forgot. Simple as that. I let down my guard with Mason before and Alice got killed. Now I'm sitting next to another woman I've let down.

"It's my fault." Now I really want a cigarette or ten. "Sorry."

She closes her eyes and seems to drift away, still flying high on whatever Kinski slipped her in that dried fruit. Her breathing becomes shallow. Her heart slows down. Then it blasts from around sixty up to a hundred and twenty. She looks at me and starts yelling. "My boss's head was talking to me without a body. But when I told you, you didn't even seem surprised. What the *fuck* is going on?"

"Yeah, that." Suddenly I'm a single dad about to explain the birds and the bees to his kid. "Do you believe in God?"

"Damn. First you say you're an ex-con, now you're Jerry Falwell. Who are you really?"

"Do you believe in God? Lucifer? The afterlife. Any of that?"

"I don't know. My mother used to take me to church when I was little."

"Remember the stories about miracles? Water into wine? Plagues of locusts?"

"'Course. Everyone remembers that. About when all the rules and commandments got boring, someone would walk on water or turn a city into salt. It was cool. So what?"

"What's a miracle but another word for magic?"

"Don't quiz me. Just say what you want to say."

"Magic. I'm talking about magic."

"Oh, man." She stands up, walks across the room, and drops into a beanbag chair held together at the seams with duct tape. "You know, when I first met you, the ex-con thing aside, I thought you might be all right. But you really are just another snake, aren't you? I mean, either you're here to scam me or fuck me while I'm high, or you're just plain crazy. Any way you cut it, goddamn. Me and men." Her voice trails off and she sinks into the chair, nervously rubbing at the bruise over her left eye.

"You just told me that the decapitated head of your dead boss was talking to you tonight. What do you call that?"

"How do you know so much about that stuff?"

"I do magic. Not Vegas magic. The real stuff."

"You're like a witch or a wizard or something?"

"Harry Potter's a wizard. I do magic. I'm a magician."

"This is a really strange night."

"Wait. It gets better. Kasabian's a magician, too. So is Parker. He's the guy I'm pretty sure attacked you tonight."

She sits up and looks at me hard. "Do something. Show me some magic."

"What do you want to see? What will convince you?"

"Blow my mind. Make that table float in the air."

"I'm not a floater. I used to be able to do the cute stuff, but most of the magic I'm good at now isn't furniture-friendly."

"So, what can you do?"

I think for a minute and pull Azazel's knife from my jacket. Allegra's pupils dilate a fraction of a millimeter. I'm getting used to seeing these things.

"Here. It's for you." I hold the knife out to her, hilt first. She takes it tentatively, holding it with both hands like it weighs fifty pounds.

"What am I supposed to do with this?"

I go over to her walking on my knees, like a kid. Staying lower than the eye level of an opponent often has a calming effect on them. Maybe it will work on a nervous friend.

When I'm at the foot of the beanbag chair, I hold up my left hand and say, "Try to stab me."

She cocks her head to the side like she's trying to figure out if her cat suddenly started speaking French. "No, I don't think I'm going to do that."

"It's okay. Don't hold back. I know you're pissed at me. Let me have it."

She just stares down at the knife in her hands. Maybe I was wrong. Maybe the knee walk made me look too silly to stab. There's a way to fix that.

I lean right into her face and scream, "Stab me, dammit!" as loud as I can. She lunges. And jabs the knife all the way through my left hand.

"Oh my God! I'm so sorry!" she says, covering her mouth with her hands.

What most people don't understand about being hard to kill is that just because getting shot or stabbed or set on fire doesn't kill you, it doesn't mean that you don't feel it. When someone shoves a big knife through my hand, it feels like anybody else's hand getting stabbed. This is a nice way of saying that when Allegra pigsticks me with the bone blade, I want to scream like a little French girl and roll around on my back demanding a thousand cc of Jack Daniel's, stat. But I don't do any of that. I calmly pull the knife out of my hand. I wipe the blood off on my pants leg. I don't want to piss her off more by bleeding on her carpet.

Allegra finds a couple of paper napkins next to a half-eaten sandwich on a plate on the floor. She presses the napkins hard against the hole in my hand.

"Thanks. You're being nice for someone who thinks I'm crazy or a snake."

"Shut up. Now I know you're too dumb to be a snake. You're probably too stupid to be crazy. I don't know what you are."

"I'm magic," I say. I pull the napkins away from my hand and wipe off the last of the blood. The wound is already closed.

She shrugs. "That just makes you a freak, not the Wizard of Oz. Or maybe it was a trick knife."

Tough crowd at the Angels' Hideaway. "Go get one of yours."

She goes to the kitchen, rattles some drawers, and comes back with a hefty butcher knife. Nice. She's getting into the spirit of things.

"Now what?" she asks.

"Try to stab me again."

"What is wrong with you? If you want a girl to hurt you, there's professionals for that in the phone book."

I hold up the hand she just stabbed. "One more time. Come on. Have fun with it. Most people don't live long enough to do this twice."

I don't have to shout this time. She shoves the blade straight into my hand. But it sticks there, only about an eighth of an inch into the skin. There's no blood at all. She keeps trying to push the knife through. Really starts leaning on it. I have to take the knife out of her hand and set it on the floor. She takes my hand and examines it, looking for blood or a new wound. All she finds is a fresh red scar from where she stabbed me a couple of minutes ago.

"My whole body is kind of magic. Once you attack me a certain way, it doesn't really work all that well again."

"So, no one can ever stab you again?"

"I wish. The new scar you gave me just means that this hand is protected from being stabbed like that."

"Is that what all those scars are from? Getting stabbed?"

"That and other things. Kasabian shot me when I walked into his store, so I have some new ones from him. It's not so bad. Some people wear a crucifix or a pentagram for protection. I wear my protection right in my skin."

"Talking heads and magic scars. That's not what I thought magic would be like."

Allegra's looking a little pale right now and I don't think it's the concussion. My little magic show might have gone too far too fast for her. I root around in my memory for magic that doesn't involve anything blowing up. I come up with half a little spell. Something I would have done at lunch in grade school. I've always been lucky at making partial spells work, so I silently recite the words I remember, then tack on my own ending, careful to recite only human words and not the Hellion that keeps trying to sneak out.

Nothing happens. Then I feel a fluttering in my chest, like the old days on Earth when the magic was flowing.

I hold up my stabbed hand and blow across the fingertips. Five yellow flames flicker to life, one on top of each of my fingers. Candles made of flesh. The fire is real, but it doesn't burn me. I take a cigarette from the pack in my pocket and light one off my index finger, blowing the smoke up into the air.

Allegra glances from me and back to the flames, her eyes wide and staring. She reaches over my burning fingertips and snatches her hand back a second later.

"It's hot."

"That's why they call it fire. Put up your hand," I tell her. "Palm toward me."

She holds up her right hand. I touch my hand to hers and say a few words. The flames drift down my fingertips and over to hers.

"Blow on your fingers lightly."

She does it. The flames disappear.

"Do it again, only blow harder this time."

She puffs her cheeks and blows. The flames reignite.

"I can feel it. It's warm, but it doesn't hurt."

"Blow really hard."

The flames flare, from one to six inches. The moment she stops blowing, they shrink back to birthday candles.

"Is that magic enough for you?"

"Yeah, I'd say that covers it."

I blow lightly on her fingertips and the flames fade away.

"Now you've got a little charm on your hand and you can do that fire trick anytime you want. So, next time you start doubting, you'll know that what you're seeing is real because part of you is magic, too."

She stares at her unburned hand for a minute.

"Tell me about Mr. Kasabian's head. Is he dead? Did you do that to him?"

"No to the first question, and yes to the second."

"Tell me about it."

For the second time tonight, I'm confessing my sins. This time it's easier because it's not just my bad moments, but also Mason's, Kasabian's, and the rest of the Circle's. Plus, I'm lying. Just a little. I tell her that Mason sold me out, sent me to a dark and rotten place. I just leave out Hell and the hitman part.

"So, that guy tonight—Parker—he killed your girl?" she asks.

"That's what Kasabian said."

"Damn. Was Mr. Kasabian in on it?"

"He's too much of a jellyfish for murder. And he's too afraid of me to lie about it. But he was there for the rest of it."

"I'd have cut off more than his head if he'd done that to me or mine."

"Then you know why I'm back."

"You're Clint Eastwood in the *Outlaw Josie Wales*. Max von Sydow in *Virgin Spring*."

"I don't know who that second one is, but if he was out to fuck up the people who fucked up someone he cared about, then, yeah, okay, I'm Max. And that's why I'm leaving."

"You're giving up?"

"No. I'm leaving Max Overdrive. I'll crash with the meth heads in Griffith Park. I'm too dangerous to be around actual human beings. I should have left that first night."

"No way. No damned way," says Allegra. "I'm in."

"In what I'm doing? No way, girlie."

She crawls off the beanbag chair and sits beside me on the floor. "Listen, I've been looking for something extraordinary my whole life, but I kept getting it wrong. I ended up in bad places with bad people, bad drugs, bad lovers, and a lot of other bad shit I don't want to think about. But this, right here, this is it. You're it. The thing I've been looking for all my life. I want in."

"Tough. I didn't come back here to be your guidance counselor."

"Yes, you did. That's exactly what you're here for. Maybe not the whole reason, but part of it."

"You're not a killer and you don't have any magic. You manage a video store."

"So, teach me."

"Teach you what? I can show you a few tricks, but when it comes to the hardcore fuck-you-up magic, you're born with that or you aren't."

"What about your friend, Vidocq?"

"He's an alchemist. It's not the same thing."

"I could learn that."

"You could have died tonight."

"I don't care."

"I'm not dragging you into this."

"You already did. And you'll take me along cause you need me."

I don't say anything. I get up so that I'm standing right over her. Earlier, I'd set the bone blade beside me on the floor. I pick it up and scabbard it inside my jacket.

"For eleven years, I've been worked over and abused in

ways you can't imagine by things you don't want to know about. I've killed every kind of vile, black-souled, dead-eyed nightmare that ever made you piss your pj's and cry for mommy in the middle of the night. I kill monsters and, if I wanted, I could say a word and burn you to powder from the inside out. I can tear any human you ever met to wet rags with my bare hands. Give me one reason why I could possibly need you?"

She looks straight up at me, not blinking. No fear in her eyes.

"Because, you might be the Tasmanian Devil and the Angel of Death all rolled into one, but you don't even know how to get a phone."

I hate to admit it, but she has a point.

LATE AFTERNOON THE next day, I knock on Vidocq's door, which I still can't help thinking of as my door, which makes my brain spin around like a blender full of ball bearings. Fortunately, I'm good at ignoring a lot of what my brain does.

Beside me, Allegra bounces on the balls of her feet. She's wearing shiny boots with thick soles and a belly-revealing T-shirt tight enough to be have been spray-painted on. Probably because I told her that Vidocq is French. She looks cute enough, but one side of her face still sports a dark purple bruise and her cheeks and jaw are a little puffy, so she's also trying to distract people's eyes from her face to her body. It's working.

She's doing a lot better than me. I crashed at her place to keep an eye on her. All I can tell you is to never fall asleep on a beanbag chair. My back feels like someone beat me with a pillowcase full of tuna-fish cans.

Vidocq opens the door and does a comical little eyebrow raise.

"There you are. And you've brought a friend."

Allegra puts out her hand and gives Vidocq a smile that would make a dead man swoon.

"I'm Allegra," she says. "Stark's new zookeeper."

"I'm François Eugène Vidocq. Lovely to meet you."

She looks over his shoulder into the crowded room. "Are all those books and potions yours?" She steps past him into the room like she'd just bought the place. Vidocq turns and gives me a conspiratorial look.

"Forget it. Just a friend," I say.

"Then you are a very foolish boy." He nods at her examining his ingredient racks. "What happened to her face?"

"Parker."

"Brave girl."

"It's why I bought her here. If Parker knows who she is, then she's already part of this. But she's a civilian. She doesn't know magic or charms or anything. Think you could teach her some of what you do?"

"You want to trust her with me? After what I've done to myself?"

"If she's on Parker's list, she could do worse than be cursed with immortality. And she needs something. I can't teach her what I do. I won't."

"What's this?" Allegra asks. She holds a small vial up to the light. It's red, but it shimmers like mercury.

"That's the blood of a Chimera. A rare beast that, it's said, can change its shape to anything it eats. It's also said that its blood can give a man that power, too, but I've never been able to make it work."

"You have so many amazing and beautiful things here. I don't know how you can remember them all."

"The trick is not to try and remember. You learn what the ingredients are and how to use them, what to mix or never to mix. You learn how to distill the essence and find the true heart of each ingredient and potion. As you learn those things, you learn the names and the methods, which books are good for one type of potion, which instruments produce the best results. You don't try to remember. You just learn. Once you've done that, your hands will remember what to take and what to use and which books to open."

She picks up a parchment scroll and opens it. It's a diagram of a woman's body, but she has wings and an eagle's head. There are diagrams and small, precise handwritten notes all around the drawing.

Still holding the scroll, Allegra asks, "You can read Greek, too?"

Vidocq glances at the scroll and nods. "German and Arabic, too. Some Sumerian. A bit of Aramaic and some others. There are so many books to read, and I've had a lot of time to fill."

"Do you think that I could learn this?"

"Alchemy? Why not? People have been learning the craft for thousands of years. Why not you?"

Allegra looks over Vidocq's endless racks and picks up a crystal box with what looks like bugs moving around inside. "What's this?"

"Babylonian scarabs. Very powerful. Very wise."

The old man goes off on a lecture of the virtues of these particular bugs above all others. Allegra hangs on every word of his spiel. I leave them alone and wander into the bedroom. They don't need me. It's geek love.

The bedroom I used to share with Alice is now completely Vidocq's. The walls are painted a bright arsenic green and are covered with protective runes and sigils. The Goodwill and surplus store blankets are gone from the bed and replaced with a dark red velvet comforter and pillows that don't look like they were found under a dinosaur's ass. There are books everywhere, tins of fresh tobacco, bottles of sleeping potions, and bowls of hallucinogenic mushrooms. On a sideboard are framed pictures—fading ink silhouettes, a crumbling daguerreotype, and even a few faded photos. Most of the images are of women. He's never talked about any of them.

I check the floor of his closet and the shelf at the top. I look under the sideboard. I find what I'm looking for in a box under the bed.

It's full of Alice's things, whatever things Vidocq could salvage from whatever happened to her that night. I know that the box will be safe to open. He wouldn't have saved anything with blood on it, but it still takes a minute to work up the nerve.

There are neatly folded T-shirts and panties on top, which is funny because I don't think Alice or I ever folded anything in our lives. Under those are her favorite shoes, a pair of glow-in-the-dark leopard-spotted Chuck Taylors. There are pesos and taxidermy frogs playing toy instruments we got on a road trip to Mexico. Tucked in a corner near the bottom is a pair of vintage Ray Bans she'd hot-glued back together after a bouncer knocked them off her face for slamming too hard at a club in Culver City. These days, I would have pulled the guy's spine out through his ass, but I wasn't such a hands-on type back then. A simple Sumerian spell gave the bouncer the worst case of food poisoning he'd have in this or any other lifetime.

When I piled it all on the bed, a small white box that had been stuffed in with the T-shirts fell out. When I opened it, I recognized the box instantly. It was that stupid magic-shop box with the hole in the bottom and the fake bloody cotton inside. The one she'd used to show me that she could do magic, too. I put the magic box in my pocket and the rest of her stuff back in the big box and carry it out into the living room.

Allegra and Vidocq are still taking inventory, but pause long enough to grin at me.

"Eugène says that I can be his apprentice and learn to be an alchemist."

"Congratulations. Just don't forget that we had a deal.

I'm letting you into the other world, the Sub Rosa, but you still have to help me with a few things, too. And you can't abandon Max Overdrive. It may not be much, but it brings in money and, unless things changed while I was gone, that's what makes the world go round."

"I'll remember. We'll go out tomorrow and get you a phone."

"And the Internet. We need to get that, too."

"First thing, never say 'Get the Internet.' You sound like the Beverly Hillbillies. You 'use' the Internet or you 'access' it. You never 'get' it."

"See? That's why I hired you."

She turns to Vidocq. "Don't listen to him. He didn't hire me. I blackmailed his ass."

"Is this true?" he asks.

"Ignore her. She's schizophrenic and a pathological liar. I only let her work at the shop to keep her from swindling widows and orphans."

"You just can't handle the truth, can you?"

"And what's that?" I ask her.

"That I totally made you my bitch."

"See? Not a word of truth can pass her lips." I take the box with Alice's things and go to the door. "I don't know how long it'll take me to pay you for the Spiritus Dei."

"I was going to bring that up. I know someone who can help with both the Spiritus Dei and provide some work. Work that's more in line with your talents than your video store. The fellow's name is Muninn. Mr. Muninn."

"Why do I want extra work? I have a job. Killing Mason."

"And how is that money you stole from the man near the cemetery holding up? How much did that jacket and those boots cost you?" Vidocq crosses to the window and pulls back the curtain. Clouds have softened the sunlight, but it's still all billboards, brown hills, and asphalt below. A couple of burly kids in baggy denim jackets are doing a brisk trade in what the buyers will be hoping is crack, but in this part of town is probably baking soda and plaster. Across the street, a couple of leathery-skinned old men are selling oranges and watermelons off the back of a pickup truck. They're probably illegals and new in town. They don't know which neighborhoods are profitable and which are dead zones. Or maybe the orange and watermelon Mafia muscled them out of their territory and this was the best they could do.

"You see it, right? Even here, where there is very little, this is a world that runs on money. There's no arena here for you to fight in. No rich fallen angels to pay your bills."

"Fallen angels?" Allegra asks.

"It's just an expression," I tell her. Turning back to Vidocq, I say, "In case you hadn't noticed, I live in a store. Allegra runs the store. Stores bring in money."

Allegra says, "Not really."

"What do you mean?"

"The store's never really turned a profit. There's a Blockbuster and some other big chains just a couple blocks away. The porn keeps the doors open, but most of the real money came from Mr. Kasabian's bootleg business, and now that's gone."

"Stop calling Kasabian 'mister' all the time. He doesn't deserve it." Out the window, the crack dealers are buying oranges from the old men in the truck. The cultural divide between homegrown American entrepreneurism and immigrant ambition is being bridged right before our eyes. It's an inspiring moment. Maybe the old men will let me sell oranges with them off the back of their truck when Max Overdrive closes and I'm homeless again.

"What's this guy's name again?" I ask Vidocq.

"Mr. Muninn."

I nod like the name means something to me. "Okay. Let's meet him."

"I want to show my new apprentice a few more things, so we'll do it tonight."

"Sounds good." I start to leave, but Allegra calls me.

"How am I supposed to get back if you take the car?"

"You take it. I jimmied the ignition, so you can start it with a flathead screwdriver. Vidocq will give you one. Ditch the car at least ten blocks from the shop."

The sound of shots comes through the window and we all turn. The two crack kids are on the ground in widening pools of blood, and a powder-blue Chevy lowrider is speeding away. Oh well. It's like the real estate people say, "Location, location, location."

"How will you get back?" asks Allegra

"I know a shortcut." I go out into the hall, step through a shadow next to the door opposite and come out in the alley behind Max Overdrive. I go in through the back and straight upstairs. The morning crew has cleaned the place up pretty well and taped the front-door glass back together reasonably well. Some customers look at me, but I don't look back.

In my room—this is my room now; that other place is Vidocq's—I put the box with Alice's things on a shelf in the closet where I'd kept Kasabian's head. I wish he was still here. I'd put one of Alice's T-shirts over his head at night, the way old ladies drape parakeet cages. Sleep tight, moth-erfucker, with my murdered girl's shirt for a nightcap.

I wonder where Parker has taken Kasabian and what he's done with him. Only one thing makes sense. Parker has killed him. After I set off the trap back at Mason's place, he and Parker realized I was back. They checked on the rest of the Circle and found Kasabian was gone. Know-ing what a rancid little worm he was, Mason would figure that he'd start blathering secrets sooner or later. It would be simpler and easier just to kill him. Sweet dreams, Kas. I might not have killed you, you know. You were just too damned pathetic. Leaving you to your little store and the dreams of the power the others swindled you out of might have been punishment enough. I could have been happy to see you live another fifty years trying to make lemonade out of your misery.

I take the little magic box from Alice's things and set

it on the table beside the bed. I don't dwell on it sitting on that crap table in this nowhere room. *Let it go. Don't think. It's what you're best at.*

I'd picked up the habit of playing movies on the monitor Kasabian used to make his bootlegs. Mostly I watched old Shaw Brothers chop socky stuff. *Five Deadly Venoms. The 36th Chamber of Shaolin. Dirty Ho.* Or spaghetti westerns. *The Good, the Bad and the Ugly. The Great Silence. Four for the Apocalypse.* The sound of fighting, even movie fighting, is weirdly comforting when I'm falling asleep. Something else is playing now, and I don't remember having left the set on. It's *Fitzcarraldo,* a German movie about a crazy Irishman who tries to drag a riverboat over a mountain in the Amazon. It almost kills him. Is this a message? Did Parker leave this playing for me? After he broke in, why didn't he wait to ambush me?

I take the Veritas off its chain and do something I wanted to do last night. I flip the coin and ask, "Is Doc Kinski for real?" When it I catch it, the Veritas is showing a symbol it's never displayed before. A calopus. Imagine a flying wolverine covered in porcupine quills dripping with enough poison to give God himself a sore ass. That's a calopus. Written in Hellion script around the edge of the coin's face is, *If assholes had assholes, Kinski is the shit that would come out of that asshole.* I've never see the Veritas say that about anyone before, Hellion, angel, human, or beast.

Like every sentient creature in the underworld, the

Veritas has strong opinions. Using the Veritas well means being able to separate facts from its horror-show editorials. This is good news. There's only one reason it would hate anyone like that.

Kinski is one of the good guys. Okay. Time to take the doc's advice.

I leave *Fitzcarraldo* running with the sound off and dig around on the worktable until I find a creased AAA map of L.A. After I unfold it on the floor, take out the piece of lead the doc gave me, and start drawing a magic circle around it, I can't remember any specific locator spells, but the idea is pretty simple and I know I can fake my way through one.

The circle is complex. Hellion magic is always complex—either that or so simple, Fungus could do it. There's not much in the middle when Hellions are in charge.

When it feels like the circle is done, when the map is completely enclosed and I've loaded in every luck, hunting, and eavesdropping charm I can think of, I reach up for more junk off the table. A piece of string and some foil from a burrito wrapper. I wad up the foil and tie it to the bottom of the string, making a pendulum. Then I take my knife and slice across the palm of my left hand. Squeezing hard before the wound closes, I sprinkle blood around and inside the magic circle.

Hell doesn't run on prayers or promises. Downtown magic is about reaching out and grabbing what you want, and that requires payment. An offering. Blood. Black magic on Earth isn't so different and it's why so many dark magicians dress like cashiers at Hot Topic. Black is a good color anytime you're flinging around blood.

I start chanting, a free-form mix of Hellion and English, ordering whatever Lurkers, spirits, magical pinheads and old, forgotten gods who happen to be nearby to turn down *The Price Is Right* and listen up. *Show me where Mason is. I paid you my blood, now give me what I want. I command you. Give me what you owe me. I have the key to all the doors in the universe. You don't want to even dream of cheating me.*

The foil ball on the end of the string begins to move, making little circles where I hold it over the map. The movement becomes steady and strong, pulling my hand and my whole arm in circles, too. Then it stops. The foil slams onto the map like it's magnetized. I pull the pendulum away and look at where it landed. Just a little north of Hollywood Boulevard and Las Palmas, right on top of Max Overdrive.

Cute. I should have seen that one coming. Mason stuck a reversal gag on anyone stupid enough to look for him with magic.

On the floor, the map wads itself up and bursts into flame. A lick of fire reaches up like a burning claw and snatches the pendulum from my hand. Both the map and pendulum disintegrate into ashes and drift away on a breeze blowing in from some other part of Creation.

That was an *Amateur Hour* move. Now I know why Parker didn't go for me the night he took Kasabian. Why should he bother? I've proven that I'm dumb enough to walk into a bear trap marked with a big flashing neon sign that says WARNING: BEAR TRAP. I'm a killer who hasn't managed to kill anything. And it must be clear to everyone paying attention that I'm not Sam Spade. I don't know what I'm doing. I'm running on instinct and hunches.

Killing is a funny thing. Even if it's killing a Hellion general, one so psychotic that even other Hellions want him dead, the first time you commit murder, you're going to get sicker than you've ever been in your life and it's going to last for days. The second time you commit murder, you're going to get just as sick, but you're going to be over it the next day. The third time you commit murder, you change into that extra shirt you brought along, the one that's not covered in blood, and you go out for a drink. After that, killing doesn't feel like much of anything at all. Of course, I haven't killed a human yet. I'm not sure how I'm going to feel about it when the time comes.

Maybe it's not such a bad thing that Alice isn't here to see what I've become.

I sit down on the edge of the bed and pick up the magic box, roll it around in my hands, then set it back on the table. On the TV, some poor Indian has just died hauling Fitzcarraldo's boat over the mountain. The Indian's friends are gathered around his body, but Fitz is screaming for them to keep pulling his boat. He's the hero of the story and he's completely nuts. This isn't going to have a happy ending.

I lie down for a while, trying to get the kinks out of my back, but I'm too restless, so I walk over to the Bamboo House of Dolls. Carlos says hi, but I just sort of grunt at him. Being a good bartender, Carlos sees all and knows all. He brings me a double of Jack, along with some rice and beans with warm tortillas. Then he leaves me alone. The music isn't Martin Denny tonight. It's someone named Esquivel. It sounds like what James Bond's dentist must play in his waiting room. I try to relax, enjoy the food, and let the ludicrous sound wash around me. After two or three more drinks, Esquivel is really starting to grow on me.

When Carlos comes over to take away the empties, I ask, "What about me on a yacht in a white tux? Could I be James Bond's stunt double?"

Carlos takes the glasses away before he says, "Only if Bond fell into a wood chipper first."

He asks if I want another drink. I tell him I need a cigarette more and go outside and light up. It's around eight. Maybe nine. Ten's a possibility. Anyway, it's dark out. Time to get back to Vidocq's. I head for an alley across the street where I can slip unseen into a shadow. Halfway there, I spot a Ducati parked down the street. The twentysomething hipster TV producers love these sleek Euroracers, but like the Melrose Harley boys, it's mostly for show. The Ducati's tires are clean enough to eat off of. Doesn't anyone in this town actually ride their bike?

It'll be nice to feel some wind on my face. I take out the knife, jam it in the ignition, and I'm gone.

RULE ONE WHEN you get back from Hell and haven't ridden a high-performance in eleven years is not to get on the bike after three or five Jack Daniel's. Rule two is not to try a stoppie—grabbing just the front brake so that your rear end pops up. When you're drunker than you think you are, which is pretty much always, you're going to lean too far forward and pull the rear end of the bike up and over onto your dumb ass. Lucky for me, even six or seven sheets to the wind, I still have impressively inhuman reflexes, which means I can jump off the bike before it comes over and snaps my neck. The downside to jackrabbit reflexes is that while they get you out of the way of obvious and imminent danger, when you're going forty miles an hour on your front wheel, those reflexes will simply launch you into the air like a squirrel on a land mine.

Off to my left, the bike is pinwheeling down the empty street, kicking up, sparking, and shedding its plastic and chrome skin as it flies apart. It's kind of beautiful, turning from a machine into an ever-expanding shrapnel flower.

Then I hit the street and start tumbling. Then sliding. Then tumbling again. I vaguely remember that there's a proper way to come down after laying down a bike, but my head is bouncing off asphalt and manhole covers and

I'm way beyond technique at this point. I just roll up into a ball and hope that I don't break anything important.

And I don't. I just come away with some road rash on my hands and legs. Chalk one up to Kevlar scar tissue. My leather jacket is nicely scarred, which is fine by me. There's nothing more embarrassing than new bike leather. However, my jeans look like they were attacked by a pack of wolverines. The bike is a total loss. I drag what's left of it and leave it between a couple of stripped cop cars. I'm only a couple of blocks from Vidocq's, so I walk the rest of the way.

AT THE DOOR Vidocq hits me with the resigned look of a father who knows that no matter how much he tries, this son probably isn't going to make it to thirty. He shows me mercy by letting me in without saying a word. Allegra is grinning at me like the little sister who's thinking the same thing as the father, but finds it funny and not pathetic.

"Are there any of my old clothes around?"

"I think there might be some in one of the cabinets. Wait here and try not to bleed on anything."

"I showed Eugène that fire magic you taught me," Allegra says.

"That was barely magic at all. More of a trick. And I didn't teach you anything. I charmed your hand and gave you about one molecule of what I can do. That's not the same as learning magic. You need to remember that or you'll get hurt."

Vidocq comes out of the bedroom with a familiar looking pair of beaten-up jeans.

"Thanks," I tell him. I take off my shredded pants, toss them in a corner and put on the clean jeans, then remember that while modesty isn't in high demand in Hell, you're not necessarily supposed to do that kind of thing up here. But they're both still looking at me like I stepped off the short bus, which is pretty much what I just did.

Vidocq leads us into the hall, stops, and looks at me.

"Allegra is with us now," he says. "She needs to see and understand the things we do. You're too drunk to safely steal another car tonight, though I know that's exactly what you'd like to do. Instead, you need to show this girl your true gift and prove to her that you do things besides hurting yourself and other people."

"Where are we going?"

"Third Street and Broadway. The Bradbury Building."

I hold out my hand to Allegra. "You ready to do the next thing?"

"What is it?"

"This isn't an asking situation. This is a doing situation. Either you're ready or you're not."

A moment of hesitation, then she takes my hand. "Show me."

Vidocq takes her other hand, and I pull them both into a shadow and into the room.

"What is this place?"

"The center of the universe."

"What does that mean?"

"You can go anywhere you want. Any street. Any room. Anywhere. Across town, the moon or Elvis's romper room."

"If you can go anywhere you want anytime you want, why are you always stealing cars?"

"Because ghosts walk through walls. People drive cars."

"Mr. Muninn is waiting," says Vidocq. "We should move along."

I take Allegra's hand as Vidocq touches her shoulder and we all step out onto Broadway together. We're right next to the Bradbury Building. It's late enough that the only people who might see us are a couple of winos and some master-of-the-universe business types so in love with their cell phones that a nuke could go off in their pants and they wouldn't notice.

Allegra looks around and punches me in the arm hard enough that I can tell she means it.

"You shit! You could have done this last night, but instead you made me stab you."

"I didn't think you were ready for it."

"Like I said, if you want girls to hurt you, there's plenty of professionals in the phone book."

The inside of the Bradbury Building is a giant Victorian diorama. It looks like aliens dipped one of Jules Verne's wet dreams in amber and dropped it in Los Angeles. The place is all open space in the middle, with masonry walls and wrought iron catwalks leading to offices and shops.

We step into an iron elevator that looks like a cage for an extinct bird the size of a horse. A couple of guys get in behind us. Grim expressions. Dark suits. Shades that look like they've never been taken off and, in fact, have been soldered to their faces. They wear those things in the shower and when they're fucking their best friends' wives. Mostly the guys in the suits bug me because they give off a whiff of bacon—cops earning a little extra money under the table by working as security guards. They might be off duty, but a cop is always a cop and being caged up with them makes me want to chew my way out of this steam-powered rattrap. The funny thing is that while their presence is sending my blood pressure to Mars and back, their heartbeats are rock steady. So is their breathing. Cops make me nervous at the best of times, but when I've been ripping off people and cars every couple of hours for days, and I'm packing a Hellion knife and an incredibly unregistered handgun, it brings out the bad side of my personality. Vidocq hits the button for the fifth floor. One of the men in black presses the button for three. If either of these guys even blinks funny, I'm going to be painting the walls with livers and spinal cords.

But nothing happens. The elevator hits three; the cops get out and walk away without even looking back. The fucked-up part is that I'm actually a little disappointed. I was so ready for a fight that now that it hasn't happened, I feel like I've been tricked. Teased and let down. I desperately want to break something. It occurs to me that I might still be a little drunk and that the only thing that will cure me is a cigarette or random violence. Or maybe a glimpse of the ugliest furniture in the known universe.

There's a home-decor shop right across the elevator. Some kind of high-end Pier 1 nightmare selling faux-exotic crap for dot-com cokeheads with too much money and no shame. There are life-size porcelain cheetahs with gilt eyes. Fake antique Chinese furniture. Plasticine Buddhas. Paint-by-number Tibetan thangkas. The sight of the place is the kind of horror that will kill you or sober you up. Fortunately, I'm hard to kill.

Vidocq closes the elevator door and we start up to the fifth floor. Before we get there, he pushes the stop button and the car rattles to a halt. Using two fingers, he pushes the one and three buttons on the elevator keypad.

"What did you just do?"

Vidocq says, "We're going to the thirteenth floor."

"There is no thirteenth floor," says Allegra. "Look at the buttons. This building only has five floors. And if it had more, it wouldn't have a thirteenth floor. It's bad luck. No one would move in."

"If you say so," he says, and pulls out the stop button. The car begins to move down. It stops at the third floor.

"See? We're on three again." Then something moves by the home-decor shop.

The window where the porcelain cheetah stood just a minute earlier is dark and lit only by candlelight. The big window is caked with a century's worth of dust and impacted grime. In the cheetah's place is a bell jar at least six feet tall. There's a woman inside. She's transparent and drained of color, nearly black and white. Her hair and dress billow around her, blown by some invisible storm. She screams and claws at the glass walls of her prison. When she sees people getting off the elevator, she goes quiet and stares at us like a lion tracking a herd of zebra. A second later, she's pounding on the bell-jar glass again and showing yellow, sharklike teeth.

The interior of the shop is dark and crowded and has the musty smell of an attic that hasn't been opened in fifty years. A shadow moves out of the shadows. It's a man. He's small, round, and black. Not the way Allegra is black, but black like a raven or an abyss. He's wearing an expensive-looking silk robe and holding a brass telescope.

"I see you've met my Fury," he says. "She's a very recent acquisition from Greece. Of course, I've had all three Furies at one time or another, but never all at once. That would be a coup." I look back at the Fury and out the dirty window. Women in business clothes and men in suits and carrying attaché cases pass, completely unaware of the Fury and the strange store.

"Nice to see you all," says Mr. Muninn. "I was beginning to think that you'd forgotten about me."

"Never, my friend," says Vidocq. He introduces Allegra and then me.

Muninn takes my hand and doesn't let go.

"I've heard a lot about you, my boy." He stares up at me like he's trying to see out the back of my head. "Interesting. I thought I might see bit more of the devil in you. Perhaps it's best for us all that I can't."

"Vidocq said that you might have work for us."

"That I do, my boy. I'm a trader and a businessman. Merchandise comes in and merchandise goes out. I'm busy, busy, constantly busy. There's always work here for those who want to work and to earn a decent wage."

"We were hoping for more than decent."

"Then we'll have to find something indecent for you to do."

"You have so many beautiful things," says Allegra, picking up what looks like a basketball-size pearl with a map of the world caved on it.

"These are just baubles, shiny things to bring in the curious. Come. Let me show you the real store."

He sets down the telescope on a table overflowing with pocket watches, an orrery with the wrong number of planets, and a box of glass eyes, some of which are larger than the palm of my hand.

Muninn takes us through a steel door marked EMERGENCY EXIT. Beyond the door, the walls are rough, chiseled stone, like we're in a cave cut into a mountain. There's a stone stairway that's so narrow at points that we have to walk down single file. And it's not a short walk.

The trick getting into and out of a place like this is

memorizing landmarks. Anything will do. Anything you can remember. A loose stair. A breeze from a hole in the wall. A crack in the rock face that looks like a sheep blowing the eagle on the presidential seal.

If it's too dark, like it is on Muninn's stairs, you can always steal a handful of rare and ancient coins from a bowl in a guy's shop and drop them like bread crumbs all the way until you get where you're going.

The most important thing to know about caverns is to never go in one without having a pretty good idea of how to get out. And never let yourself be led into said cavern by a stranger who owns his own Fury. That last one isn't absolute. It's just a good rule of thumb. It also helps to have a friend vouch for the guy, which is the only reason I'm still stumbling down a set of crumbling stairs dropping doubloons and drachmas behind me.

Just before we hit the bottom of the stairs, I can see where we're headed. It's huge. Like Texas huge. I can see the cavern's ceiling, but not the far walls. There's a junkyard of old tables, cabinets, and shelves at the bottom of the stairs. About fifty yards beyond that is what looks like a stone labyrinth that twists, turns, and snakes away into the distance. Can't see the end of that, either. It's like standing on the beach at Santa Monica and trying to see to Japan.

"Where did all this come from?" I ask.

"Oh, here and there. You know how it is when you stay in one place too long. You tend to accumulate things."

Shelves, dressers, and old tables are piled with books, old photos, jewelry, furs, false teeth, pickled hearts, and what might be dinosaur bones. Those are the normal bits. Sticking up over the top of the labyrinth's walls are parts of drive-in movie screens, the masts and deck of an old sailing ship, a lighthouse, and strange carnivorous trees that snap at the flocks of birds circling the ceiling.

"How long have you been here?"

"Forever. I think. It's hard to be sure about these things, isn't it? I mean, one ice age looks pretty much like another. But I've been here a long time and that's why everyone comes to me. I have all the best things. For sale or for trade. Buyer's choice."

"That's why we're here. I used up some of Vidocq's Spiritus Dei and need to pay him back."

Muninn glances over at Vidocq.

"Eugène, I didn't know that you knew the sultan of Brunei."

"What does that mean?" I ask.

"You're not the sultan? Perhaps you're Bill Gates or the czar of all the Russias?"

"No."

"Then trust me. You can't afford Spiritus Dei."

The little man wanders to a nearby table and picks up a wooden doll that looks like it was pulled out of a fire. He winds a key at the doll's back. It stands up and begins to sing. The song might be a hymn or an aria from an opera I've never heard of, which is all of them. The doll's voice bounces off the walls, high, perfect, and heartbreaking. With a soft click, the key in its back stops moving and the doll falls over. Its voice echoes for several minutes, bouncing off the labyrinth's thick walls.

"Of course, we might be able to do a trade," Muninn says. "There's a certain someone who would like a certain something in the possession of certain other people in our little town. I would like you to help Eugène procure this item for me. If you're successful, I guarantee you a flask of Spiritus Dei and a not inconsiderable amount of cash. Eugène told me that you'd like money to be part of your payment. Is that right?"

"Money is good."

"Money I have."

Muninn brings over a set of blueprints he'd hidden behind a collection of canopic jars. He spreads the blueprints on the only relatively uncluttered table in the room, first pushing animal teeth, Mayan vases, and a box of lenses and prisms out of the way.

"The place you are invading is called Avila. It's a gentleman's club in the hills."

"What does that mean, 'gentleman's club'?"

"Just what I said. A gentleman's club. In the old sense. A place to drink, to eat, and to gamble with friends. It's also the most exclusive and expensive bordello in the state. Perhaps the country. Avila's clients are film producers, software billionaires, local politicians, and foreign heads of state. Only the highest of the high can get inside. Except for you two, of course. You'll be the rats in the walls."

The building on the blueprints is round and the interior is laid out in concentric circles.

"While Eugène is an accomplished thief, Avila is heavily guarded. It might take days or even weeks for him to figure out how to penetrate the defenses. However, I understand that you can easily get him inside and out again."

Avila is laid out with the offices in the outside circle. Food and a bar one circle in. Gambling one more level in, and the bordello one after that. The center of the blueprints is blank.

"At this time of year, there are parties every night, leading up to their New Year's Eve party in a couple of days. You'll want to go in there as soon as possible. Now, there will be enough chaos to make your work easier, but on New Year's there will be too much."

I point to the building's blank center.

"What's in there?"

"No one knows. Perhaps you'll find out."

"Does it pay extra?"

"Let's see what you bring me."

I'm trying to keep my mouth shut, but it's really pissing me off that I have to give up the hunt for Mason so I can play cat burglar for an Oompa-Loompa. But that's exactly what I have to do if I want to keep Max Overdrive open and have a place to live. I don't have a choice. I don't think Vidocq would be happy having me planning mass murder at his kitchen table.

"I'm in," I say.

"Good boy," says Vidocq. "I'm in, too."

"Me, too," says Allegra.

"Forget it. No amateurs on this bus. Only criminals."

Allegra starts to say something, but Vidocq cuts her off.

"He's right, even if he's rude about it. What we're doing is criminal and dangerous. This isn't the time or place for you to learn about such things."

"Fine," she says. "Have a boys' night out. I hope you and your dicks will be very happy together."

I look over at Muninn and he has two tuxedos on hangers.

"Gentlemen's disguises for a gentleman's club."

WE STEP FROM the room and into Avila without anyone noticing, which is something I've always wondered about. How can you see two guys dressed like ushers at Liberace's funeral walk out of a wall and not react? My guess is that no one sees us or remembers us. The room or the key or some combination must temporarily blind or switch off the memories of anyone nearby. Otherwise how could I have sent so many of Hell's A-team killers down to Tartarus, the special Hell for the double dead.

Avila is a palace designed by Martians. A rip-off of a rip-off of a rip-off of a Victorian men's club that some set designer saw in a Sherlock Holmes movie when he or she was six. Still, the scale of the place is impressive. They must have cut down half the Amazon rain forest to get the dark wood for the bar. The Rolexes in this one room could pay off the national debt.

The place is full of sloppy, well-dressed drunks laughing and screaming in a dozen languages. Happy hour at the United Nations of Money. Half-naked and just plain naked hostesses serve drinks and tapas and hold out silver trays piled high with white powder, syringes, and glass pipes, whatever the partiers want. Perfect. Who needs magic to sneak around when you've got Caligula's bachelor party going on down the hall?

Vidocq's thief instincts are cranked up to eleven and he finds the office in the time it takes me to stop looking at the girls. He's no fun at all when he's in business mode. He pushes me into the office ahead of him and closes the door.

After all the rumpus-room fun, the office is kind of a letdown. It could be the office of a bank president or a Beverly Hills real-estate tycoon. There are lots of awards on bookshelves. Lots of celebrities smiling down from the walls. Some of their eyes are so glazed it looks like you could go ice skating on them. Over where Vidocq is working on the safe is an oak desk the size of a Porsche and probably more expensive.

"How's it going over there?" I ask.

Vidocq is rattling little bottles together as he pulls potions from the pockets of his tux.

"It's as I thought," he says. "The safe is ordinary, but it's protected by a number of protective spells."

"Want me to help? I'm good at breaking things."

"Be quiet. I have to understand exactly what's at work here and eliminate the spells one by one and in the proper order."

I'm already bored and annoyed by Avila. It's not that I have anything against bad behavior. I'm all for it. But this incestuous, backslapping, heavy-money-party cabal scene is everything I hate about L.A. in particular and human beings in general.

Those pricks down the hall, flying high above it all on this hillside, they're the kind of people whose faces end up on money or a new library so that kids will have a new place to hang out while realizing that no one ever taught them how to read. Their wealth doesn't insulate them from the world. It creates it. Their bank statements read like Genesis. Let there be light and let a thousand investment banks bloom. They shit cancer, and when they belch in a bowl valley like L.A., the air turns so thick and poisonous that you can cut it up like bread and serve it for lunch at McDonald's. A Suicide Sandwich Happy Meal.

There must be a hundred of them just ten steps away. I wonder how many I could kill before the cops got here.

Vidocq is mumbling over his vials and potions across the room. I drop down into the desk chair and look through the pile of envelopes in front of me. Aside from a few charity begging letters, suck-up notes from politicians, and more bullshit awards, the rest is just bills and ads. What do you know? Even the gods get junk mail.

I toss the pile back on the desk and pick up a photo in a silver frame. From TV, I recognize one guy as the current mayor of L.A. and the other as a guy who was almost elected president. There's a woman standing to one side and the governor is handing her yet another award. All three beam from the picture, showing their teeth. A pack of happy wolves.

Something fun must have just happened at the party because the crowd suddenly got loud and then died down again. I bet I could take out everyone in that room and be gone before anyone figured out what's happening.

A little switch clicks in my brain. I pick up the framed photo and show it to Vidocq.

"Recognize anyone here?"

He shoots me a look.

"What? *Oui*. Politicians. Fuck them. Let me do my job."

"Not them. The woman."

He looks again. Then gets more interested.

"I know her. Is that your friend Jayne-Anne?"

"Yeah. This must be her place. She was always a crazy social climber. Avila is her gift for standing by Mason."

"It's a very funny coincidence that we're here."

"Isn't it just?" I get up and walk around the desk.

"Where are you going?"

"To kill someone."

Vidocq comes over to me and grabs my arm hard. Two hundred years of work has given him a strong grip.

"Don't you dare. Be a man! Hold your temper and do

the job you agreed to do. You know where she is now and you can come back for her another time."

"You're right. Sorry. I just lost it there for a minute."

"Stay there and make sure no one comes in."

"Got it."

The second Vidocq turns his back, I'm out the door.

A few minutes ago I was feeling like an idiot in the tux, but now I'm glad Muninn insisted that Vidocq and I tart up like a couple of players. No one looks at me twice as I plow like an icebreaker through the crowd, just another horny drunk, bumping his way through the human waste, running down his rightful share of first-class drugs and free pussy.

I didn't have much of a temper before I went Downtown. Maybe I never needed it up here. The first time I felt it was a few weeks after I got tossed into the arena. I kept winning fights. Barely, but I won. This surprised me as much as it did the crowd. Azazel was my owner by then, but he didn't pay much attention to me. My novelty had worn off and waiting for me to get beaten to death was the only amusement I had left to offer. Every time I didn't die it seemed to piss off the handlers Azazel had sent to keep an eye on me.

They always walked me out of the arena in chains, on my wrists, ankles, and neck. It was a joke. I could have just killed some poison-spitting sphinx thing, but I was the wild man-beast that had to be leashed. Hellion humor. Big laughs every time the chains went on.

One night, Baxux, the tallest of my three watchers, got a little frisky with my chains. He held them behind me like reins and whipped me with them like I was a four-dollar mule. There was a half-broken *na'at* embedded in the dirt floor of the arena. I don't even remember picking it up, but I must have because all of a sudden Baxux's belly was as open as the Holland Tunnel and his angelic guts were lying at my feet. The crowd went apeshit, which might have been the nicest thing anyone did for me the whole time I was in Hell. The roar distracted my other two attendants for long enough that I could swing the broken *na'at* hard enough to extend it to almost its full length, taking off the head of attendant number two with my first swing and one of attendant number three's arms with the next.

The bad news was that attendant three still had three arms left and now he was pissed. He *lucha-libre* leaped on top of me, all five or six hundred pounds of him, collapsing the *na'at* to its noncombat length of about eighteen inches. Then he started pounding me with three big fists like granite jack-o'-lanterns. Every time he set me up for one of his John Wayne haymakers, he pulled his body away from me and up in the air a little, just far enough for me to smash the end of the *na'at* into the ground.

The *na'at* has a spring-loaded mechanism that extends it full length in a nanosecond. I mean, a working one does. This *na'at* was badly damaged, so it took a dozen good raps on the ground for the thing to go off. When it did, the look on number three's face was almost worth the beating.

He stood up, which was a lucky break. I couldn't have lifted the guy off me with a hydraulic jack and dynamite. He stood there swaying and looking down at the shaft of the *na'at* that now went into his chest and out his back.

I whipped the *na'at*'s grip around clockwise, which extended thick barbs that bent backward, getting a good grip on my opponent's flesh. Then I pulled. I put all my weight into it and spun my body as I fell back, using the *na'at*'s razor edges like a drill to open up the wound even wider. The last big pull hit the spring lock that made the *na'at* collapse back into itself. The force knocked me flat on my back, but that was all right, because it also pulled out attendant number three's black heart and part of his spine.

Do I even need to tell how the crowd reacted to seeing one of their own eviscerated? The cheer nearly melted my eardrums. I was Hendrix at Woodstock.

But just killing my attendants isn't what taught me that I had a temper or what gave Azazel the idea that I might have the stomach for serial murder. It's what happened next.

I piled dead attendant one on the body of dead attendant two, climbed up both of them, and grabbed one of the torches off the arena wall. Fire in Hell isn't like Earth fire. It's more like Greek fire or burning magnesium. It burns long and hot and is practically impossible to put out.

While attendant number three tried to crawl away from where I'd left him, I shoved the lit torch into the hole in his chest where his heart used to be. He didn't just have jack-o'-lantern hands anymore. His whole body lit up, burned, and burst like the Hindenburg.

I used the *na'at* to slice through the chains and made a break for the door. Not that I ever had a chance of making it. Twenty armed guards came pouring into the place. I had enough full-tilt crazy left that I killed three or four of them before the *na'at* flew apart in my hand. It was all country music after that. Those Hellion guards square-danced all over me. It was Azazel himself who broke up the party and kept the guards from killing me.

They threw me in one of the arena's punishment cells and put a couple of guards on the door. At the time, I thought that was overkill. I was already three-quarters gone. There was no chance I was going to even try to escape. Later, I realized that the guards were there to keep other Hellions from getting in and finishing me. That cell was where I first realized that I was officially hard to kill.

I went in there bleeding and slashed, and with half my bones sticking out through the skin. Three days later, I could stand up. A day after that, I could walk. My guards didn't like this one bit. When they thought I was asleep, they'd sneak peeks at me through a sliding panel in the cell door. There was something new in their eyes. I should have been deader than dead. But I wasn't. They thought I was a monster. And no one bothered me until a few days later when Azazel sent a friendly little homunculus with sweet Hell fruit and Aqua Regia and a request that I join the general for dinner that night. Naturally, I said yes.

That's the upside of a temper. The downside is that it makes you do stupid things, like not watch where you're going.

I'm stalking through the party, trying to catch a trace of Jayne-Anne, when I walk straight into someone, knocking his drink all over his $10,000 suit. The guy gets up and starts to call me an asshole, but only gets out, "Assh—" before he chokes.

It's Brad Pitt. Not the actor, but my favorite crackhead from the outside cemetery when I first got back.

I say, "Where you been, man? I've missed you."

"Security!" he yells.

"I've been meaning to give this back to you."

I pull his stun gun from my pocket and zap him in the ribs, just for old times' sake. He goes down like a sack of lug nuts and I drop the stun gun on top of him. It won't do much good against what I know will be here in a second.

I'm not entirely stupid. I start back for the office when security comes tearing around the corner before I can get very far. Five or six of them. Buzz-cut heads and necks as wide as manhole covers. They look as stupid in their suits as I do. But they have more guns. They all draw down on me, but don't make a move. A woman walks around them and heads right for me. She has no idea who I am. Until she does.

"You're dead," she says.

"Not as dead as you're about to be."

Jayne-Anne backs off, yelling, "Kitty! Bennett!"

A starlet-skinny blonde in an off-the-shoulder designer *schmata* and a fop who looks like Ziggy Stardust in a purple velvet suit come around from behind the guards.

They reek of magic. It comes off them like heat ripples over desert asphalt.

So, to recap: we have five or six guns, a couple of hoodoo hipster killers, an old friend who wants me dead, a lot of drunks and naked showgirls, and me in a borrowed suit. I'd duck through a shadow, but with the crazy lighting in this place, there's nothing dark or deep enough for me to dive through.

Even my stupidity has its limits. I turn and run.

Fire and lightning explode behind me. Burning golden sparks rain down on me like a thousand lit matches, burning through the suit and into my skin. Best of all, ducking and bouncing off the walls to keep from getting hit is making the bullets in my chest very angry. They scrape my ribs and prod my lungs. I can already feel blood in the back of my throat. I'm never going to outrun these idiots.

I drop to my hands and knees, breathing hard through the froth in my throat. Blondie and the fop stop and look at each other, a couple of good hunting dogs who just ran down the fox and are about get their reward.

I've got their reward.

I shout guttural Hellion syllables, coughing up blood with every word. I push every ounce of power I have down through my arms and legs. I spit and my blood soaks into the expensive carpet that lines the hallway. Then it's gone. So is the floor. But I knew that was going to happen. Jayne-Anne's magicians and her armed linebackers didn't. They fall straight through where the hall floor used to be, roll down the hillside and into the trees. Jayne-Anne's and my eyes meet just long enough for me to give her a little wink. Then someone grabs me from behind and drags me back into the office that I wasn't supposed to leave in the first place. Plenty of shadows in here. I grab Vidocq's shoulder and we walk out through a photo of Jayne-Anne glad-handing the pope.

Pray for us sinners now and at the hour of our death.

WE STEP OUT of a shadow and into Muninn's cavern. Vidocq turns and punches me in the gut. I go down on one knee.

"You fucking child! You could have gotten us both killed."

This isn't the first time Vidocq has been mad at me, but it's the first time he's ever gotten physical. Good job. I'm about to lose one of the few friends I have on this rock.

When I don't get up he says, "Don't play with me. I

didn't hit you that hard." Then he must see the blood. "What happened to you?"

"You hurt me bad, Pepe LePew," I say.

"You child," he says, and helps me to my feet. The bullets are rattling around inside me like gravel in a tin can.

Muninn looks like a little kid on Christmas morning when Vidocq hands him a small golden box with what looks like delicate grasshopper wings on top.

"Perfect. Beautiful," he says over and over. He takes the box over to what looks like solid rock. But with a few touches and turns to specific stones, the rock face swings away, revealing an enormous vault in the side of the cavern. Muninn takes the golden box inside, comes back out, and seals the vault so that it's invisible again.

"You've done a splendid job, gentlemen." He gives me an indulgent smile. "Well, one of you has been splendid. The other has ruined his suit. Don't worry. I have a million of them. Literally."

"You didn't tell us that they were using magicians as security at Avila," I say.

"Are they? That's new. But you rose to the challenge and completed your mission. I look forward to doing more business together."

"What else do you know about Avila? You know what they're hiding in that blank spot in the blueprints. Don't you?"

Muninn looks troubled.

"You don't want to know about these things. I don't

want to know about them and I've seen whole civilizations turned to salt or buried in ice."

"What's in there?"

Muninn shakes his head.

"A bordello. The secret one. A celestial bordello full of creatures seldom seen here on Earth. But the real reason those so inclined go there, risk their lives and their souls, is for the pleasure of abusing captive angels. These are the injured ones who fell to Earth during Lucifer's uprising and new ones that they've captured since, though I have no idea how one goes about capturing an angel." Muninn looks at me. "There. Are you happier knowing? Will you sleep better tonight? Young man, there are some things in the world so profane that their only real value is in not knowing about them."

I wipe blood off my lips with my tuxedo sleeve while Muninn brings over a bottle dusty enough to have been on Noah's Ark. He pours three drinks in three crystal glasses. When he raises his, Vidocq and I follow.

"To God above," he says, and tosses the drink over his right shoulder. Vidocq and I do the same. He pours three more drinks.

"To the devil below." He tosses the drink over his left shoulder. So do we.

Muninn pours three more drinks, each twice as full as the first two.

"To us. The ones who did real work tonight while those other two were off playing tiddledywinks with poor fools' souls." He raises his glass and knocks the whole thing off in one gulp. The stuff burns like rose-flavored battery acid, but I don't taste blood anymore.

Muninn sets down his glass, takes a blue bottle from the end of the table, and sets it in front of Vidocq.

"Spiritus Dei, my friend."

Vidocq beams. "Thank you. That's more than I was hoping for."

"If you have extra, can I have some?" I ask. "I want to put it on my bullets. I might have to shoot things that don't die easy."

Muninn goes to a shelf and comes back with a smaller version of the bottle he gave Vidocq.

"On account," he says.

"Thanks."

"And I owe you some cash, too, I believe."

"That would be nice. Do you have an ATM down here under all these clocks and bones?"

Muninn walks to a corner of the room piled twenty-feet high with boxes of bills and chests overflowing with gold and silver coins. The little man pokes through the pile like an old codger trying to choose just the right ripe peach at the grocery store.

"Ah." He pulls down a box marked U.S. TREASURY and hands me a neatly banded stack of brand new bills. I riffle the stack, enjoying the feel of money in my hands. The bills are all hundreds. Next to the counter girl at Donut Universe, it's the most beautiful thing I've seen since coming back to Earth.

Over Muninn's shoulder there's a glass decanter with a small blue flame, not much more than a match head, hovering at the center.

"Is that what it looks like?" I ask.

"What does it look like?"

"It looks like the Mithras. The first fire."

"Right you are. The first fire in the universe. And the last. There are many in this world, and others, who believe that at the end of time the Mithras will escape and grow until it has burned down all of Creation. The ashes of our existence will fertilize the soil for the universe to follow."

"How much is something like that worth?"

"It's not for sale. And if it were, not in this lifetime or with the accumulated wealth of your next thousand lifetimes could you afford it. Don't be too ambitious too quickly, my friend. If we're able to do business more regularly—and I think that we can—then your payment will increase and become considerably more interesting."

I put the bills Muninn gave me into the inside pocket of the tuxedo jacket.

"Who were we working for tonight?" I ask.

"That's confidential."

"Not even a hint?"

"Answers are easy, but hints cost money. Save yours for now. You're going to need a new suit," he says, fingering a hole in my sleeve where some of the golden sparks have burned through.

We say good night and start back up the steps to Muninn's store.

"Would you mind picking up those coins you dropped?"

I wave to him and pick up each one as we pass. When we reach the shop, I drop them in the bowl I'd stolen them from.

In the elevator, Vidocq asks, "Why do you care who Muninn's client is?"

"That's was a big coincidence walking into Jayne-Anne's place tonight. It's the second time since I've been back that I happened to stumble into a member of the circle. I want to know if I'm being set up."

"Muninn will never tell you. It's a matter of honor for men like him. We must be more careful."

The elevator reaches the ground floor and Vidocq slides the brass gate open.

"This is going to get worse, you know. That run-in with those goons tonight? That's nothing."

"*Inter urinas et faeces nascimur.* We are born between piss and shit," he says. "Many wanted to kill me back in my day in France. The criminals I sent to prison. The local police who never believed I was anything other than the rogue and thief I was in my youth. Even the Sûreté, the special police force I built for Paris, one based on true scientific principles—even they were corrupted by those in power and turned against me. Most of what I've built or had has been taken away from me by liars and curs, so if you're going to tell me to go away or that I don't have to stay for what's coming, kiss my arse. The things that

Mason and his friends do—they are the things of men. Mason has power, maybe more power than any magician in history, but he is still a man. I am not afraid of any man."

"Let's go get drunk."

"And piss on our enemies from a great height."

I'M SITTING AT the bar in the Bamboo House of Dolls, playing with the Barbie-size keyboard on my new phone. Phones are like toys now. They fit in your pocket, light up and vibrate like joy buzzers. Plus, you can get—I mean, "access"—the Internet and find anything you want. Music. Maps. Porn. Anything. If cell phones came with a cigarette dispenser, they'd be the greatest stupid invention ever.

"Googling yourself?" asks Carlos.

"What's that?"

"Searching for yourself on Google. Find out how famous you are. How many places you're mentioned. They call it 'ego surfing.' Just put in your name."

The first thing that comes up is an old *L.A. Times* article on Alice's murder. It's just a filler piece with no details because who cares about one more dead punk? It's kind of insulting, but I'm grateful not to know too much about exactly what happened to her. I'm still not ready for that.

Carlos is right. I'm on Google, too. Apparently, LAPD is looking for me as a "person of interest" in Alice's murder. So much for ego surfing.

I put in *Mason Faim* and get another *L.A. Times* article on the fire at his house—the first one. Not the one Vidocq and I started. There's a sketchy obituary, too. Sounds like they found a body in the mansion; it was so far gone that they couldn't check dental records and get a decent DNA sample. My guess is that the body was the Circle's resident hippie, poor, dumb TJ. Mason isn't the type to let a perfectly good corpse go to waste if he can use it to convince people that he's dead.

Another search and I find Jayne-Anne's name mentioned in about a million places. Mostly society-page party and charity events, political fund-raising, and movie premieres. Anywhere she can get up close and personal with the masters of the universe.

I put in Cherry Moon's name and get a link to a Web site. Click on the link and there she is, in perfect Sailor Moon drag, a rhinestoned cell phone in one hand and a pink teddy bear backpack in the other. She looks even younger than she did before I went Downtown. When I left, she could pass for twelve or thirteen. Now she looks like she's eleven, tops. I hope it's done with makeup, but I have a feeling it's something else.

I click the enter button and go to her site. It's the same thing inside. A pretty little girl's pretty little diary, full of gossip about her cool friends and the neat things they do together. Plus pages and pages of pictures of her in maybe a hundred different Gothic Lolita outfits, everything from Shirley Temple pinafores to pirates to a kimono-clad vampire with fake fangs. It's a pretty convincing little girl's site, only Cherry is about my age. If I didn't know her better and know that this was all an act, I'd think she was retarded.

There's a links page with buttons that lead to you to the sites of the rest of her prepubescent coven. At the top of the page is a big link to a site called Lollipop Dolls. That was the name of the creepy girl gang she hung out with while we were in the Circle. Now Lollipop Dolls seems to be an expensive store on Rodeo Drive selling imported Japanese anime and monster-movie toys, games, and custom Gothic Lolita clothing. Now I know what Mason gave Cherry as her reward. I check the address one more time, go the bathroom in the back of the bar, step through a shadow, and come out on Rodeo Drive.

It's sunny on Rodeo. It's always sunny on Rodeo. When rich trophy wives with platinum AmEx cards and endless supplies of Vicodin float down the street like Prada parade balloons looking for $20 lattes and $2,000 jeans, it goddamn well better be sunny.

Cherry's store is at the end of the block. I've got my knife, a gun, and I'm wearing the motocross jacket with the Kevlar inserts. The perfect accessories to go shopping for a Hello Kitty lunch box.

LOLLIPOP DOLLS IS like some weird little girl's hunting lodge. The heads and faces of every Japanese cartoon character and monster are hung on the walls like trophies. Their plastic guts are in model kits on the shelves and their skins are draped on padded hangers in long rows of animal prints and Little Bo Peep frills. When I turn around, there's a platoon of twelve-year-old Cutie Honey types staring up at me, letting me know that I'm extremely not welcome. It's *Village of the Damned* with ankle socks.

I say, "I'm looking for Cherry Moon."

One of the Lolitas walks over to me. She barely comes up to my chest.

"Who the fuck are you?"

It's exactly what I thought it would be, and now that I know, it's even worse. What comes out of this mouth of Lolita in a pink ball gown and yellow ribbons isn't a cartoon squeak, but the voice of a thirtysomething bar chick who's had too many late nights and smoked too many unfiltered Luckies. That's the other thing Mason gave Cherry. The power to be twelve forever and to do the same thing to her creepy entourage. A terminally fucked-up fountain of youth.

"I'm an old friend of hers. We both knew Mason way back when."

"Are you stupid or are you fucking stupid? No one talks about Mason around here, cocksucker."

I've never been chewed out by a fourth grader before. It's all I can do to keep from laughing. She must see it in my face because the next thing I know, she's snapped out a white furry-handled tanto knife and is pressing it under my chin hard enough to break the skin.

"Why don't you get out of here, Grandpa? We have

a reputation and you're driving down property values. Cherry doesn't want to talk to you. And, by the way, you look like a faggot in that jacket."

Even with her cute move with the knife, I'm guessing that she's not a real blade fighter. If she was, she'd be holding the tanto under my ear, where she'd be right above a major blood vessel.

I sweep my arm in front of me, faster than she can see. All of a sudden I'm holding the knife and she has a sore wrist. The first thing she does is register surprise. Then fury. She steps back into the pack and they all strike cartoon fighting poses. A few more of them have knives out. They might look like little girls, but they stink of magic, Cherry's or their own. I can't tell. Either way, I don't like the idea of duking it out with a dozen windup dolls. This place probably has surveillance cameras and alarms. I don't want to have to explain to the cops why I'm going Mike Tyson on a bunch of pink-cheeked cherubs.

I hold up my hands so they can see I'm not going for a weapon, and start for the door. There's a pen on the counter. I use it to write down my cell number on a receipt.

"She can call me at this number. Tell her a dead friend is back in town and that she better call him soon or he's going to come back here and spank her." I hold up the tanto to the girl in the ball gown. "You get this back when she calls me."

I walk out of the store and drop the knife into the sewer grating on the corner.

I hear something over the noise of the traffic. Someone is calling my name. I turn around, thinking at first it's one of the girls from Lollipop Dolls, but no one is there. It's a man's voice coming from across the street. I have to shield from eyes from the damned sun, but when I do, I get a good look at him. It's Parker, not more than fifty feet away.

Parker isn't big. Parker is a Disneyland attraction. Lay some track across his back and shoulders and he could give the kiddies a wild ride. I go for him straight through traffic. Cars are zipping along Rodeo, heading for the green lights at both ends of the block. I hop across the hood of the closest car, drop down, and cut behind the next. Then I'm up on the trunk of another, but slip and end up on the hood of the car behind it.

Everything is very calm and quiet inside my head. In the distance, halfway across the solar system, I hear squealing tires. Grinding metal. Shattering glass. People are yelling. But I'm back on my feet and moving. My blood is pumping and I feel a heat spread from my belly to my arms and legs. For the first time since I crawled out of the fire and back onto this rock, I feel like myself. Parker is dead ahead and I know exactly what I'm doing.

On my left, a storefront explodes, knocking me off my feet. I make a nice dent in the front passenger door of a Cadillac parked at the curb. People are screaming. The store is on fire. I look up in time to see Parker tossing what looks like a flaming basketball from hand to hand. He throws it in my direction. I roll away from the Caddie, but Parker misses the car and hits a bus stuck in traffic. More broken glass. More screaming.

I get to my feet and run at him. He backpedals down the street. Something is wrong. No matter how fast I go, Parker stays ahead of me. When he spins on the balls of his feet and really turns on the speed, I can't come close to keeping up.

By the time I'm on the next block, he's gone. I keep turning around, like a drunken ballet dancer, hoping to catch a glimpse of him.

Something hot explodes against my chest and it feels like a bulldozer is trying to park on top of my lungs.

Parker has thrown another one of his plasma balls, but show-off that he is, he missed by an inch and took out a mailbox. It's snowing *People* magazines and liposuction flyers. The front of my jacket is scorched down to the Kevlar and a little voice in the back of my brain is telling me to let one of the fireballs hit me so that next time they won't hurt. Only if one of them hits me, I'm not all that sure there will be a next time, so I tell the little voice to shut the hell up and go to Plan B.

I spring forward from a crouch and slam my shoulder into a parking meter. The pavement cracks. Two more slams and the meter is loose enough for me to pry it from the ground. I creep along the sides of the cars, keeping below window level. Parker has disappeared again. I try to reach out with those weird, new senses that keep telling me people's secrets, but I can't feel him. He's probably too powerful for something as crude as my kindergarten mind-reading experiments. Besides, I'm distracted by the smell of burning shops. The sound of crashes and women screaming.

Then I see him, behind a Hummer two cars ahead. He's juggling another plasma ball and the glow is visible under the parked cars. I sprint forward, hoping that I'm faster than he is at this distance.

When he steps around the car to knuckleball the burning plasma, I'm already there. I swing the parking meter up and catch him square in the chest with the end that's still hanging on to a nice chunk of concrete. Parker goes flying, smashing into the half-inch-thick glass of a bus kiosk, where he leaves a nice bloody spot on the shattered glass. I'm amazed, but he manages to crawl to his feet. That's something new. The old Parker was tough, but there's no way he could have taken a blow like that and lived, much less stood up. Then he surprises me again. He starts running away. Not as fast as before, but fast enough that I have trouble keeping up.

At the corner, he cuts left onto Wilshire and blows down the street at his inhuman pace. I'm fast at short distances. My reflexes are quick enough to snatch a knife out of a moppet's hand or yank the eyes out of a Hellion's head. But I'm not a marathon runner. Parker is a receding dot. I'm losing him.

Desperate to keep him in sight, I do the only thing I can think of. I grab the knife and slam the blade down as hard as I can lengthwise on the street. This one block of Wilshire shudders and an inch-wide crack slices the sidewalk in both directions. It's not exactly ten-point-oh on the Richter scale, but it makes Parker stumble. He looks back and, for the first time, seems a little nervous. He takes off running across the street to a tall, glass-and-chrome office building. I take off after him, but stop in the middle of the street.

When Parker reaches the office building, he doesn't go inside. He doesn't stop running or even break his stride. He takes one big leap and goes from the street up the side of the office building and keeps running. He doesn't crab up the side like Spider-Man. He sprints standing straight up, like the Flash.

My brain might have been cracked at the beginning of the fight, but now it breaks. I lived in Hell for years, and I never saw anything like this. I stand there as the traffic flows around me. Horns honk. Drivers give me the finger. Bus drivers scream at me to get out of the street. I crane my neck as Parker, the Human Fly, skitters up the side of a building, getting away.

My brain explodes like ice dropped in boiling water.

I sprint forward and get right under him.

Fuck magic.

I pull the Colt Peacemaker from under my jacket and blast all six shots into Parker's back. As each bullet hits, he slows down. When the last of the big .45 shells slams into his spine, I can see bones through the hole in his back. He stops running, stands drunkenly on the side of the building for a couple of seconds. Then his body goes limp. He starts to fall.

I step far enough away from the building to avoid the splatter when he hits. I have the knife out, ready to drive it into his heart to make sure he's really dead.

As Parker falls, his body seems to drift away like smoke. He becomes transparent. Two floors above the street, the last of him blows away like morning mist. I keep the knife out, ready for a trick. Nothing happens.

I walk back to the front of the building, looking up, hoping that Parker has somehow scrambled around to another side. He's not there. He's gone. I hear someone laughing nearby.

Across the street Mason is leaning against a lamp pole. The sun shines on him. A slight breeze blows his hair. He's smoking a cigarette. He doesn't look at all like the dark god of Los Angeles. He looks like Mason. A smug, handsome rich kid, but entirely human. A shadow slides from behind the lamp pole and joins him. It's Parker. His clothes are perfect. His shirt is pressed and clean. His bones are back inside his body. Both men are laughing at me. Mason points his index finger at me like a gun, and then snaps his thumb down as he pulls the imaginary trigger.

I take a step forward as two crows dip silently toward the street. When the birds pass, Mason and Parker are gone.

I HEAD BACK to Max Overdrive to change my scorched party clothes. I'm an Evel Knievel doll that a kid lit on fire and tossed on Dad's barbecue. Good thing I bought the motocross jacket with Brad Pitt's money. Otherwise, I'd be really pissed off. At least my boots are all right. And I still have the silk overcoat. Thanks, Brad. Hope Avila's security goons didn't confiscate your stun gun.

Going through the door at Max Overdrive, even the back door, usually feels good. It's boring and normal. Burned up like this, I don't bother. I step through a shadow and straight into my room. For the few seconds I'm in the room, there's noise coming from behind every door, especially the thirteenth. Something seismic is rippling through the aether, giving the universe indigestion. Good.

I take off my ruined clothes, toss them into the far corner of the room, and dig out a hoodie and pair of black jeans that I picked up with Muninn's cash. Then I walk the few steps through a dark patch in the wall to Vidocq's apartment.

I knock and let myself in. Allegra is holding an old book that looks like it weighs more than she does. Vidocq is reading it over her shoulder, with a couple of potion vials in his hands. They look up when I come in. Allegra doesn't say anything. Vidocq turns back to his worktable. I don't need super magic sense to figure out that something isn't right. He takes a set of keys from his pocket and hands them to Allegra.

"Would you take the car and get us some lunch?"

I walk into the room. "You own a car?"

"I own and do many things you don't know about. You don't know anyone anymore. You don't listen. You don't care."

Allegra walks to the door.

When she passes I ask, "Cat got your tongue?"

She turns to me. "You fucked up good, man." When she leaves, I look over at Vidocq, but he won't look at me.

Quietly he says, "You and your cowboy bullshit. There's no excuse for what you did today. It was too public and too reckless. You could have been killed. You could have killed others."

I sit down on the arm of the easy chair. "Right. It's all my fault because Parker was being so careful not to hurt civilians."

"You should never have gone after him, Mason, or the others like this."

"If I didn't, which one of you was going to? You were a detective once. Why didn't you track Mason down?"

Vidocq shakes his head, turns away, ands flips pages in the book that Allegra had been holding when I came in. "I tried for a while, but I saw things. I heard things. Don't ask me what."

"You people have had eleven years to deal with Mason and, as far as I can tell, you haven't done a goddamn thing. You think he grabbed all that magical power so he can retire? You should be on my side, trying to snuff him."

"People were here earlier. Representatives from the Sub Rosa." Vidocq finally looks at me. "They came to me because they know that you and I are close."

"Are we still? I can't tell lately."

"They're done with you over that debacle. There were so many people. So many security cameras in the stores and on the street. Tourists with more cameras. There's only so much they can do to cover it up."

"They have a story yet?"

"A publicity stunt for a movie. Equipment malfunctioned. There are many Sub Rosa in the film industry. They'll pay any fines and lawsuits this time. But they won't next time." Vidocq makes a face like he can smell two-week-old garbage from the apartment next door. "In this matter, no one is on your side."

"Are they going to kick me out of the magic union? Take away my 401?"

"This isn't a joke." Vidocq slams the book closed. "These are powerful people. Medea Bava was here. She left this for you." He hands me a small white linen bundle tied with horsehair. Crow feathers inside. And wolf teeth spotted with blood.

"An Inquisitor? That's a fairy tale. They don't exist."

"That lady sure existed," says Allegra. "Her face was more messed up than yours."

Vidocq says, "These people can hurt you."

"Let them try." I get up and go to the door. "Tell those Sub Rosa and their meter maids that they have three choices if they want me out of L.A. They can help me. They can stay out of my way. Or they can kill me."

Out in the hall a guy with two overflowing bags of groceries stops dead in his tracks, his key halfway to his door lock. With Vidocq's apartment being invisible to civilians, it must have looked like I appeared out of thin air.

"Oh. Hello," says the guy.

"Good-bye," I say, and disappear through a shadow right in front of him.

CARLOS HANDS ME a plate of rice, beans, and enchiladas in a thick mole sauce. I tear right into them. I'm starving after the fight, and Carlos's food is so good I want to marry it.

"You been doing your ninja thing again?" Carlos asks.

"What makes you say that?"

"One side of your face and your hands are all red, like a burn."

I look at my hands. They're scraped and raw-looking, like I've been juggling cinder blocks. "No big deal. They'll be fine by morning."

"I have aloe in the back if you want some."

I shake my head. "Thanks anyway. Another scar or two isn't going to ruin my pretty face."

"Right."

"Carlos, are you being polite? That's not what I come here for. I know I'm not Steve McQueen."

"My lady is totally in love with him. Lucky for me he's dead or I'd be in trouble."

I hold up my glass of Jack Daniel's in a toast. "Here's to all the guys better looking than us. May they all die first." Carlos picks up his glass, clinks mine, and we drink.

For the first time since I've had it, my cell phone rings. I don't even know what it is at first. It feels like a rat is having a nervous breakdown in the pocket of my hoodie. When I get it out, it takes me a second to remember which button to push to answer it.

"Hello?"

"Jimmy?"

"Who is this?"

"It's me. Cherry. I heard you were at the store. I didn't believe her."

"So, you called someone you didn't think was alive?"

"I called because if you *were* alive, I need your help."

I don't answer for a minute. I eat a forkful of enchilada.

"Jimmy?"

"Don't call me that. I don't like it."

"What should I call you?"

"The guy you helped send to Hell for eleven years of torture." I get up and walk over by the jukebox, speaking quietly. "The guy who is seriously thinking about redecorating the inside of that store of yours with your guts."

Now it's her turn to not talk.

"I know you must hate it."

"Hate doesn't come close to it."

"I heard about your fight with Parker."

"Everyone has, apparently."

"Did you know Jayne-Anne is dead?"

"When?"

"Last night. Parker did it. At least, that's what I heard."

"That's why you need my help. I go after Jayne and Parker kills her because she probably has information that could lead to Mason. TJ and Kasabian are already out of the picture. That just leaves you."

"Will you help me?"

"Give me a reason."

"I know where Mason is."

I walk back to the bar and away from the music. I don't want to miss any of this. "I don't believe you."

"The reason no one can find him is that he isn't in this reality. He's somewhere else. But I guess that if you got back here from Hell, you can find a way to get to him."

"How do I know that Mason isn't standing next to you right now, telling you what to say?"

"How do I know you won't shoot me in the back like you did Parker, once I've told you where Mason is?"

Mason or Cherry. If she's telling the truth, it isn't much

of a choice. Especially after today. I wouldn't mind giving bloody noses to some nosy Sub Rosa hall monitors, but with Parker and Mason dogging me, it's dumb to go begging for unnecessary trouble.

"Okay," I say. "It's a deal. When and where should we meet?"

She doesn't say anything for a few seconds. "Someone's coming. I'll call you later."

I put the phone in my pocket and go back to my food. Carlos has already refilled my glass.

"Let me guess. You were talking to a woman. I don't need to hear the words. It's all in the tone," he says. "They call when they want something, then they're the ones who cut you off."

"It's not women. It's humans. Can't live with 'em. Can't kill 'em all."

I go back to my food, and wonder about Cherry. Her breathing sounded nervous on the phone, but I can't be sure. I guess my new Spidey senses don't work over wires. But if she's setting me up, wouldn't she have suggested a time and place to meet right away? I can go round and round like this forever, looking for secret meanings in every syllable and pause in the conversation. If I am being set up, I want to go in with an edge so I don't end up eating one of Parker's fireballs. Normally, about now, I'd go and ask Vidocq for advice or maybe a protection charm. Today doesn't seem like the day for that.

It takes me a minute to notice that the music has

changed. It's shifted from tiki drums and bird calls to something more somber. All slow bass and breathy sax. Then a singer.

> *"It's dreamy weather we're on*
> *You waved your crooked wand*
> *Along an icy pond with a frozen moon*
> *A murder of silhouette crows I saw*
> *And the tears on my face*
> *And the skates on the pond*
> *They spell Alice."*

I go to the jukebox to see what's playing.

> *"Set me adrift and I'm lost over there*
> *And I must be insane, to go skating on your name,*
> *And by tracing it twice, I fell through the ice*
> *Of Alice . . ."*

"Who put this song on?" I turn and look at the room. It's early enough that the place isn't packed yet. There are maybe a dozen people scattered at different tables. "Who put this song on?" Not a word. My heart is pounding. I go back to the bar, keeping an eye on the room, not sure what to do. I want to start throwing furniture and people, but two sets of civilian casualties in one day is probably two too many.

I ask Carlos, "Did you see anyone by the jukebox?"

"Sorry, man. No. I didn't even know we had the song. Never heard it before. The service guys change the tunes every now and then, when they come in to empty the coin bins."

"Next time one of them comes in, tell them to take it off."

"You got it. Here. Have another drink." Carlos starts to pour me one, sets down the bottle, and grabs a baseball bat from under the counter.

"Get the fuck out of here, *rulacho*. You got no business here."

I look at the door. One of the skinheads from the other day is there, black eyes and his arm in a sling. He comes inside and stands by the bar, tall and cocky, but his heartbeat says he's scared, and he's keeping an eye on Carlos and his bat.

"The *Blut Führer* wants to see you," he says, nodding at me.

"The bloated what?"

"*Blut Führer,*" says Carlos. " 'Blood leader.' The boss to these Nazi bitches."

"Shut up, spick. White men are talking."

I have one hand around skinhead's throat and I'm squeezing the juice out of him. This is exactly what I need to work off some tension. When I let go, the skinhead falls on his ass on the floor. So much for tall and cocky.

"The *Blut Führer* . . ." he rasps.

"Blood leader?" I say. "When did you guys start playing Dungeons and Dragons? Tell the blood fart to kiss my ass."

Himmler grabs a bar stool and pulls himself to his feet. "I told him about that black knife you used on Frederic. That's why he wants to meet you."

"Why do I care what he wants?"

"The *Blut Führer* says he knows the original owner."

Azazel? A third-rate Colonel Klink impersonator knows Azazel?

"How does your boss know the owner?"

"I don't know. He just said he wanted to meet the man with the power to have that particular knife. He promises you safe passage in and out."

"Thanks, but I think I can find my own way in and out of your mom's basement."

"Don't trust this little bug," says Carlos. "Let me call the cops."

"No. If he knows about the knife, I want to meet the guy."

The skinhead says, "There's a car outside."

When he turns, I wrap my right arm around his neck and squeeze. I have the knife against the side of his throat.

"If you're lying to me, I'm going to cut out your eyes and cut off your balls. Then I'm going put your balls in your eye sockets and staple your eyes in your ball sac. So, let me ask you one more time, are you absolutely sure you're telling me the truth?"

The skinhead tries to nod. "He said he just wants to meet you and that no one will bother you."

I take off the Veritas and flip it. It lands showing a burning cross and *Sieg Heil* in phonetic runes.

"Okay, Princess." I put the knife back in my waistband under the hoodie. "But remember—no tongues on a first date."

THE NEW REICHSTAG is an abandoned furniture warehouse near Sunset and Alvarado. A dozen American junker cars with white-power bumper stickers are parked outside. Another dozen chop-shop Harleys are lined up just beyond the cars. At least now I know who rides in this town.

My Nazi best friend knocks on the door and a girl skinhead with a Luger in a shoulder holster lets us inside the clubhouse.

No one has opened a window in this place for ten years. The room stinks of beer, piss, and sweat. It's packed with roid rage Hitler Youth, but I can't take my eyes off the girl who let us in, fierce and skinny, sporting a wife beater, shaved head, and a gun. I want to tell her, *Baby, you're my punk-rock dream date. Let's get drunk and break stuff.* Then I remember that she's not like the girls I knew way back when. Proud to be scum. She's waiting to be swept off to Valhalla by goose-stepping Dolph Lundgren look-alikes.

She asks, "What the fuck are you staring at, asshole?" and moves a hand to the gun.

I smile at her. "Spank me harder, Eva Braun."

She spits at my boots but misses. My Nazi pal says, "Shut up, Ilsa." He leads me to an office door marked PRIVATE. He knocks twice and we go inside.

While the main room is a piss-soaked junkyard of broken furniture and overflowing garbage cans, the office is as clean and organized as an operating room.

Behind a gray metal desk, a blond man is writing with a fountain pen on a yellow legal pad. High forehead. Sky-blue eyes. Cheekbones like the prow of an icebreaker. A perfect Aryan wet dream. Hell, even I want to have this guy's babies.

His desk is surrounded by neat piles of white power pamphlets, slim books on how Jews and blacks are really extraterrestrial invaders, event sign-up sheets and CDs with pictures of bare-chested bands covered in swastika tattoos. At one corner is an impressive pile of weapons, knives, knuckle-dusters, and pipes wrapped in electrical tape. Mixed in the pile of metal, I'm pretty sure I see a couple of Hellion weapons that I used in the arena.

He looks up at me and gives me a smile that would melt a car salesman's heart. "Sorry. Just making some notes for a speech I have to give this weekend. Please, sit down."

I sit on a padded metal folding chair. My weight makes it squeak. Only the Führer gets the good furniture. I've gotten used to being able to read people, their breathing and heart rate, but I can't get a fix on this guy. He's not even too calm to read. It's like he's not there at all.

"What's the story, Siegfried?" I ask. "Why are they all shorn sheep out there, but you get to have hair?"

"In the group, I'm called Josef. I'm the face of the movement. It's all about media these days, isn't it?" He points to a box of recruitment DVDs and tapes. "Tattoos and shaved heads scare people. Looking like the prom king brings the newspaper and local TV around, and gets our message out to more potential recruits."

"I know about your message and don't want to hear more. I've had enough crazy talk for this lifetime."

"I'm sure you have. They don't think much of the human race down in the pit, do they? I know Azazel doesn't." He watches me when he says it, waiting for a reaction. I don't give him one.

"How do you know what Azazel thinks?"

"Because I've talked to him. He's not happy with you killing him with his own knife. Tartarus is a bleak place compared to Hell."

"How could you talk to Azazel? You can't do a summoning on anyone as powerful as Azazel, and only Lucifer can walk in and out of Hell on his own."

"Who says I'm on my own?" He opens his hands in an expansive gesture, like something a preacher would do. "What's that old line from Luke? 'My name is Legion: for we are many.'"

"Who's 'we'? Not those idiots out there."

"Of course not." Josef gets up and walks around the desk. He's wearing chinos and a polo shirt. He doesn't look any more dangerous than a salesman at RadioShack. "Who we are doesn't matter. *You* matter. You got out of Hell and that makes you special. But why are you special? You don't even smell like other humans. What are you?"

"I'm no one. I'm just me."

"I think you're being modest. Let's see."

Before I know what's happening, Josef has one hand on my shoulder and the other inside my chest. I'm not bleeding and my bones aren't cracked. He's just got his hand *inside* me. I can feel his fingers moving over my ribs and between my organs. I try to throw him off. Punch or kick him. But I can't move. He finds one of the bullets. Turns it between his fingers.

"Oh," he says. "That shouldn't be there. You should have that looked at."

Josef's human facade cracks like old paint, drops in flakes, and peels away in long sheets, falling on the floor. There's a black void beneath his skin, but the blackness doesn't hold and I can see what's inside him. Josef is the hands and eyes of the operation, but he's not alone. There are other creatures in there, too. Their outlines aren't entirely solid. They're vague, like ghosts. Like Josef, they glow from the inside, a pale blue white, like a slug crawling across the bottom of the ocean. They remind me of angels, if angels were candles that you left in a locked car in Texas in August. Their faces are fish-belly white and soft. Half formed. The fact that the creatures are almost beautiful makes them even harder to look at. I can't read them the way I can a person, but I don't have to. They remind me of insects. They might pounce on your next move, or they might wait for a million years, until they think the moment is right. It's all the same to them. They're patience and hunger with a side of fury.

I'm sick and freezing. It's like I'm icing up from the inside. There's a bitter smell and taste. Like a mouthful of vinegar. I want to throw up, but I can't move.

"What's this?" The question comes from far away and in a thousand discordant voices.

Josef takes my heart in his hand. His fingers glide through my flesh and touch Azazel's key. Josef goes rigid.

All those voices again. "What is that? Is that your secret? I want it!" He leans forward and pulls on my heart. This time I scream. He's trying to pull it out through my chest and it feels like he just might make it. But it's not my heart he wants. It's the key inside. He gets his fingers around it and tries to pry it out.

I don't black out. I don't scream. My vision collapses to a small point and settles on the floor, which opens up beneath me. I can see the outlines of Lucifer's palace, Pandemonium, and the city around it. The smaller generals' palaces and the arena where I fought. Individual Hellions drift up through the chaos at the edges of Hell, flying toward me. I know what this is now. I'm dying. Until now, I wasn't even sure I could die. Now I know better.

The Hellions are getting closer. Soon I'll fall right into their waiting arms. I hope they let me fight in the arena again. What else am I good at?

Josef screams and pulls his hand out of my chest. The human fingers are black and charred.

"What did you do to me? What is that thing? I want it."

The floor is suddenly solid beneath my feet. He's let go. I'm not dying anymore.

Josef grabs me with his good hand and pulls my face close to his. He looks human again. "A man couldn't do that. Tell me what you are."

"I'm the Gingerbread Man. I'll run and run as fast as I can."

Josef swings me around and throws me, one-handed, over his desk. Books, papers, and CDs scatter around the room. I slam into the wall. Some of the knuckle-dusters and knives that had been on his desk now dig into my back. I roll over on my belly knowing that I'm useless. I have a demonic knife under my shirt and I'm lying on a pile of shiny killing toys, but I couldn't go two rounds with a kitten right now.

When I try to get on my feet, my hand comes down on one of the taped pipes. It feels familiar and heavy, like Hellion metal. It's a *na'at*. Of course. Josef said that he's been to Hell. He definitely knows dark magic. He's the one who gave the Devil Daisy to the skinhead in Carlos's bar. I stay on the floor, slip the *na'at* inside my shirt, and wrap my arms around myself so he won't see it.

I say, "Don't stop now, sweetheart. It was just getting fun." Then I puke.

I hear Josef open the door and bark orders at someone. My Nazi pal and some of his friends come inside and haul me to my feet. I stay bent over so that they can't see the *na'at.* Not that I can stand up straight yet. I still feel Josef's fingers inside my chest.

The skinheads perp-walk me to the door, but Josef stops them. He leans over and whispers, "My name is . . ." and he makes a sound like a snake getting ready to strike. "Remember me. We're going to meet again."

This trip through the skinhead's playhouse isn't as fun as the first. It feels like every one of them spits on me or bounces a beer can off my head. My punk girlfriend at the door grabs my balls and squeezes until I collapse and get my first chance to admire the warehouse's lovely linoleum floor.

That's it, honey. We've officially broken up.

The trip back to the Bamboo House of Dolls is a blur of elbows and knees as the skinhead boys play Frisbee with me in the backseat. The good news is that the meth head driving gets us to the bar in record time. The bad news is that he barely slows down when we get there. The boys push me out of the backseat while the car is still going thirty miles per. I land like a sack full of Silly Putty, rolling and bouncing down the street until I hit the curb in the front of the bar.

Before anyone can call the cops, I crawl under a parked car, drop into the shadow, and stumble through the room back to Max Overdrive.

I don't even get into bed. I lie on the cool floor. Try to catch my breath and shake off the feeling of those fingers scrabbling around in my chest. I take the *na'at* out from under my shirt, feeling its familiar weight in my hand. If I was a better liar, I'd say that scoring the weapon was worth the beating, but I'm not and it wasn't. On the other hand, coming away with a working *na'at* and leaving a demonic skinhead with nothing but a burned hand and a pile of puke can give you a feeling of accomplishment at the end of a long day.

I WAKE UP with Mount Rushmore lying on my chest. My body feels like it weighs about a million pounds and it's telling me that I shouldn't move until at least the next ice age. Then I could forget all about L.A., get a job sweeping up Muninn's labyrinth, and live in the dark and the silence forever. Or, more likely, until Baphomet or some other Hellion redneck finds a loophole in the universe's cosmological rule book and wiggles his way out of Hell for the simple pleasure of gnawing my head off.

I think I might have gone a little too far down this road to call a press conference and announce my retirement. But what would I say? *Ladies and gentlemen, I'm hanging up my key and my guns and will follow my bliss to lead a quiet life, devoting myself to my nonprofit organic-vegetable farm cooperative, where I plan on going slowly out of my mind and strangling every goddamn human being and chicken within one hundred miles.* I really hate chickens.

THE BURNS ON my hands and face are gone, but my chest is a Jackson Pollock mess of black and purple bruises. Every time I take a breath, the tissue around Kasabian's bullets feels like someone is trying to check my oil level with a cattle prod. If I'm still alive when this is over, I'm definitely going to see Kinski.

My phone is beside me, blinking. I thumb the on button and find a text message from Cherry, with the address of a little taco place called No Mames on Western Avenue and a time when she wants to meet. The good news is that I have a few hours to get cleaned up and pull myself together. I want a cigarette and a drink, but I can't smoke in the shower (trust me, I've tried), and if I started drinking now, I'm fairly certain that my brain would finally give up, get a new roommate, and move to Redondo Beach without me.

I can still feel Josef's fingers inside me. I dreamed about that room in the back of the Nazi playhouse. And the arena in Hell. About the black and empty creature that Lucifer once ordered to leave the arena. For all I know, it could have been Josef or one of the legion I sensed was there inside his body with him. If it even was a body. When he split open, his insides felt more like an empty portal than a real entity. I don't want to ever meet him or any of his friends again.

I strip down to take a shower and see that I've ruined another set of clothes. This time it isn't my fault. Those Nazis owe me a new pair of jeans for shoving me out of that car. I'll have to go collect on that sometime. That will be fun.

The shower feels so good I almost faint. I can't get over how these little things still thrill me. If I was the spiritual type, being so pleased by little pleasures would mean that I was one of those penitent saints who live in a cave and only eat gruel once a week. In my case, it's my secret shame that the most exciting thing I can think of is clean socks.

After I get cleaned up, I put on the last pair of unshredded jeans I own. I put on the trashed motocross jacket figuring it will keep tourists from asking directions to Disneyland.

None of my guns will fit under the jacket without sending waves of pain through my body. I don't think Cherry is going to get cute about anything, but if she does, the knife ought to be enough to take her down. I take off the Veritas and toss it. Should I go? No words this time. Just the image of a winged bug on a small hill. A fly on shit. That's how I'm attracted to these things. In Hellion speak, it means that the answer to the question is inevitable, so why bother asking? It's right. Why bother?

THE GRILLED FISH tacos at No Mames aren't half bad. The place is minimal inside. A few folding tables and cheap white plastic lawn chairs. It's a pleasantly anonymous atmosphere. I eat three tacos and drink strong black coffee and wait.

And wait. When Cherry is officially an hour late, I go outside for a smoke. (I know she's officially late because Allegra told me that the time on my phone is set by a goddamn satellite thousands of miles up in space. Apparently, while I was Downtown, people decided that they needed to know the exact time on Neptune.) I call Cherry every ten minutes for the next half hour. I text her. Nothing. Finally, I get fed up with the car exhaust and the rancid pot smoke from the dealer by the pay phone. Cherry probably grew some brains in the night and hopped freight out of town. Smart move.

I was too tired to steal a car on the way over, so I scan the traffic for a cab. A Yellow and a Veteran's show up a minute later, and I start waving at them. The Veteran's cuts across two lanes, aiming right at me. When it's one lane away and about to turn into the curb, three black Ford SUVs come blasting around it from behind and cut it off. The middle one pulls up in front of me and a tall man in a dark blue suit and tie and white shirt steps out, flashing a badge. It's one of the two men in suits who rode the elevator at the Bradbury Building with Vidocq, Allegra, and me.

"Excuse me, sir," he says in a West Texas drawl. "I'm U.S. Marshal Larson Wells. There's a Homeland Security matter that we need to speak to you about."

I should have known something was up when I saw three Ford vans rolling down the street together. Is there any other time you see so many expensive American vehicles in one place? It's always a presidential motorcade or a bust. Who else would buy those rolling tugboats when they're so easy to steal? American cars are like condoms. Use them once and throw them away.

I step back and reach for my knife. The van doors swing open wide. It's bright out and all I can see inside are silhouettes. There are at least six of them and I bet every one of them has a gun pointed at me. I'm not exactly in shape to get shot fifty times right now. I bring my hand forward and hold it up. Nothing palmed there. Everybody stay cool.

Wells takes my arm and leads me to the middle van. Just before I step inside, he slaps cuffs on my wrists in one smooth motion, like maybe he's done this before. He pushes me inside and joins me in the rear seat, keeping himself between the door and me. All three vans shoot straight down Western, turn right on Beverly, and keep going.

"Is this about those library fines? I swear I meant to pay them, but I was ten at the time and had a lousy credit rating." The marshals in the front ignore me. Wells checks his watch and looks out the window. I pull on the cuffs. There's barely any give. I might be able to break them and get them off, but not without shattering bones and peeling most of the skin off my hands. "For a Sub Rosa hit squad, you hide it well. I'm not picking up any magic vibes. I don't see a binding circle or any killing charms. Did you hide them in the headliner?" I reach up and touch the vinyl, feeling for lumps or ridges that might give away hidden evil eye booby traps.

Wells snaps, "Don't touch that." He's still not looking at me. "And the Sub Rosa can kiss my ass. I don't work for pixies and necrophiliacs."

He says "pixie" the way a redneck says "faggot."

I say, "I think you mean 'necromancers.'"

"It's all the same to me, Merlin. A bunch of middle-age Goths playing with Ouija boards, and talking to spooks and fairies. Or playing Martha Stewart with their Easy-Bake Oven potion kits."

"You keep bad-mouthing them like that, one of those pixies is going to turn your guts to banana pudding with one hard look. Or don't you believe in that kind of thing?"

"Oh, I believe. I just think those absinthe sippers are a joke. Half the Sub Rosa are out-of-their-mind party animals. The other half dress up like the Inquisition and have committee meetings on how you pixies should live and behave around normal humans. You people are all either drug addicts or the PTA with wands."

"They sound like a lot more fun than I remember."

"I bet they're in love with you, boy. You must have missed the memo about keeping a low profile."

"If you're not Sub Rosa, tell me why I shouldn't be killing you right now."

Wells finally turns and looks at me, giving me his best

El Paso squint, trying to drill a hole in my head with his eyes.

"Because if I shoot you, you're not going to hop up and decapitate me. Just because I don't work with the Sub Rosa doesn't mean that I think all nonhumans are worthless. For example, the guns my men and I are carrying were designed by a coalition of human engineers and certain respectable occult partners. What I'm saying is that if you sneeze or blink or do anything even slightly annoying, I'll burn you down with the same holy fire that the Archangel Michael used to blast Satan's ass out of Heaven and into the Abyss."

"If you're not Sub Rosa, who do you people work for?"

"I told you. Homeland Security."

"The federal government monitors magic in California?"

"Not just California. The whole country. It's our job to keep our eyes on all freaks, terrorists, and potential terrorists, which describes all of you pixies, in my opinion."

His heartbeat and breathing are steady. His pupils aren't dilating. He's telling the truth. Or he thinks he is.

"Are you spooks local? 'Cause I just met this funny little Nazi named Josef. Know him? Blond. Good-looking. Not even remotely human."

"We know about Josef and his goose-steppers. They're irrelevant to our current concerns. And we're not spooks. The CIA are spooks. We heard you and Josef got into a little dustup."

"It wasn't so much a dustup as him beating me about three-quarters to death. He also showed me that I can die and how it'll probably happen. So, how was your day?" Wells checks his watch again. He's not as cool as he looked at first. Something is worrying him and it's not me. "That probably doesn't make much sense to you."

"I've read your file. I know all about you. You've haven't exactly been inconspicuous since you got back to town."

"You guys have been watching me?"

"From the moment you walked out of the cemetery. At first, we thought you were just another zombie, and were about to send out waste disposal. But when you mugged that crackhead and didn't eat him, we decided just to keep an eye on you."

"How?"

"Radar. We've got all you pixies on radar."

"More respectable magic?"

"Our friends understand the security issues at stake."

"Radar and death rays. Where do I sign up? It doesn't seem fair that you get all the fun toys."

"Cry me a river. Anyway, with all your fun and games, my superior asked me to bring you in for a talk."

"Seems like my week to meet bosses." The cuffs hold my wrists together, which makes my arms rest on my sore chest. I shift around in my seat, trying to find a more comfortable position. I glance out the window and see that we're crossing La Cienega. "I notice we're not going to the courthouse."

"What makes you think you deserve a day in court?"

"You're a cop . . ."

"U.S. marshal."

"Fine. A cop who can read. Isn't there something in the law or the Constitution about everyone getting a day in court?"

"That only applies to the living, son."

"I'm sitting right here."

"Technically, no. Not in any legal sense. Legally, you're a nonperson. You've been a long-gone daddy out of this realm of existence for eleven years and change. A missing person can be declared dead after seven, which means that you've been legally dead almost four years."

"You're not serious."

"Look at the bright side. If you were alive, you'd still be the prime suspect in your girlfriend's murder. If you were alive, the IRS would want to know why you haven't been filing taxes. Ask me whether I'm more afraid of Hell or the IRS, I'll go with the IRS every time."

"So, you know who I am and where I've been."

"I know every inch of your sorry waste of a life. My boss might want to talk to you, but to me, you're a parasite. A waste of space and air. It makes a person wish the earth really was flat. Then we could take all the people like you, load you in a garbage scow, and push you over the edge and out of everybody's hair."

"If you know where I've been, then you know why I'm back. Let me go and let me do what I came here for. I'll get rid of some very bad people for you."

"How? By blowing up Rodeo Drive?"

"That was a mistake."

"Was it? Thanks for clearing that up. The truth is, I don't give a damn about some Hollywood lawyers' wives and their shoe stores. What I care about is you. What you represent and the kind of trouble you bring with you. You're a walking calamity."

Now I feel it. His heart rate is picking up and there's the slightest whiff of perspiration coming off him. One of the G-men in the front of the van has turned to watch our conversation. He and Wells smile at each other, sharing some private joke.

When Wells speaks again, he does it with the kind of phony casualness that lets everyone in the room know that you're about to tell the bad joke they've all been waiting for. Wells says, "So, what the hell kind of a name is Sandman Slim anyway? You think you're some kind of superhero?"

I turn and look at him, "You lost me there, Tex. I don't have any idea what you're talking about."

"Don't be modest, we've all heard of you. 'Sandman Slim. The monster who kills monsters.' I have to admit, it's kind of catchy. Did you come up with that or did some Hellion ad firm shit that out for you?"

"Listen, cop. I've never heard that stupid name before. Stop calling me it. And tell me where we're going or I'm getting out."

Wells and the marshal in the front laugh. "I wouldn't

try. I'm dead serious when I tell you that I could put a bullet in your head right now and go have a sandwich."

"What kind?"

"What kind of what?"

"What kind of sandwich? What's a murder sandwich taste like? Does it come with extra cheese or chili fries? What tastes better after murder, Coke or Pepsi?"

"You are working my very last nerve, cocksucker."

"I'm going home." I reach across Wells for the door, shoving him back into the seat with my shoulder. The marshal goes for his gun.

When you're facing down multiple attackers, you always want to make the first move. It lets them know that you're ready to fight and that you're crazy enough to get the party started. One rule of thumb in fighting is that crazy can often overcome skill and numbers, because, while a trained fighter might actually enjoy going up against another trained fighter, no one really wants to wrestle with crazy. Crazy doesn't know when it's winning. And crazy doesn't know when to stop. If you can't pull off crazy, if, for instance, you're handcuffed in a small van with six armed assailants, stupid is a decent substitute for crazy.

Wells still has his hand inside his jacket when I slam my elbow into his throat. He freezes, trying to remember how to breathe. Before the boys in the front of the van get any ideas, I swing an elbow up over his head and bring the arm down on the other side, getting the cuffs around his throat. Then I fall back across the seat, pulling Wells on top of me. The G-men in the front of the van have all drawn their guns out by now, but I'm not sweating. If they want to shoot me, they're going to have to blow a lot of holes in the big man first.

"Stand down," shouts Wells. Then, quieter, to me, "That got you far, didn't it, shit-for-brains?"

"It got me your neck. That's a start." I tighten the cuffs across his throat. Just enough so that he can feel it, but not enough to make him pass out. "You're not the first bunch that ever kidnapped me, but you're definitely the least fun."

"Boy, you just attacked a federal officer. I'll have you swinging from your balls at Gitmo."

"Who you going to arrest? I'm already dead." Wells goes for his gun again. I spring forward and slam his head into the door frame, spinning him at the same time so that his body stays between his boys and me. I've got four guns on me and one guy is still driving.

We're somewhere south of L.A., near Culver City. The van turns into the parking lot of what looks like an aircraft assembly plant that hasn't seen action in twenty years. There are diamond-shaped hazardous materials warnings and rusted DOD signs on all the fences and buildings.

The van slams to a stop and the side door opens. I tighten the cuffs on Wells's neck and pull him back to use as a shield against whatever is coming into the van.

A woman in a crisply tailored power suit leans her head inside.

217

"I can come back later if you two gentlemen need a moment alone," she says.

I let up on Wells's neck, but still keep hold of him.

"He's the one getting grabby," says Wells.

The woman nods. "That's what he does. All those years in the Abyss have left him with some impulse control issues. It's all in his file." She looks at me. "Let Marshal Wells up right now. No one is going to shoot you. And, Larson, uncuff this man. You look like a couple of third graders."

"Sorry. Who are you again?" I ask.

The woman shakes her head, and then walks away. The G-men have holstered their guns. I lift my arms so that Wells can wiggle out from under the cuffs. He gets out of the van without looking back at me and starts adjusting his suit and tie. I follow him outside and hold out the cuffs. He takes his time, playing with his jacket and tie like a bad Vegas lounge comedian. Finally, he digs a key out of his pocket and unlocks me. There are red marks on my wrists, but there are corresponding marks on Wells's throat, so I guess we're even.

I take out my cigarettes and Mason's Zippo. When I thumb the lighter, all I get is sparks.

"Anybody got a light?" I ask.

"You can't smoke here," says Wells.

"We're in the open in the middle of nowhere. Why not?"

"Are you stupid?" asks Wells. "That's Aelita. She's

an angel. They're very sensitive to things like cigarette smoke."

"Cool. I've never seen an angel in disguise before." I follow her to the old assembly plant.

Aelita isn't what I imagined an angel would look like. She's about as ethereal as a zip gun. She walks like she's about to call in an air strike or buy Europe. Donald Trump in drag with her enemies' balls in a candy dish on her desk, right next to the stapler.

The complex's main building is huge. Probably a Cold War–era industrial assembly line. Aelita opens a side door and I can see inside. Absolutely nothing. Concrete floor and metal walls. Shadows of smashed and abandoned machinery. Not even lights.

A few steps into the building, I hit a kind of barrier. It's like walking through warm Jell-O. Then I'm suddenly in Times Square on New Year's. Humans in suits, and different kinds of nonhumans, are moving huge diesel engines on automated chain lifters. Others are driving forklifts with pallets loaded with cedar and mugwort. Silver ingots and iron bars. Industrial drums of holy water. They're assembling armored vehicles and what look like weapons. Shiny superscience versions of old pepper-pot guns.

I look back at the entrance. There are angelic runes chiseled into the concrete floor. Overhead some kind of massive machine hangs bolted to the ceiling. It hums like a beehive and gives off a shimmering fluorescent-green light.

"It's called a Phylactery Accelerator," says Aelita. "The

holy relics and sigils in the floor form a protective talisman."

"But not one powerful enough to hide all of whatever the hell this is."

"Please don't use profanity in here. The Accelerator captures the energy released by charmed-strange mesons as they decay into protons and antineutrinos, and uses that energy to amplify the talisman's blessed essence."

"You lost me after 'profanity.' But I think I get the idea. You're the respectable magic committee. You've got a real Norman Rockwell vibe here. Except for all the guns."

She looks right through me. Suddenly I'm thinking that maybe I would have been better off if the guys in the van had been a hit squad.

"Come with me."

She takes me into a soundproofed side room. After the noise of the factory floor, the room is spooky quiet. There are stained-glass windows suspended by wires from the rafters. More angelic script cut into the floor, this time in the shape of a cross. There's an altar at one end of the room. The other end looks like Frankenstein's lab. There are celestial maps of the universe looking down from Heaven (I'd seen the reverse maps Downtown). The machine that surrounds the operating theater could be anything. Part of a personal nuclear power plant or one of the alien rooms from *Forbidden Planet*.

I wait for the angel to say something. I want to know why she had me dragged here, but I'm not about to be the first one to blink. I turn and find her over by the altar, brushing Communion-wafer crumbs into her hand. She gently drops them into a trash can beside the altar, then bows her head and crosses herself. Now I know why Lucifer and his wild bunch ended up down below. If I had to take my boss's kid so seriously that I was required to salute his dandruff, I'd go stab-happy, too.

"Have you been enjoying yourself since your return?" she asks with her back to me.

"Not particularly."

Now she turns. She smiles. A beaming, monstrously insincere angel smile. Probably another part of her job training.

"I only ask because it seems to me that you've been having a lot of fun. Cutting people's heads off. Beating up people in bars. Blowing up whole shopping districts. Shooting people on the street in the middle of the day. It sounds terribly fun to me. The kind of fun that I'd expect to appeal to someone like you."

"Is snatching people off the street your idea of fun? God gave you wings, so you have an everlasting get-out-of-jail-free card. You can do anything you want because everything you do is holy. Is that it?"

"Yes. As a matter of fact, it is."

"Is everything your army does holy, too? They didn't all look like angels to me. Was Marshal Wells sweating holy water? I must have missed that."

"Marshal Wells is a good and dedicated man who is

willing to give his life in the cause of good. What are you willing to die for?"

"To kill the people I came here for. And to not be fucked with along the way."

"What if I told you that I could help you find what and who you're looking for?"

"I wouldn't believe you."

"Why?"

"Because I rode here with a gun to my head."

"Have you ever heard of the Golden Vigil?"

"Sounds like a community-college Goth band."

"We're an ancient order. A coalition of celestial beings and humans dedicated to protecting the world and mankind from its greatest enemy."

Get ready for the Garden of Eden Sunday school lecture.

"Don't try and sell me the snake oil you fobbed off on your Ghostbusters out there. I've met Lucifer. I've killed his generals. Those idiots are too busy stabbing each other in the back to be much danger to mankind."

"You're right. I agree completely."

Aelita walks to a long wooden table and picks up what looks like a piece of thick brown cloth. When she gets closer, I see that it's vellum.

"Lucifer is a eunuch and his armies are buried at the bottom of Creation. No, our real concern is the world's true enemy, the Enerjik Kissi." I'm not sure I catch the first word, but she pronounces the second one "Kee-shee." She holds up the vellum and a sigil has formed there. One I've never seen before. It's not like the usual angelic or even Hellion symbols. It's practically a Rorschach blot, like someone spilled ink on the vellum, and then tried to wipe it off.

"Let me tell you a story," she says, and goes and sits at the wooden table. "All little boys like stories."

As much as I want to get out of here and away from this crazy angel and her mercenary zealots next door, I'm still feeling too ragged to bolt or put up too much of a fight. So I do the next best thing, and surrender. I go to the table and sit down across from her. She spreads the vellum on the table between us. As her hands pass over it, the sigil fades away.

"At the beginning of time, the Lord God made a mistake. Frankly, to some of us, He made two mistakes, but since He likes you talking monkeys, we can't fix that one. So we turn our attention to the first great mistake."

She passes her hand over the vellum and images of rough glass globes appear, like pen-and-ink drawings. As Aelita talks, the drawings begin to glow.

"When the Lord bought life to the universe, He did it by spreading His divine light throughout the dark. He breathed His light into glass vessels that He hung in the sky like the stars that would come much later. We, the angelic order, were born from this light. And we helped to spread it throughout Creation. Once, as the Lord blew light into a vessel, He blew in a bit too much and the vessel shattered. His divine light fell into the void and onto the worlds we were building. That falling light was the beginning of life in the universe."

Like a Disney cartoon, the vessels on the vellum crack open, turning into squirming little one-cell organisms.

"But not all of the divine light landed on the worlds. Some fell into the deep unformed void that was nothing but boiling chaos. Since the Lord was now enchanted by the life growing on His worlds, we never bothered to put anything into the far void. We all now regret that decision."

She waves her hand and the vellum images disappear, like lines on an Etch A Sketch. She lays her palm on the vellum, and a roiling, crawling blackness seeps across it.

"As both angels and lower life"—she nods in my direction—"were born from divine light, so was something else. In the chaos grew another sort of life, very much like angels, but different. Wells and some of his men describe them as 'anti-angels,' which is as good an explanation as your little brains can grasp."

I put my hand on the black vellum that's now roiling and writhing like liquid obsidian. It looks like the knife I have under my coat. The knife is supposed to be bone, but I never found out what kind of bone.

I say, "The anti-angels are the Kissi."

"Yes." She moves her hand again and the bubbling black is gone. As she talks, other images appear from under the hand resting on the vellum.

"The Kissi don't hate life. Life fascinates them. The energy. The unpredictability of it. The chaos of life. When they found early humans, they settled right in, creating more chaos. Helping one tribe create weapons.

Teaching language to another. The Kissi were born in chaos. It's what they're made of. It's what they consume. Humans create a particularly appetizing sort of chaos to the Kissi.

"Eons ago, there was a war between us angels and the Kissi that raged from the earth all the way to the gates of Heaven. Neither side won."

"Was Lucifer already in Hell? If you'd asked for his help, he might have come through. I don't think he'd like a bunch of mad dogs eating up Earth, either. If we were gone, who else would he screw with?"

"No one would ask the Prince of Lies for help. Don't be stupid."

"So, it was an option? But you didn't go for it. Isn't pride one of the seven deadly sins?"

She looks at me like my mother used to look at me right before she smacked me on the ear. Like Mom, she gets hold of herself before the big explosion.

"As I said, there was a war. Neither side could defeat the other, so we struck a bargain with the Kissi. They could stay and, since humans were naturally chaotic creatures, the Kissi could satisfy their appetites for chaos and destruction within certain specific limits. The Golden Vigil was created to monitor this truce.

"The truce has held for millennia. But lately things have changed. The Kissi activities are becoming more bold and reckless. They openly attack humans. They are involved in wars. Terrorism. Drug and weapons trading. Something has upset the balance." She takes her hand off the vellum and starts folding it up. "When we heard that Sandman Slim had come to Earth, naturally we thought that he might be the cause of the trouble."

"Wells called me that name in the car. What the hell was he talking about?"

"Please don't use profanity here." She sets the vellum aside. "The marshal was talking about you, you fool. You're Sandman Slim. The monster who kills monsters. Do you think we don't know what you were doing in Hell? Fallen angels are still angels. We notice when someone kills them. You have quite a reputation in the celestial realms. That's why you're here."

"I'm not a monster. I'm just a man."

"You're a monster to someone. In the Inferno, you're the bogeyman who frightens the bogeyman. And you've bought your talent for destruction back here to Earth. That's why you're here. In case you hadn't noticed, this is a job interview."

That's the single scariest thing I've heard anyone say since I came home. And this angel is making my skin crawl in ways that even Mason can't.

"I already have a job, thanks. I run a video store."

"You're weak. I can smell the damage from your recent injuries. That's the only reason you're here and alive. When we thought that you were in league with the Kissi, there was a death warrant on your head. But after your encounter with Josef, that seems doubtful."

"He's a Kissi."

"Of course. I thought that you would have understood that by now."

"I think I met one in Hell once. In the arena. Is that possible?"

"Unlike the Hellions, the Kissi can move anywhere in the universe, including into and out of Hell. So, yes, you could have easily met one. What happened?"

"Lucifer was pissed. He threw the thing out."

"No doubt hoping it would return to Earth to wreak havoc and leave his disgusting kingdom to him alone. How brave."

"He did walk right up to it and order it out. Have you ever walked right up and started a fight with a Kissi?" She doesn't answer. "Anyway, if something's upset the balance of the universe, it probably means that we're looking for the same person. Mason Faim."

"Excellent. We have a common enemy. You'll join the Vigil and we'll fight the forces of chaos together."

"No thanks. Your little war sounds like fun, but I have my own work to do."

Aelita says, "This is God's work."

I get up from the table and walk away across the room. I need to be careful. I don't want to say the wrong thing when she knows that I'm hurt. The bullets in my chest are playing soccer with my ribs. I'd filled Mason's lighter earlier, so I take out my cigarettes and spark one. Take a couple of big puffs and flick the ashes onto her altar. I'll admit it. I'm not good at careful.

"Where was God when I was stuck in Hell?" I ask her. "If you knew about Sandman Slim, then you knew I'd been dragged down there alive and was being tortured. But you hosanna-singing sons of bitches couldn't spare one lousy angel to help me out?"

"Maybe God thought you were where you belonged."

"He was right. You know why? Because I got to see exactly how the wheels turn in that part of the universe. Now you've given me a little snapshot of Heaven. You Heaven-and-Hell types are just the same shakedown artists in different uniforms. I've only been kidnapped twice in my life. Once by Lurkers and now by an angel."

"You understand that since none of Lucifer's fiends can leave Hell, it must have been Kissi who dragged you down, probably in league with your friend Mason."

"Thanks. When I'm done with Mason, I'll know who to go after next." I grind the remains of my cigarette into the altar and leave them. "All of you celestial pricks. Lucifer's psychos and God's lapdogs, you're out for yourselves, just like everybody else. You don't care about the world. You cut a deal with the Kissi. I wonder why?"

Aelita stands, very tall and straight, with her hands folded in front of her.

"Tell me. Enlighten me, Sandman Slim."

"Because they made it to Heaven. Got right up to the gates. So, you cut a deal. You sent the wolves down here among the sheep and asked the wolves to behave. And if they didn't, oh well. It's just a few ewes being slaughtered. But now the wolves are hungrier than ever, and you know that sooner or later, they're going to come knocking on Heaven's door."

Aelita shakes her head and gives me that creepy, benevolent-angel smile again.

"You make me so sad, James."

"Don't call me that."

"All right, Sandman."

"Don't call me that, either."

"I hadn't realized how all those years in the Abyss had warped your mind. You've completely lost your ability to feel empathy. I've told you what's coming for humanity, yet you won't lift a finger to prevent it." She's walking over to me, like a kindergarten teacher about to take the white glue away from a kid who won't stop eating it. "Don't you feel anything for anyone?"

"No. The only person I cared about was murdered. And you didn't do anything about that, either, did you?"

"I can help you heal. Your body and your soul. You were an empty vessel when you went into the Abyss and the devil filled you full of poison. Let me fill you with the Lord's divine light."

She's throwing some hardcore angel hoodoo my way. Trying to get control of my tiny, expendable monkey brain. Candy was better at the soothing talk trick—she really had me going back at Kinski's. But Aelita isn't getting anywhere. Maybe the difference is that I kind of liked Candy, but Lucretia Borgia here isn't my type.

"Let me help you, my son." She reaches out and takes both of my hands in hers. "Become part of God's great plan."

"No."

Aelita's face turns red and she screams. Tears are streaming down her red face. She takes my hand again and then drops it.

"Abomination," she whispers. Then she screams, "Abomination!"

Downtown, one of the things Hellions used to complain about was how Heaven had disarmed them before tossing them into the garbage dump. Every angel is born with a weapon. Not something they can lose, but something that's part of them. A flaming sword. They manifest it with a thought and use it like a handheld nuke. I'd never seen one before Aelita manifested her sword in the soundproof chapel.

I'm still looking at it, kind of hypnotized by the thing, when she sticks it through me. I can feel it go through my chest and come out my back, burning and freezing at the same time.

Then I'm on the floor. I have a weird hallucination that Vidocq and Allegra are standing over me. Then I'm dead.

I DREAM THAT I'm back on Earth. I dream that I've escaped from Azazel and all the pain and madness of Hell. I'm home and I'm drinking beer with Alice, sweaty and happy in bed. I struggle to open my eyes and I see blue skies. I'm waking up in a cemetery. I am home. It isn't a dream. But why is the moon out during the day?

It's not the moon. It's a light.

That's not the sky. It's a blue ceiling. I know the smell of this place, but its name is lost down some darkened detour in my brain.

"I WAS DEAD."

"Pretty much," says Kinski. He's leaning over me, shining a light into my eyes as I lie on his exam table. "But Eugène poured a whole bottle of white nightshade elixir down your throat. It kept your soul from wandering away. After that, it was just a matter of kick-starting your body. How do you feel?"

"All right. Tired, but all right."

Several of Kinski's rocks are arranged around the wound in my chest. Others around my head, arms, and legs. The doc takes the stones off me, one by one.

Vidocq and Allegra are at the other end of the table. "I saw you there," I say. "I thought I was dreaming, but you were there."

"Yes," Vidocq says. "I'm so sorry for what happened."

"You knew those cops were going to snatch me, didn't you? You told them where I'd be. You set me up."

"You've been so out of control lately. I thought meeting the Golden Vigil and seeing their work would help you to focus your energies. You're going to kill yourself or some innocent person."

"So, you handed me over to Homeland Security and a psychotic angel. Is that your idea of group therapy?"

"I had no idea this would happen. Aelita was just going to talk to you."

I swing my legs over the edge of the table and try to stand. My vision blurs and my head swims. I sit back down.

"I crawl all the way out of Hell just to get kidnapped and sold out by friends all over again. But you know what the funniest thing about this is? Mason didn't get me killed. You did." Vidocq is sweating and cold. It's a fear reaction. Fear and guilt. "How long have you been working for them?"

"I work *with* them, not *for* them. It's been a while. Half a year. A little more, maybe. You don't know how things have been getting here. It's bad and getting worse. Things are quieter now. I don't know why. But they'll turn bad again and then you'll see why I did what I did."

"Were you working for them before I went Downtown?"

He shakes his head. "No. I'd barely heard of them back then."

Kinski hands me a glass of some stinking brown tea.

"Drink that down. All of it. Don't sip it."

I down the tea in three long gulps. It's thick and hot and I can feel little bits of twigs and leaves in my mouth. I hand the glass back to Kinski.

"Thanks. That was disgusting." I look at Vidocq. "At least your lie is a new lie. That's something. Small mercies, my father would say."

Allegra is holding on to Vidocq's arm, like she's supporting an old man who's had a stroke but is too proud to use a cane. Her heart is racing. Her pupils are like hubcaps. She's afraid, but not of me. Of everything. It might not have been such a good idea to bring her into the Sub Rosa world. She's seen a lot in just a few days. "Were you in on this with him?" I ask.

She looks at Vidocq, then back at me.

"He told me earlier. Look, after the thing on Rodeo and Medea Bava with those feathers and teeth, it didn't seem like such a bad idea."

"Okay. Thanks. You can leave with him."

Vidocq comes around the table. The bottles of potions and poisons sewn into his coat tinkle as he walks. "No, Jimmy."

"Yes, Jimmy. Get out of here. Both of you."

"Eugène saved you," says Allegra. "Aelita about killed your ass."

"Maybe next time she'll get lucky and save you two the trouble of selling me out."

Kinski says, "Why don't you ease up on these people a little? You brought some of this on yourself." I can't read Kinski. His eyes are steady. I can't hear his heart or breathing. He's hiding them from me somehow. Maybe Candy taught him some Jade tricks.

"Thanks for saving me, doc. I mean it. I'm going to need to sit here for a while. After that, I'll be out of your hair. But until then, please stay the fuck out of this."

Candy is over in the corner of the room. I missed her before. She's got her back to the wall and is trying to make herself small.

Looking back to Allegra and Vidocq, I say, "You two need to leave now. I don't want to look at you anymore." Vidocq starts to say something, but I cut him off. "I should have seen something like this coming. Hell's a circus run by mental patients. Heaven's a gated community where we're the bastard stepkids the real kids hate. Daddy's little mistake. Where does that leave us on this rock? I believe Aelita's story about the broken glass starting life. Trash falls from the sky and no one cleans it up because the trash starts talking. Why should anyone expect anything from anyone? How can trash trust trash?"

Vidocq nods. "Right, then." He looks at Allegra and they walk out together, closing the door to the exam room behind them.

Kinski and Candy start putting things back in cabinets. Bottles. Bundles of dried plants. A tray of desiccated sea horses. Kinski wraps his rocks up in their silk covers and quietly stows them away.

"What's wrong with your arm?" I ask. His left arm is bandaged up to the elbow. Spots of blood have soaked through the dressing.

"That's nothing. A couple of kids jumped me last night. They must have been high or something. They weren't very good robbers. They didn't get anything. Maybe they just wanted to beat someone up."

"Did they grab you or did they just start pushing you around?"

"What difference does that make?"

"If they grabbed you, it was probably a robbery. If they started whaling on you, then they were just looking to kick someone's ass. Which was it?"

"I guess they sort of grabbed me, at first."

"Then it was a robbery."

"Yeah, but they didn't ask for my wallet or pat me down. They just kind of held on and dragged me around."

"Were they trying to pull you toward a car or into one of these stores?"

"Like they were kidnapping me? No. I don't think so. They were just high."

"Who've you pissed off? You owe anyone money?"

"No one. It was nothing. Just life in the big city." He puts the last of the rocks away and turns to me, half smiling. "Look who's quizzing me about pissing people off. I think you took the gold, silver, and bronze in that event."

I waited for a minute, not sure I was going to say the next thing.

"I figured out one of your secrets."

"Which one would that be?"

"The rocks you used on Allegra and me. They're glass, aren't they? The glass from Aelita's story. Glass all full of divine light. Where did you get them?"

"You can find anything on eBay."

"Or from Mr. Muninn," says Candy.

"He has some nice things, no doubt."

"Why did you want them?" I ask. "You don't seem like a hippie New Age type. And you seem smart enough. Why aren't you a regular doctor?"

"What do I keep telling you? We'll talk when you let me take those bullets out."

"Then it was a bad move using those rocks on me. I don't even feel them anymore."

"You will." The doc keeps moving around the place, putting little things away. Examining others before handing them to Candy. He drops things, clumsy with just the one good arm. Candy leans against the end of the exam table. I pull my legs back so she can sit down. "Keep running around things and you'll feel them soon enough." Kinski picks up some green stems with small white blossoms on top. Candy leans over and takes them from him. "See? I told you we had some veratrum," he says.

"That's why you're the doc," says Candy.

The doc looks at me and crosses his arms.

"You might want to ease up on Eugène. He stood up for you while a lot of folks around here want to see you sent right back to where you came from, but he stood up for you."

"You one of them?"

"I'm on the fence."

"That's why I don't know if I trust you to cut me open."

"Imagine how I feel having you in my home, Sandman Slim."

I hadn't thought of that.

"Thanks again for fixing me up. I owe you."

Candy says, "You're going to have a nice new scar for your collection."

I rub my chest. She's right. There's an almost-healed burn near my heart, right where the sword went in.

"It's a good one, too. I think I'll be immune to nukes after this." Candy's heart has slowed, but her pupils are still wide. "Listen. I was an asshole the other night. I had no call to talk to you the way I did. I'm sorry."

"It's okay. Jades freak out a lot of people."

"Not me. I know better than that. When I was Downtown, I met Hellions more honorable than ninety-nine percent of the people I have to deal with up here. And I met human souls as vicious and treacherous as any Hellion. So for me to say that stuff to you, that was double shitty. My father would have smacked me and I'd've deserved it."

"I forgive you. We'll all be freaks together. A blood-sucker who doesn't suck blood. A human who thinks he's a Tasmanian Devil driving a tank. And a two-armed witch doctor with only one working arm."

I ask Kinski, "Why don't you use the glass to fix yourself?"

He shakes his head.

"They don't work the same way on everybody and they can't fix everything. I've got my herbs and my ice packs. I'll be fine."

"It's funny, you got mugged by people who didn't know what they wanted and I sort of did, too."

"You mean the angel?" asks Candy.

"Yeah. One minute, she's doing the hard sell and then she's coming over all beatific and Mother Teresa. Then she suddenly goes batshit psycho. Screams, 'Abomination,' and stabs me."

"You're sure she said 'Abomination'?"

"She was screaming it right in my face. I'm sure."

Candy makes a face and says, "Angels can be such pricks."

"That they can, darlin'," Kinski says. "Listen, you're going to have to watch your back. Just because Eugène stopped Aelita today doesn't mean he'll be able to do it again."

"You think she'll come after me?"

"Angels don't use the word *Abomination* lightly. You're the lowest of the low to her. Worse than a Hellion."

"So, if Parker or Mason or Hellions or Homeland Security don't get me, she will."

"Don't forget the Sub Rosa," says Candy.

"Thanks, sunshine. The Sub Rosa, too."

"You can always come here if things get too hot. I know people who can help get you out of town," Kinski says.

"I'll remember that." I slide off the table and try out my feet. What do you know? I don't fall over or want to throw up. It's the little things that make life special. "I should go. Do you know the number of a cab company?"

"I've got one in the desk. I'll go look." He goes out and

Candy and I are alone in the exam room. She gets off the table and brings me a plastic bag full of what looks like mulch.

"Doc wants you to boil this stuff and drink it once in the morning and once at night until it's gone. Don't worry. It doesn't taste any worse than a boiled doormat."

"Thanks. Is this what the doc gives you to wean you off being a Jade?"

"My tea tastes a lot worse than yours."

"How's sobriety working out for you?"

"You know. One day at a time."

"Were you bitten or something? How do you become a Jade?"

"You're born to be a Jade. The gift, or affliction, depending on who you ask, descends through the female line in the family. I can trace all my Jade ancestors back to the First Crusade."

"If it's your nature to eat people, doesn't it feel funny to go against that? And against a thousand years of your family history?"

"We drink people. We don't eat them. And giving it up isn't so bad. Everything has to evolve, right? We're monkeys in trees one day and the next we're monkeys with dental hygiene and cell phones. Best of all, we don't throw shit at each other anymore."

"Speak for yourself," I say, and Candy laughs. Her heartbeat goes up a little. "Do you think that if the doc can get you off drinking people juice, you'll feel like a regular person someday?"

"Project much, Sandman Slim? What you mean is that if doc can make me less of a monster, can he do it for you, too?"

"I didn't say you were a monster."

"But I am. By any human definition, I am a monster. And I always will be, so, no, I don't think I'll ever feel like a regular person. I'll just be a monster who chooses to be a little less monstrous. Who knows? I might fall off the wagon and start drinking people milk shakes again. But I'm going to try not to. Are you asking because you want to see if doc can turn you into a librarian when all this is over?"

I'm walking circles around the table, trying to get my sea legs back. Candy cranes her neck around to watch me. It's weird being alone with her.

"I don't know exactly what I want. I know that no one outside of Hell can stand what I am. I'm not wild about it most of the time myself. But I can't picture being something else."

"Try. Just imagine it for a few days. See how it feels."

"Why not? But I'm lazy. When it's time, I'll probably go for a simpler fix."

"Like what?"

"Going back to Hell isn't the worst thing I can imagine. I know the place. I have a rep. I can probably get my old job back, fighting in the arena."

"Are you talking about killing yourself?"

"Nah. I'm not the suicide type. I just mean that if I get

to pick my moment, it might not be so bad. That was the problem last time. I wasn't ready. I didn't get to pick the moment. I could this time."

"I hate to break it to you, but planning your own violent death, whether it's you murdering yourself or letting someone else do it, is still suicide."

"You think so?" I shake my head and lean against the wall, suddenly out of breath. "Ignore me. I'm babbling. I'm tired. My only friends narced me out to Norman Bates's mom. And every time I get up close to death, I think about Alice."

"You know she's not down below. You let yourself be killed and you'll be farther away from her than ever, and it will be forever."

"Point taken. Truth is, enough people want me dead that I'm probably never going to have to make that choice."

"See? Things are looking up already."

"Let's see if my cab's here yet."

I WAKE IN the early afternoon, wander into the bathroom, and see myself in the mirror. Candy was right. Aelita's sword has given me one of my best scars. It looks like a rattler set itself on fire and did a GG Allin stage dive into my chest. This scar is a work of art. It deserves an Oscar and a star on Hollywood Boulevard. It deserves its own power ballad. Now I sort of know how Lucifer must have felt when that last thunderbolt hit and he fell out of Heaven's cotton candy clouds and into the deep, deep dark.

Aelita seems to have given me something else, too. Back in Hell, each new scar was a gift. Protection against a new attack. That attack in Aelita's chapel seems to have left me with something besides a new scar. She's given me some part of her angelic vision. Or maybe she just tore open my third eye, the one that's been sensing other people's moods and heartbeats. Whatever it is, I see with different eyes now and I see what she was trying to tell me. The Kissi are everywhere.

There's graffiti on the alley wall behind Max Overdrive. It's painted on the buildings and street corners. Store windows and telephone poles. The marks aren't in any language I know, but I can almost understand them. Like a name on the tip of your tongue that just won't come. The marks are greetings, warnings, and messages. Hobo signs for eldritch hicks.

The Kissi wander the streets ghosting the holiday merrymakers. Giddy families window-shop, trying to fill some of their desperate hours together with anything that gets them out of having to talk to each other. In some of those families, Mom or Dad is a Kissi. Or possessed by one. A little Kissi girl follows her parents, holding her big brother's hand, literally draining the life from him as the family stops to admire a blinking LED wreath outside a Burmese restaurant.

There are Kissi as pale and tenuous as vapor from a car

exhaust. They whisper lies into people's ears. Slip hotel receipts into a husband's wallet. A phone number into a wife's jacket pocket. They merrily plant little cells of paranoia that grow like a melanoma, because what's more fun at this time of year than a holiday family slaughter?

I have to get off the street. I can't stand looking at this. Regular people are bad enough, but regular people being made worse by chaos-sucking bottom feeders is something I can't take right now.

What's going on in the street doesn't look much like a détente to me. The Kissi don't care who sees them. The Vigil might be right about the Kissi breaking the treaty, but they don't seem to have a clue how to do anything about it.

There are plenty of cops out, too. Unis and plainclothes. More than I'd expect around Christmas. Aren't people supposed to be nodding off on tryptophan, eggnog, and fascist Santa's order to be merry? Maybe the cops know something the rest of us don't know. Maybe they just feel the undercurrent of craziness in the air. They try to blend in with the holiday wanderers, but they're as inconspicuous as spiders on a birthday cake.

I just want quiet, a cup of coffee, and no one talking to me. I head for Donut Universe.

Some genius has installed a TV on the wall behind the doughnut counter. Those of us stupid enough to want to sit and drink our coffee inside get a complimentary twenty-four-hour-a-day slice of weather, sports, and genocide with our glazed old-fashioneds. When the local report comes on, it confirms more of what Aelita told me. Robbery. Murder. Rape. Arson. They're spiraling up and out of control. The local politicos and law dogs don't have a clue why or what to do about it. Sounds like someone moved Devil's Night to December and forgot to tell the rest of us to duck and cover.

The green-haired pixie counter girl I've seen before is working today. She's good at her job. Chats up the customers. Smiles and listens without looking fake or like a mental patient. At another time and place, I'd steal a car for her every night and leave it in the parking lot with the keys in the ignition. But here and now I can't keep falling in instant love like this. It's embarrassing and distracting. If Vidocq was around, I'd ask him for a potion. A temporary lobotomy, please. Just something to get me through the holidays, and maybe kill off this idiot nineteen-year-old who still lives in my head.

I look up from the pixie girl to burning houses in East L.A. Crying mothers. Screaming kids. There's blood in the water, so the TV reporters swim up with blank eyes and a mouthful of shark's teeth. They stick microphones in the faces of new widows and ask, "How does it make you feel?" I love L.A.

I wonder if things have always been this way. Are the Kissi the devils on our shoulders? Or do they just like us because our devils are so loud and hard to miss? I see why Heaven and Hell want to control the Kissi. They can't ever let regular people hear about them. After the panic, it'd be too easy to pin all of humanity's bad habits on them. Plus, someone would have to explain where they came from. That means people finding out that God is a fuckup and the devil doesn't matter. Neither side wants that.

I wonder if the Kissi are strong enough to jack an angel? Maybe. If they really are anti-angels. Muninn said someone was dragging angels up the hill to Avila. That sounds like urban-myth bullshit to me. Like that kid down the street who made a funny face and it stayed that way, so his family had to move away. If someone is snatching angels, it's probably the Kissi. I don't think even Mason could mug Aelita.

Two guys come in from the parking lot. I can feel them from all the way across the room. Heat and crazy breathing. Their hearts are going off like machine guns. But they look boring. An older guy in a gray suit. A junior high boy with a skateboard under his arm. They're bent over the counter ordering doughnuts. I can't get a look at their faces. They order a few dozen. A whole box full. The green-haired girl rings them up, and when she tells them the total, the guy in the suit pulls a .44 from his jacket and shoots her. And he keeps shooting her. He has to lean all the way over the counter to get off the last few rounds.

I'm up while he's still concentrating on the girl. Junior drops his deck, pulls his own piece, and aims it at me. I stop. They're both Kissi.

This isn't a good time. I'm weak. I don't want to get shot right now and they know it. They laugh at me.

The guy in the suit says, "You naughty boy."

"You stole our *na'at*," says the kid.

"And after we invited you into our home so nicely and politely."

"Some people have no manners."

"No manners at all. That's all right. We'll do you a trade." The man points to his chest, then mine. "Hold on to whatever that is in there for us. We'll be back with a doggy bag."

"Happy holidays," says the kid. There's blood all over the box of doughnuts. The kid opens it and takes out an apple fritter. "You really ought to try these. They make 'em fresh every morning."

They stroll out the door like they just won the lottery.

Behind me, an old lady is screaming. I hear cell phones beeping as people fumble with the keypads trying to make their fingers hit 911. I look over the counter at the green-haired girl. She's dead. As dead as anyone I've ever seen.

Is that what Alice looked like?

Good-bye, green-haired girl. How many more of you am I not going to save?

THERE'S A GOLD Lexus parked around the corner. Ten seconds later, it's mine. I pull into a no-name indie gas station and buy a pack of cigarettes, two plastic gas cans, and a T-shirt with MANN'S CHINESE THEATRE on the front. I pay for four gallons of gas in advance, fill the two cans, and get back in the car. I've always been pretty good with directions. Hell made me good with them even when I'm getting my ass kicked, so I know where I'm going. Fifteen minutes later, I'm parked down the block from the furniture warehouse where the skinheads party.

I slice the T-shirt in half and dip each piece into the can, letting them soak up the juice. Then I stuff them in the cans' mouths and head for the clubhouse.

A fat man in a Hawaiian shirt and khaki shorts is walking the other way. As we pass I say, "You should call 911."

He stops. "Has there been an accident?"

"Not yet."

There's no one outside the clubhouse. Why would there be? Who's going to play games with a building full of methed-up headbangers?

I light the rags in each can with Mason's lighter. I knock on the door politely. My other adolescent crush, Ilsa, the skinhead girl, opens up. She smiles at me like you smile at an old dog that can't help shitting on himself.

She asks, "What the fuck do you want?"

I kick once, slamming the door open and her out of the way. I sling the gas cans underhanded, aiming at the opposite ends of the room.

They explode, one a fraction of a second behind the other. Flames splash across the walls like a flood of hellfire. It's an instant riot inside. Screaming. Punching. Skinheads and their white power girlfriends clawing past each other for the one exit. I pull the door closed and kick a garbage can in front of it.

The first one out is the big gorilla I stabbed in the leg at the Bamboo House of Dolls. He trips over the can and face plants just outside the door. The next few drowning rats trip over him. Fall in a screaming pile of bodies, blocking the door. It's the Keystone Kops with third-degree burns.

Eventually, enough people inside push forward that the bodies and the door get kicked out of the way. The panicked, burned, and smoke-choked master race pours outside and collapses in the street.

Josef comes strolling out last. His clothes are smoldering and his face looks like a hamburger someone forgot to take off the barbecue. Ilsa and a dozen of Josef's steroid lapdogs get up and follow him.

Josef doesn't even look around. He knows who did this. He comes right for me. I can see the beast under his skin. I can't tell if he was ever human.

When he's a few feet away, he starts to say something. It's going to be some Kissi threat or demonic one-liner. Who cares? I slash his throat with the black blade, giving the knife a little twist. Unlike Kasabian, when Josef's head pops off, he's totally, one hundred percent dead.

I pick up the head by its singed blond hair and push it into Ilsa's chest. It takes her a minute to figure out that she's supposed to take it. I wait for one of the big boys to make a move, but they're mostly staring at the raspberry-colored lake forming around Josef's body.

I say, "You tell the rest of these animals and any Kissi you run into to stay away from my doughnut place."

I go back to the Lexus and floor it out of there before they come to enough to realize that there are fifty of them and only one of me.

IF YOU DO it right, cleaning your guns is a form of meditation. There's the precise disassembly. Attaching a cotton swatch to the end of a ramrod, soaking it in solvent, and passing it through the gun barrel from the breech end and out the front. Cleaning the nooks and crannies with a soft toothbrush. Carefully applying a few drops of gun oil. Then wiping the gun down and reassembling it before starting on the next gun, moving from smallest to largest. It's a calm, quiet, and satisfying process. I'm ashamed that I've neglected the guns this long. I should have cleaned them the moment I dug them out from under the floorboards at Vidocq's. Wild Bill would be ashamed of me.

I'd picked up the cleaning kit at an upscale gun club in West Hollywood on the way back to Max Overdrive. Also a can of WD-40 to clean the *na'at*. On the night table next to the bed is the bottom half of a Coke can I ripped in half. There's an inch of Spiritus Dei floating in the can and I dip each bullet into it before reloading the guns.

That encounter with the Kissi back at Donut Universe woke me up. I need to be more careful now that I don't have any real backup.

I can't get the bloody image of the green-haired girl out

of my mind. Every time I think I've pushed her away, Alice drifts in to take her place.

No wonder I'm so popular.

There's a knock at the door. I stay sitting on the bed, but hide the reassembled .45 under one leg, where I can get it quickly. I don't say, "Come in," but she comes in anyway.

Allegra only takes a couple of steps into the room, like she's afraid there are snakes under all the furniture. She sits on Kasabian's old bootlegging table, knocking over a couple of stacks of DVDs that I'd stolen from the racks downstairs. I soak another cotton patch in solvent and go back to cleaning the guns.

"Why didn't you tell me before about what happened to you? What Mason did?"

"Vidocq told you my little secret? Is he in some contest I don't know about? Rat out your friends three times in a day and win Springsteen tickets."

"He just wanted me to understand why you're the way you are."

"And now everyone knows. Did you come up here to gloat? I give up. You win. You and Vidocq showed me up for the chump I truly am."

"That's not what this is about and you know it."

"Princess, I only know two things. One is that I'm going to kill Mason and Parker, and nothing human or inhuman is going to stop me. And two, I'm on my own."

"Don't play that martyr shit with me. I've seen how you are."

"You don't get it. You think I'm saying this because I'm still mad. I'm not. I just understand things better now. A friend laid it out for me. I'm not one of you. The only thing I live for now is to kill as many people and break as many things as I need to, to get what I want. By the standards of most sane people, that makes me a monster. I'm fine with that. And, if I'm alive when this is over, I'm going back to where the monsters live."

"Hell?"

"It's where I belong. It's where I want to be."

Allegra reaches down, picks up one of the piles of DVDs, and begins to straighten them.

"Eugène loves you," she says.

"That's nice. My father loved me. He tried to shoot me once."

"What?"

"We were out deer hunting. It was just after sunup and cold enough that I could see my breath. I'd spotted a six-point buck ahead in the tree line. I led the way, up front a few yards, with my father right behind me. I spotted the buck in a clearing, signaled my father to stop. I raised my rifle and took the shot. Just as I pulled the trigger, I heard another gun go off and something hit me on the side of the head. My father's shot had missed me by maybe an inch and hit the tree where I was leaning. I looked back at him, blood coming down my face where flying bark and splinters had hit me. He came running up apologizing, saying it was all an accident, asking if I was okay. But behind all the panic in his eyes, there was nothing but fear and loathing. He hated himself for taking the shot, but he hated me more for still breathing."

"I'm so sorry."

"Just because someone says they love you doesn't mean they're not going to fuck you over the first chance they get."

"What about Alice? Did she fuck you over, too?"

"No. She's the one who didn't."

Allegra empties a couple of overflowing ashtrays into a metal trash can on the floor.

"Doesn't that mean anything?"

"No. I told her I loved her about a million times. It didn't save her. It's what got her killed."

"But you both loved each other. You still have that."

"You loved your drug-dealer boyfriend. I bet he told you he loved you every day. How'd that work out for you?"

"This isn't about me."

"You're right, it's not. So, why don't you run along back to Vidocq and let me finish my work so I can get all of you and this town behind me?"

She shakes her head, pushes more junk from the table into the trash, and starts for the door.

"After I'm gone," I tell her, "as far as I'm concerned, you can have Max Overdrive. Parker's killed Kasabian by now, so he's not going to want it back. I'm sure Vidocq can come up with some kind of glamour that'll make it look like you owned the place all along."

She drops the trash can by the door. Lets it fall over

and spill food wrappers, empty cans, and cigarette butts on the floor.

"You know what? You're not a monster. You're just a motherfucker. Eugène should have let Aelita put you out of your misery."

"Good-bye, Allegra. Go tidy up at Eugène's."

She kicks the can out of the way and slams the door. I can hear her stomp down every single step, like she's punishing the staircase, like God's tiniest tyrannosaurus.

WHEN ALLEGRA IS gone, I finish cleaning and reassembling the guns. When that's done, I take old newspapers and paper bags from under the bootlegging table and lay them out flat on the floor.

When you stretch out a regulation *na'at* to its full length, it's ten feet of very sharp Hellion steel teeth, spikes, and spines. Some are spring-loaded and ready to go whenever you pick up the *na'at*. Others only open up when you trigger them from the grip.

Traditionally, you use a *na'at* like a spear or a staff, but there's another trigger that collapses the central shaft. Suddenly the *na'at* is as loose as chicken chow mein, a metal whip that can strip the skin off a rhino like peeling a grape. Not that I've ever peeled a rhino or a grape, but you get the idea.

I only mention this to explain that your basic *na'at* has a lot more intricate mechanical parts than anything any human has ever manufactured. When you decide to WD-40 your *na'at,* you need a lot of room and a lot of newspapers to soak up the excess oil. You should also open a window before you start spraying lube and solvents around your bedroom, something I almost always forget to do.

I drag the newspaper and the *na'at* across the room and out of the way. I stash the guns under the mattress and wash the WD-40 off my hands in the bathroom. I've trashed enough clothes that I'm back down to video-store T-shirts and jeans. I throw on the silk overcoat I've been avoiding and slip the knife inside. On the way out, I push open the three big windows on the wall opposite the bed.

The short walk to the Bamboo House of Dolls clears the stink out of my nose and head. A drink and a cigarette later and I'm happy to be back on Earth. When Carlos brings me my food, I drink to his health. I haven't done much for him lately, except maybe cooking and decapitating some skinheads, but I can't exactly talk to him about that. He brings up sports and I try to say something that doesn't sound stupid, but I didn't know much about sports before I went Downtown. Finally, he gives up and walks off to serve other customers.

I haven't talked to him much lately. I haven't wanted to talk much at all. It seems like a good idea to let the guy know that I appreciate him, his bar, and his food. Right now Carlos is about the closest thing I have to friend on this planet. With Cherry, Jayne-Anne, and Kasabian gone, so are all my ties to Mason, leaving me right in the middle of downtown with nothing to do and nowhere to go. When you're in that neighborhood, you need at least one person on your side. Preferably one with a bar.

I finish off two more drinks before it becomes dangerously clear that if I hang around much longer, I'm going to have to talk to someone.

I time the walk back to Max Overdrive perfectly. I get to the door right on the last puff of my cigarette. Flicking the butt into the Dumpster, I let myself in the back way.

Inside, the oily solvent smell is gone, but now there's something else. Alcohol? Disinfectant? The staircase smells like a hospital waiting room.

I find out why a minute later. By then I'm already on the floor and the world is a shivering Slip and Slide, so there's no chance of me getting up. I have a feeling that the robot ghost in the dirty trench coat that's waving a baseball bat in my face might have something to do with it.

Pieces of the world start falling back into place enough for to me to see that the robot ghost isn't really a robot or a ghost. It's Kasabian, and he's held together with a lot of metal rods and screws. There's a metal band bolted around his head, held in place by steel dowels that are attached to a brace on his chest. A traction halo. It holds his head onto his body well enough for him to stand up, but the rig makes him move like a rusty windup toy. Still, for a kid's toy, he's doing a pretty good job tuning up my ribs.

I deflect a couple of the blows with my arms, which feels just as good as it sounds. Kasabian is so stiff, he has to stand in one place to work me over. Lucky me. I swing one of my legs around and catch him behind the knee. He goes down on the knee, but refuses to fall over. Just keeps smashing me with the bat, teeth gritted, sweating and red-faced. But he's working from close range now, so the shots hurt a lot less than before.

I swing my leg again. This time I hit the top of the metal halo. That gets his attention. Kasabian drops the bat and crab walks his way back, putting some distance between my foot and his head.

Except for the first surprise shot on the back of my skull, he hasn't hurt me too much. Kasabian moves like he's half frozen in ice. Can't get up the strength to do any real damage. If he wasn't up and walking around, I'd swear that his body was in rigor mortis. Maybe he's afraid that if he wiggles around too much, his head will pop off. Let's test that theory.

Still on the floor, I throw a kick at his head. Kasabian tries to move out of the way, but I'm faster than him. But I still miss. Okay. So that first smack on the head scrambled my brain a little more than I thought.

I go for the guns under the mattress, but my aim is still off. It gives Kasabian a chance to drive the bat into my ribs again. I'm breathing hard, trying to take in air every time it gets knocked out with another rib shot. I could probably throw a spell at Kasabian if my head was clearer and my chest wasn't hurting. I can feel every single bruise from the Kissi attack. And all this wrestling around is waking up those bullets again. Fuck Kinski for being right about them getting angry again.

When Kasabian tries to jam me with the bat again, I move faster and get my hand on it. One twist and it's out of his hands and bouncing off the floor. Kasabian backs up and braces himself against the wall. He reaches for something under his dirty trench coat, but he's not fast enough. The world is settling down. Becoming firmer around me. I grab the bat and swing. It smashes into his halo, buckling and scattering the metal dowels.

Kasabian screams, "Fuck!" His head is hanging free, held on by just the stitches and the couple of remaining dowels. He gets his feet under him, braces his back against the wall, and pushes himself up until he's standing. His eyes are wide. Not so much in anger anymore. He's remembering what it was like the first time his melon came off and he doesn't like the picture. That's why his hands are shaking and he's muttering, "No, no, no," when he pulls what looks like a short tree branch out from under his coat. It wraps around his arm from the wrist to his elbow.

Now it's my turn to scramble back. The skinhead at Carlos's bar tried to shoot me with a Devil Daisy, but he didn't know what he was doing. In a room this small, even a crippled, half-dead wreck like Kasabian couldn't miss me. But I'm more worried about something worse.

I yell, "Stop!" and put up my hands. Kasabian just looks at me. I guess he wasn't expecting such an easy surrender. He face splits into a big grin. He waves the Daisy around a little, stabbing the air with it, trying to intimidate me. He does, but not for the reasons he thinks.

"Listen to me, Kas. I know that Parker and Mason gave you that thing. If you use it, you're going to die. For real this time. No second chances."

"Kiss my ass, man. They helped me. Parker took me out of here. He and Mason gave me back my body."

"Nice job they did, too. You look like Frankenstein's ball sac. You can barely move. Don't you think if they liked you they could find a spell to put your head back on for real?"

"That's your fault! You and your goddamn knife. It left some kind of residual magic behind. No matter what we tried, my head wouldn't go back on. Parker put together this traction rig for me. It sucks, but it's better than spending the rest of my life in that closet watching infomercials until you decide to shoot me."

"You're right. I got a little more extreme with you than I meant to. Sorry. I wanted Mason, but I had you. You got some of the grief I was saving up for him. That wasn't right. So. You know. Sorry."

"Sorry? Even if you didn't cut my head off, you came here to kill me. You think sorry covers that?"

"I'm not so sure you want to know the truth about that."

Kasabian hoists the Devil Daisy up to face level. I take a couple more steps back, until I'm on the other side of the bed. Still in point-blank range.

"Tell me," he says.

"When I got here, yeah, I planned on killing you. But after ten minutes, I was pretty much over that. I mean, how much more could I do? Mason did a pretty good job of wrecking you before I ever got here."

"Yeah, but I stood up to you and he's on my side again."

"No, he's not. He's never been on your side and he never will be. You think he gave you your body and sent you back here to get me? This is a setup. You're here to kill yourself. Me, too. But mostly you."

"Look at you. Look how scared you are. You'll say anything."

"Ask me how Jayne and Cherry are. I double-dog dare you."

"Why? Is that a trick question?"

"Yeah. Because they're dead. Parker killed them. He's killing everyone connected to him and Mason. If he gave you that weapon, it'll probably kill me, but I guarantee that it'll kill you."

"You are such a liar. Not even a good one. Look how scared you are."

"I'm scared you're going to do something stupid."

He pushes the Daisy in my direction.

"Don't call me stupid!"

"Sorry. Just don't do anything you—we—can't take back."

He starts to nod, but catches himself. The nod turns into a twitch as he pushes his shoulders and head back against the wall. His heart is a trip-hammer. His pupils narrow. Now that he's done something dumb in front of me, he's angrier than ever.

"Kas, Mason and Parker are using you."

"Keep talking, dead man. I hear there's a bunch of imps waiting for you with knives and forks."

I take another step back. He's going to do it. It's building inside him.

"Don't do it, man. You'll die, too."

The grin is back on his face.

"This is nice. This quiet moment before you die. Thanks for lying and whining. You made it really special for me."

Oh, hell.

I know it's coming, so I don't wait. I dive for the floor. When he fires the Devil Daisy, I'm behind the bed collapsing the *na'at* to its spear configuration. I dig one end into the floor and, staying low, angle the shaft over me.

The first wave of dragon fire hits, tries to tear the *na'at* out of my hand. The intricate Hellion web of edges, angles, and teeth along the weapon's body spreads the fire out and over me. Then the second thing happens. The one I've been worried about.

The Daisy explodes. The room turns into Dresden, burning under the Allied planes. It's Rome while Nero fiddled and pissed on the panicked mobs. It's Hamburg and Chicago and the Hindenburg all going off at once in my room. It's all I can do to hold the *na'at* in place and channel the supernova on the other side of the bed anywhere but on top of me.

And it's over. No fire. No smoke. No nothing. The Daisy has swallowed the remains of the fire. The room is a wreck. Lath is blown off the walls. Part of the ceiling is down. The junk on the bootleg table is scattered around the room like a hurricane blew through. All the windows are gone.

I pick up the charred bed and push it out of the way. Kasabian is lying under it. Considering how he looked before the explosion, he's not looking that bad right now. His right arm is gone. The Daisy took that off when it blew. And his head has fallen off. I get down on my knees and push random junk out of the way. I spot it a minute later under the bed.

Poor stupid, idiotic, goddamn Kasabian. If he was still alive, I'd strangle him. Right now I kind of don't mind him coming after me with the bat. I was pretty hard on him. He really did get me down on my knees and speaking in tongues for a minute, so he got at least a little of his own back before he made the big mistake of trusting Mason. Kasabian was an idiot, but he wasn't stupid. He must have known that Mason hated him at best. Considered him an insect at worst. Did Kasabian really not know what was going to happen when he pulled that trigger? Or did he want to go out in a sexy murder-suicide that would make it onto the local news? Idiot reporters would get it all wrong. They'd think it was an insurance scam gone wrong. Or that we were clumsy terrorists. More likely, they'd go with the sexiest choice, a lovers' quarrel gone nuclear. It's more than an even bet that he wanted to kill us both. At least then, one person would know that he'd done something right. I'd know that he'd gotten me, that I was truly dead, and that there was nothing I could do about it.

I stand very quietly for a minute, listening for sirens. If I had time and a clear head, I could probably come up with a spell to keep everyone away or send them off in the wrong direction. But that's not going to happen. I wait.

The sirens don't come. The fire was here and gone so fast that while the Daisy wrecked the place, it's sparing me from having to explain the headless body, all the guns, the video bootlegging gear and me. Who am I? Also technically dead, thanks. Just ask Homeland Security.

Someone's cell phone goes off. It's not my ring. I pat down Kasabian's body. Pull his phone from a coat pocket. It's one of the cheap prepaid models. I flip it open and wait.

"Well," someone says. "What the hell, man? Is it done?"

"Who is this?"

There's a pause. Then a low laugh.

"Stark? Is that you? Oh my God. What an asshole. I give Kasabian a flamethrower and a bomb and he still can't kill you. Where is he?"

"All over the place. He's in pieces."

"One thing went right tonight, at least. You must be

feeling pretty good right now, huh? Pretty proud of yourself. You kicked a headless guy's ass. Thank you, masked man. You saved our city."

I listen for signs of strain or stress in his voice. I wish I could see his eyes. Or catch a whiff of his sweat. But on the crap phone, Parker sounds thin, distant, and far away. Like he's calling from the Marianas Trench.

"You're the one who sent a half-dead guy to kill me. What did you think was going to happen?"

"I expected you to die, Mr. Bond," he says in a bad German accent. "Actually, Mason and I had a bet. He thought Kasabian might be able to do one thing right one time. He told the fat man to his face how much faith he had in him. I guess I won that bet."

"What happens now? You going to send more cripples after me? Blind guys with blowguns? Grandmas in wheelchairs with chain saws? What's your next brilliant move? All I've seen you do so far is get your pitiful excuse for an assassin blown up and yourself shot in the back. How did that feel, by the way? Were you awake when you fell? I'm glad Mason saved you. It means I get to kill you all over again."

"Calm down, sweetheart. You're getting all worked up. Trust me. You'll get your chance. We're going to see each other again. Not here. Not now. But it'll be soon. Cross my heart."

"I can't wait."

"You don't have to. Mason is sending you a late Christmas present. Don't worry. No more explosions or ninja attacks tonight. Just a token of his and my esteem for staying alive this long. How did you stay alive down there, by the way? Did you suck demon cock all day every day, or did you get weekends and holidays off?"

"Pucker up, tough guy. You'll know all about it soon enough."

The line goes dead. I toss the phone into the corner of the room. At least I know one thing now. Parker took Kasabian to wherever Mason is hiding. He was with both of them. He's seen their hideout and might have even heard them talking about what they're planning next. Mason thought Kasabian was an idiot and knew that one way or another, he was going to be dead tonight. Why not talk in front of him? Make him feel like he's part of the plan. If Mason convinced Kasabian that he'd been promoted and was going to get to play with the big boys, Kas wouldn't have asked any questions, but would have run along like a dog to please him.

I need to talk to Kasabian. But I can't get to him when he's in Hell. No way I'm setting foot Downtown. I need to get to him before he hops the ferry.

I only know one way to do it and it's really going to suck.

The Daisy has saved me the trouble of having to move the bootlegging table. I just push it up against the wall so it's out of the way. I kick broken, powdery lath, boxes of DVDs, dirty clothes, cigarette butts, and Jack Daniel's bottles out of the way until I clear an area about six by six on the floor. Aside from the furniture, most of the junk is pretty light. It's easy to sift through until I find something that's heavy. The lead Kinski gave me.

Start by drawing thirteen circles, six on the outside, and six on the inside, and one in the center. Take the lead and, at the outer top circle, draw a line across to the farthest. Then draw lines to the other circles on the outer rim so that they're all connected. Now do the same thing with the other five outer circles. Wash, rinse, repeat on the inner circles until you have seventy-eight lines that connect all thirteen circles. Ladies and gentlemen, meet Metatron's Cube. One of the holiest of holy glyphs. The soul of the angel Metatron, the voice of God. Good for keeping away imps, flesh-eating zombies, and ants at a picnic. It slices. It dices. It has a thousand and one uses. A thousand and two if you draw it on a brick and throw it through the windshield of your ex-girlfriend's new boyfriend's car.

Kasabian's head is still under the bed. I pull it out and set it on his chest, then grab his body by the ankles and drag him into the Cube. I straighten the arms and legs, set Kas's head back on its shoulders, and generally try to make him look more like a respectable human being and less like a big pile of loser jerky.

Under one of the windows are the remains of the warning bundle Medea, the Inquisitor, left for me at Vidocq's place. I leave the wolf teeth. All I need are the crow feathers. Pretty much any part of a crow is useful. Especially when you're dealing with the dead. Crows are psychopomps.

They guide the dead from this world to the next. There are quicker, more direct ways to get through to dead souls, but crow's feathers are the smart way to go if you don't want some clever boots to come along and pluck your soul out of your body while you're distracted, waiting on line one for dead Aunt Lily to pick up.

I rip open Kasabian's shirt, dip the feathers in his blood, and paint a smaller version of Metatron's Cube on his chest. Then I open his mouth and put one of the feathers inside. I dip a finger into his blood and, with it, paint a circle over my third eye.

The one remaining unopened, unbroken bottle of Jack is under the mattress with the guns. I crack it open and have a couple of long drinks. Whatever I thought of Kasabian, whatever I thought that I might do to him when I tracked him down, painting him with his own blood and wearing some of it myself was never on my original agenda. One more drink and I'm ready to hit the road.

I lie down in the Cube next to Kasabian so that our shoulders and feet are touching. I use the black blade to cut one of my wrists, deep enough to really get the blood flowing, but not so deep that I lose control of my hands. I upend the bottle for one more shot of liquid courage, and then slice the other wrist.

Nice and relaxed now. Warm and drifting. The Jack and the flowing blood are doing their job. I'll be unconscious soon. Just before I lose consciousness, I put the second crow feather between my teeth and hold it there.

I'm standing on the floor of an empty desert. The alkali plain is cracked and glistening. There's a shaft of light at the horizon, but it never moves. It's always just before sunrise or just after sunset. Take your pick. The air is thick and hard to breathe. The light is a watery blue green.

Kasabian is standing a few yards away wearing the same Max Overdrive T-shirt and chinos that he was wearing the night he shot me.

"So, this is it?" he asks. "This is death?"

I walk across the packed earth to where he's standing.

"Not really. You're kind of in between worlds right now. There really isn't a desert and there really isn't a sunrise or sunset. This is just something to look at while you wait. You're sort of on hold and this is the Muzak."

"While I'm waiting to see if I'm going to Heaven or damned to Hell, this is the best the all-knowing occult powers that run the universe could come up with? Talk about being underachievers."

"Be fair, man. Everyone knows where you're headed. Maybe they just didn't break out the A material for you."

Kasabian nods.

"You're right. Why bother? I fucked up my life and I even fucked up dying."

"So we're clear, you know that wasn't me who killed you just now, right? It was Parker."

"I should never have trusted those guys. Why would Mason help me after all these years? I thought it was different now. I thought that with you back, he'd need me again."

"Where is he?"

"Listen, you were straight with me before. You know, saying you were sorry for locking me up in that closet and everything. I want to be straight with you."

"Don't worry about it. There isn't a lot of time. Where's Mason hiding?"

Kasabian looks over his shoulder to the mountains in the distance. There's a low rumble of thunder. It won't be long now. He turns back to me.

"I knew something was up that night. I knew Mason had something waiting for you. I thought he was just going to hit you with a leech charm or something. Suck out all your power and keep it for himself. But when those Lurkers showed up . . ."

"Kissi. They're called Kissi."

"I didn't know he was going to do that."

"What did you know about Alice?"

"Nothing. I'm not into doing stuff like that to women. And a civilian? That's messed up."

"Would you have told me if you'd known?"

He shrugs. Looks down. Shakes his head.

"Come on, man. That's not even a real question. Going against Mason feels like you're going against the devil."

I can't read a dead man like a living one. No heartbeat. No breath. Fixed pupils. But I don't need any of that now.

"I believe you," I tell him. "And Mason isn't the devil.

He just likes to play dress-up. Tell me where he is and I'll get him for both of us."

"I don't know where he is exactly. It was sort of like here. Spooky and wrong, but a lot weirder. Somewhere far away and dark. Not regular dark, either. Dark like it had no idea what light even was. Like light was Kryptonite to the place. There was no one there, but it wasn't empty. In fact, it was crowded. But it was full of nothing." He holds up his hands in frustration. "If any of that makes sense."

Thunder rolls down the mountains again. A dot of light appears at the base of one a couple of miles away. A door has opened. I take Kasabian by the arm and start walking him that way.

"Listen, when you get to Hell, look up a guy named Belial. He's one of Lucifer's generals. Tell him I sent you and ask him for a job. Tell him I said not to send you to the pits."

"The pits?" asks Kasabian. "What pits?"

"When you tell him who sent you, make sure you tell him it was Sandman Slim. And remind him that the Sandman knows where he lives."

Kasabian gives me a look.

"What the fuck is Sandman Slim? It sounds like a Japanese cartoon."

"Just tell him," I say, and let go of his arm. "This is as far as I go. I have things to do back in the world."

Kasabian looks at the door and then at me.

"I know," he says. He turns and heads for the mountain. "I'll see you around."

"Probably."

Flat on my back again. I gulp and the crow feather almost goes down my throat. Rolling over, I spit it onto the floor. Home again, home again, jiggity jig.

I'm not bleeding anymore, but I'm a mess. Again. Besides getting my ass kicked, my main accomplishment on this trip has been to massacre an incredible number of completely innocent clothes. I'm the Joseph Stalin of laundry. I take off the shirt, toss it onto a pile of other junk, and slip on the silk overcoat.

My ears are still ringing, but I'm pretty sure there aren't any sirens headed this way (the crackheads aren't going to call it in and who else hangs out here at night?). But some passing Joe Citizen could call in the noise. And the morning crew will be opening the place at eleven tomorrow. I can't leave Kasabian's corpse lying here. First, I have to find something.

I find it under the splinters of the bedside table. Alice's magic box. It's been crushed a little by the blast. Inside, the bloody cotton has come loose, but it's still in one piece. I put it under the bed, near the wall.

I pull the blanket off the bed, roll up the body, and use some duct tape I get from behind the counter to hold the blanket tight. I take Kasabian downstairs and out the back way. Also grab a couple of cinder blocks that the day crew uses when they're on a cigarette break. I'm trying very hard not to think about anything I'm doing. Of all the iffy things I've ever done in my life, I've never had to ditch a body before. While it's giving me a migraine right now, I think the fact that I'm not an expert on corpse disposal says a lot of good things about me and my life choices.

About a block away, I find a shiny new BMW SUV, which is way too many random letters strung together. It makes me feel less guilty about stealing it.

I drive it around the block, pull up to Max Overdrive, and load the body and the cinder blocks in the back. Then I drive to Fairfax and turn south. At Wilshire, I make a left and hit the gas until I see mammoths.

Animals have been falling into the La Brea Tar Pits since the last ice age. Not so much recently, since the pits are fenced in and part of a pretty slice of upscale urban green called Hancock Park. There's a big museum. A lot of wolf skulls and bird bones. A gift shop. And, soon, a dead video store-owning ex-magician.

There's not a lot of traffic on this part of Wilshire late at night. I hop the curb and pull the van up onto the brick walkway that leads to the museum. When I figure out which light pole I want, I gun the engine and smash the BMW into it at full speed. The van's windshield and front bumper are totaled. Steam billows from under the hood. The good news is that the pole with the surveillance camera is now a big aluminum toothpick by the museum's front door.

If you ever need to weigh down a dead body, remember that it's not hard duct-taping cinder blocks to a stiff, but it is hard getting them balanced right. I'm sure that with enough time and practice, I could come up with a corpse-cinder-block arrangement stable enough that a tightrope walker could use it, but I don't have time for that now. I'm parked on a major thoroughfare in a stolen van. I have no shirt, an expensive overcoat, and fresh scars on my wrists. And I'm dragging around a dead guy accessorized with building materials. This is not a precise or subtle situation. This is a situation for mindless violence and brute force. First good news I've had all day.

I get Kasabian's weighted body onto my shoulder and haul it out of the van. I drop him on his back a few yards outside the fence. I stoop and grab the body by the ankles, then I start spinning, holding the body like the hammer in a hammer throw. After a few revolutions, I'm dizzy, but have a pretty good head of steam up. When I release him, Kasabian goes flying. He sails through the air end over end, like some long-forgotten Russian space probe returning to Earth, off course and out of control.

The body hits the tar with a thick, dull *thunk*. At first, it doesn't move. Kasabian floats on the surface defiantly, a corpse burrito refusing to sink. Demanding to be eaten by one of the local dinosaurs lying at the bottom of the pit. Finally, he realizes how unreasonable he's being, and starts to go under. Slowly. Very slowly. Kasabian's head disappears. Then his gut. When all that's left of him above the surface are his shins and feet, I leave. Even if the surface of the tar lake is disturbed in the morning, I think the police will be more interested in the stolen van.

It's a long, exhausting walk back to Max Overdrive. When I get back to the room, all I can do is flip the mattress clean side up. I don't bother taking off the overcoat. I lie down in it and get some clean towels from the bathroom to use as a pillow.

All night long, the song someone played once at the Bamboo House of Dolls loops in my head.

> "Set me adrift and I'm lost over there
> And I must be insane, to go skating on your name,
> And by tracing it twice, I fell through the ice
> Of Alice . . ."

Are there people smart enough to know how doomed they are before the world crashes down on them, the way pianos fall on people in old cartoons? There must be, but I've never been one of them. Before my trip down the rabbit hole, I figured that I could joke, lie, and bullshit my way through pretty much anything. That's what's known as being a professional brat, and I was Superman at that.

Alice never liked Mason and didn't really trust the rest of the Circle. Neither did I. At least the old, sharp-tooth reptile part of my brain didn't, but that just made playing with them and being better than them more fun. Especially being better than Mason. Alice could never see the fun. She talked about the Circle like it was crystal meth and I was an addict.

"Didn't your mommy and daddy teach you that if

you play with the bad kids, you're going to be kept after school?"

"My mom told me I was the handsomest boy in the world. My father taught me to shoot and how to smile while getting the back of someone's hand. That's pretty much all I remember."

She was wearing a white wifebeater and black panties. She was making coffee, but stopped, came over, and sat on my lap.

"That's why I love you. You're Norman Rockwell's perfect boy. Don't go out with those magic assholes tonight. Stay home with me. We'll eat apple pie and fuck on a flag."

"I've got to go. Mason's got something big to show us tonight. I need to be there to piss on his parade."

She got up and went back to the kitchen.

"Fine. Go, then. Go and show a bunch of losers that you're better than them. That's huge. That's a fucking accomplishment."

"This is important. You don't understand. If you had the gift, you'd know. Most of the Sub Rosa are rich dicks or Goth kids without the clove cigarettes. But I need to be around magic people sometimes. People I don't have to explain myself to."

"You need to show off to them more than you need to be with me. They're dangerous and they're going to suck you into something dangerous and stupid, like summoning the devil or something. And when they get killed or thrown in jail, you're going with them."

I grabbed my jacket and went to the door.

"I need to go. I'm late."

"You know, trying to still be the precocious one isn't that cute after you're old enough to buy beer. Grow up. Stop being such a fucking child."

Walking out, I said, "You know, sometimes you sound just like those regular jack-offs out there. You say you don't care about the magic. You say you're not jealous, but you are. You want what I have or you don't want me to have it at all. Fuck that."

Later that night, Mason played his little trick on me and I never saw Alice again.

Only now she's standing at the foot of the bed, staring at the wrecked room. She doesn't have to say a word. I know what she's thinking because it's what I'm thinking. That the mess is a kind of metaphor for my life. She sighs. Picks up small things, drops them, then picks up something else. She shakes her head in wonder at all the junk until I feel ashamed and stupid.

I know that none of this is real. This Alice is a golem. The present Parker said Mason would be sending me. This sighing ghost isn't Alice any more than the slab of meat I tossed into the tar pits was Kasabian.

The golem's eyes are milky gray. Its skin is cracked and stained with red, green, and brown lichen, like old granite. Its broken teeth ooze blood. Golem Alice's fingertips are bare bone, like something has been gnawing at them.

275

Unfortunately, knowing that something isn't real doesn't mean it's going to go away or that it doesn't affect you. When she isn't eyeballing the wreckage of my mini Pompeii, Alice is leaning over me and whispering in my ear.

"You wouldn't throw me into the black tar, would you, Jimmy? There's no air down there. And it's so dark. You wouldn't do that to me, would you, baby?"

THE MORNING CREW arrives like a herd of baby elephants jacked up on lattes and enough mutant energy drinks to give a rhino a stroke. The crew is an ever-shifting posse of film school hipster dudes. I don't know any of their names and I don't want to. They're just Blond Surfer Dude. Billy Goat Beard Surfer Dude. Dreads Dude, etc. They really are dudes. Sleepy eyes. IQs drowning in bong water. They invent complicated filing systems for the movies because the alphabet baffles them.

One of them knocks on my door. I open it without putting on a shirt. My wrists have healed, but there's dried blood on my hands. I hope I didn't ruin the overcoat. Time to look for a dry cleaner.

It's Billy Goat Beard Surfer Dude. He smells like he used bong water for aftershave. My lack of a shirt and the blood don't even register.

He says, "Um, a bunch of the shelves in the porn section fell down last night. What do you want us to do?"

For a second, I wonder if he's kidding. Then I remember who he is.

"Maybe one of you should go and clean it up."

"Okay, but I'm the only one who can work the register. Bill's allergic to dust and Rudy just got born again, so he's a no-porn zone till he gets over it."

"So, none of you is capable of walking to the back of the store and picking up the movies?"

"I guess not. Plus, there's cracks in the ceiling. Looks like there's cracks in there, too," he says, pointing into the room. I pull the door closed a little.

"Fuck it. It's porn. People who want it will paw through it wherever it is. Hell, they might like it better down there. Maybe we should put the whole porn section in a big pile on the floor."

"What?"

I forgot. The only things that are funny when you're as buzzed as Billy Goat Beard are cartoon animals and seeing other people get hurt.

"Never mind. Just open the store and let me get dressed."

"When is Mr. Kasabian coming back?"

I look at the kid. Does this doe-eyed weed monkey suspect something? Am I going to have to lobotomize this twerp?

"When he's damn good and ready," I say.

"Okay." He walks away, like he's already forgotten the whole conversation.

I throw the dead bolt when I close the door. Need to start locking the room up all the time. Too many weapons in here. Too much blood on the floor. Too much residual magic in the walls. All I need is for some stoned teenybopper to take a post-weed nap in Metatron's Cube and wake up with his soul on a hook in some stalker's trading booth in the souk.

I clean up in the bathroom. There's a brownish-red ring around the drain. I need to get some bleach before all the blood I've been leaking into the sink stains it permanently. I wonder if Kasabian had any accident or maybe earthquake insurance. I saw official-looking papers in one box—I'll have to track that down. It'd be nice for Allegra to be able to get the place fixed up when I'm gone and she takes over.

The overcoat is wadded in a ball at the end of the bed. It looks pretty rough. Praise Lucifer that my jeans are black. Blood's not so obvious on them. I find a box with the last of the Max Overdrive T-shirts in my size and slip it on. The only thing I have to wear over the T-shirt that will hide a weapon is the half-burned motocross jacket. I'll look a little crazy in it, but it's still wearable. Because it's such a wreck, I don't have any regrets about tearing the lining open so I can slip the *na'at* inside. I'll still pack Azazel's knife for backup, but from now on, my primary weapons are the ones that will keep attackers the hell away from me. I didn't crawl back to Earth just to go bankrupt buying new shirts.

It takes me a minute to find where I stashed Muninn's money. I slipped it into the back of a Val Lewton box set that was blown against the far wall. I take a wad of bills from inside and toss the box on the bed.

With the overcoat tucked under my arm, I lock up the room and slip out the back without any of the dudes seeing me.

Aelita is waiting in the alley, standing there like the angel of death in librarian drag. I drop the coat and take a couple of steps into the alley so my back isn't pinned to the wall.

I say, "You're big on the *Fortune* magazine look. Know any decent dry cleaners around here?"

She shakes her head and shoots poison darts at me with her eyes. Or she wishes she could.

"The Vigil saw you last night. What you did with that man. You're disgusting."

"I'm an Abomination. What do you expect? If you clowns really did have me on your radar, you'd know I was just taking out the trash and that I didn't kill Kasabian. He was killed by someone you should have dealt with a long time ago."

"You followed the poor man into death and tormented him even there."

"I talked to him. I gave him a job recommendation. I helped him more than you ever helped me."

"I offered you help just yesterday. Help and redemption."

"You helped me so much that I had to get glued back together again by Doc Kinski."

"Don't speak that name in front of me!" she shouts. "He's the only creature alive more vile than you."

"Thanks. You hating Kinski makes me feel a lot better about the guy. Maybe I'll let him cut me open after all."

"Why wait? I can do that for you right now."

"Yeah, but when Kinski cuts me, he won't have a hard-on while he's doing it."

"You dare speak to an angel of the Lord that way?"

"If I hurt your feelings, get God down here so I can tell Him to His face."

"Maybe you are worse than Kinski."

"You're the most useless thing I've ever met. Even the worst Hellion has a purpose. What's yours? You can't keep a treaty from falling apart that might destroy the world. You don't even go after Mason. Why is that?"

"Don't you dare interrogate me. We've been looking for Mason for many years."

"But that's not the same as finding him, is it? I mean, the way no one seems to be dealing with the guy makes me wonder if there isn't something else going on."

"We are agents of Heaven and do its bidding."

"And while you do, you let Parker roam around free, slaughtering people, hoping he'll lead you back to the big boy. How many people has Parker killed in the last eleven years and you didn't do anything about it?"

"You're suddenly so concerned about death? People die

around you every day and you barely seem to notice. What does that make you?"

"Fuck you, angel. Fuck you and all God's little prison bitches. He slips you some cigarettes and a con job smile and you run off to do his dirty work for him. Go and scare some sinners. No one's listening to you here."

I can't read an angel the way I can a human, but I can read a fighter's body. Aelita shifts slightly, sliding one foot back a few millimeters at a time, letting her weight settle on her back leg.

"God can still save you, Abomination. He can't change the vile thing you are, but through me he can save you from perdition."

"If it's all the same to you, I'd rather go to Hell."

"So be it."

Aelita must have been holding back yesterday. She manifests her flaming sword incredibly fast and shoots forward like a bullet. Thing is, I'm pretty fast, too. Especially when I know what an opponent is going to do. Before she charges me, I already have the *na'at* out, extended, and I'm sidestepping her. When she blasts forward at me, she also impales herself on one side of the *na'at*, like she's run onto the cutting edge of a chain saw.

Aelita freezes for a second, stunned to find her angelic body sliced through. That gives me a chance to give the *na'at* a slight turn so that the barbs lock into her. She lets out a monstrous roar, something to rattle Heaven's gates. Buildings shudder and car alarms go off. I can't let go of the *na'at* to cover my ears. Her scream is like a vise crushing my skull.

She swings her sword at my head and tries to move forward, but she's stuck on the *na'at*. I push a stud in the handle and step back, locking her in place while extending the *na'at* so her sword can't reach me.

Aelita is strong. She lunges at me, but each time she moves she just drives the *na'at*'s razor edge deeper into her body. She stops moving and stands there bleeding. Turning pale. After a few minutes, her sword dims and flickers out. She refuses to fall. She won't submit to an Abomination. If I didn't hate her so much already, I'd probably like her.

Then she crumbles all at once. Like someone pulled the plug and shut her down. When she's flat on her back, I turn the *na'at* to release the barbs, pull it from her chest, and retract it.

Slipping it back inside my jacket, I go over to have a look at her. Her eyes are open, and even though she's looking up, I know she's not looking at the sky. She's looking a lot farther away than that. I wonder what she sees.

"You'll suffer for this, Abomination. Do you know that? God sees everything and He sees you."

"Does He see you? I have an idea. Call God to come down and save you." I look up at the sky with her. "Nothing." I look down again and shrug. "I guess you're expendable, too."

"I hate you more than anything I've ever seen or known."

"There we go. The truth. You hate me. Not for God's sake, but for yours. Feels good, doesn't it? Feels human."

I wonder if an angel can die the way humans do. I wonder what happens to their bodies. Does their spirit go back to Heaven or Hell or do they just evaporate?

I kneel by Aelita's head. She looks up at me, sort of blank.

"I've been thinking about it. Remember when I asked you why God left me in Hell and you said that He probably thought I was where I should be? Maybe He thought I should be here today. To face you down in this alley. Maybe He wants me to finish what I came here for, only to do that, I had to get past you first. It's something for both of us to think about."

Aelita straightens out her arm and tries to manifest her sword. A fighter to the end. Maybe I do like her a little after all. No. I don't.

I don't really believe that angels can die the way we do. And God wouldn't let an important one like Aelita go so easily. Wells and his Golden Vigil buddies and half of Homeland Security are probably on their way over right now. Time for me to find a cleaners, buy some clothes, and generally, not be here.

THERE'S ONE GOOD way to always get what you want from someone who doesn't necessarily want to sell you something. Pay in advance and pay too much. When you're dropping off a coat covered in blood and plaster dust, it's no time to cheap out. The old lady behind the dry-cleaning counter gives me a I-might-call-the-cops look over the tops of her glasses. I slip her one of Muninn's hundred-dollar bills, and just like that, all is forgiven. The coat will be ready later tonight. Civilians really need to remember this. Cash is the magic that anyone can do.

Where did all the Kissi go? The streets were lousy with them yesterday and now they're as gone as a Friday block-buster with a bad weekend gross.

What the hell is wrong with L.A.? Full of magicians, alchemists, bloodsuckers, soul suckers, the Golden Vigil, and federally funded angels, and no one's been able to touch Mason? That doesn't make any sense. It stinks of protection. It smells like a conspiracy, but I don't believe in conspiracies. Guys will say anything to get laid. If some CIA guy thought he could get a little action by showing a coed how he was the guy on the Grassy Knoll, he'd do it and we'd all know about it by now. But if there's no conspiracy, what does that mean? Maybe there's an ass-hole A-list that no one told me about. Shake hands with the forces of darkness and get a gift bag from Neiman Marcus and a free pass on murder and apocalyptic power plays.

Is Mason bulletproof because he's tight with the Kissi? Is everyone really that afraid? What did he have to do to cozy up to that celestial vermin anyway? What did he have to steal? Who did he have to kill? What Lovecraftian sewer slug did he have to blow to get up close and personal with God's bastard kids?

I don't believe in conspiracies, but I do believe in bullshit and I believe I'm up to my balls in it right now.

I throw the Veritas and it comes up showing a tangle of what looks almost like barbed wire. The thorn forest in Sheol, Downtown's wild western region. Caatinga thorns will strip and debone anything that wanders into them faster than a piranha with a chain saw. Roughly translated, the Hellion script around the edge of the coin reads, *It's not too late to go back and get your GED.* I can't tell anymore if the Veritas is giving me advice or just making fun of my doomed ass.

I've pretty much used up any sense of charity or obligation I might have had in this lifetime, but I don't want to turn into just another L.A. dick looking out for number one. I get out my cell and dial Allegra's number. She doesn't pick up. I dial my old number, but no one picks up at Vidocq's. I text Allegra the way I'd seen her text her friends: *Keep yr doors locked. Mason 3's suicide bombers.*

I wonder if Wells and his G-men have picked up Aelita. It couldn't hurt to make a quick check. The Chinese believe that having a funeral home near your store is bad luck in general and lousy for business. How bad must a dying angel outside your back door be?

I pick up a Jag outside a raw food restaurant next to a tanning salon. Isn't a tanning salon in L.A. like a frostbite salon in Fairbanks?

There's no one is behind me, so I can do a slow drive-by at Max Overdrive and get a look in the alley. Aelita isn't there. There's no blood. No scorch mark from her sword. No sign that anything has ever happened there. Thank you, Marshal. I'll drink to your health on New Year's.

I'D BE A happy camper if between now, when I kill Mason, and when I'm back Downtown, I didn't have to speak to anyone. But that's not how this is going to work out. I drive the Jag over to Allegra's apartment and pound on her door. Do it loud enough and long enough that one of her neighbors comes out and explains to me that she hasn't been home in a couple of days and that I should fuck off. I drive over to Vidocq's and ditch the Jag a few blocks away. There's a little bodega on the corner. I step into a shadow beside it. Two gray-haired men sitting on plastic milk crates and drinking beer ignore the weird white boy doing weird-white-boy stuff.

Vidocq's door is open. That's not so bad all on its own. The door opens and closes all the time when he goes in and out. But now it's standing open and the vaguely diffuse glow that signals a glamour is gone, like someone took soap and water and washed it off.

"When did they put an apartment in over there?"

A nosy neighbor stands down the hall staring at the open door. He wants to see it, but he won't get any closer, like maybe the place is radioactive.

"Stay here," I tell him, and reach under my jacket for the *na'at*. The day I don't pack a gun, that's when I really want one.

"Should you go in there? Should I call the landlord?"

I throw him a quick keep-talking-and-you'll-be-shitting-out-your-tongue look and he backs off.

There's something really wrong with the apartment. Like the one out-of-tune string on a guitar. I can feel it before I even get inside. When I step over the threshold, something else hits. A taste and a smell. Vinegar at the back of my throat. Josef smelled like that when the Kissi revealed themselves. Not that I need another clue that there's something wrong with Vidocq's place.

The walls, ceiling, and floor are covered in twisting, spiky ideograms and letters, intertwined with endless spirals. Spirit faces or maybe images of God the Father, looking more like some saucer-eyed alien than a deity, are smeared around the room. The colors run from rust to a snaky, metallic green, but I've smelled enough dried blood in my time to know what the basic ingredient in all these pigments is.

I stop and I listen, waiting for something. The nosy neighbor is so freaked out, I can feel his heart and breathing. *Don't stroke out, guy. We've got enough problems here.*

Or not. I don't feel anything. There's nothing alive in the apartment. I can't read the Kissi, but between my own heightened senses and the new sight that Aelita has given me, I think I'd know if there was a Kissi lurking in the corner with a lamp shade on its head. As much as I don't want to wrestle anything magic for a while, not finding a single Kissi is a letdown. Finding the body is worse.

It's a man's body. Naked. Nailed face-first to the wall about six feet off the ground. Someone has carefully peeled back the outer layers of skin. Let them fall back like pale, fleshy leaves on a plant, leaving the muscles and bones untouched. There are only two or three drops of blood on the floor. At least I know where the blood for the frescoes came from. And that whoever peeled and drained a body that cleanly really knew what he or she or they were doing.

The body is nailed the wrong way around for me to see the face. I can tell from here that it's the body of a middle-aged man. Vidocq has been in his fifties for two hundred years. Is that still middle-aged? I wish the old bastard had some tattoos I could look for. The body is too badly beaten up to look for scars.

I know I should take the body down. All I have to do is stand on a chair, yank the nails from the hands, and it's taken care of. But I don't want to get near it. I can't look away, either. I had the same reaction seeing my father at the funeral home. I couldn't get near him and I couldn't move away. My brain knew that I needed to react, but my body wouldn't go along with any of it. I only got over it by forcing myself to go to my father's body and touch his face. Looking just vapor-locked my brain. I had to feel that he was dead.

There's a stepladder next to the refrigerator in the kitchen. I bring it to the living room and open it up right below the body. Before I can start the dirty work, out of the corner of my eye I see the nosy neighbor sticking his nosy face in where it shouldn't be.

"Oh God. Oh my God. I'm calling the cops."

I move fast. Fast enough that I scare him more than the body does. Before he can finish dialing, I snatch the cell phone out of his hand and perp-walk him to a window. Lean him out and make him watch as I drop his phone into a Dumpster several floors below.

I say, "Go get it. Then you can call."

Nosy Neighbor looks at me like I just told him that I'm Darth Vader and I fucked his sister, but he doesn't say a word. He heads straight for the stairs.

Back at the body, I pull the nails from the feet first. They're some kind of heavy concrete nail. Perfect for going through muscle and bone and into a wall stud.

With the feet free, I can get the body down on the ground. I climb onto the top step of the stepladder. Yank one nail out of one hand and the other out of the other. Suddenly free, the body drops heavily into my arms. The limbs flop. The head tilts, snaps, and falls off.

Too much. I let go and it hits the ground.

I should have seen it the moment I started to move the body, but I was distracted, trying to decide between collapsing into a queasy heap or pulling a John Wayne to see what was right in front of me.

Kasabian's corpse is lying on the floor. That's why the

body is so beaten up. The Kissi didn't torture Vidocq. They just stitched back together what Parker blew apart last night.

How do you steal and clean a body from the bottom of a ten-thousand-year-old tar pit? *Why* do you steal and clean a body from the bottom of a ten-thousand-year-old tar pit?

And if Kasabian's boomerang corpse is here on the floor, where are Vidocq and Allegra?

My phone rings. I thumb it on.

"Boo. Fooled you with your own dead guy." It's Parker. "I bet right about now you're wondering where your friends are."

"How are you seeing me?"

"Look around you, shit for brains. There's eyes everywhere."

"The paintings."

"There's this thing called magic. Maybe you've heard of it."

"Where are Vidocq and Allegra?"

"Relax, sweetheart. They're fine. In fact, we're having a New Year's party tonight and you're invited."

"At Avila?"

"How do you walk around with that big brain? Yeah, Avila. It'll be a blast. We're gonna raise a little hell. Get your ass there before midnight."

"I'll be there."

"This is a personal invitation. No guests. No plus ones.

If I see a cloud of dust behind you, Señor Frog and that little slice of cherry pie go right in the wood chipper."

"I'll be there."

"Before midnight. That's twelve. When the big hand and the little hands are straight up."

"Either one of them gets hurt, I'm going to personally teach you the Tombstone Dog Paddle."

"That another scary trick you learned in Hell?"

"No. Wild Bill told my great-granddad about it. It's where I take you down the river. Someplace the ground is soft and wet. I break your arms and legs. You fingers and toes. Your neck and back. I dig a hole in the wet, soft ground, put you inside, and fill it back up. Then I have a cigarette and wait for you to dig your way out."

"Before twelve," says Parker, and hangs up.

IF I LEARNED anything Downtown, it's this: the only real difference between an enemy and a friend is the day of the week.

I go back to where I abandoned the Jag, jam the knife in the ignition, and aim the car west, then south, heading back along the same surface streets I traveled with Wells once before. A good sense of direction can get you into or out of a lot of trouble.

Who's higher on the food chain? The Golden Vigil or Homeland Security? The feds are probably picking up the tab for the operation, but that probably has more to do to with Washington control freaks and politicians who want their names next to supersecret intelligence groups. Wanting to put *Ran CIA* or *Busted terrorist cell* on your résumé when you run for president seems obvious, but would telling people that you run angels and G-men who keep the world safe from chaos creatures on the edge of the universe help your political career or get you a syringe full of Thorazine and a lifetime supply of adult diapers? What does whoever runs the Vigil back in D.C. put on their quarterly work reports? At least, the people that person reports to must know what the Vigil does. But what do you tell oversight committees and budget fascists? "We need that extra billion for a gun that will turn vampires into dog food and dark angels into the filling for Bavarian cream doughnuts." Who runs this sideshow and what do they want?

If what I'd read was right, it was all a joke anyway. Before the morning herd came into Max Overdrive this morning, I looked up the Golden Vigil on an occult encyclopedia Web site. The Golden Vigil has been around at least since the First Crusade in the eleventh century. That's when the Brits and the French started writing about it.

According to some of those stories, the Vigil was a splinter cell of the original Hashishin, the frat-house assassination cult that was the Al Qaeda of its day. While the regular Hashishin stuck to *Dirty Harry* jihadist political power-structure attacks, the Golden Vigil went after invisible enemies.

The French chroniclers insist that the Vigil is much older than most people realize, and that its origins might actually explain how and why some of the first tribes stopped chasing game up and down the Fertile Crescent and settled down to build the world's first trailer parks along the Euphrates. If the Kissi have been here for as long as Aelita said, it makes sense. It means that the Vigil has been around for at least eight to ten thousand years. Even longer, if the tribes were negotiating with the Kissi when they first wandered up out of Africa. That would push the Vigil's origins back to around seventy thousand years, according to another encyclopedia site.

Which brings us back to the question of who's the big meat eater along this food chain, Homeland Security or the Golden Vigil? Whoever controls the money is in the driver's seat. The gray-suit guys back east might pony up the money now, but I have a hard time believing that if Washington pulled the plug, the Vigil couldn't support itself. You can stuff a lot of loot into the cookie jar over seventy thousand years.

WHEN I PULL into the parking lot of the Vigil's warehouse, a couple of G-men dressed like rent-a-cops hold up their hands for me to stop. Being highly trained security professionals with keen powers of observation, they leap and lurch out of the way when they see that I'm not slowing down. By the time I'm up to the warehouse entrance and out of the Jag, six of them have surrounded me and each one of them has an identical Glock 9mm pointed at my head. I hate Glocks. Guys who love Glocks love Corvettes. Not because it was a hot car, but because it was cool forty years ago and they once saw a picture of Steve McQueen in one. Their dad probably had a Vette when he was young, but he was never cool. But if they have a Vette, maybe they can forget the fat man who made them mow the lawn when they should have been out with their friends sneaking into R-rated movies, and who embarrassed them in front of their first girlfriends. Maybe their dad was the guy driving fast and locking lips with Faye Dunaway in *The Thomas Crown Affair*. Maybe their dad was cool after all and maybe that made them cool, too. That's what Glocks are. High-precision killing machines that scream "Daddy Issues."

They come on attack-dog fierce, but no one seems eager to pull the trigger. Lucky me. I don't want to get shot. Lucky them. I know these guys are just the hired help, but right now I really want to hurt someone.

A couple of them are talking into their sleeves, nodding to the air. Another minute of the silent Sergio Leone standoff and Wells comes out of the warehouse, banging the door open.

"I ought to let these men shoot you. You drove straight here, shitsack. Did you, even for a second, think about who might be watching or tailing you?"

"Not even for a second."

He nods to his men.

"Bring him inside."

"I want to talk to you, not your Boy Scouts."

"I don't want to talk to you at all out here. Shut up until we're somewhere secure."

I keep my mouth shut. I don't need any more enemies. Well, any more enemies who want to see me turned into chum any more than they already do.

We pass through the electric Jell-O interior barrier and the work floor appears. It's different inside. Like Vegas on the Fourth of July. All lights, machine noise, a din of voices, welding sparks like fireworks. Vigil members are trying out new weapons. Some look like modified guns. Others are like metal parasites attached to their backs, wrapping around their arms and waists. Across the warehouse, they're prepping vehicles. I don't see Aelita, but then, there's no reason she'd want to see me.

Wells says, "We're kinds of busy right now, so talk fast."

"I thought you'd like to know that a couple of civilians have been kidnapped and dragged up to Avila."

"Friends of yours? Then I doubt they're civilians, in the true sense of the word. I mean, in the sense that anyone gives a rat's ass about."

"You're going to leave a couple of innocent people hanging because you have a beef with me?"

"I don't think you'd know innocent if it rode up and bit you in the balls. And, for your information, I don't leave innocent people hanging."

"Then what are you going to do about it?"

Wells sweeps his arm around at all the activity.

"I'm going back to work. We're a little busy right now. Thanks for stopping by."

He turns away, but I put my hand on his shoulder. Hard. Come up right behind him, close enough to snap his neck. When I feel him tense, I know he knows it. I say it all quietly and evenly.

"I can go up there and tear Avila apart on my own. I'm far from bulletproof and they have enough firepower that I'm pretty sure they'll kill me, but I'm going to take a lot of people with me, including every magician in the place. A fight like that, it can't be helped if some of Avila's rich clientele gets burned, including the richest, most important ones. Imagine the shitstorm when all those old-money families and the Sub Rosa find out that you knew what was going down and did nothing about it. Or, you and your Mouseketeers can come with me and we can take the place down together."

"You're a day late and a dollar short, Chuck. What do you think all this is? We're hitting Avila tonight."

"If you're not going for the civilians, what are you going for?"

"We're trying to stop the end of the world, asshole. Which, by the way, is entirely your fault."

I let go of him. He turns around and faces me, rubbing where I held him. He's not lying. I can see that right away. His heart is hammering like a car running third at NASCAR. He smells like anger with a little fear mixed in, but no lies.

"Keep talking," I say.

"You know why you piss me off? It's not that stunt on Rodeo Drive, your schoolyard threats, your pixie friends, or even you wanting to kill every living thing in sight. It's that you think you're alone in the world and that there's nothing going on except for you and your problems."

"Enlighten me. What, are you and your cowboys going up there with your Flash Gordon toys to make them turn down their music?"

He looks over his shoulder, then back at me.

"Do you even know what Avila is? What's going on up there?"

"I've been there. It's the best little whorehouse in Purgatory. So what?"

"Yeah, to the college boys and businessmen in the dumb-ass front rooms, but Avila is a lot more than that to insiders. Avila is a dark-magic power site in a city that's one big power site. What's today's date?"

"I have no idea."

"That's what I mean. You don't know anything. It's New Year's Eve. It's not just another frat party. Tonight is a ritual night. *The* ritual. At midnight, you know all those angels they've been fucking in the back room? They're going to sacrifice each and every one, and when they do, they're going to open up the gates of Hell and let your pal Lucifer and all his Hellion armies stroll through L.A. like it's the goddam Easter parade."

"That doesn't make any sense. Mason runs Avila; why would he want to destroy the world? It could be the Kissi.

They'd love the chaos, but why would they want competition from Hellions?"

"Avila was built for this one purpose. They've been kidnapping and turning angels into whores for as long as anyone can remember."

"And how is this any of my fault?"

"Because you wouldn't stay put. Because you were in Hell, which is the only place that damned key you're carrying around is safe. But Mason got you back here by killing your girlfriend, the one thing he knew you couldn't let go of."

"Would you have let him get away with that?"

"It's not me or my girl we're talking about. You bringing that key to Earth is like opening a tiny crack in the universe. The ritual tonight is going to kick that crack wide open. That's why he killed your girl now. He needed you to get the key to Earth before New Year's."

"So, let's go up and hurt some bad guys."

This time, he puts his hand on my shoulder and turns me to look round the room.

"Wait. There's more, sunshine. Do you see Aelita? No, you don't. You know why? Because some hothead fucked her up and left her in an alley where the Kissi could find her, and they carried her on up the hill. That's right. Aelita's in Avila right now and they're going to kill her in a few hours. So, pardon me if I don't get all choked up about you and yours. I've got my own people to worry about."

I nod, a little numb. I have absolutely no reason to feel

bad about what happens to someone who's tried to kill me twice. But I don't like the idea of throwing anyone, even a crazy, homicidal angel, to Mason. Besides, anything Mason wants, I don't want him to have.

"Okay, Tex. You wanted me, you got me. And before you call me an asshole and tell me to get out, listen: I can give you something that no one else in the world can."

"What?"

"I can walk you and your troops straight inside Avila. Past security and alarms, magicians, and whatever goblins or devil dogs they've hired as lookouts."

Wells looks at me. I can practically see the hamster wheel turning in his head. He so wants to tell me to get out, but he's read my file and knows that I've gotten to some of the best-protected Hellions Downtown. It's fun watching a cop squirm.

"You'll use the key? How? I need to know that my people will be safe."

"I'll walk them straight in. If there's a shadow anywhere, I can get in through it."

"Show me."

"I'm not going to do magic tricks for you. Do you want my help or not?"

He stares at me. Chews the inside of his cheek. He wants a cigarette. He's a secret smoker. I can smell it in his sweat.

"Know what, Tex? I don't need you giving me the pig eye. You need me a lot more than I need you. I can wait until you and the cavalry charge in through the front door and get blown to rags. I'll stroll in after and use your corpses for shields. Have fun getting slaughtered."

"Okay," he says. "This one time."

"One more thing. We have different agendas. I'll get you in, and if I can, I'll step up and help you save the world and all that Boy Scout crap, but not until I get my friends out of harm's way. Deal?"

"The world could end tonight and you're determined to go out a selfish bastard."

"Being up close to you godly types just brings it out in me."

"We have a deal."

I can tell that it's killing him to say it. This is better than ice cream *and* cake for dinner.

Wells says, "But when this is over, you have to have a face-to-face with Aelita over what you did."

"I'll be there. When do we leave?"

Wells checks his watch. Looks up at a big digital countdown clock on the wall. Preparations are picking up in pace. The animals are getting worked up. Attack dogs doing lines of crystal meth, hoping that if they do enough, their teeth will turn to razor blades.

"We figure the last important guests will be there by ten, so we'll go in a little after."

"I'll be back before then."

I start out the way we came in, but I get stopped by a beautiful sight. A heavy metal clothes rack on wheels with a row of brand-new, state-of-the-art body-armor vests. At least fifty of them. I take one off the rack and hold it up.

I yell back at Wells, "I'm taking this."

"Fine. Go." Then, "Wait. One thing."

"What?"

"Stop calling me Tex. I'm from Sparks, Nevada."

"You know the only thing worse than a Texan?"

"What?"

"A pretend Texan."

"Be back before ten or we go without you."

THE KISSI ARE still nowhere to be seen. Something is definitely up. I look out the Jag's window at a couple waiting at a red light, not talking to each other, glaring off in different directions about a stupid fight they just had. A couple of kids in front of a newsstand are picking on another kid. Teen gangsters in training hang on a corner by a liquor store passing a joint around. I want to lean out the window and tell them that world is about to end and they should get their shit together, but why bother?

Does anyone really know what goes on in the world? I used to think these people were a joke because they only believed in their concrete reality and never dreamed of looking below the surface of the world. Most of them, even if they ran face-first into a bunch of Sub Rosa necromancing John the Baptist, Billie Holiday, and Wild Bill back from the dead, they'd never believe or understand it.

I don't understand anything, either. My brain is bouncing back and forth between asking why Mason wants to open up Hell and wondering if that's what's really going on at all. It seems like opening Hell, or pretending to open it, might be a nice distraction. While everyone's looking one way, he does a slip and slide around back and pulls something else. But what?

Mostly, I'm trying not to think at all. I'm never going to get inside Mason's head. I might have been born a better magician, but he's always been smarter. That's why he's going to end up running the carnival and I'm going to end up biting the heads off chickens. But that's thinking, too. I want silence. Big, blank, Zen silence. I need to get back to that calm quiet moment I'd have before I went into the arena. No thought. No action. Thought and action as one. I control my breathing and focus on the road ahead. I can feel the calm coming on.

That's when the siren starts and the light bar pops behind me. Colored lights reflect off the rearview mirror and right into my eyes. A cop's garbled, amplified voice echoes off the glass buildings. I can't understand a word, but I know how to translate this cop haiku: *You're driving around in the same stolen Jag you should have ditched an hour ago. It's not like there aren't other cars in L.A. to steal. But you started thinking and you got distracted and now look what's happened.*

This is really the last thing I need right now. I wonder if they'll let me off with a warning if I tell them I'm going to be trying to save the world later tonight?

The cop voice booms again. They hit me from behind with their searchlight. About a billion candlepower. I stop the car and put it in park.

Thanks for the shadow, Dick Tracy. It's a tight fit, but I can just slip through. I drag the body armor in behind me. I hope that one of the cops sneaks up on the driver's side window in time to see my feet disappear into the dash-board.

I step out into the lobby of the Bradbury Building. The place is dark. Shut down tight. I get into the elevator hoping they haven't cut the power over the holiday. I hit the button. The car shivers and rises, and I can breathe again.

It goes up a floor and stops. I press the one and three buttons at the same time and the car starts moving. I get out when it stops, not sure I did it right. Then the Fury in Muninn's window lunges at me from inside its glass cage. I blow her a kiss, go inside, bump my way through the clut-ter, and head straight down the stairs in back.

Muninn is waiting for me at the bottom.

"My boy! I heard the bell and wondered who'd be coming here tonight. This is usually a quiet evening for me."

"Sorry if I'm keeping you from a party or something."

Muninn laughs.

"My boy, when you've seen as many new years as I have, the last thing you want to do is throw a party for the damned thing."

He takes me by the arm and leads me to a table cov-ered with neatly laid out groups of bones. Fingers. Toes. A whole hand or foot.

"Relics," he says. "Each bone and appendage belonged to one saint or another. I have a client who wants to build a summer home in the form of a sort of ossuary. But only with the bones of saints. No commoners allowed. As you might imagine, that takes quite a lot of bones. I'm just cataloging this batch tonight."

He goes to a shelf and takes down the same dusty bottle we drank from after Vidocq and I got back from Avila. He gets two small glasses and pours us each a drink.

"Thanks," I say, and shotgun it. "I'm in kind of a rush tonight."

"Of course. Sorry," he says. "Just because I ignore the new year doesn't mean you do. My apologies."

"No problem." I clear my throat. "Mr. Muninn. I want to make a deal with you. A big one."

"I'm always open to a good trade. What would you like?"

"It's not what I want. It's what you want. You're going to want this." I reach under my shirt and take off the coin. I set it on the table and push it toward him. Muninn looks at it without touching it.

"Is that a Veritas?"

"Straight from a Hellion general's pocket."

"You've had it all this time?"

"I brought it back with me."

"My boy, I could have made you a very rich man by now, if I'd known that. Does it work?"

"Like a charm. Take it for a test drive."

"You're the experienced one. What's the proper way?"

"There's no trick to it. Just hold it and ask your question. Say it in your head, not out loud. Saying it out loud won't ruin the magic. Just makes you sound like a mental patient."

Muninn picks up the Veritas slowly, like it might shock him. He makes a fist and closes his eyes. A moment later, he opens his hand and laughs at what he sees.

"Well?"

"I asked if buying it would be a good deal. It presented me with a lovely view of Abaddon's bottomless pit, lit in such way as to look like a large, not terribly clean sphincter. Along with that is a message on one side of the coin telling me that I'm an impotent, flatulent, fat, old fuck, and on the other side, telling me that it's a good investment only if I like having hot coals shoved down my throat by Hellion cocks."

"What do you think?"

"I think it's brilliant. I must have it. What do you want for it? Money? I know you like money. I'll give you a lot for this. Enough for this lifetime and for your children's children."

"No. This is too big for money. I want something special for the Veritas. Something cool. Something apocalyptic."

Mr. Muninn smiles at me like he might end up celebrating New Year's after all.

HAVING LEARNED MY lesson with the Jag, I go through the room to Max Overdrive. Upstairs, I toss the bedroom like a nervous B&E guy, shoving broken furniture and video players against the walls. It's nice to be strong at moments like this. I shove the bed frame and all the furniture into one corner of the room without breaking a sweat. Eventually, when I've tossed enough junk into enough piles, I've found all my guns. Then the bullets and shells. Then the bottle of Spiritus Dei. I guess the stuff really is as magical as Vidocq said. The bottle is sitting upright and is perfectly clean. Everything else in the room is covered in plaster dust and lying on its side.

The pistols are already loaded with bullets dipped in Spiritus. I go downstairs and find a paint-caked hacksaw in the little storage room behind the porn section. I take it upstairs and start sawing down the Benelli shotgun. Sawing down a simple double-barrel model is easy. You can cut the barrel down all the way to the front of the shell. Turn your long-range shotgun into a short-range blunderbuss. I don't want to go that far with the Benelli. I just saw off most of the stock, down to the curved part of the grip, so that it fits into my hand like an oversize pistol. I find a ball of heavy twine from under the bootleg table and tie a tight knot around the grip, then tie off a loop so that the gun can hang off my shoulder under my coat. Simple, crude, and deadly. What Clyde Barrow and Bonnie Parker called a Whip-It gun because you could whip it out from under your coat before anyone knew what was going on.

I'm moving, staying in motion, doing things that feel like they make sense, but how do you accessorize for the end of the world? When you're not sure what to bring, I figure you should bring everything. Four handguns, a shotgun, a Hellion knife, and the *na'at* feel like a good look for me.

I dip each shotgun shell into a little Spiritus and chamber it. Eight rounds in all. Then I sprinkle Spiritus on the shotgun itself. Why be stingy? I sprinkle Spiritus on all the guns, keeping my thumb over the top of the bottle to control the flow. I'm Martha Stewart spritzing my orchids. While I'm on a roll, I toss Spiritus onto the body armor and my coat, and wipe the rest on my hands.

Wild Bill might have been the greatest shootist of his time, but he had a habit that's come back to bite me in the ass. Wild Bill didn't believe in holsters. He carried his Navy Colts tucked in a red sash he wore around his waist, a fashion back then. I didn't grow up using holsters, either. It's easy to tuck one big gun down the back of your jeans, but it's not so good for four.

Time for a sacrifice. I slit both side pockets on my coat a few inches, long enough so that the Colt .45 and the LeMat can rest inside, but far enough out that I can quick draw them. When I get the cuts the right length, I reinforce the interior and sides of the pockets with duct tape.

This is one of the reasons I'll never own a car. I'm hard on things. Everything ends up broken, ripped apart, modified, stuck together, or shot to shit. I'd be naked as Adam and cold as a polar bear if it weren't for duct tape.

If anyone ever asks you what a desperate man looks like, you can tell them that he looks like this: He's down on his hands and knees, digging through the ruins of his exploded bedroom, looking for a cigarette. If he looks hard enough, he might find a real treasure, like a bent, but only half-smoked butt. I hold it up like the Holy Grail, blow off as much of the dust as I can, and fire it up with Mason's lighter. Like my grandmother used to say, "I am blessed and highly favored."

I get out my cell and dial Kinski's number. Candy answers.

"Are you always the designated phone answerer over there?"

"Stark? Doc doesn't like phones. He thinks they're too disembodied."

"I'd love to be disembodied. All my problems solved at once."

"Ghosts don't smoke or get to drink Jack Daniel's."

"Forget it, then. I'll live forever."

"That's a better plan than what you had the last time we talked."

"That's why I called. I wanted to ask about some of that. I know you're taking the cure and trying to stay clean and all, but we're still a lot the same, too. Still monsters under the skin."

"Why do you want to talk about that?"

"I was wondering if maybe you'd like to go do something with me tonight. Some friends and me, we're going to crash a New Year's Eve party and kill a whole bunch of people."

"Why, Stark. Are you flirting with me? You bad boy."

"We're going to stop a mass sacrifice, so there's going to be a lot of bad guys. I figure that having as many experienced killers as possible will help even out the odds. But it sounded like Doc Kinski's clipped your wings. You haven't tasted a human in a long time, have you?"

"Doc makes me this amazing cocktail. My iced frappuccino people substitute, I call it. I haven't fed on anyone in two years, three months, and eight days."

"If you've ever had the itch, here's your chance. And this time when you're killing, you'll be on the side of the angels. Literally."

"You sure know how to turn a girl's head." She doesn't say anything for a minute.

"Candy?"

"I'll have to talk to Doc first. I can't lie to him."

"I understand. It's up to you. My friends and me, we're going to be at Club Avila a little after ten. You know where that is?"

"Everyone knows where Avila is."

"This party is going to be special. Assuming the world doesn't end, no one is ever going to forget it."

"I'll try to be there."

"One more thing."

"Yes?"

"Thanks for treating me like, you know, a person through all this shit. I know that isn't always easy."

"You do have a habit of pissing on other people's welcome mats. But, when a gentleman gives you a booty call to a massacre, it's easy to forgive him. Ciao."

I finish my cigarette and start getting ready. I strap on the body armor, which feels tough enough, but closes with Velcro strips. I know this is state-of-the-art gear, but I'd feel more confident if it wasn't held together with the same stuff they use to fasten kids' sneakers.

I'm going to feel really bad if this all falls apart tonight. I don't want the last thing I say to Vidocq and Allegra to be "Get out."

I tuck the Navy Colt and the Browning into the back of my jeans.

Two more dead like Alice. Two more who don't deserve it.

The looped cord on the Benelli Whip-It gun goes over my shoulder and the coat goes on over that.

Will Avila be full of Kissi? If that's who's waiting for us, this is going to be a very bad, very short night for anything with a pulse.

The Colt .45 and the LeMat pistols go in the coat pockets, butt ends out.

They must be partying hard Downtown tonight, waiting for the velvet rope to come down and the doors to the VIP section of Creation to be blown off their hinges.

What's going on in Heaven? Are all the ranks of the angelic throng on their knees, praying for humanity's faith in the Word to pull them through? Me, I bet it's more like a sports bar the night before the Super Bowl. Crowds of drunken, winged frat boys with team hats and big foam fingers. Maybe that's why Heaven is silent and God doesn't speak to Man anymore. Heavenly intervention would blow the point spread.

THERE'S TOO MUCH weird, magic-cloaking static and protection hoodoo around the Vigil's warehouse. I don't have time to find a straight path inside through the room, so I have to use a shadow a few blocks south and run the rest of the way.

A line of low-profile, matte-black transports warm up their engines in the parking lot. They're nearly silent, and where their bodies touch the dark, they disappear. Stealth party vans. If I'd known about these, I wouldn't have bothered stealing all those cars.

The rear hatch of the lead van is open. Wells motions me over, squinting at me like a constipated Clint Eastwood.

"Why'd I know you were going to cut it short? Two more minutes and we'd have been gone."

"Your damned Flatulence Accelerator has the whole area fuzzed out. I had to walk halfway here."

Wells holds up a hand. "Wait. You couldn't even get

here with the pixie hocus pocus you're going to use to get us into Avila? I am not filled with confidence."

"Relax. I've already broken into Avila. They don't have anything like your setup."

"And what if they have? What if they've brought in a load of technology and dark magicians?"

"Then we do it your way. Blow the place open. Take heavy losses. Get inside. We're walking into the O.K. Corral. You want a guarantee that your hair won't get mussed, Marshal Wells?"

"You get any of my people killed unnecessarily, I'm coming after you."

"Take a number."

Wells steps up into the transport. I take a quick look around the lot. No sign of Candy. Guess she really has taken the cure.

I get in the transport and squeeze into a seat next to Wells.

THE TRANSPORT MIGHT have been quiet outside, but inside it's like sitting in a washing machine. None of the Vigil crew is talking. A few are praying, but most probably don't want to have to shout over the noise.

Wells's G-men are wrapped up in weird electronics and nylon webbing, and holding strange guns. Some are in aluminum-coated full-body suits like foundry workers. The rest are in black pants and skintight tops that stretch over their heads like balaclavas. The ones not carrying guns are wrapped up in metal exoskeletons like they're being raped by robots.

I lean over and shout into Wells's ear.

"Seriously, you people should try to learn just a little magic. I saw celestial types working at your warehouse. They could teach you something. I know you civilians can't handle any really heavy magic, but maybe you could pick up something useful so you wouldn't have to dress up like the Terminator's retarded cousin."

Wells shouts back, "Learn your kind of magic so I can spend eternity in Hell with people like you? No thanks. I'll stick to the weapons Heaven's given us."

"You'd think if Heaven was that completely on your side, it'd be a little more helpful."

"Aelita, God's hand on Earth, is on our side. You'd be able to understand that if you didn't have a soul dirtier than a hobo's boxer shorts."

"All I'm saying is that I don't trust either side. Heaven just might be hedging its bets."

"I'm sure that's what you think, but our weapons have never failed us yet."

"Suit yourself. But with magic, I don't ever run out of ammo."

"No, just brains."

WE STICK TO backstreets until we get north of the city, then cut overland through the hills and canyons until we cut south near the Stone Canyon reservoir. Come down through Bel Air, paralleling North Beverly Glen Boulevard. The drivers up front wear helmets like fighter pilots, with night vision and heads-up displays. Monitors over our heads show us what they're seeing. It's nothing special. Trees as we mow our way through the hills. Flares and pinpoints of light when we come close to a housing development. This is either the worst amusement park ride in history or I'm back in Hell.

Soon we're at the bottom of one especially tall hill with lights like a piece of the sun is sitting on top. That's how Club Avila looks through night vision. To anyone driving by, it would be just another gated mansion.

There are six transports in our convoy. Four of us stay put while two drive onto Beverly Glen so they can roll up to Avila's front door.

Wells say, "We're flanking them. A-team will initiate the attack at the front, drawing the club's security that way. You're going to get us inside so we can attack from the rear."

I nod.

"Listen to me," says Wells. "I don't want this to be the last night of the world, so I'm going to ask you one more time, are you sure you can get us all inside? There's still time to catch up with the other team if you can't."

I say, "I was in a rush earlier. I didn't take the time to find a good way in. But I can walk into Heaven or Hell or anywhere in between. I can damn sure walk us into this place."

"You know I'm going to shoot you if you say you can and you can't."

"That won't kill me, but I tell you what. If I can't get us inside, I'll show you what will."

Wells looks back, nods at his G-men, and then turns back to me.

"Let's get going."

I swing up the Whip-It gun and pump a shell into the chamber.

"What was all that BS in the transport about you only using magic?"

"This *is* magic. Wild Bill magic."

"Just get us inside, Sandman Slick."

"Hold on to my shoulder and keep your eyes shut. Tell the guy behind you to do the same thing and all the way down the line. Whatever you do, don't open your eyes or let go of me until you're completely inside Avila. You don't want to be stuck with half your ass sticking out of a hill."

Wells passes the instructions down the line. I should have bought blindfolds. I hope I scared Wells and his crew enough to really keep their eyes closed. The Vigil just wants to get inside the club. I don't need everyone who works for them knowing about the Room of Thirteen Doors.

Wells comes back a minute later and thumps his hand on my shoulder.

"Time for you to redeem your sorry ass."

"Okay, Dorothy, click your heels together three times and say, 'There's no place like home.'"

I step into the dark at the bottom of the hill. I've never tried to walk this many people in and out of a shadow before. I hope I don't kill everyone.

A second later, we're inside Jayne's office in the club. It looks pretty much the same as when Vidocq and I were here a day or two ago. I doubt anyone has been inside since Jayne turned up dead.

"You can open your eyes," I say.

"Gabriel's swinging blue balls, boy. You did it. You actually did something."

"Thanks, Dad."

The room fills up fast. Vigil members gasp and cross themselves when they open their eyes and see that they're still alive. I pull Wells over by the office door so that we'll be the first ones out. If there's an ambush outside, I don't want him to miss a second of it.

"What do we do now?" I ask.

"Wait. I'll tell you when to go."

It gets hard to move as the last of the Vigil crew comes through the room.

"This isn't a raid. It's a Marx Brothers movie."

"Shut up."

A blast rocks the whole building. Another blast hits a second later. Avila shudders, like the building is floating on water. I reach for the door, but Wells grabs my arm.

"Wait," he says.

Thunder in the hall as people stampede past the office. Harsh voices yelling over the noise.

"Move! Security! Out of the way!"

There's a sizzle and a wave of static electricity pulses through the wall, making the hairs on my arms stand up. That was a magician, clearing the hall the quick way. The smell of the burned bodies makes some of the Vigil crew gag. I smelled enough of it Downtown that it's familiar and even sort of comforting. I really hope there aren't any mind readers with us.

"Okay," Wells says.

I step into the hall, shotgun first. Wells is behind me, ordering his troops to split up and head out in different directions.

I wait until he's done and say, "I got you in. That was our deal. Now I have my own to do."

"This is the world we're fighting for."

"*You're* fighting for. I'm here for my friends."

He shakes his head and moves off with some of his people to the back of the club.

I keep my head down and move in a slow lope to the front, where the fighting is the loudest. I have no idea where to start looking for Vidocq or Allegra, but if I can get hold of one of the human security guards, I bet I can make him sing me a song.

It's all *Scarface* gunfire and flashes of murder magic up front. A young magician in a bloody tuxedo shirt sprints around the corner, sees me, and shrieks a death hex. A swirling vortex like black smoke shoots from this chest. I fire the Benelli twice. The Spiritus-dipped shot rips through the smoke, tearing it to pieces, before slamming into the magician's chest. He goes down and doesn't move.

I run straight into the chaos. I don't even bother shooting the human security. Why waste supercharged ordnance on civilians? Their gunfire can't get through the Vigil's body armor, which gives me plenty of time to work. I elbow one security guard in the throat, crushing his windpipe. Get my arm around another's head and plant my knee in his back. Pull and push, and his spine snaps.

There are still plenty of magicians firing wildly, hitting as many of Avila's men as the Vigil's. Three or four of them spot me in the middle of the firefight. They fire their deadliest spells all at once.

A crawling wave of red lightning rimmed with bright blue sizzles across the floor and ceiling. A smoking death-spell vortex spins through the center.

In the Old West, they called shotguns "street sweepers," and that's how I use the Benelli. I open up, firing into the eye of the shitstorm, sweeping the gun barrel from left to right.

The magic breaks apart. Flies like shrapnel in all directions, burning anything it lands on and turning some human security guards into pillars of fire.

Blowing their curses apart catches the magicians off guard. The shotgun blasts three of them dead. The last one, a blond, blue-eyed, fashion-model type, falls over backward, minus her left arm. She's flat on her back, bone jutting from her shoulder, still screaming curses. They swarm from her mouth and carpet the floor in an army of fat, blue-eyed spiders.

The Benelli empty, I rip the cord off my shoulder and drop it, while pulling the Colt .45 and the LeMat. I dive to the side, getting off one shot with the Colt. It catches Twiggy at the base of the throat and she falls back dead. Her spider army turns to dust.

The Vigil are holding Avila's killers off, but I need to get out of here and into the back rooms to look for Vidocq and Allegra. All I can do is hunker down and go *Wild Bunch* on the room. I'm faster than just about anyone else at Avila, so I put my head down and sprint through the gunfire. To anyone else, I look like I'm running scared and firing at anything that moves, but I'm carefully aiming and killing the last few magicians I can find.

Something hits me in the knee. It feels like it's on fire. I tuck and roll so that I don't go down on my face. When I get my balance, I'm looking up at another magician ten yards away. A huge, ancient, heavyset man. He could be Lawrence Tierney's stunt double. I bring up the Colt and pull the trigger. *Click*. Damn. The LeMat does the same.

If I had another thirty seconds, I know that I'd be able to stand again and kick Lawrence's head to Argentina. But I don't have thirty seconds. The old man is so close that I can feel the hex building up inside him. As he starts to shout the spell, his jugular explodes.

Something is on top of him, ripping at his throat. It digs its claws into his chest and cracks him open like a boiled lobster. Lawrence doesn't move after that. A blur, the creature spins and grabs my ankle, dragging me behind a grand piano in a corner of the room. I twist around and grab the Browning .45 from behind my back just as it turns on me. I have the trigger half pulled when I realize that the rib cracker is Candy. I twist my arm just in time to pop off the shot in the air.

"Miss me?" she asks. Candy is covered in blood and things I don't want to think about.

"How did you get here?"

"I came up through the woods. When I saw those black trucks, I hitched a ride on top."

I've never seen a Jade in full feral mode before. Candy's nails have curved out into thick claws. Her eyes are red slit pupils in a sea of black ice. Her lips and tongue are as black as her eyes. Her mouth has a slightly different shape. Like she has a few more teeth or the ones she has are wider and sharper than before. A mouthful of pretty white shark's teeth. She's the most beautiful thing I've seen in eleven years. I want to have monster babies with her right here and now. But something explodes, someone screams, and I remember my other friends and the end of the world.

"Parker probably has Vidocq and Allegra at the center of the club, near the sacrifice," I tell her. It's just a guess, but with D-day going on in the front parlor, it's where I'd go.

Candy helps me to my feet. My knee is knitting itself back together. It can almost take my weight, but it's not there yet. Candy slings my right arm over her shoulders, puts her left arm around my waist, and practically picks me up. I didn't know that Jades were that strong. So far, this is the best first date ever.

I talk Candy through the twists and turns I remember from Muninn's blueprints. There isn't much action in the inner rooms. Mostly, it's half-naked civilian assholes cowering behind the furniture, trying not to listen to the slaughterhouse noises from the outer rooms.

Candy and I are almost to the door of the central room.

And about to be monumentally dead.

A couple of Kissi are sitting and smoking on the stone steps outside the sacrifice room. The father-and-son murder act that killed the counter girl at Donut Universe.

"Look what the cat drug in," says the kid.

"Dragged in, but won't drag out," says Dad.

"Let's eat him this time. Eat him and get the shiny thing inside."

"You don't mind, do you?" Dad asks me. He seems to notice Candy for the first time. "Oh, look, he's bought dessert."

"What is she?"

"A filthy, dirty monster, son. Maybe you should nibble her first. I want to see what Mr. Shiny Chest tastes like."

The Kissi aren't carnivores, like the Jades. There's a hint of game playing in their voices. Fear and confusion are the Kissi's favorite snacks and words are a good way to tenderize the meat. Candy takes her arm from around my waist. I can barely stand, but I manage.

The young Kissi circles Candy, but I can't watch long.

Dad is coming for me. My knee still isn't back yet, so I have to stand my ground. It's not my favorite place to be, but I've been here before. You can't avoid an attack, so you hang back, leave yourself open, and let the attacker show you what he's going to do.

The Kissi goes straight for my bad knee. I pivot the best I can to bring the butt of the Browning down on its neck. But he tricks me. Feints for the knee and lunges up at my chest. I'm crippled and off balance. I can't get out of the way in time.

Daddy Kissi plants his shoulder in my sternum and knocks the wind out of me. He's on top of me, pinning me down with his weight. I know what's coming. Fingers inside my chest, like spiders crawling over my ribs. Then he'll pull out my heart and the key with it. When I fell, my arm twisted behind my back. I can't use the Browning or reach my knife.

I get ready for the pain. He brings his hand down hard. But just sort of punches me in the chest.

I look down, then at him. The Kissi looks as surprised as I do. He rears back and slams his hand down again. It just bounces off the body armor. I have a feeling that this isn't part of the armor's original design. But my heart and the key are still where they should be, so I'm not complaining.

The Kissi screeches, "What are you doing? Stop it!"

When he rears back for another try, his weight shifts enough for me to get my hand out from under my leg.

This time, when Daddy Kissi slams into my chest, I wrap my arm around his neck, shove the Browning under his chin, and blast away. The Spiritus bullets blow the Grand Canyon out the back of his head.

I shove his carcass off and look around for Candy. She's on her stomach, tearing out chunks of Avila's polished wood floors with her claws while Junior is on her back with both hands buried inside her spine.

I can move enough to limp up behind Junior, shove the Browning in his ear, and blow half of his head off. Junior falls one way. I fall the other. Candy pushes herself up onto her elbows, crawls over, and collapses on top of me.

"The sacrifice is in there," I say. "We can't stay here."

"I know," Candy says. She sits up and pulls me up with her. We're both streaked with human and Kissi blood. Candy grabs my head and plants a hundred-thousand-volt kiss on my lips. There's something in her saliva that feels like spider venom and speed. Her black tongue draws my tongue into her mouth and her razor-sharp shark teeth slide down the full length of it.

Candy lets go and smiles. She uses her thumb to wipe off some of the blood she's smeared on my lips.

"Thanks for getting him off me," she says.

"Anytime."

She helps me to my feet. I'm still shaky, but I can walk again. I can tell that Junior hurt her, playing around in her lungs. I give her the Browning and the Navy Colt pistols. I pull the *na'at* from my coat. Twist the grip to collapse the center shaft so that it hangs like a whip.

I point to the doors.

"Open sesame," I say.

Candy brings up both guns and blasts open the twin doors.

Inside, it's almost comical. Don't devil worshippers have any imagination? It's like a Hot Topic Halloween party. There's a circle of men wearing long, black, hooded robes. Each man holds a silver dagger. Between each of the men is a drugged, naked starlet wannabe with an inverted pentagram cut into her chest. Up at the altar, the head priest holds a shiny kris over an unconscious angel. The angels are what make the scene not funny. There are thirteen of them. The ones who've been at Avila the longest are filthy. Cut up, pale, and bruised. The newer, less abused ones are hog-tied with bright, diamond-like cords.

With Kissi guards stationed outside, it probably didn't occur to the devil's nitwits to have some security inside. Candy and I are pretty beat up, but they don't know that. Plus, we're armed. Plus, we're covered in enough blood and filth that we look like Hell arrived in the room a little sooner than they expected.

One of the robed satanists takes a swipe at Candy with his dagger and she blows a manhole in his chest with a blast from the Navy Colt. More men charge as the big clock over the altar hits the first midnight chime. Candy wades into the crowd and blasts anyone who gets near her. I swing the *na'at* over my head, let it extend to almost its full length, and crack it like a bullwhip. The high priest's hand and kris knife fly off in different directions. He screams and falls to his knees. Bye-bye, gates of Hell.

The rest of the old-boy coven doesn't seem to notice that they've already lost. They swarm us. Suddenly I'm back in the arena. Swinging the *na'at,* feeling it shear bones just right. Bring my arm up and sweep it down. Let the *na'at*'s own momentum carry it through anything in its way. I could go on killing these guys all night. But I can't go completely wild. The glassy-eyed starlets are standing around like drugged sheep. I muscle them off the killing floor when I can. They fall over like bowling pins with tits.

More satanists are running out of the room than are staying around to fight, which is fine by me. My knee burns me every time I take a step. Candy isn't using the guns anymore. She's back to teeth and claws, a meat grinder in tight jeans and Chuck Taylors.

I collapse the *na'at* and hold my arms out at my sides. The last few hard cases come at me with their daggers. I don't even fight them. I don't have to. They stab and slash and all they hit are my scars. Each knife thrust hurts, but not enough to matter, and none draws blood.

And then it's over.

The last satanists are dead or limping off into the club where the Vigil is waiting for them with hot cocoa and Tasers. The drugged starlets stare at each other trying to remember exactly what they're auditioning for and when wardrobe is going to arrive.

Aelita is lying hog-tied and unconscious at the far end of the altar. The black knife cuts through the diamond cord around her wrists and ankles. I free Aelita, then hand Candy the knife and tell her to free the others.

I pick Aelita up off the bloody floor and carry her back to the front room.

I'm not one hundred percent certain, but I think that two monsters just saved the world. And I couldn't care less.

Parker was supposed to be in the sacrifice room. And he should have had Vidocq and Allegra with him. If they're dead, the world should be, too. It's only fair. But I learned a long time ago that fair doesn't have much to do with how the universe works. If things were fair, Lucifer wouldn't have had to rebel. Adam and Eve wouldn't have been card-sharked out of Eden. The big man's kid wouldn't have been nailed up at Golgotha. And the Kissi would be just another pack of boring angels. And nothing that's happened in the last few days would have happened.

Wells and his crew have Avila secured when I get up front. They're already sorting the living from the dead, the inner-sanctum bastards from the gentleman's-club morons. All the club members still alive are sitting on their asses in the front room, arms and legs locked together with plastic restraints. Politicians, movie producers, stock-market czars, and fair-haired heirs to Babylonian-size fortunes. If the Vigil really wants to do the world a favor, it'll burn Avila down with them inside.

I don't see a single magician among the living. Maybe that's all the fairness I'm going to get tonight. It's better than nothing.

I must look worse than I thought. Or maybe it's because I have Aelita with me. Either way, the entire Vigil crew stops and stares when I carry Aelita in and hand her to Wells.

"She's okay," I tell him. "We stopped the thing before it happened."

"We?"

"My friend Candy and me. She's back there freeing the rest of the angels. You might want to send some of your people back to help her. And bring some bathrobes."

Wells nods and some of the Vigil crew head off the way I came.

Wells kneels and sets Aelita on the floor. He takes a small bottle of what looks like holy water out of a jacket pocket and pours a few drops over each of Aelita's eyes. The angel's lids open a fraction of an inch. She begins to breathe. A Vigil medical team pushes Wells and me out of the way. They wrap Aelita in a Mylar blanket and give her drugs from bottles that look older than the world.

I take off what's left of my silk coat. It's just rags with a hundred bullet holes, a thousand knife slashes, and enough blood to paint a Camaro.

I strip off the body armor and hand it to Wells.

"You should check this out. Either you accidentally made armor that's Kissi-proof or you can make the armor Kissi-proof with some Spiritus Dei."

"Thanks."

I pick up a jacket someone's dropped on the floor and use it to wipe the filth off of my face.

"I never found my friends," I say.

"I'm sorry. We got a lot of bad people tonight, but we lost your pal Parker."

"Parker was here?"

"Yeah. He took off pretty early in the assault. We lost him in the trees below the house. I don't know how."

"Mason probably gave him something to make him invisible or to transport him someplace. Was he alone?"

"As far as I know."

"How well have you searched this place?"

"Well enough that if there were two people who knew you, we'd have found them by now."

I nod toward the line of bodies on the other side of the room.

"What about the dead?"

"We've been watching you, remember? I know what your friends look like. They aren't here."

"I'll need that body armor back for a while."

"Why?"

"I'm going to go get them."

"Be realistic. Parker took off. If he had them, he's killed them. That's what men like Parker do."

"No. They're alive. He wants me to come and find them. Then he can have the fun of killing them in front of me. I think I know where he has them."

"Where's that?"

"The Orange Grove Bungalows on Sunset."

"We used to have that place under surveillance. Sub Rosa kids used it for magic and sex games for years."

"Yeah, we did."

"No one goes there now. It's just pathetic civilians. Strictly crackheads and whores these days."

"It's where he'll have them. It's his idea of a joke." I look at the body armor. "Can I have that back?"

To my surprise, Wells hands me the armor. I put it on and go to the line of corpses. Find a guy a little bit taller and fatter than me with a decent-looking jacket. I slip the jacket off his body and try it on. It fits across my shoulders and is loose enough that when I button it closed, it covers the body armor.

I ask Wells, "You find any usable shotguns?"

"Around the corner. There's a whole pile—help yourself."

I find a nice sawed-off double barrel, about twelve inches long.

"I'm taking this," I say, holding up the sawed-off.

"Be my guest."

Vigil members come from the sacrifice room, carrying angels on stretchers. Candy trails behind them looking more than a little uncomfortable.

I steal a clean cloth from the medical kit of the crew working on Aelita. Go over to Candy. She looks completely human now, except for all the blood and dirt. I put the shotgun in her hands, push her head back, and gently wipe her face. She laughs.

"You sure know how to show a girl a good time, Mr. Stark."

"I try to keep things interesting for my friends."

"So far, so good."

If I was a regular person and Candy was a regular girl and this was a regular moment, I'd be kissing her, but we're not and this isn't. She looks at me like she knows what I'm thinking.

"I should probably give doc a call and let him know everything's all right."

"Yeah. He's probably worried."

"You look like you're going somewhere."

"I know where Parker has Vidocq and Allegra. I'm headed down there now."

"I'll go with you."

"No," I say. "I could be wrong. If I am, I want someone here I can trust to look out for them."

"Okay," she says, sounding a little hurt.

"I should get going."

She looks at the medics working on Aelita. The angel is sitting up now.

"I'm going to call doc in a minute and then I'm going home to him because that's where I belong. I'm going to tell him most of what happened tonight, but not everything. But I want you to know that I'm not sorry for what we did."

"Me neither," I say. "The one good thing about an awkward moment like this is that, with the way we look, the longer we stand here torturing each other, the more likely we are get to get some of these Vigil nervous nellies to pee themselves."

Candy smiles.

"Go," she says. "I'll keep an eye on things here."

"Thanks."

I take the sawed-off from her hands, nod at Wells, and step through a shadow behind the dead magicians. Still the best first date ever.

THE PHONE BOOTH outside the Orange Grove Bungalows hasn't changed much since I was here eleven years ago, except that now there's a guy living in it.

The Orange Grove is a collection of about two dozen small cabins that were twenty years past their prime before I went Downtown. Now they look like a condo complex in Hiroshima the day after the bomb. The bulletproof glass in front of the check-in counter has had a good workout. In eleven years, no one's painted anything or cleaned the pool. There are things wiggling down in the stagnant backwash that I don't even remember seeing in Hell. This is where David Lynch groupies go to lose their virginity on prom night.

There's one specific cabin where we used to party, but I can't remember the number. I walk up and down the concrete walkway that snakes between the cabins. It's New

Year's Eve, so the place is crawling with skinny hookers with black meth teeth and equally skinny johns who can't walk straight. A lot of smells in the air. Pot. Stale cigarettes. There's a lot more piss and the weird burning plastic stink of bad crack. Those are the least offensive.

I spot the badness near the back of the third row. It looks just like the others, but to my eyes, it pulses with chaotic energy. The energy fields around the window and front door are brighter and the colors are more intense than the rest of the cabin. When I put my hand out, the brighter energy morphs into teeth, like a giant cartoon version of the bear trap, and snaps at me. When the civilian hookers and their johns wander by, nothing happens. A tired looking hooker, in a miniskirt way too short for her veiny legs, wanders by alone.

I say, "Hey, darlin', want to make some quick money?"

"I'm done for tonight, honey."

"No hanky-panky. I'm pranking a friend. I just need you to go over there and bang on that door real loud."

"How much?"

I pull out a wad of Muninn's money. What the Hell. It's New Year's.

"Five hundred dollars."

Suddenly Miss Done for Tonight is all smiles.

"Hell, I'd suck the shine off the doorknob for that."

I give her the money and she stuffs it in an inside jacket pocket in case I change my mind.

"Don't do anything until I tell you. Then bang on the door as hard as you can and take off."

I leave her by the door and go around to the back of the cabin.

I hold up my hand, drop it, and say, "Now!"

The hooker takes a step forward and gives the door six or seven good raps. She looks at me and I motion to her to get the hell out of there. Then I step through a shadow into the room. I go through it fast and to the Door of Memory. I make sure the sawed-off is still there. I left it by the door when I came through from Avila. I had a feeling that Parker would have spells up that could detect weapons.

Through the door and into the cabin. Parker is up front, hands on the door, trying to feel who's out there.

I'm in the bungalow's bathroom. Allegra and Vidocq are on the floor, their mouths closed with duct tape and their hands tied in front of them. I put a finger to my lips for them to keep quiet.

There's a wooden plunger behind the toilet. I grab it and sprint at Parker. Just before I reach him, I snap the plunger's wooden handle and bury the sharp end of the bigger piece in his back.

Parker screams in pain and the sound of his voice knocks me back against the far wall.

Parker turns and smiles at me. Slams his back against the wall so that the sharp end of the wooden handle punches all the way through and comes out his chest. Then he reaches up, pulls it out, and drops it on the floor.

"How fun is that, huh? That's the kind of thing you would do. Mason knew you'd find me, so he juiced me with a Kissi power enema. Is this how you feel, Sandman

Slim? It's like I could tear the world apart with my hands. Let me show you."

I bark a Hellion phrase and Parker sinks halfway into the carpet, which is sucking him down like quicksand.

Parker isn't shocked or scared. He presses his hands into the melting carpet, whispers a few words, and the quicksand reverses itself, pushing him up out of the floor. Before I can get out of the way, he throws one of the plasma balls he was using on Rodeo Drive. Hits me square in the chest. I hit the back wall hard enough that some of the studs snap, leaving the wall bowed out. The body armor keeps my ribs from cracking, but I feel like I got hit by the same meteor that killed the dinosaurs.

Parker comes over and takes a good long look at me on the floor.

"This is the best New Year's ever. Yeah, you messed up our little Hell surprise on the hill, but that's okay. Mason's got lots more ideas, and let me tell you, hanging out with the Kissi is a blast. Those boys really like to party."

With a superhuman effort I try to push myself to my feet, but only get as far as propping myself on my elbows like a white-trash Sphinx.

Parker smiles and shakes his head. I've never seen him so happy. He disappears into the bathroom and comes out holding Allegra by the arm. She holds her hands up in front of her face like she's afraid he might hit her.

"Is that your new bitch here? Alice two-point-oh? She's about as pretty as the first Alice."

He pulls the tape off Allegra's mouth. Grabs her by the hair and gives her a peck on the lips. Still holding her, he turns back to me.

"You're the definition of a loser, Stark. You know what a loser is? Someone who can't keep his women alive." He winks at Allegra. "Know what I mean, sweetheart?"

When Parker leans in for another kiss, Allegra puffs out a stream of air across her fingers. Flames burst from her fingertips, right into Parker's eyes. He screams and falls to the floor.

I yell "Get out!" to Allegra and she steps back into the bathroom.

Still blind, Parker screams hexes that shoot around the room, blasting holes in the walls and roof. He pulls a pistol from under his jacket and shoots wildly in all directions. I keep my head down until he's about an arm's length away. Then I reach into the shadow under the bed and pull out the sawed-off. Press it against his forehead and give him both barrels.

One minute Parker has a head and the next minute he doesn't.

I hope Kasabian makes you into his ponyboy in Hell.

Allegra helps me up, then goes into the bathroom and unties Vidocq. When he's on his feet, he comes over and grabs me like only a two-hundred-year-old Frenchman can.

"It's good to see you, boy," he says. Allegra is saying, "Thank you." I'm calculating the odds that the motel manager or a scared john has called the cops. No reason to wait and find out. I grab both of them and half walk, half fall into a shadow by the door, pulling them with me.

We come out in the hallway by Vidocq's place. The door is closed and yellow-and-black crime-scene tape is tacked up over the entrance. Allegra tears it down and opens the door. Vidocq helps me to the sofa, where I collapse. He drops to his knees and rummages in the potions and elixirs scattered across the floor. Comes up with a cracked blue bottle, goes back out to the hall, and runs a line of liquid all the way around the door frame. There's the faint aetheric glow of the glamour as it turns the door back into a blank wall.

Allegra comes back from the kitchen with a cold cloth. I lie back and she drapes it over my forehead. I run a body check, like I used to do after a night in the arena. Flex, move, feel, and evaluate each part of my body, starting with the feet and moving up. Feet and legs work. Knees bend (one is still a little stiff). Gut and ribs are about the same. Arms, neck, and skull intact. Hands and fingers flex. I'm all right. I'm just having a hard time getting my breath after Parker's fireball love tap. I shrug off my coat, peel off the ruined body armor, and drop it on the floor.

Vidocq is on the floor again, clinking bottles together, looking for usable potions. He comes back to the sofa with a couple.

"These aren't my first choices, but they will do. Drink this."

"What is it?"

"Mustika Pearl. From Turkey. You'll feel stronger and heal faster."

"Christ. It tastes like boiled goddamn roadkill."

"Have some of this—now. You'll feel very good and it will help wash away the taste of the other."

He's right. The second one is warm and earthy, with a slightly bitter edge.

"That's nice. What is it?"

"Vin Mariani. Red wine and cocaine."

I don't know if it's the Vin or the Pearl, but within a few minutes, I feel sort of like myself again. A shaky, hot, glued-together version, but definitely me.

"Don't tell anyone," I say, "but every rotten thing that's happened since I got back is my fault."

"What does that mean?" asks Allegra.

"Wait. It gets better. I could have gone after Mason and the Kissi a long time ago. But I was flat-out chickenshit."

Vidocq asks, "How is that possible? You didn't even know about the Kissi until two days ago."

"I knew about them. Not their name or what they were, but I knew there was something like them right in front of me. What did the Kissi want from me, the moment they knew I had it? The key. Mason would have told them about that. When I followed Kasabian into the Twilight, he told me that he'd been with Mason and Parker somewhere dark. Not empty, but filled with nothing. That's why Mason and the Kissi want the key."

"Because they're in nothing?" asks Allegra.

"Because they want *me* in nothing. I've been through twelve doors in the Room of Thirteen Doors. I've never gone through the thirteenth. I've always been afraid of it. All the other doors are marked with a symbol. A sun. A crescent moon. A frozen lake. Only the thirteenth door is blank. There's nothing on it. It's the Door of Nothing. That's where the Kissi and Mason will be. And I could have gone there anytime since Azazel gave me the key. Years ago. But I was too afraid of that blank door."

"You're going to go there now?" asks Vidocq.

"I should be there already." I pull a wad of bills out of my pocket and hand them to Allegra. "There should be around a thousand dollars there. The rest of Muninn's money is in an envelope under all the junk upstairs at Max Overdrive. If I don't come back, it's yours. If I do come back, I'll need some of it back. The place needs a little fixing up."

Their heart rates and breathing are all over the place. The stress is going to kill them quicker than Mason or the Kissi. They both want to say something. I make sure I have my knife and step through a shadow before either of them can get out a word.

THE THIRTEENTH DOOR looks older and more battered than the others. If the other doors are portals to different planes and places in the universe, the thirteenth is the entrance to a prison. Strange sounds leak through it. Growls. Vibrations. A faint stink of vinegar. What could be the wind or voices whispering. A slow but relentless scratching, like something is trying to dig its way out.

I throw the bolt and open the Door of Nothing.

The name is pretty damned apt. Some of the other doors, I still can't figure out. What does the Door of Abandoned Melancholy mean? Not much. But the Door of Nothing is right on the money.

There's nothing beyond on the door. Not darkness. Not emptiness. Nothing. It's the total and absolute absence of everything. Especially light. I step inside and pull the door closed. Immediately I hear sounds all around me. Scurrying, secret sounds. Bugs under dry leaves. Something wet pulling itself through mud. Hungry things, chewing their claws and grinding their teeth. Things touch me in the nothing. They crawl on me and try to work their way under my clothes. I can't move. I don't know where to go. Then I remember the thing Mason left for me because he knew that sooner or later, I'd be standing here. I take out the lighter.

Let there be light.

The Zippo flares, looking like an oil-well fire in all that lightless empty space. A billion soft, pale, half-formed anti-angels limp back into the dark. Their big blank eyes glitter like black chrome. The Kissi are crowded into every inch of their chaotic nonspace. They live piled on top of each other, like dead and dying angels. The piles of bodies look like pictures of Auschwitz. This is what Heaven must have looked like after Lucifer's war.

When I start walking, the wall of Kissi bodies parts like the Red Sea, then closes in behind me.

I'm moving just to move. Standing still feels like asking for trouble. But every direction looks exactly the same to me. I can't tell if I'm walking on something solid or just the idea of something. One minute, it feels like I'm on hard-packed dirt, then the next, I'm sinking into sponge cake. I don't stop or slow down. I keep walking, like I know exactly where I'm going.

A Kissi puts its glowing hand on my arm. I look at it like I talk to zombie angels every day. Its face is half-baked dough. I can't quite bring it into focus.

"I told you we'd meet again."

The Kissi's face rearranges itself for a second. Turns into Josef's Aryan poster-boy mug. "He's waiting for you. Straight ahead. We've all been so looking forward to this."

"Hang around, ugly. When I'm done with Mason, the two of us can get some dim sum before I kill you again."

Josef laughs, turns his sluglike head, and dissolves into the writhing mass of Kissi bodies. They pick up his laugh and it spreads out across the colony, so that in just a few seconds the sound surrounds me. Thunders down on me from a billion throats like a storm. It rattles every molecule in my body. I'm being mugged with sound. I turn and shove the lighter straight into the heart of the closest group of Kissi. They shriek and scatter. Shove the lighter in another group. And another. They still surround me, but they're not laughing anymore. And they keep their distance.

Straight ahead is the Faim family's Beverly Hills mansion, a Tudor playhouse standing in a universe of nothing. I don't bother knocking.

Head straight downstairs to the basement. Mason's magic room. The room where he sent me to Hell and where I found the lighter.

I open the door at the bottom of the stairs and, like that, it's eleven years ago.

The room is exactly the way I remember it. Even the circle drawn on the floor in lead is the same. I never figured Mason for the nostalgic type.

"I know you're not going to believe me, but it's really good to see you, Jimmy."

Mason sounds exactly the same. He looks the same, too. I can't tell if he's keeping himself young with magic or if time works differently here.

"When you've spent as many years as I have with no one to talk to but Parker or the Kissi, it's a real thrill to run into someone with some brains. Who isn't here to kiss my ass or be my Renfield."

"That's funny. I always thought you and Parker were best buds. Not Vlad and Renfield."

"You used to call him my attack dog. Maybe that's a better way of putting it. A dog is man's best friend, but it doesn't mean you're going to talk to it about anything important. You pet a dog. You feed a dog. You put it out back to guard the henhouse. Reward it when it's been good. Punish it when it's been bad. That's pretty much it."

"Your plan is working out great, if your plan was to sit out here in an empty house in the middle of fuck-all, surrounded by talking army ants. Wow. You really are a genius. I never saw that one coming."

"You see? Anyone else, I'd want to strangle by now. But noise like that. Criticism. It's all right coming from you. Because I respect you. You really are the only other Sub Rosa I thought had any real talent and style."

"That's why you had to kill me."

"I didn't kill you, did I? I could have and you wouldn't have seen it coming any more than the other thing."

"You can't even say it? You sent me to Hell. Say it."

"I don't want to reopen old wounds. That's not why I brought you here. And before you tell me that you found me on your own, we both know that I made sure that Kasabian knew just enough about where we were to help you finally figure it out."

"If you wanted me here so bad, why didn't you just send up a flare or have one of your Kissi forward me a Google map link?"

"Because I had to know that you could do it. I haven't seen you in eleven years. Maybe the air in Hell or all those knocks on the head in the arena turned your brains to butterscotch pudding. I had to see you work it out and here you are. And since you got rid of Parker, I have a staff opening right now. A nice midlevel executive job. Good hours. Terrific benefits. Possible deification. Interested?"

"Keep talking. The more you yammer, the more I want to kill you. That's the only reason I'm here, in case you forgot about what you did to me and Alice."

"Alice was Parker's thing. I just wanted to make sure she wasn't going to make too much of a fuss after you were gone. He took it too far."

"He was your dog. You sent him out to hunt. Your responsibility."

"What if I told you that you could get her back? Exactly as she was. And the two of you could live together forever. What would you say?"

I'm not at all surprised by his arrogance and bullshit. What's so strange about Mason is how young he seems. Like he's exactly the same little show-off he was all those years ago. Has he really been sitting here alone for eleven years? That's worse than what happened to me. I'm the old man now, but I saw and did a few things. I didn't just crawl up my own teenybopper ass for a decade. Imagine eleven years, sitting in a dollhouse version of your childhood home, reading magic books and not talking to anyone but your pet thug and talking roaches. If Mason wasn't crazy before, he's definitely joined the banana army now.

"What are you talking about? How could I get back Alice?"

"That's why I had to make you solve a puzzle to get here. I had to know if you could keep up once the project got rolling. Stage one is why I formed an alliance with the Kissi. To take control of the world."

He smiles at me like he just got all A's on his report card.

"Why would anyone want to run the world?" I ask. "It sounds like a huge pain in the ass."

"That's just stage one. If all I wanted was to take over the world, believe me, the Kissi and I could have done it already."

"What do you want the world for?"

"In any military campaign, you need a few basic things. Troops. Equipment. Support staff. Supply lines, that kind of thing. Earth is the perfect staging area for that."

"When I knew you, all you wanted was to prove that you were the best little magician in Candyland. Now you want to be Patton, too? What is wrong with you?"

He goes to a large ebony desk, piled high with books, writing paper, and maps of the universe like Aelita had, from Heaven looking down and from Hell looking up. Mason grabs an old book about the size and weight of a bag of cement and shows me the pages he's been studying. A single word crosses the two pages of the spread: L'Infernus. Below that is a detailed map of Hell's topography.

"We're invading Hell. I have the troops and the plan. You know Hell's strengths and weaknesses. You've already softened the place up for invasion. How many of Lucifer's generals have you killed? A dozen? Two? More?"

"You want to rule this world, a not particularly great place, so you can take over an even worse place? Is that basically it? That's why you ruined me, killed Alice, and fucked over everyone who ever trusted you?"

"Firstly, fuck all those people who trusted me. Except for Parker, every one of them was greedy and then turned jellyfish the moment you stuck your nose out of the grave. I gave all of them their heart's desire and they folded the moment things got a little weird."

"You didn't exactly give Kasabian his heart's desire."

"Yeah, I did sort of screw him, didn't I? But admit it. There's the opposite of love at first sight. There are people walking the earth that the moment you meet them, you want to punch them and keep punching them."

"I can't argue with you about Kas, but what do you want with Hell? It's already on the verge of a civil war. You want to walk into the middle of warring Hellions?"

"With the Kissi and you to back me up, yes. I really do. Because with our combined strength and your contacts with Lucifer's generals, we could find which to kill and which will make good allies. Then march in and take Hell, just the way we took Earth. Once we've secured the place, we'll combine the armies from Earth and Hell with the Kissi. Then go to stage three."

"You want to invade Heaven."

"I want to storm Heaven. I want to rip open the Pearly Gates and throw them from the firmament. I want to see all nine ranks of angels on their knees bowing down to the humans that conquered them. And I want to throw out that senile old fart that runs the place. Ship Him off to a retirement home for old deities. He can get a duplex with Zeus or Odin. He ruined the universe at the beginning of time and He's been ruining it ever since. He needs to be off playing golf in Boca and power walking at the mall, not running the fundamental laws of time and space. One day, He's going to forget where he put the remote, get all distracted, and forget about gravity. Then where will we be? I know you know I'm right. I know how you think."

I look at him. I don't know what else to do. He's right, of course. I agree with pretty much everything he said about Heaven and Hell. I wouldn't mind seeing God and Lucifer stuck on a cruise ship—shuffleboard, all-day buffets, a decent band in the bar, and a passable magic act in the lounge for all eternity. But the idea of replacing the current fuckups with Mason? That part doesn't scan and he knows I'd never go for it.

"So, I help you become the new Yahweh, and what do I get out of it?"

"The world. It's yours. And Alice. You and she can live forever. If you want her to. Once we're in charge, we'll control that kind of thing."

"Who gets Hell? The Kissi?"

"Who better to run the place of torments than a race of natural-born torturers and killers?"

This isn't what I was expecting. I don't know what I

thought would be waiting for me here in Never Never Land, but it wasn't this. I came ready to fight Genghis Khan and I walk in on a shut-in playing the biggest Dungeons and Dragons game in history.

"You're right. I can't think of anyone better suited to run Hell than the Kissi."

I walk around the room, admiring how detailed his memory must be to have built this place. I stop at a bin full of maps that runs from the floor to the ceiling. City maps. World maps. Maps of time and celestial mechanics. Maps of the edges of the universe. I'm still holding Mason's lighter. I flick it and hold it to one of the maps.

"What are you doing over there?"

Old maps are printed on good, heavy paper stock. They burn well. Old ones are dry enough to burn fast. When Mason runs to the maps, I use the lighter to fire up the books and papers on his desk.

"Stop it!" he yells.

I hold the lighter to a book on his lectern. The book is written in Aramaic. It looks very rare and expensive.

"Stop it!"

That's the one I'd been waiting for. He's losing his shit. Getting sloppy with his power. The demonic boom of his voice knocks the house off its foundation and cracks the walls. Books, globes, and old specimen jars fly off the shelves. I lose my balance and knock over a spiderlike Kissi skeleton.

"The problem, Mason, is you only know me from the old days when breaking things was more fun. Your plan is so completely brain damaged that I might have gone for it back then. But all that matters now is one thing. *You killed Alice and I'm going to kill you.*"

I set fire to anatomy charts and diagrams of mystical automata.

He uses a throw rug to smother the fire on the lectern.

"When I'm sitting on my golden throne in the sky, I'm going to make you and your bitch my special project."

Mason blurs across the room at me, faster than I could ever move. He knocks me out of the way so that he can rescue the papers I've set on fire. He's working really well for a few seconds, but then the black knife that I stuck in his side when he cuffed me away really starts to hurt. He reaches around to take the knife out. But I'm pretty fast, too. I leap and roll, jam my boot heel into the knife hilt, plunging it another six inches into his side. Mason groans and falls on his face.

I climb on top of him and rip the knife out with my left hand. Get my right arm around his throat and stab up, slipping the blade between his ribs and into his heart. Mason shudders and so does the house. The walls and ceiling crack. Bricks, lath, and plaster rain down on us. I push the knife in farther and hear the upstairs collapse.

A bookcase comes loose from the wall and crashes down on me. Mason throws an elbow and knocks me onto my back. Then he's on top of me. I get the knife up in time and jam it right back between his ribs. But Mason does a trick I didn't know he could do.

He's been doing more with the Kissi than exchanging sea stories and brownie recipes. He slips his hand through my body and right into my chest. Instantly I'm cold and nauseous, remembering what it was like in Josef's office. With every wave of pain and sickness, I twist the knife deeper into him.

The mansion walls are dust and the floor is sagging under our weight. A great, black dome of nothingness hangs over our heads. Then even the floor is gone and we're in the dark, surrounded by the chittering, scuttling noises of the Kissi, the only reminder that we haven't fallen out of the universe completely.

I shout Hellion control curses and poison hexes into Mason's ear. He digs his hand into my chest and gets his fingers around the key. The whole universe shifts, like a car sliding on black ice. I drag the black blade between Mason's ribs. Throw attack spells. Mason chatters in Kissi, trying to fill my head with dread and confusion. Luckily, I'm already confused and full of dread, so the spell is kind of redundant.

The darkness shreds around us. Streaks of something leak through the opaque wall of nothing. A billion Kissi scream as light burns into their hiding place.

We're falling. Or things are swirling past us. I can't tell which. I catch glimpses of the Room of Thirteen Doors. Every time Mason tries to rip the key from my chest, the room shifts at the center of time and space, warping the universe.

Time flows like lava. Mason pulls on the key and the pain lasts a million years. The room swirls by, larger than the whole universe. One door. A dozen. A million. A blinking zoetrope as doors open, close, appear, and disappear.

We're crushed to the size of atoms. We expand to fill the Milky Way. I jerk the blade from Mason's side and sweep it through the center of a star. Slash the white-hot blade through the thin fabric that separates the Kissi's chaos realm from ours. The Kissi scream and scatter as light floods inside. They try to patch the holes, but I keep slashing new ones. The Kissi's bubble of nothingness swells and explodes, scattering their burning bodies away from the light and into the frozen void on the far edge of the universe.

The next time the room appears, I raise the knife and slice down through Mason's arm. His screams shake the nearby planets. I pull his severed hand from my chest and dive for the room. Get one hand around the edge of the Door of Shadows and pull myself inside. Mason hangs on with his one good hand. I have to drag him inside with me.

We collapse on the stones. I catch my breath and get to my feet. Mason is on his back, cradling his severed arm to his chest. He's pale and shaking, shirt soaked through with blood. I've been looking forward to killing Mason for so long and now he's spoiling it. In my fantasies, I kill the bullyboy, arrogant Mason. But this little guy on the floor, shivering like a goldfish that's fallen out of its bowl, isn't the monster I came to slay.

Mason says something, but I can't hear him. He says it

again, but still too low to hear. I lean my ear to his mouth when he says it again. It's Kissi. I can't understand the word, but there's a crunch that I heard enough in the arena to know that it's either the sound of a bone breaking or being magically knit back together. This being Mason, of course, it's a bit of both, with something worse thrown in just for fun.

Something white and larvalike protrudes from where Mason's right arm used to be. Sounds come from beneath his skin, like termites eating glass. A final crunch and Mason's arm rips from his shoulder as a faintly glowing Kissi arm emerges to take its place. Mason's eyes pop open. Suddenly he's back to being the monster I've dreamed of killing. However, there's something about this new Mason that makes every cell in my body decide simultaneously that it would like to be at least a continent away from him.

Mason sits up and smiles. He knows exactly where he is. The space is too small and he's too fast for me to try taking his new arm off. There's an old saying among fighters in the arena, "A retreat is a good as an advance, especially if your opponent just grew an angel's arm."

I open the nearest door, slam it shut, and start running. I hear Mason behind me a second later. There's a sort of town square up ahead. I keep running, knocking people out of my way. At the far side of the square is a makeshift bar selling Aqua Regia. I jump on top and kick the drinkers' glasses in their faces. A Hellion infantryman lunges at me with his spear. I sidestep him and snap it in two with the black blade. Thanks, man. Anyone who wasn't sure who I was before, just saw Azazel's knife and now knows for certain.

"Hello you shit-sucking sulfur monkeys. In case you haven't guessed, I'm Sandman Slim and I crawled back down to perdition's ball sac for just a moment of your time. And if you don't believe I'm Sandman Slim, step up closer and I'll take a lot more than a moment from you.

"Now, I know what a lot of you would like to do to me, but I want you to think about this first: I might be the monster who kills monsters and the biggest bastard in existence, but that's your real enemy right there. The man who followed me here. Look at his arm. He's Kissi. And he's been chasing me all over Creation because he wants me to help him bring a Kissi army down here to turn you into the slaves you refused to be in Heaven. I didn't bring his army, but I brought him. And I'm giving him to you. A New Year's gift from Sandman Slim."

By now, most of the crowd is fixated on Mason and his arm. He transforms it to look human, but that just pisses them off even more. They press in on Mason from every direction, but no one wants to make the first move. I pick up one of the Hellion beer mugs and, just when I feel a wave of tension pass through the crowd, smash it. There's something magical about the sound of breaking glass. Especially around a mob. It works for both humans and Hellions. If you want to start a riot, throw a bottle.

The moment the mug shatters, the crowd surges forward, banshee-howling, crushing Mason at its center.

Hellion gendarmes are heading toward the square. That guarantees a full-scale devil's night party riot. I duck, stay low, and move from table to table until I'm out of the square. Then I take off running for the Door of Fire.

I make it through and just about have the door closed when someone grabs it from the other side.

A skinny Hellion adolescent in a uniform I've never see before gets as close to the door as he can.

"You killed my master, Abaddon. I'll get to your world somehow someday, and I'll avenge him."

"Why don't you come out here and tell me all about it, sweetheart? Oh, wait. You can't come out here, can you? Magic is such a tease. When you figure out how to get yourself on the other side of this door, be sure to look me up. Until then, stay in school. Say your prayers. And just before you fall asleep tonight, pucker up and kiss my ass."

I pull the Door of Fire closed. I know I probably ought to be worried, but I can't get worked up about one more Hellion who hates my guts.

I step out of the room and into Vidocq's apartment. Allegra is on her knees, sorting broken potion bottles from ones she can salvage. Vidocq is in the kitchen making coffee. They both look at me.

"If I just did to the Kissi what I think I did, I might have just saved the world twice in one night."

"And Mason?" asks Vidocq.

"Last I saw, he was being torn limb from claw by a bunch of highly motivated Hellions."

"How are you?" asks Allegra.

"My chest hurts, but I'll be great as soon as I get a cigarette, a drink, and a lobotomy."

A FEW DAYS later.

It's sunny out, a tourist postcard L.A. afternoon at Donut Universe. I'm still not great at paying attention to dates, but I know it's a Sunday. A perfect day for a date with an angel.

I push the tissue paper at her.

"Have an apple fritter. A friend told me this place has the best in town."

"Thank you."

Aelita looks at the fritter like I just passed her a dog turd.

"The food's better at the Bamboo House of Dolls, but you didn't want to meet there."

"I don't drink."

"We didn't have to drink."

"I don't like the smell of liquor."

"What about all the wine in the Church's holy magic shows?"

"Wine isn't liquor. It's the blood of our Lord."

I take a sip of coffee. It's hot and good, but good coffee in restaurants kind of depresses me. I always wonder why it doesn't come in a cigarette flavor for places where you can't smoke.

"The state of California disagrees, otherwise teenyboppers would ask me to buy stuff for them at twenty-four-hour blood stores."

"This is exactly the kind of talk I'd expect from you."

"An Abomination?"

"Yes."

"I'll get you a thesaurus next Christmas. You need to expand your vocabulary."

"Some things are beyond redemption."

"I thought anyone could get through the Pearly Gates if they repented."

"No. Not everyone."

"Maybe I should take back my fritter."

Aelita sighs and looks out the window. She'd rather be having lunch in a volcano than sitting here with me.

"Not everyone deserves God's grace, but everything in existence has a purpose and a use. Even the abhorrent. Given that, I've come here to ask you one more time, will you work for the righteous cause of the Golden Vigil?"

"When you ask so nicely, it makes me feel all nonabhorrent."

"This is your chance to redeem yourself, if only just a little."

"Sure. I'll work for the Vigil. But on a freelance basis. And I want to be paid. In cash and in advance. I don't exactly trust holy rollers."

"You want money for doing God's work?"

"Yes. A lot of money. You practically have Area 51 tucked away in your warehouse. You can afford it."

"I didn't think you could possibly be more vile, but you've managed to surprise me."

"I know. I'm worse than the bogeyman and tooth decay. But the offer still stands. I don't have a business card, but you know where to find me."

I take my own apple fritter out of the bag and take a bite. The Kissi was right. It really is that good.

"Every day you're alive is like someone spitting in the face of God. I showed you mercy when I let Eugène save you. You won't get mercy from me again."

"I saved your celestial ass the other night."

"You put me in that awful place."

"No. The Kissi did. Or did you forget about them?"

She pushes her fritter and coffee across the table.

"This food smells like death. I'm sure you love it. I don't think we have anything more to say to each other. I'm leaving."

"You going to hide and massacre me in the parking lot?"

"It's tempting."

"No, it's not, and here's why. I went to some people and I traded some things. Got myself a kill switch."

"What is that?"

"They have them on trains. Tractors. Some other equipment. It's a button the operator has to hold down for the machine to work. The operator has a heart attack and dies, he lets go of the button. The switch kills the engine and the machine stops. A kill switch."

"Are you thinking of becoming a train conductor?"

"Better. I'm keeping an eye on this." I take out a small wooden box I bought the day before, a pyx, and slide it across the table to her. "You know what that is. It's usually for a consecrated host, but I put something better inside. Take a look."

Aelita looks at me for a minute, and then touches the box. Probably doing some angel magic to see if it's poison or a bomb or a poison bomb. Finally, she opens it and looks inside. There's a tiny light on the bottom. So small, a human couldn't see it.

"What is this?"

"Look closer, angel. Don't you recognize it?"

She drops the box.

"A piece of the Mithras."

"That's right. A fragment of a fragment of a fragment. I put the rest in the Room of Thirteen Doors. As long as I'm alive, it's safe. But if you ever run me through with that sword again, the glass holding the Mithras will break and burn its way out through all thirteen doors."

"You're lying."

"You kill me and I'll torch this whole little puppet show. Then, when Heaven itself is burning, you can explain to your boss how it's all your fault."

"Even you aren't this mad."

"There's an easy way to find out."

I put the pyx in my pocket and get up. Slide her pastry and mine into the paper bag and roll it closed.

"You don't deserve a fritter."

I leave Aelita there in the booth with the sun coming through the window, thinking about doughnuts and the end of everything.

I DIAL DOC Kinski's number and he picks up.

"Damn. When did you start answering phones?"

"It's a recent and very temporary development. What can I do for you?"

"How's Candy doing?"

"Still a little overexcited. When someone falls off the murder wagon, it can take 'em a while to calm down."

"That's why some of us don't ever stop."

Silence. Nothing. Crickets.

"That was a joke," I say.

"I'll take your word for it. That's not all you called about, is it?"

"No. I'm calling about the bullets. You said you'd take them out when things calmed down. Things have."

"Okay. Come by today."

"When?"

"How about right now?"

WHEN I PULL into the minimall, Kinski is outside smoking a cigarette. I park the stolen Mercedes SLR McLaren at the rear of lot, behind a pizza delivery van. The McLaren's doors don't open out. They flip up like insect wings.

Kinski drops his cigarette and grinds it out with his boot.

"You couldn't find anything more conspicuous to drive over here? Maybe a blimp or an ocean liner?"

"No one can see it from the street."

"I suppose. You ready for this?"

"Yeah. I'm sick of things banging around inside me every time I sneeze."

"All right, then. Let's get them out."

He leads me back into the clinic. Nothing has changed in the reception area. Even the magazines are sitting exactly where they were the last time I was here. If this was anybody else's office, I'd guess that he was a bookie or selling dope out the back door.

I wait while the doc washes his hands.

"Take off your shirt and lie down."

When I'm on the treatment table, I ask, "You going to use your magic glass rocks on me?"

"Not this time, I'm afraid. This is more of a hands-on procedure. I'm going to have to go in there and get those slugs out manually."

I watch him dry his hands on a small towel covered with pictures of palm trees. The word *Orlando* is printed in bright red letters in one corner.

"A Kissi ran his hands around inside me. I didn't like it."

"This won't be like that. For one thing, you won't feel it. I have some special salve that'll numb you up good."

"I like the sound of that."

"Let's just get started."

He takes a stoppered bottle from the counter, opens it, and pours something thick, like Karo syrup, in a line down my chest. Then he takes a sponge-headed brush and paints the stuff across my body, from my neck down to my stomach.

He puts the brush back on the counter and says, "Tell me when that stuff gets warm."

"I think it's there already."

"Close your eyes for a minute."

I close them and he says, "Feel that?"

"No. Did you already put your hand in my chest?"

"Does it feel like I did?"

"No."

"Good. Then you're ready. Feel free to keep your eyes closed."

"Are you going to wear gloves or something, at least?"

"Of course I'm wearing goddamn gloves. I'm not a god-damn Kissi."

"Sorry."

"It's all right."

There's a clank. Like metal on metal.

"What was that?"

"That's bullet one."

"That was easy."

"See? We could have done this a long time ago and saved you some pain."

"I'll call you after my next shooting."

"Or you could try not getting shot."

"Where's the fun in that?"

He laughs a little.

"That's why you and Candy get along. That's what she'd say."

Candy is the last thing I want to talk to Kinski about when he has his hands in my guts.

"What's the going rate for magic surgery?"

Another piece of metal drops.

"It's on the house."

I don't say anything for a minute.

"How the hell do you make a living? You never have any patients and you don't charge me for surgery or for dragging my friends in here. What's going on?"

"You're tensing up. Relax. Every time you move, the bullets shift."

"Okay."

"And for your information, how I make a living is my business, not yours. As for why I don't charge you, let me ask you a question. Have you ever asked yourself how you survived all those years in Hell? Do really think you lived with Hellions and survived the arena because you're that much of a badass?"

"I don't know. I used to think about it, but I could never find any reasons. And I was kind of busy getting my ass kicked, so I stopped worrying about it."

"Well, you're back and there aren't any monsters chasing you right now. Tell me how it is that you, by yourself, managed to stay alive all those years."

"I don't know."

"Guess."

"I don't know. I'm nothing special."

"You think so? You fell into the bottom of the cesspool of Creation, survived and crawled out again. Doesn't that sound just a little special?"

"I don't know."

"Yes, you do. A regular person, a civilian, wouldn't have lasted a day down there, much less eleven years."

Another piece of metal falls.

"What does that mean?" I ask.

"Maybe it means you're different. Maybe it means that you're not who you think you are. Maybe it means you're not entirely human."

I open my eyes and look at him. No matter how hard I look and listen, I can't read him. Can't hear his heart or his breathing. Nothing.

"I don't like where this is going, doc."

"Another minute. We're almost there."

I close my eyes and try to calm my breathing. I didn't like seeing his hands moving around under my skin.

"You haven't answered the question. Are you human or not?"

"If I'm not human, what am I?"

"Same as me. An angel not quite fit for heaven or hell."

Another piece of metal falls. The fifth bullet.

I feel Kinski lean back. Hear him walk to the sink and wash his hands.

He says, "You can put your shirt back on."

I sit up on the table.

"What did you just say to me, man?"

He wipes his hands on a towel and says, "It's going to be harder for you than it is for me. I made concious choices that got me here. Half the universe hated you before you were born."

He moves slowly, choosing his words carefully. That much I can see. He's not high or drunk and he doesn't give off a Looney Tunes vibe. Still.

"Put your shirt on. Let's go have a smoke."

I follow him into the parking lot. The sun hurts my eyes after having them closed. I watch the doc, looking for any signs of obvious craziness. I could make a break for the Benz, but I'm a little woozy from the surgery.

Kinski is looking at me. He takes out a cigarette and offers me the pack. I take one.

"If you don't want to hear this, I'm not going to force you. I just thought that maybe you'd like to know who you are, why certain things have happened to you, and why certain other things are going to happen in the future."

"I'm listening."

"I'm sure Miss Aelita told you about God's great fuckup at the beginning of time. The thing is, there are other stories regular folks aren't supposed to know about. One is about how in the early days of the world, after what happened in Eden, yet another great fuckup, God sent angels to Earth to look after humans. These angels didn't float around in the sky with big white wings and harps. They lived as ordinary people. Had jobs. Farmed. Fought in wars. All the things regular people do. The only thing they couldn't do was fraternize with humanity. They had to remain apart and aloof so that they could be watchful."

I smoked my cigarette and watched the smog rim the clouds with funny shades of blue and gold.

"The problem with this plan is that you can't take anything, even angels, put them in a human body, give them a human life, and not expect them to start feeling and acting just a little human. Even falling in love. Even having children.

"The children these angels had with mortal women were called *nephilim*. There were a lot of them around once upon a time. Now, not so many."

"Why not?"

"They were killed. So were the angels who fathered them and the mothers who gave birth to them."

"Why?"

"They had to. There had to be no record, no trace that they ever existed. Most of those doing the killing didn't call the children *nephilim*. They had another name for them."

"Abomination."

Kinski nods.

"Smart boy."

"If you're not Doc Kinski, who the hell are you?"

"They took away my real name when they kicked me out of Heaven. Normally, when an angel falls from grace, that angel ends up with other fallen ones in Hell. That would have been too embarrassing in my case. See, I was an archangel. Uriel, the Guardian of the Earth. If they'd sent me all the way down, they knew what would happen. Lucifer would have thrown me a ticker tape parade. God wasn't going to let that happen. So, here I am. I run a little under-the-radar human fix-it shop next to some nice ladies who do other ladies' nails."

"What did you do to the kicked out of heaven?"

"I killed another angel."

"Why?"

"He deserved it."

I flick the remains of my cigarette out into the parking lot.

"Can I get another?"

The doc offers me one from the pack. I light it with Mason's lighter.

"Does Vidocq knew about this nephilim thing?"

"You mean, does he know what you are? He's a smart man who's read a lot of book. He can do the math."

"This is fucking ridiculous. I'm no goddam angel."

"Sure, you're a perfectly normal boy. You were born able to do more magic than most Sub Rosa learn in a lifetime. You survived Hell. You saved the world and you corraled the Kissi. Typical underachiever."

A skinny kid in a striped shirt and backward baseball cap comes out of the pizza joint, carrying a pile of boxes to the delivery van.

The doc nods toward him. "That kid is smarter than both of us put together. He's got a car and all the pizza he can eat. What more does a man need?"

He smiles at his own joke. It's the first time I've seen him be anything but serious.

"If I believe all this, where does that leave me?"

The smile fades.

"Not anywhere good, I am sorry to say. You're an Abomination. You'll always be an Abomination. Hell hates you for being more than a human and Heaven hates you for being less than an angel."

"No wonder I couldn't get a date for the prom."

"There's something else you need to know." He looks at his watch. "I should call Candy soon. See how she's doing. I have her on double doses of the blood substitute."

"Is she going to be all right?"

"Hard to say. It's hard to fight your own nature. I couldn't do it. Angels are creatures made to love and protect humanity, only we weren't supposed to fall in love. But I did. Candy's a predator. A killer through and through. She's trying to change that and I'm trying to help her. Maybe that's a mistake."

"I thought it was you who was making her give up the kill."

"No. She came to me."

"I wouldn't have guessed that."

"Like I said, I'm not sure I'm doing the right thing by helping her. There's something else you ought to know about the *nephilim*. Not all of them were killed off by God's hit squads. Your kind is mostly gone because you tend to kill yourselves. You're not the most stable being, but I guess you knew that."

"Is that how you got that wound on your arm? Those

guys who tried to shove you into a car. Those were angels trying to kill you?"

Kinski laughs.

"No, boy. Heaven doesn't worry about me anymore. Those were Kissi. They were shopping for one last angel for their New Year's party."

I look at him hard, trying to read him. Wanting a final, for-real take on him. But he's a blank wall.

He smiles at me.

"I know what you're doing. You can't read angels like regular people. Even angels can't always read other angels. Otherwise we would have never had that little dustup with Lucifer in Heaven."

"Can you read me?"

"Of course."

"What am I thinking?"

"You're afraid I'm crazy because that's one more person you can't count on. And you're afraid I'm telling the truth 'cause that means you were screwed before you ever drew your first breath."

That's exactly what I'm thinking.

"Will I be like you? Will I be able to read you someday?"

He shrugs.

"It's hard to say. With *nephilim,* it's always different. Some are more human and some are almost angels and can do almost anything angels do. You'll know what you can do when you can do it. That's all I can tell you."

"Let's say I believe this story. Could you fix me up with a cocktail like Candy's? Make me like a regular person?"

"I wouldn't even try."

"Why not?"

"You always had magic, but you came into your real power in Hell. You were running wild, not holding yourself back like the *nephilim* that grew up around humans. You found yourself and accepted what you could do without all the angst and bullshit that they went through."

"And what is it I can do?"

"*Warrior* is the nice word, the traditional word, but that's just a polite way of saying that you're a natural-born killer. You're Sandman Slim, the monster who kills monsters. I'm not going to drug you up to change that."

"Even if I wanted to change it?"

"Especially then. How many angels showed up to save the world the other night? Did Aelita and her little quilting bee conquer the evil at Avila's heart? No. It took a monster to walk between all the forces massed there and to beat them all. No one else could have done that."

"There were two monsters there," I remind him.

He nods.

"Right. Two monsters."

The pizza delivery boy brings out a second pile of pizza boxes, loads them in the van, backs up, and heads into the afternoon traffic. He gives us the finger on the way out of the parking lot.

"I can feel a lot of stuff pinballing around in your head. You want to tell me what you think about all this?"

"If your story is true, then one of my parents fucked an angel. Which one?"

"Why does that matter?"

"It doesn't, but I want to know."

"Your mother."

"I thought so. My father was gone a lot on sales calls. Mom was lonely and pretty. I guess that explains some things about my father."

"If you say so."

"He knew I wasn't his."

"But he still raised you. Give him credit for that."

"He wanted me dead."

"Hell, boy. At some point, all fathers want to kill their sons. Just like all sons think about killing their old man. They're too much alike or the're not enough alike. It doesn't matter. What's beautiful is that they don't do it."

"Are there other *nephilim* around?"

"It's not like there's a newsletter or anything, but as far as I know, you're the only one."

"I used to worry all the time about being boring. Suddenly boring looks pretty good."

"Try not to sing too many sad songs for yourself. The universe already hates you. Self-pity isn't going to help."

Whenever the hammer has come down in my life, I've always wondered what my father would do. Then I usually do the opposite, but I still always think of him first. But now I'm seeing my mother's face instead of my father's. And I'm thinking about Alice. And Candy. And Allegra breathing fire into Parker's eyes. And Vidocq, who isn't a father, but who makes being a man easier than any of the men in my family.

I flick my cigarette butt at a rat that's stalking a couple of pigeons in the parking lot.

"You know what I'm thinking right now?"

Kinski is silent for a minute.

"That you really want a drink."

"Yeah, but that's too easy. I always want a drink. Guess again."

"You're back wondering if I'm crazy or not and leaning toward crazy."

I nod and take few steps in the direction of the Mercedes.

"Actaully, I'm not. I'm leaning toward I don't give a goddam. I'm sick of Heaven and Hell and angels and *nephilim* and all the rest of it. I knew what I was doing there. And no one told me that I'm not who I am. Be a fallen archangel if you want, but leave me out of it. I don't want to be part of your soap opera. I don't want to be mythological."

I start back for the Mercedes, but it looks ridiculous to me now. A brain dead cross between a giant grasshopper and a Cubist Corvette. I walk past the car and into the shadow of a lampost at the corner of the lot. Kinski watches me go. As I slip into the Room of Thirteen Doors, for just a second, some annoying part of my brain whispers, "You know that thing that you're doing right now, going from a parking lot to the center of the universe and out again? That's pretty seriously mythological."

THERE'S ONLY ONE problem with L.A.

It exists.

L.A. is what happens when a bunch of Lovecraftian elder gods and porn starlets spend a weekend locked up in the Chateau Marmont snorting lines of crank off Jim Morrison's bones. If the Viagra and illegal Traci Lords videos don't get you going, then the Japanese tentacle porn will.

New York has short con cannibals and sewer gators. Chicago is all snowbound yetis and the ghosts of a million angry steers with horns like jackhammers. Texas is crisscrossed with ghost railroads that kidnap demon-possessed Lolitas to play strip Russian roulette with six shells in the chamber.

L.A. is all assholes and angels, bloodsuckers and trust-fund satanists, black magic and movie moguls with more bodies buried under the house than John Wayne Gacy.

There are more surveillance cameras and razor wire here than around the pope. L.A. is one traffic jam from going completely Hiroshima.

God, I love this town.

I NEED FOOD. I need booze. I need to smoke a cigarette outside a bar where you can hear people dry humping in the alley behind the Dumpster.

I walk from Max Overdrive to the Bamboo House of Dolls, sucking down stage-six smog-alert air and lingering over a sunset as bloody as the fall of the Roman Empire.

People stare and point at me as I go inside. For a second I have that anxiety-dream paranoia that I'm not wearing any pants. But no one's laughing and I've got a pocket full of money and a knife tucked in the back of my jeans, so I think I'm covered on the pants thing.

More girls smile at me going into Bamboo House than have smiled at me in my entire life. There must be a scar-fetish convention in town.

An older guy in a purple velvet Edwardian jacket holds the door for me when I go inside. Scratch the scar convention. We've been invaded by Renn Faire rejects on acid. I stand for a minute in the alcove. Let my eyes adjust to the dim inside.

The place goes dead silent. Carlos even kills the music. My balls shrink up inside my body and my hand sneaks back for my knife. I open my eyes and about a hundred schizophrenics start applauding. In a minute, they're all chanting "Sandman! Sandman!" There's a banner over the bar. In silver glitter it says DING DONG, THE WITCH IS DEAD. There's a framed picture of Mason with a black wreath around it on the bar. Someone's drawn a mustache and devil horns on him in Magic Marker.

People rush forward and start shaking my hand. Patting me on the back. Women kiss me. Guys with funny accents kiss me, too. Some are dressed like ordinary businessmen and women, students, hipsters, and adolescent neopunks. Others look like they're on a weekend pass from an asylum in Oz.

Holy shit. The Sub Rosa have taken over my bar.

Word must have gotten around about my cage match with Mason and the Kissi.

Fuck me. I'm a rock star. And all I really wanted was a burrito.

I belly up to the bar and Carlos beams at me.

"Your friends are a blast!" he yells over the din. "Why didn't you bring them in before?"

"I didn't know they were my friends."

He keeps smiling. He can't hear a word I say. He motions me to get closer so he can whisper something to me. I get right up to him and he says, "Some of these people, no shit, can do magic."

"Can you magic me some rice and beans? I'm hungry enough to eat Orange County."

Two minutes later, Carlos brings me enough food to feed the Pacific Rim. I hold up my tumbler full of Jack and Carlos and I toast each other. He looks extremely happy. The Sub Rosa might be a bunch of lunatics, show-offs, and bureaucrats, but they're a big part of the underground economy that keeps California afloat. And they're not shy about splashing around cash. If the Bamboo House of Dolls stays Sub Rosa central, Carlos will have enough money to retire by Friday.

I try to eat, but people keep coming up and introducing themselves. If I need anything at all, don't hesitate to call. About fifty different women slip me their phone numbers. So do at least that many guys. I don't remember anyone's name. It's one big lovefest blur, and as nice as these people are being, it's really getting to me. I pretend that I'm going out for a smoke, but what I really need is a shadow to disappear into.

On the other hand, I really need a smoke, too.

I light up by the side of the bar. A woman walks over to me. She's dressed like Stevie Nicks in her how-fast-can-I-burn-out-my-nose-with-coke period. When she gets closer, she becomes really interesting. She has the whitest skin I've ever seen. And there's something strange about her face: it moves whether she talks or not. Her face is like the phases of the moon, going from a gorgeous bride-to-be to an old woman with a face like shattered granite.

"Are you having fun inside?" she asks.

I shrug.

"It's nice, but it's a little much. I'm going to finish this and sneak off."

"I'm glad I caught you then. I'm Medea Bava. Did you get the package I left with your friend Vidocq?"

Feathers. Wolf teeth. Blood.

"I got it. And it was after Christmas, but you still cared enough to get me something."

The young woman's and the old woman's faces turn serious.

"You might be a hero to those fools inside, but you're not to me. To me, you're a dangerous man. A criminal for sure. Possibly a wild dog that needs to be put down."

"You're from the Inquisition, aren't you?"

She laughs.

"My boy, I *am* the Inquisition. And from this moment onward, I will be watching every move you make."

"Isn't that a song by the Police?"

"That's exactly the kind of thing that will get you another package. Only this one will be a bit more, let's say, lively."

"Lady, I've seen Hell and I've seen Hollywood and I have a pretty good idea what Heaven looks like. So, take your threats and shove 'em straight up your deviated septum. For me to worry about your finger wagging, I'd have to give a damn about something, and I've pretty much reached my limit there. Anytime you want to get all junkyard dog, give me a call. You might kill me, but trust me, you're going to have a limp and that face of yours isn't going to move so easily anymore."

She keeps looking at me. No reaction. Nothing. Just her stare shifting through the phases of the moon.

"Have a nice party, young man."

"Leave a light on. Maybe I won't wait for you to come after me."

That makes her laugh. A high titter, like crystal wineglasses tinkling together.

That's enough fun for one night. I throw my cigarette into the gutter and look around for a comfy shadow.

"Littering is a crime, even in L.A."

I'll be hearing that drawl in my dreams for the next hundred years.

"U.S. Marshal Wells. Come to party with the pixies?"

"Don't be obscene," he says. "I can smell the crazy on these people from here."

"Don't knock it. You might get lucky. Some of them inside are going to love a man in uniform."

He shakes his head.

"I don't like wasting my time talking to people too crazy or stupid or addled to understand what I'm saying."

"Then maybe what you were going to say, it's not worth saying."

"No. It is. You did a good thing the other night. I don't know that we could have stopped the ceremony without you."

"And Candy."

"Yes, your sidekick monster. So, are you Batman and Robin now?"

"I think that was our first and last date."

"Too bad. You might have been good assets."

"I'll tell her we have Homeland Security's blessing. And you can hire us, if you want. I'm sure for the right price, I can get her out of retirement."

"Aelita told me about your business proposition. I'll never understand people like you. You respect nothing. You value nothing. But you went out of your way to take on the biggest evil this city has seen in a good long while."

"I value plenty. Probably just not things you'd care about."

"You might just be surprised."

He looks away. His heartbeat is up. He's hiding something.

"It's okay to be in love with an angel. Trust me. You wouldn't be the first."

He nods, but he still won't look at me. There's a package under his arm. He holds it out for me.

"I thought you might want this. We found it when we were searching Avila. There was a whole room of similar items. It's your girlfriend's ashes."

And there goes L.A., dropping down fifty thousand feet right under me. Swallowed up by the San Andreas fault. My head swims, but I don't want him to see that. I start to say thank you, but nothing comes out.

"Don't say anything. It's okay even for an asshole to get choked up. Trust me. You wouldn't be the first."

He walks away and gets into one of his blacked-out vans. I step into the first shadow I can find.

I WANT TO steal a car. Something big. Something ugly. A Hummer or a director's decked-out Land Rover. Reinforced suspension, emergency winch, and self-sealing tires, like he thinks he can four-wheel his way out of the Apocalypse. I want to steal something bright and shiny and stupid and expensive, set it on fire, climb into the driver's seat, and pile-drive it into the ocean at a hundred and twenty. Feel the windshield cave. The crack as the safety glass pops out, hits me in the face, and snaps my neck. I want to feel the cold black water swallow me up and spit me out on the sandy bottom of the world. Just blind crabs and bone-white starfish down here. I don't want death. I know what's waiting for me when I die, and Hell is too bright. Too loud. I want oblivion. I want to not exist. I want to feel something that's not pain.

I want Alice.

But Alice wouldn't want me to disappear. She didn't like me stealing or breaking other people's things, so I won't do any of that tonight.

See? Even dead she makes me a better whatever-the-hell it is I am. A less stupid person. A more considerate monster.

I step out of a shadow and onto Venice Beach. Alice is under my arm in a brown plastic box. There are bonfires fifty yards down the sand. A boom box pumps out something that, at this distance, is just beats and the buzz of overloaded speakers. People cop drugs on the street behind me. Couples grope and sweat in the dark.

I knew a drug dealer from Marin County. A hippie, but the kind who slept with a .45 under his pillow. When he got into organic pot farming, he stopped using the toilet. He'd shit on a black plastic tarp behind his house, staked out in the sun, so his droppings would dry out and he could use them to fertilize his plants. He told me that he got the idea from a friend who made sun dried tomatoes.

He did the fertilizer experiment for a year. Collected each dried-out nugget after a month in the sun. He told me that at the end of that year, everything he dropped on the tarp fit inside one shoe box.

I don't know why I think of that, except that the only person I ever loved now fits into something about the same size as that dead hippie dealer's shit box.

There's a crescent moon out. Does that mean it's a good night to let Alice go or a bad one? If I was better at magic than murder, I'm sure I'd know.

The water is cold and calm. Low tide. I have to walk out a good ten or twenty yards to feel the waves on my legs, boots sinking into the wet sand all the way out. I wade into the sluggish waves until I'm in waist deep.

Pop the top of Alice's plastic sarcophagus. Her ashes are in a plastic bag, like something you'd put your lunch in. I hold out the bag so that the bottom is about an inch underwater. Pull the black knife and slit the side.

The waves lap at the bag, washing out her ashes. Alice floats on the surface of the ocean, a white cloud spreading out in all directions. When the bag is empty, I drop it and the box into the water. I wade out, following the ash cloud as it's drawn away with the tide.

I want to follow her all the way out, over my head, and keep on going. But she wouldn't like that, either.

I stop when the water is up to my chest and watch Alice spread out into the black Pacific. Scoop up a handful of her ashes, but they wash away when the water runs between my fingers. That damn song is stuck in my head again.

> "It's dreamy weather we're on
> You waved your crooked wand
> Along an icy pond with a frozen moon
> A murder of silhouette crows I saw
> And the tears on my face
> And the skates on the pond
> They spell Alice."

My legs are good and numb when the last of her drifts out of sight. I'm not even cold anymore, but I can't stop shaking.

Good-bye, Alice. I know you probably don't like the idea of me killing, but it's all I have left to give you. And I've gone too far to stop now. When I'm sure about Mason, this thing is done. I'll go back down where I belong and dream about you in Hell. Till then, sleep tight.

WHO WOULD HAVE guessed that Kasabian had his act wired tight enough to have accident insurance? Allegra found the papers in the bottom of the safe when she was closing up the one night a week she still works at Max Overdrive.

Drop cloths, ladders, and paint cans are stacked along the edge of the staircase leading to my bedroom. The broken walls and ceiling have new drywall. In the morning (not too early; I tipped the foreman not to show up until after eleven), the crew will start plastering one end of the room and start painting the other.

I'm lying in bed after a shower, staring up at streaks of drywall tape and mud, the long white scars that hold the new ceiling panels together. I'm trying to talk myself into getting my ass out of bed and down to the Bamboo House of Dolls for some decent food.

"Knock. Knock."

I have the Navy Colt up and cocked in a fraction of a second. Lucifer is standing in the doorway, holding a red-and-white-checkered bowling bag. I lower the Colt's hammer and set it back down on the bedside table.

Lucifer says, "Don't get up. This is just a social call."

The Prince of Darkness is dressed in a tailored charcoal-gray suit that looks like it cost more than this building. He sets down the bowling bag on the bootlegging table and leans back against the door frame.

"Careful. That might not be dry," I say.

"Thank you." He stands up and checks his jacket for spots. "I was in the neighborhood, so I thought I'd drop by and congratulate you on outfoxing Mason. I honestly didn't think you had it in you."

"Up until he was gone, neither did I."

"It was clever how you tricked him into following you to Hell. It's just too bad that when you locked him in, you probably gave him exactly what he wanted. You don't really think that ritual at Avila was to let me or my kind out of Hell, do you?"

"No, it was to let him in. I didn't figure that out until later. So, the mob didn't rip him to shreds?"

"Of course not. Mason won't die that easily. And now he's free to crawl around down below, like a viper at my bosom, and conspire with my generals to overthrow me."

"It's going to be a lot harder for him now that he doesn't have the Kissi to back him up."

"Maybe."

"You telling me that the Prince of Darkness can't handle one lousy human? You've done it before."

"Not when he's protected by my entire general corps and the aristocracy. Things were chaotic enough before his arrival. I could gather the troops who remain loyal to me, find and kill him tomorrow, but I'd have to destroy half my kingdom to do it."

"That's not my problem."

"Not yet."

Lucifer takes out a pack of thin black silver-tipped cigarettes.

"Do you mind?" he asks.

"Damn. Are those Maledictions?"

"Right. You can't get these up here." He tosses me the pack. "Keep them. I have more."

"Thanks."

I tap a Malediction out of the box, fire it up, and puff. It tastes like a tire fire in a candy factory next door to a strip club. The best cigarettes in the universe.

"I heard a funny story the other day. Doc Kinski told me one about angels and human women and something called a *nephilim*. He says I might be one. You know anything about that?"

"I know all about Uriel and his disgrace. Do you think an archangel could fall without me knowing? I'd hoped that Heaven would cast him all the way down to me. I would have thrown him a ticker-tape parade."

"So, he was telling the truth?"

"Of course. I'd heard stories about the *nephilim* over the centuries, but I'd never seen one. I wasn't sure they even existed. When the Kissi dropped you down with us,

I wasn't terribly interested. Unlike my brethren, I'd seen more than my share of humans. Then days passed and you refused to die. That's when you got interesting. I moved you from household to household. Put you in direct conflict with powerful Hellions. Decided who you would fight in the arena."

"I was your science project."

"You still are."

"What does that mean?"

Lucifer looks away and picks up an import DVD of Lucio Fulci's *Zombi*.

"This looks fun. May I take it?"

"Happy New Year. It's yours."

He throws back the drop cloth and starts going through the stacks of discs on the table.

I say, "I've been wondering, just how much of everything since I got back was your doing?"

Lucifer keeps going through the stacks of movies.

"The Veritas aimed me straight at Kasabian. Then some mysterious buyer wanted Muninn to get something for him, only Muninn needed my help and that sent me to Jayne-Anne and Avila, which led me to the Golden Vigil and Mason. Don't you think that's an awful lot of coincidences?"

He holds up a copy of *To the Devil a Daughter*.

I shake my head. "Don't bother."

He makes a disappointed face and tosses the disc back onto the pile.

"You're too hard on yourself, Jimmy" he says. "I'm sure

you're simply a much better detective than you give yourself credit for."

"Really, I'm not."

He holds up a copy of *L'Inferno,* a 1911 silent version of Dante's *Inferno.*

"You'll love that one," I say. "Why would you tweak things so they ended up with me still alive and Mason in Hell? Either you never saw it coming or you were lying before and you really wanted him Downtown."

"Why would I want Mason where he'll cause me the most trouble?"

"I haven't figured that out yet."

"Don't overthink things. It's not your strong suit. I do have an ulterior motive for coming here tonight, besides raiding your movie collection. Now that you've beaten Mason and the Kissi, there's really no reason for you to be concerned with the Room of Thirteen Doors. I'd like to buy the key from you."

"How much?"

"Name a figure and don't be shy. You can be the richest man in the world. The richest man ever."

"No thanks. Sounds like there'd be a lot of paperwork."

"If you're worried about getting hurt, I'm not a butcher like the Kissi. I can take the key out and you won't feel a thing."

"But I have a feeling I might need it again sometime. You just said that Mason's busy conspiring with your generals. I might have to do something about that, and the key came in handy when I had to to kill a few of them. Besides,

I'd still like another shot at Mason, so, thanks, but I think I'll hold on to the key for now."

"Suit yourself."

Lucifer turns away. Starts flipping through another pile of discs. I wish angels weren't so impossible to read. I know that he's got to be pissed, but I can't tell how much.

"But I'll work for you, if you want."

Lucifer turns and looks at me.

"Strictly freelance. On a case-by-case basis. Cash up front. And I have to not object to the job."

"Is this the same deal you offered to Aelita?"

"Exactly."

"All right. But I'd still rather have the key."

I go to the bathroom and take some pebbles from a pot in the window holding the remains of a dead flower. I take the stones back to the bedroom and hand them to Lucifer.

"You can have these."

He looks at them and gives me a big, toothy Prince of Darkness smile.

"Seven stones. Seven stones to chase away the devil. Are you trying to prove that you're not afraid of me, Jimmy? That's adorable. And how very Old Testament. Don't tell me that you've gone and read a book?"

"I saw it in an old monster movie."

"Phew."

Lucifer picks up a stone between his thumb and forefinger, takes my hand, and drops the stone into it.

"Keep it. You just might need it someday, Sandman Slim."

I don't know what that means, but the way he says it makes the hairs stand up on the back of my neck.

He looks at his watch.

"I've got to run. Thanks for the flickers."

He gives me a wink and starts down the stairs.

I yell down after him, "You forgot your bowling bag."

Lucifer looks up at me.

"That's for you. I wasn't entirely sure I was going to give it to you, but after you gave me this lovely gift"—he holds up the stones—"I think you deserve it."

That doesn't sound good. But if he wanted me dead, he could have done it without me even knowing he was there. I open the bag. Kasabian's head looks up at me from inside.

"Hello, asshole."

I slam the bag shut.

"I can't make these personal calls all the time," Lucifer says. "Kasabian here will be my voice when I want to get in touch. Of course, you can also relay messages to me through him."

"And the rest of the time he'll be your spy."

"O ye of little faith."

Lucifer vanishes from the stairs.

I can hear Kasabian's voice from inside the bag. I open it about an inch.

"Come on, man. You think I wanted this gig? You told me to ask for a job."

I open the bag the rest of the way and take Kasabian out. Clear a spot on the table and set him down.

"Is that a Malediction?" Kasabian asks. "Can I have one?"

I take mine, put it between his lips, and let him puff.

"So what's being dead like?" I ask.

"Eh. I've felt worse."

"You know. I thought I'd be dead now. That's how I always pictured it. When the Circle was gone, I was supposed to be gone, too."

"Aw. Dying didn't work out for you? Boo hoo. Shove your James Dean wet dreams up your ass. At the end of the day, you're still Sandman Slim and I'm still a head in a bag that smells like someone used it to store an extra ass."

"I miss Alice."

"I miss my balls." Kasabian looks around. "Who fucked up my room?"

"It's my room now and you did. When you blew yourself up."

"Oh, right. That sucked. I heard you got Parker."

"Yeah. Back at the old motel."

"I haven't thought about that place in a long time. You think it hurt when you killed him?"

"Definitely."

"Good."

I take a puff of the Malediction and let Kasabian finish it off.

I say, "Maybe us being stuck here isn't the worst thing imaginable."

"No, it is. It really is."

"I felt so guilty about everything that's happened. Then

I remembered that half of this shit is just because humans are jokes to Heaven and Hell. We're the punching bags in their family psychodrama. I know I can't change that, but I can make it more fun. A mosquito can't kill an elephant, but it can drive it crazy. Maybe that's enough. Fucking with Lucifer's bullyboys and God's Pinkertons. Maybe that's a good enough reason not to be dead."

"That's really beautiful. Why don't you go and knit that on a sweater, Heidi? Here's an even better idea—don't talk anymore. Put on a movie."

"What do you want to see?"

"Porn."

"There's no way I'm watching porn with you."

"You're such an old lady. What's on top of the player?"

"*Master of the Flying Guillotine* and *The Good, the Bad and the Ugly*."

"*The Good, the Bad and the Ugly* first. Then *The Flying Guillotine*."

I take Kasabian to the bedside table, hit on, thumb play on the remote, and lie back on the bed. The no-copying warning comes up.

"Can we order in pizza later?" asks Kasabian.

"Can you eat?"

"I can chew."

"I'll put a bucket under you."

"Shut up. The movie's starting."

RESURRECTION SUCKS.
SAVING THE WORLD IS WORSE.

'The best B movie I've read in at least twenty years. An addictively satisfying, deeply amusing, dirty-ass masterpiece.'

WILLIAM GIBSON

OUT NOW AT ALL GOOD BOOKSHOPS